WHEN TOUCH
BECOMES
A LUXURY

Devin Wright

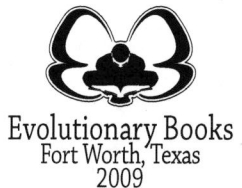

Evolutionary Books
Fort Worth, Texas
2009

PUBLISHER'S NOTE

This is a work of fiction. Names, places, characters, and incidents either are the product of the author's imagination or are used fictitiously, and any resemblance to actual persons, living or dead, events, or locales is entirely coincidental.

When Touch Becomes A Luxury

ISBN 978-0-9845821-4-3

For more information please visit:

www.EvolutionaryBooks.com

Humanity has evolved to the point where personal contact is no longer necessary, and touch has become a luxury. When human contact becomes trivial, instead of necessity, something is wrong...

In The Background

From my parents & To my children

. . .

In memory of Roosevelt

    & to all those bold enough to fight both on the spiritual and the physical plane until their last breath.

In dedication to my father, Will

    & to all the warrior class, the rebels, and the revolutionaries who embody the fighting spirit that shall never extinguish until the people are free.

WHEN TOUCH
BECOMES
A LUXURY

Mark

Chapter 5

1. And they came over unto the other side of the sea, into the country of the Gadarenes.

2 And when he was come out of the ship, immediately there met him out of the tombs a man with an unclean spirit,

3 Who had his dwelling among the tombs; and no man could bind him, no, not with chains:

4 Because that he had been often bound with fetters and chains, and the chains had been plucked asunder by him, and the fetters broken in pieces: neither could any man tame him.

5 And always, night and day, he was in the mountains, and in the tombs, crying, and cutting himself with stones.

6 But when he saw Jesus afar off, he ran and worshipped him,

7 And cried with a loud voice, and said, What have I to do with thee, Jesus, thou Son of the most high God? I adjure thee by God, that thou torment me not.

8 For he said unto him, Come out of the man, thou unclean spirit.

9 And he asked him, What is thy name? And he answered, saying, My name is Legion: for we are many.

10 And he besought him much that he would not send them away out of the country.

11 Now there was there nigh unto the mountains a great herd of swine feeding.

12 And all the devils besought him, saying, Send us into the swine, that we may enter into them.

13 And forthwith Jesus gave them leave. And the unclean spirits went out, and entered into the swine: and the herd ran violently down a steep place into the sea, (they were about two thousand;) and were choked in the sea.

14 And they that fed the swine fled, and told it in the city, and in the country. And they went out to see what it was that was done.

15 And they come to Jesus, and see him that was possessed with the devil, and had the legion, sitting, and clothed, and in his right mind: and they were afraid.

16 And they that saw it told them how it befell to him that was possessed with the devil, and also concerning the swine.

17 And they began to pray him to depart out of their coasts.

18 And when he was come into the ship, he that had been possessed with the devil prayed him that he might be with him.

19 Howbeit Jesus suffered him not, but saith unto him, Go home to thy friends, and tell them how great things the Lord hath done for thee, and hath had compassion on thee.

BOOK OF SIGHT

Psalms 82:6

I have said, Ye are gods; and all of you are children of the most High.

1 : 1

It's happening. It's in the air. I can feel it. They've gone too far to stop it, and we've let it go too far to stop it. The question is no longer if but when - when exactly? As what I've so long wished for nears, I honestly wonder if I even want it. I've wished for the results of it while conveniently leaving myself out of the active process, when removing myself is the most important part of that process. The level of self-sacrifice demands that who I am must die so the next can live, in one way or another. It's scary. Although I can't say that I've been a big fan of life and I've wished it away many times, I fear I'm afraid to lose it. I know what fear feels like, and I'm confident that this is fear that I'm feeling as this climate intensifies. I dare not tell or show the others, though. I've been self-medicating more to hide my anxiety, because fear is addictive, and I'm no saboteur.

Like a well-developed strategy, it can be seen but never seen through. Those experiencing it can only become subject to it, and if lucky, they'll understand it when it is complete. The same is this stain upon this glass, frosted scales that catch the light and appear as a wall of water gently vibrating upon the face of the citadel. Stain is considered aesthetically pleasing. Beyond its placement in art, a stain is a liability and a detraction from value. The glass is stained. It scatters light like ocean ripples in the day, and does the same to the establishment's inner glow in the night. None can make out what's beyond its mosaic, but upon it, if the viewer stands back a ways, the fractal of multicolored stained shards become well-shaped and well-placed, serving function in form. As a braid or a lock, many pieces together make what one strand cannot, and these glasses together create a white robed, white winged, White man holding a double-edged sword in his right hand. Surely, it's the archangel Michael. He protects those that gather in this space and the activities they've involved themselves in behind him, behind the glass. Should any press their forehead against him and line their hand across their brow in an attempt to peer beyond him, he's been divinely instructed to let the blade fall to protect God's work.

Along with this mural of stained glass, the front face of the establishment is covered in flaking paint upon stucco that's cracked egg shell in some places, partially exposing mesh grating and wood framework so weathered it appears as gray shale. To the left of the front entrance is one of these places. There's always a new crackle of shell scratching beneath the opening and closing doors that mark the cement in chalky arcs, ghost trails that make the doors the guiding paddles of a pinball machine that have been swinging away from the spirit home. Welcoming, it is not. It was, when home to another kind of spirit, the holy kind, and alcohol was only served for communion, decades ago. The spirits have multiplied, and alcohol is now served daily. It's a quaint bar, frequented by few because the prices are not competitive, it's not on a main road, and it is not lit well enough for the type of women that attract men to choose it. A really sexy bartender built like a pinup with choice body parts flowing over and from under her painted on uniform could possibly help, but Toni, the owner and a poor replacement, prefers manning the bar. Getting rich was never the goal, getting by was. There are many things more valuable than money, like peace, quiet, and the time to think and plan. Located deep enough in the brush, some days the only knocks upon the establishment come from the pecans that land and rattle down the roof tiles, shaken from the trees by the breeze.

Its location is barely urban, but defined as because urban is only a mile or so away. It is close to urban, by location and by stage in development, but it was arrested in mid-state change because of poor planning. Businesses arrived before the residents, residents who never arrived, never quite buying the promise of the developers. In a receding wave the city that had swelled here, retreated, leaving most of the infrastructure except the traffic lights and the dreams of what it could have become because there was more money to be made in the new direction of the wave. Replaced by stop signs, the traffic lights followed the current to the places with traffic, and this section of the city was left to dry up. It's not often that a church fails, but when the foam of the wave refuses to return, it hasn't a choice. A church was left, acres of cleared land, complete and incomplete concrete structures, and trees. No amount of prayer could change the church's fate. So, it's a church no longer.

A new kind of fellowshipping is taking place, behind the frost and the stain and the sword. It is said that when three have gathered in His name, He is there, and the inclusion of a man of the cloth, though extremely unorthodox, makes this consistently so. So maybe it's appropriate that they meet in what used to be a church sanctuary. It is after hours and the front door is bolted shut - the bolt assists the archangel in his duty, and three, including Toni, nestle within the poorly lit structure, passing the conversation between one another like a rubber ball on a playground. The ball is in Toni's possession, and it's tossed in an intense whisper.

"Well?" The men sit silently, trading glances, ignoring the question as if it was rhetorical. Toni's eyes are covered by a frustrated index finger and thumb massage, paying particular attention to the nose bridge. It's the hand sign of a hidden headache; it could be physical or emotional. One scratches his head, teases with his hair, and plays with his ear while tracing his tongue along the crest of his upper teeth and back around along his top lip, making slow laps around his loaded, *I told you so*, smile. He enjoys this. No one is anxious to fill the awfully fertile space beaconing before them like a bitch in heat, mangy and wet. Stern faced, with his brow pinched and jaws locked in a flex, one cuts through the tension with the sharpness of his stare. They are all thinking. *See no evil*, *hear no evil*, and *speak no evil* meet in confidence in the back of the bar.

While sitting in the eye-pinching, wanting darkness, Toni continues, "Well, it's here… What we been waiting for, right? Another BUM. Black, Unarmed, and Murdered, with another cop story that doesn't make any fucking sense. And right in our back yard this time…"

One slowly raises his finger to intervene, and Toni leaves him space. "I apologize, but I was so exhausted after the last, I, regretfully, haven't looked into the latest episode of cops gone wild. I just know he was Black and unarmed."

Toni affirms with a nod and a shrug. "Didn't even get out of his truck, shot up through the driver side window. Classic ambush, let The Ears tell it. The street account differs from the official one, of course... Cops watched him, boxed him in, from the front and the rear as he tried to pull out his driveway. He'd just walked out the house, unaware he was being hunted, and they converged on him. Cop story is he tried to back into one of the officers with his truck, the officer dove out of the way, and a second officer ran up and shot him..."

"Bullshit," the third speaks as if his tongue was forced to balance rancid meat upon it. He's calm in his disgust, with his disgust refusing to come out smoothly. He's been working on his anger, and like a war, his face shows it. "This unsubstantiated, self defense story, making a victim the aggressor, 'cause dead people can't testify."

"Right... I got questions. If he was boxed in, how could he back up and hit the officer? Was she behind him, between his truck and the cop car? What sense that make? Who walks there unless grabbing something out the bed of a truck? They approach driver side, guns drawn, walking toward a vehicle, always, but they want us to believe she walked up from directly behind a boxed in truck?" Toni pauses to let the lack of logic sink in. "Then he tries to back over her. He's boxed in! How much space is he working with? Run her over? Pin her to the car behind him, maybe, but I can't imagine enough space to do anything else, which really limits the time she has to dive, and makes walking between the vehicles even more ridiculous... She dives out the way, her partner runs up, murders him, so he wouldn't still run her over. Still? She dove. He's was boxed in. How was *still* possible? And allegedly backing up, in a truck! We can even drop the boxed in part for a moment, because it just complicates things. Follow me."

Toni illustrates in the dimly lit space, head turned as if looking through the back of a truck window, left hand on a steering wheel. "Imagine trying to back into a person, and they dive out of the way. Imagine the coordination you would need to redirect this truck to, still, back over them, especially when you can't see 'em anymore." Toni returns from the illustration posture and back toward the small audience. "It's a truck... If she dove out of the way, she's no longer standing up, the driver, whether looking through the mirror or back window, can't see her. The truck bed's in a way. No way he could keep sight of her, without losing her at least a moment, but let's say he's just that good. Now!" Toni nods, "add that he's boxed in back to the story. He's epic. And how long did all of this take? Was the cop who murdered him already walking toward the truck from the front while she approached from behind the truck bed, or did he just appear out of nowhere? They do things in concert, usually. So while knowing there is at least one more cop in front of him, he *was* boxed in, he is still trying his damndest to run this lady over? Makes perfect sense, right? I'd pay good money to see a reenactment."

"Just tell us anything… them motherfuckers think we stupid," the third responds, still struggling to remain calm.

"Right, Tuck. That's not even believable to someone with half a brain. Thank you, Toni. Basically, we've watched this happen over and over with tiny uprisings springing up across the face of this nation like, like bad acne. With the makeup of our city, poverty and education levels, the aggressiveness of our police force, we knew it was coming… I fear this is just the start."

"Exactly Liam," Toni asserts, "Damn sure ain't the end."

"It's a'ight y'all. I don't see no reason to get all riled up. Official story is fine." Tuck makes a vacuous appeal in a purposeful reveal of his character. "Cops and cop lovers understand them. Rest of us ain't evolved enough. You gotta figure the protests are starting to wear 'em down, though. Stopping traffic. Hashtags. BUMs…" Tuck stops and points at Toni. "I like that. I'm stealing that. BUMs is trending, niggas is falling like cripples, but whatever's trending is ending, if it's something bad. We got the Internet revolution happening, boots on the ground in protests, the thug, hoodie, sagging pants, smoking weed, who deserve to live and who don't, debates. It's all working if we just be patient… If you got you some good walking shoes, we can, well… y'all can set up a couple of them fine events here. I'll pull up the lyrics to *We Shall Overcome* for you, but I'll be home cleaning my guns while you marchin'. Might even go coon hunting. The sellouts need to be first to go."

Speak no evil impales an apparent nothingness with his frigid gaze, jaws flexed. He's more so allowing the ball to be passed without his direct involvement like it's going over his head, a child in the middle of a game of keep away swatting at it, unable to grasp the discussion, when in reality he can snatch it from the air at any moment. He has the authority to take the ball and go home because, metaphorically, it's his, and he averages the highest time of the possession for the three. He watches as the conversation, red and rubber, pressurized with hope, the bladder filled with good intentions, floats back to Toni.

"I'm sick, guys. The pain worsens with each new incident. Physical pain! I'm serious. Never felt anything like it before. What's going on? Cops hold public executions and people respond with pieces of poster board and markers… For what? To get on the nightly news like it's a fan-cam, with their carefully crafted political statements? Yeah, that'll teach 'em. About as useful as it is at an NBA game. When did cheerleading become the appropriate response to murder? It's like a… disgruntled spirit team, a BROKEN-spirit team! Begging, groveling for some kind of compassion. They don't understand yet that we don't like being murdered, and they would surely stop murdering us if they knew we didn't like it, so we scream chants and shake our signs in their faces like tits and pompoms. I watch it in pain. If that kind of moral appeal has to be made, they have no morality. It's a useless approach, so I say stop being pussies and suit up… Maybe. Sorry for the language, it's just…" Toni digresses. "I got a better cheer for them. Go hard, or go the fuck home! That's the least they can do."

Toni's words strike Tuck like a drum, solid on solid. His clenched fist shakes the table, stirs the smoke, like the physical manifestation of his leather being slammed into. He drops his sarcasm and resonates in his guttural bass, through the heavy gravel of his excited voice, "Yeah!! I been stockpiling for this shit. All I need is the word, y'all."

"Tuck? Toni?…" Solid on liquid, Liam vibrates in a different manner, absorbing the emotional impact and allowing it to dissipate in calming ripples. With top lip curled and eyes pinched tightly, he pierces the mood, causing it to release some of the quickly building air pressure within its membrane. "Let's not start the revolution just yet. Ok? If emotion is the conductor, I'm hopping off this train. I figure we convened to properly assess the situation and then make a decision, not to put batteries in each others' backs."

"Pssshhh! Here we go. Knew it was coming!" Tuck blows the last statement off, and there is a measurable slump in Toni's shoulders, both gestures indicative of deflation. The mood hangs. "Nig... Man! If Toni is ready, yo' ass is outvoted. I don't even want to hear this shit from you. Again?!"

Toni catches the ball, unenthusiastically. "Tuck, I'm sorry, but... I'm really just venting..."

"Aw hell." Tuck is doing a poor job of abating his anger, revealed in his earlier demeanor. "I mean, what's all this training been for then? It's been years, training, recruiting, developing strategy. Come on y'all." Tuck punches his chest like a silverback. "Legion up!"

"I notice you neglected to mention studying. It hasn't been years for you, and it may take more years, or it may take a week." Liam is calming, "I'm just saying not to let our emotions get the best of us. Graves are full of people who went out in an emotional blaze of glory. Didn't rethink their strategy until they were bleeding out with their bodies growing cold. Too much work has gone into this to throw it away with one poorly planned, poorly executed, op... because you upset." Tuck shakes his head in negation like he is keeping time for the duration of Liam's statement. Liam wrinkles his face and pans from Tuck to Toni while releasing an exhale. "Whatever."

"He's right Tuck. Let's talk this out... Alright Liam."

"Ok. Well, here's deal. Spoke with The Ears earlier. The west side is cool, like always. The American dream works better for those with pillows and beds, but the east side is unstable and on the verge of a breakdown. Winos even talking retaliation. Whatever that means. Ha. To utilize their skill set, maybe we start a Molotov cocktail unit and recruit them?" Liam laughs a little. The others don't. He uses their silence to make a point, as he continues, "Everyone else is comparable as far as readiness is concerned. Not even ready for a thumb war, yet grandstanding. Emotion will confuse you into thinking you are physically prepared, when often you are not even emotionally prepared. The sight of human blood has made the hardest rocks crumble… It's not time, and we've got to get The Mouths out there saying this before someone with the charisma to capture the people's imaginations says the opposite."

Toni nods. Tuck twists his mouth in disagreement and responds, "Fuck that. That's that Black preacher, turn the other cheek, bullshit. No Liam. Not this time nigga. Man, Toni in pain and shit and you still trippin'? It's the same story, from them AND from you. Who you work for, huh? Not the people… I really wonder about you sometimes. Not sure what you in this for. Don't act like any revolutionaries I know. Might be an agent. Don't you wonder too, Toni?" His attempt to get Toni to assist his argumentative insult falls flat. Calling one an agent, short for double agent, is an insult of the highest form in the liberation community, but also comparable to teenage girls claiming one has cooties to keep the others from associating with her. Research rarely goes into the claim. Toni says nothing, remains expressionless, listening. Tuck shrugs while looking at Toni and completes his piece, "Needed to be said."

Liam stares with question marks in his eyes and an awkward smile. "What are you talking about?" He also looks at Toni for reinforcement that he doesn't receive, and the three drift away from each other slowly and evenly. Islands.

Tuck clarifies, "Same story. If there ain't no weapon, make one. This time it was a truck. Last time pig shot an unarmed brother, punk ass cop say he tried to take his gun. Ain't no justice. Tell us one thing, do another. You want shit to make sense, but it ain't gonna. No pattern or logic you can plan around, except they shooting niggas and lying about it. Same shit, Liam. Look at Ferguson. Brother's unarmed. They scuffle. The brother retreats, getting shot at, stops, puts his damn hands up, just to be murdered… You not tired of this yet?!" Tuck is highly animated, emotionally illustrating with his hands. "Oh the official story though. Supposedly, he ran away, turned BACK around and charged the cop while getting shot at, while reaching at his waistband. Really?! Tried taking the cop's gun but had his own? Oh, he got a gun but he charging, instead of shooting back? Oh. Ok. And niggas with no guns *always* reaching for they waistband. Must got jock itch or something… Tell us anything… Just another BUM."

Tuck smiles at Toni for the involuntary assist. "Fuck them Liam. Shit won't matter until they hurt too, and you want to tell people to cool it? If that's the best you got, we can stop right now, 'cause I ain't telling my people that coward shit."

Liam flexes his jaws, strokes across his mustache and pinches his upper lip while waiting for Tuck to finish. He responds, his calmness a contrast to Tuck's activeness, "What does any of that have to do with us picking the best time?" Liam swats at the air, waving Tuck off, like knocking his argument off its Liam directed course. "Fair enough, Tuck." Liam makes a second deliberate turn away from Tuck and continues, "I just want us to best utilize this energy and not do something foolish. If we can't, considering the frequency of events like this, and how the reactions of the people are escalating, I'm tempted to say we're wasting our time."

"I've BEEN saying that. We need to hit the streets. We need to be a part of what's building and stop all this damn talking!"

Liam sighs and speaks at Tuck without turning back towards him, "I was talking to Toni… We've heard you. Again and again. Duly noted Tuck…" He returns to his point with Toni. "If we're not ready before the poster board and markers become guns, we'll be too late, but we don't want to be too early either, and unprepared. That's what I caution against."

Tuck again responds on the tail end of Liam's pass as if standing in between him and Toni and intercepting it. Toni calmly watches. "We're ready now! I figure too late'll be whenever YOU finally ready. That's my measuring stick. Anytime before that is good. Like now. I'm ready to hit the streets NOW."

"Hit them to do what? To who? And to achieve what exactly? Until you can answer questions like that, you don't have my attention. There IS a sense of urgency though. This that we've been building will all be a waste if the public executions continue, because people are getting angry, and we can't organize anger."

"Shiiid. That's exactly what we need. More anger."

"No, Tuck. You really don't know what you're talking about, still. You shouldn't even be here. Toni, he shouldn't be here." Liam's getting tired.

Tuck is not tired. "Man, fuck you! I'm here 'cause I ain't no coward, and..."

Toni interrupts, snatching the ball from Tuck, sensing a building tension and the only available release, at present, being upon each other and counterintuitive considering their goals. "Fellas, fellas! Maybe it's not time yet," Toni pauses and looks at Liam, and then to Tuck to finish, "but maybe the time is near... I think with the correct target, a shot won't begin a war; it will effectively end one. That's what we've been preparing for. Guerilla strategy. It's about precision, not force. Shows of force are for superior numbers and placing fear in the hearts of the enemy. We don't have that advantage. But," targeting Liam, "the opportune time may not be so much when we are ready as it is when our enemy is not. Precision is our God... and she will protect us."

Liam adds while slowly shaking his head in negation, "I don't believe in that God either." According to scripture, Matthew 18:20, it doesn't matter whether Liam believes, God is in attendance as the three of them, beneath a cone-shaped, single-bulb, hanging-lamp, seated encircling a small round table, talk. Shadows are also in company. There are no other light sources active besides several neon beer signs sticking to the darkness of the walls like refrigerator magnets. The shadows pull down at their protruding facial features, and they are hard to make out, but they know each other well by tone alone, and no light would be just as comfortable. All have heads of hair of various lengths, but short enough to reveal head shape like tennis balls with different levels of wear. Smoke rises from a glass ashtray resting nearer to one, but not near enough to indicate ownership. Neither grabs at the vessel, concealing to whom it belongs, if only to one, or shared by them all. It smokes untouched. It may have met its end, and it is no longer of any use like the end of a barrel of an emptied firearm. They continue to speak.

"Revolution talk though? I don't know, Toni. Right now, I believe in the revolution about as much as I believe in the *second coming*. People aren't about to do anything but pray, complain, and talk shit." His head slowly pans over to his left. "Ain't that right, Tuck?"

Tuck laughs. "I don't pray, I acknowledge, but whatever, reverend. You sound just like an ol' Negro preacher to me. Maybe not the bible, but go hide your face in one of them other books you place your faith in. We'll call on you when we need help spelling or something. It's never time, let Pastor Liam tell it. That's exactly why we don't listen to you."

"We don't listen to you either!! Or we'd be dead right now with the homies pouring out liquor for us, the revolutionaries without a revolution, fighting to protect an idea that people aren't ready for, or even aware of. Please. I'm just trying to be realistic, and when I speak of freedom, I'm not talking about my soul being liberated from my body, or any of that conscious, ancestor, energy never dies mumbo jumbo either. Fuck that."

As they talk, Toni grabs the vessel from the glass ashtray, and takes a drag while patiently listening. The size of the vessel is indicative of either a hand rolled cigarette or a marijuana joint because it is shorter than the length of a retail cigarette butt. Dangerously short. Only technique and fingernails of the proper length can handle it. The men continue to bicker without break.

"See Toni? Some of us lose before we ever pick up a gun. They got nice vocabularies though. Tell you that much. They can tell you all about the how you should fight, where you should fight, and when, but SHOW you how? They don't do no fighting. Don't have the heart for it. They're like revolution coaches, and we wait for them to send us in the game. Good coaching too, Liam. You taught me a lot, but... we can't win on the bench."

Toni places the vessel back in the tray after a couple of inhales and exhales. They continue.

"Sorry I don't share your optimism, brother. I mean that. You talk tough, but when it comes down to it, I, with all my book learning, have killed more men, no... more humans, women and children included, than you. As far as the present struggle is concerned, your body count is as blank as mine, yet you talk this *we* at war shit nonstop. With a proper target, I have no doubts about my ability to execute, but with you though, I'm guessing anyone who doesn't look like you is a target, or wearing a uniform, but your body count is as blank as mine... So, I guess *we* losing this war since one of *our* most outspoken ain't shooting off nothing but his mouth. Your little corner speeches don't excite me. I'd much rather see a target identified, and a target taken out… but keep up the good work."

"Sure you would… Tell us anything. I don't give a damn what you'd rather see. Hell, books is what you'd rather see, and a long drawn out strategy that'll only serve to convince people that we got no chance to be free. I may not use a bunch of big words, but I ain't no damn fool. I know stalling when I see it, and I also know there's a such thing as knowing too much. I know at a certain point patience becomes cowardice. The soldier that know what he fighting *for* is just as passionate as the one who know everything about who he fighting *against*, if not more 'cause one got time to get scared. Ain't no building up the enemy on my watch. No, Liam, I pass."

Toni cuts in, "Do y'all ever get tired of doing this?" It's an age-old conflict, a script written and roles already set, but new actors often fill them, and the men rehearse, their characters expressions of logic versus emotion, as if the two are in opposition instead of harmony. Sometimes they're called the conscious versus the street mentality, but oftentimes they're called the house slave versus the field slave. Both the script and the conflict is older even than western slavery, as many ancient philosophies encourage the suppression of the lower nature, emotional expression, while others encourage the acceptance of it. Toni's objection is ignored, and, without pause, they continue.

"You've BEEN passing. You ain't fighting nothing but your own sense of reality. By yourself. Suicide. Revolutionary suicide. Add that to your *neglected* reading list. Yeah, all books aren't made into movies. You just got lucky with Spook." Liam pauses. Tuck pinches his eyes at him and reaches for the smoke. Liam continues, "I'm willing to die, but hell I ain't trying to. There is no us. We haven't built shit compared to what we're against. We are few, and our potential army has been divided by the scared, the ignorant, and the locked up…"

"And the sellouts," Tuck quickly interjects from the back of his smoke filled throat, from the back of his drag.

"Of course. Yeah, them too. This is not an army, and y'all ain't soldiers. Especially Mr. Street over here. He doesn't have the discipline," Liam says in response to the sideways insult. While staring at Tuck, who pinches what's left of the flame, pinching his eyes and staring back, he finishes, "We are not ready."

Toni speaks. "Maybe an army isn't what we need. Not in the traditional sense, anyway. Of course we'll continue to recruit, but Liam makes a good point to consider, if we're serious about this. If our future army is scared, they must be emboldened, if they are ignorant, they must be educated, and if they're incarcerated, they must be freed. A revolution must start somewhere, and this gives us a place … Our clock is in the hands of the oppressor, but this gives us direction. You both agree?"

*　　*　　*

"There'd be no gate, if not for keeping something out or keeping something in … and I don't care if it's made of fucking pearls, this shit ain't natural."

This was partially thought, partially spoken in whisper, and partially exhaled as he hung from the top bunk, seconds before releasing and dropping to his knees, a short reprieve before beginning his last set of pull-ups. His arms, knotted bundles of live wiring, pulsed like they were about to short out. Every cell of blood could be felt coursing through them as they dangled like flesh without a skeleton. Counter to these limbs feeling so feeble and frail while relaxed, working against this state, they become opposite. He gathers, grabbing the lip of the top cot firmly. Like bending metal bars, pulling himself up again after so many reps already complete, it is. Once his chin reaches up to the frame, he reaches burn out, which is his goal, to completely deplete himself, saving none for the use of another. Being used by others had gotten old.

He grabs at the gate to begin his stretching, presently a feat as tricky as threading a needle. The tips of his fingers are guided to his iron anchors like he was navigating by mirror, completely under his control with sense and sensations not matching up exactly. The bars are more hot than cold, so it is early spring, maybe. By frequency, if the bars were capable of bending, they would have by now. He grabs the same ones in the same spots. They have lightened in those places. He puts them through the rigmarole, testing them, as he tests himself nightly because the rule of the animal kingdom is the weak get eaten.

He works at keeping his muscles developed and undesirably tough for those that would try to consume him, creating cuts that make the poorest cuts for consumption. Not enough fat. Not enough flavor. The butchers point with their batons at him and his kin, at the striations in their muscles like they were but 2D diagrams, meat charts, with the stitching of dotted lines between his major moving parts, while yelling out herding instructions. The chart is accurate, and they know exactly what places to point at to make an animal double over, hobble, or wince and grasp himself, should one decide to buck. Understanding, he speaks not, unless asked to do so, in the disguise of the weak heart. As the defeated, he'd acquiesce, because pointers leave purple and red watercolor like bruises, but he is not defeated.

There just weren't many outlets within the gated community for the residents to express themselves, so they might as well act as extensions of the guard's expressions, who were themselves extensions of the warden's, who is himself an extension of the state's. It isn't defeat. It is just a complicated labyrinth of expression blocking, interlocking gates, keeping things out and keeping things in, natural expression included. Expression still occurs. It is just compartmentalized, like the body parts of an inmate viewed through the bars, like the 2D diagram. Unmistakably, the gates making him into cross-sections and cuts of beef, when being viewed by those *beyond* him, are not *pearly*. St. Peter is not the name of either of the guards that make their rounds pacing up and down his cellblock. This is not heaven, and why does heaven need gates? The shit isn't natural. It can be called hell, some say it is, but inmate 7413 really wouldn't know. Although it is not a grand time, it cannot be called his worst because it is rare that he is even present within it.

Now, counting the days to when he will again be on the other side of these gates, he leans against the bars, forehead between two, arms spread across eight, feet together, upon his toes, palms open and out with the tips of his fingers curling around the bars. This is his church and his sacrifice, every second of it. He is the sacrifice, his death for the lives of others that spit upon him and call him names... or something like that. His meditative stretching includes his mimicking the man he sees every Sunday in chapel, as he convinces those watching that he has some type of soul. His Sunday soul is, hands down, his easiest con yet. It is so easy it bores him, but he tucks his boredom behind serene smiles and sanctified handclaps that match the rhythm of the hymnals. The search for God never occupied his time much on the outside, but he's found that he could even quote a couple of bible scriptures once nearly all the things making life worth living were removed from his reach. His flesh, they'd say, and he'd understand it but in his own way. His flesh was only weak in the ways that he is not allowed to nurture it, so he nurtures his spirit instead, every Sunday, and being a good Christian looks great to parole boards. That kept a lot of the guys in attendance. If it is all an act and not genuine, who, besides God, could tell the difference? Was Jesus hanging there looking through them, dying for their sins, yet perpetually undead because Gods don't die? In the boredom that formed between his hallelujahs and Amens, he couldn't help but notice while sitting there that the crucifix and the cross bar are identical. It is coincidental, or they're all puppets.

Twenty four hundred days, give or take a hundred or two, is his number. He's lost count with no hash marks, no calendars, and the use of just the seasons as his litmus. When the gates first slammed and locked, he hadn't a clue whether or not he would make it to the next week, much less the duration of his sentence, so why count? As if there is someone who is, he was definite that he was not cut out for this type of living. He was too slick, too smooth, too pretty, and all his days on the outside were preparing him not to be here, but there is always someone a little bit slicker. They got a place for slick folks too, and it looks just like the place where the stone cold murderers are put. As a matter of fact, they are one and the same. The little boys in blue must have been fast asleep under haystacks when they allowed the sheep in the meadow and the wolves.

Oblivion is timeless, and behind bars all watches are forced to stop. This timelessness would have been absolute if not for his swelling, cracking, and sweating skin adjusting to the weather. Obviously, it is quite the difficult and expensive task to keep tons of iron and brick warm in the winter, and conversely to keep it cool in the summer. The temperature swing from day to night in a desert climate is extreme. A drop of 50 degrees, without a cold front coming in, overnight is not unheard of. He would go to sleep nearly naked and sweating and wake up having to pump his fingers and rub his toes to get blood running back through them. At first, he would complain and no one would listen. Now, he *would* complain but no one would listen. He's a felon. He's in prison. No one without similar labels truly gives a damn, and those with similar labels don't care much either. It is a waste of caring for those who truly understand. That concern is better suited to adjusting to the circumstance, the terrain, of this environment using their newly gained handicap. It's like being almost human, but not quite, like slaves, demoted from the human classification and defined as merely human-like, sixty percent human, or 3/5ths. The felons relate and no one cares, so let them fry and let them freeze.

The overseers adjusted to the inmate demand for a decent, fourth-class human level of comfort by allowing them an extra, extra-thin blanket, if requested, and the guards have been especially lax on the *shirts must be worn* policy for those in cells in the summer. The first thing the inmates noticed with their small increase in freedom was how much a thin layer of cotton does to dampen odor, as their space began to smell exactly as if they were the animals those that placed them there labeled them to be. They get used to it though. They have plenty of time to. In the winter, there is much less privacy. The sheets that were often tied between the bars and the bunks when an inmate or inmates desired a little privacy were used to keep warm. The really bitterly cold days had grown men refusing to leave their cells, wrapped in their sheets with only their faces poking out from the bundles like maggots maybe, bulbous burritos, or bearded babies.

More than six and a half years, he's been behind some type of gate – beginning in the back of a police cruiser, then in a holding cell, next in a jail cell, and finally, after a wonderfully uncomfortable bus ride, prison – and he only has twenty-six days left of this state sponsored torture program and then on to his rehabilitation. They are giving him a new leash on life; it'll be longer than the present one and polished to a shine, and he'll be allowed to walk amongst the productive members of society again with the state still holding his chain of course. He's an animal still, just supposedly more obedient. They shall see. Twenty-six days.

In prison they taught him his name, pulled it from his insides and revealed it to him like a malignant tumor after a painful surgery and handed it to him like a newborn. It was his, assigned to him for the duration of his life, attached with a mugshot and lifelong stigma. His not wanting it did not matter. He has to live with it. His name wasn't what he thought it was, and he was diligently corrected like Toby was from Kunta, and like Winston was in learning that he did not hate, but loved Big Brother. The truth was already in him, the state just needed to help bring it out, and who could not love the state for that? Yes, he thought his name was what the streets called him - Dix, what his women called him - Gray, or even what his mother cried - Gary - the day *your honor* banged his gavel as though he'd been standing beneath it in his orange jumpsuit, in shackles. Instead, he was standing just moments before a woman scheduled to die years before he, her youngest child, would again see the light of day. With his back to her, he couldn't even face her, hug her, although he felt her reaching. He was too ashamed; besides, she wasn't even calling him by his real name. She wasn't aware the state had renamed him and that the drivel she murmured after nine hours of labor was no longer what her son was to be called. He was hers no longer, but state property.

Mother died sixteen months into his sentence, and something in inmate Dixon 7413, died along with her. His older brother corresponded with him through letters, telling him about Mother's deteriorating condition, and his last letter was about her death in which he attached that he didn't have the strength to keep up communications with someone so willing to throw his life away, where an *I love you little bro* or a *We all we got* would have been better received. Big brother was speaking through his pain, and Gray understood that, but he was not the only one in pain; he was at least privy to seeing her waste away. Gray was half a state away wasting away himself, and the process sped up with that final letter. A connection between the stress of Gray's lifestyle and her body's inability to heal itself was even made. He was blamed. Half a state away, in a medium security prison, somehow Gray was able strip the life away from his mother is what big brother inferred behind retelling of the family's good times, that only included Gray in his most docile years. "Mom still would be alive today and healthy if you would've pulled your pants up and not have been chasing money and women," is what he was saying, and this lie was reason enough for him to cut communication, knowing that Gray's fast lifestyle had no connection to Mom's pancreatic cancer.

That letter survived almost a week in the soup, daily increasing in acidity and disgustingness, it sat in, lodged in his metal commode. His cellmate at the time allowed this experiment only because Gray's mother had just died, because it decreased the comfort of them both, and he actually helped it along when relieving himself. When it finally released from itself like toilet tissue, Gray flushed it. As if he was not already cold enough, he resembled more the lifeless shade of his irises that inspired what the women started to call him. Lifeless for the most part, but there are imperfections, flecks of green and brown near the pupil that aren't nearly as arctic. Few have been allowed to share space with him at a close enough proximity to catch the warm spots, all were women, and women were responsible for the nickname. Phonetically, there is not much difference between *Gary* and *Gray*. Unless someone is saying it slow, or screaming it, like his mother was in the courtroom, it just melts together into a single syllable, so Gray doesn't mind being called one or the other, or both. He barely pays any attention to it. His consciousness has always been very selective in this manner, as if saving space for the important stuff and relegating the rest to the background.

Often, while standing in this position and stretching, he

thinks of Mother. With the cold, or warm, bars pressed into his fore-head with arms spread in his metaphoric cross, of them, and of all things that bind him during his nightly ritual, he thinks of her. He awaits all of the feeling to come back into his extremities, feeling that has been gone for moments and the feeling that has been gone for years, thinking. Pressed against the bars, he stretches beyond them; he escapes, like Jesus, on his cross.

"Almost out of here, huh? Won't be long now," his escape was a lot easier when he had a cell to himself; his celly of maybe 6 months spoke from the top bunk. Gray has a reputation of being more of the quiet type, a man of few words, but rather efficient in his utility, but he's given a considerable amount of voice time to young Ervin, who fucked up his life doing a run of suburban burglaries with his peers. Gray thought he was asleep, but he must have been just quietly sitting there in the dark like a weirdo. The quiet part is a struggle for him, and he was probably about to burst while waiting for Gray to burn out because to vibrate his Adam's apple and curl his tongue in speech is the nectar of life, but speaking while Gray is exercising ruins his concentration.

Gray, with his forehead still resting between the bars in stretch, simply responds to his question with, "Yup." Behind his head he can hear the springs and welds squeak with tension. Gray sighs. Not only is his cellmate awake, he is now sitting up, so he has more to say, much more. It's too late and Gray is too tired. He'd much rather think of his mother and escape, but he is being forced to be present. He has to return to his cell because young Ervin wants company. Twenty-six days. Gray ended his stretch and closed his statement with, "Well out of here at least. Twenty-six more days, but I got six months in a halfway house."

"Oh that's easy time," Ervin responds while Gray crawls into the bottom bunk. Ervin was awarded the top bunk after the first night Gray's pull-ups awakened him to a shadow of a torso and crotch rising and falling in front of him. It startled the shit out of him. They almost fought that night. All of those stories of what happens in prison sprinted to the front of his consciousness, still foggy with sleep, and he concluded Gray was trying to take his ass. He started talking fast and cussing, disturbing Gray's set. Gray released the lip of the top bunk and dropped to his bent knees, maybe six inches, and grabbed Ervin's armpit and neck with the force of punch, pinned him against the wall, and told him something about what short time meant, that he wasn't no punk, and to shut the fuck up during his set. Ervin had never heard that many words from Gray in one space, and it wasn't even that many. Pressed against the wall of a small box, a cot below him and one above him, with a hand beneath his shoulder and one on his neck, connected to arms conditioned to God knows how many reps of pull-ups, push ups and dips, which were at the time pumped from being in mid-set, all Ervin could really do is sit there and listen. He had no choice in the matter. He was welcomed to the reality of prison that night, how thin the space between one and another is here, and the respect that regulates it. They never had a problem after that night, and Gray awarded Ervin the top bunk. He didn't need any more time in this space as a result of breaking the kid's face, not a week, a day, not a minute.

"Is it easy time? I wouldn't know, but damn, just being in the company of women again, I'm sure will make whatever kind of time it is, good. And I'll be damned if they don't miss me as much as I miss them."

"Man, don't even mention bitches. I could fuck a hole in this concrete right now," Ervin raps on the wall with his knuckle, "but they'd think I was trying to break out." He begins laughing.

Gray, also laughing, adds, "And give your young ass even more time... I honestly can't even imagine what an ugly woman is anymore. After this stint, they all can be salvaged, I promise. I'm giving discounts when I hit the streets. Women who could never afford some play with Gray got a chance. Even chicks I done dissed already... I gotta have it, man. Hell, might be right back up in here for a crime of passion. Literally. I feel sorry for my first victim." Gray returns to laughter.

"I hear you. I don't even want to think on it as long as I got left. But... wait. You ain't got nobody waiting on you? Said you got a son, right?"

"Nah." Sharp and succinct, Gray's response cut into the

mood like a deck of cards. It came out colder than planned. "No one's waiting… I do have a son though, and a daughter, but nobody's waiting… except these hoes." With the final three words Gray intended to revive the mood a bit. Ervin caught it and coughed out a small laugh but the conversation effectively halted. Discomfort had been invited into the exchange; the conversation was his to finish, and he did so by amplifying the squeaks of bed springs while adjusting for comfort. The inmates faded into their heavying breaths as they fell into the trance of sleep. Not another word was spoken, and they ended this night at *hoes*. It was late anyway, Gray was burned out, and grown men, not in a sexual or familial relationship with one another, do not close the day out with goodnights. The conversation just ends how it ends and resumes in the morning.

1:2 *If only it were as simple as house slave, field slave. Simplification makes for easy understanding but only when ease benefits the problem. We are not fractions, even though once considered to be. Some field slaves want nothing more than to destroy the house, some want to take over the house, some want only to move into the house as it is, escaping the field. Some house slaves are comfortable and content with not being in the field, and some sympathize or identify with field slaves with aim to destroy the house from the inside. Many male house slaves lost their nuts, castrated as to not fuck the masters' wives and daughters. It creates a wonderful metaphor for some of the house slaves of today, but Nat Turner was also house slave. When simplified, the allegory is flawed and divisive, and the question remains as to what kind of house the system is. A broken house? A house divided? Say it's a fortress, and not nearly as easy to take from the outside. Simple this problem is not, the who or the what.*

"Fuck you gonna do with some freedom… Huh?" With the *Huh*, he clapped once, his elbow, a rough and ashy map of the Milky Way, bumped the table and all the pieces, the blacks, the whites, and the red and the black wafers, rattled and stopped as if standing at attention. The same happens with those listening. The cracking pads of his hands meet and grind into each other like Emory boards, enough energy to produce fire in his palms, as he thinks of what to say next. Speaking with the pacing of a proud southerner, a proud Baptist southerner, a proud Baptist southerner preacher on his pulpit - the sweaty Black kind, so, southern *and* Baptist, not Southern Baptist - Ol' John teases. His words are never in a rush, and they reach the congress with a similar impact as those sent in a tension-building hurry from one with less gravity, yet his carelessly float between the comblike gaps of his leaning yellowed teeth, wooden lips, and the weave of his silver-laden whiskers. Sounds as if he's stuck on a high. He always sounds as if stuck on a high, and though the occasional sack of weed makes its way behind these prison walls through a daisy chain of rectal cavities and Ol' John is established enough to get a taste, there is no way he's *always* high; it's just his sound.

Without allowing Gray an official space to respond within, in the many spaces of his cadence, he continues to hold the floor, letting his syllables hang to alert that he isn't yet done. The others sit patiently. It's like waiting for one who stutters but almost opposite. This expression of an age before beauty-like respect remains inside the containment, when prison perverts so much else. The elderly still have their respect when everyone else must earn it, especially the old timers, who've done much of their aging inside the penal system's nurturing embrace. Ol' John continues, "Knowin' you ain't ready for all that. You need to let me have that time, boy. I'd do it proper." He folds his arms and looks Gray down as the *r* hangs in the pause his cadence provides, and he continues with, though he'd never really stopped, "All I need is some contacts and about a couple muscles, and I can pass for your pretty ass. Haaaaaaa." Ol' John's laugh is more of a mule call, but it's accepted as a laugh for those who gather behind the south building in the yard at the game tables. The others join in with the laugh. Gray fights it, clinching his teeth and contracting every muscle in his face like he's being punched by the gust of inter-state air one meets poking his or her head out of the window while traveling at freeway pace. Gray waves the comment away with his left hand, too excited about the prospect of leaving this wretched place to publicly express it. Gray rarely challenged, opting to just listen and nod. He let the freedom line slide, knowing actual freedom wasn't in his future, not simply through his release; he also let that *pretty* shit slide, which is not a compliment in prison, while awkwardly pressing his lips together and dimpling his face to suppress the smile that was as hard to hide as the sun.

Not exactly old by most standards, but definitely no longer young because prison ages a man; Gray was granted a seat with the old school players, where the threat level is lower. They now confine their play to chess and checkers mostly, because of the dictates of their circumstance. Playing women often came up in conversation, along with playing the system, and even playing the fool. They were players in the truest sense of the word, and they all had been played. How else would they have ended up in prison? Gray had the best of his stories to tell when being played came up, and the strength of it cemented his initiation. His example is grand, and speaking about it helps him process the level of betrayal he'd received from someone he'd loved. It's often a counseling session at the game tables, or a trading post for those who gain advantages through their ability to quickly read others, and this game behind the games is a therapy much more useful to Gray than what goes on in chapel. Ol' John, the patriarch of the group, who loves to ask people for their story, pretty much leads it, and he has a knack for digging beneath the social callus the frequently hurt begin to form and really getting to know people. He knows many people on the outside as well as on the inside, and when Ol' John takes his last breath here, the inmates will probably dedicate a corridor to him or something.

Only the poor chess players play checkers, and they are ridiculed. Stacking one wafer upon another and calling it a king was a running joke, because, "That's how you make queens in prison." Some would even call out in laughter, "Queen me!" upon reaching the eighth rank, further blurring the lines between the two games because should one reach the eighth rank with a pawn in chess, a queen is often the desired promotion unless one needs a knight, the only piece she cannot mimic. Some groups were plotting or preparing for wars, drawing up plans in the dirt, doing body weight exercises, and securing raw materials for the manufacture of weapons, but the focus of those at the game tables was making the bricks and the fences topped with razor wire disappear, even if only for a short while. It is theater and the character is rarely ever being a prisoner for anyone but those who have lost all hope, and everyone stays away from them because these harbingers of doom only serve to remind the others about the degree of *fucked up* their lives have managed to reach, to have arrived here; inmates have been stabbed for supplying such a buzz kill. Outside, it is Gray and his old school homies discussing the game, playing games in the park, not the penitentiary yard. The beer has no flavor and the reefer is dirt, but it's as if they are smoking and drinking as they talk shit out there daily at the game tables, close to free, with Gray being the closest by far.

Gray knew how to play chess upon arrival, got better through the years, but he's nowhere near one of the best. He just can't think enough moves ahead, a problem that has proven to have real life consequences. He enjoys the challenge, and even picks up a win on occasion. When not playing, he watches the older and more seasoned players, learning strategy, and extracting lessons from the tales they share of life before prison. No one really talks of prison, only the life before and the life after. Only the hopeless, fools who have lost it all, talk about the prison life. It is an unspoken rule. *How did you get here?* is a question, *How long have you been here?* is a question, and *How long before you get out?* is a question, but actually talking about *here* is next to criminal, even for the accused and the admitted criminals. Speak of that subject gives it residence within their minds. They know where they are and how terrible their circumstance without a reminder from one too weak to try and ignore it. It is usually the new ones that don't know any better, and those who are willing to engage in the conversation about that subject with them usually do so for future sexual favors. When the line on the plantation is to ignore it, those few who tolerate it begin looking like swell individuals, when they're actually the most malevolent. If the new guys knew this upon entry, they'd probably have a lot less questions about prison life, how to maneuver within it and how to cope. Once a week, there's fresh batch of these unfortunate souls, and Gray's game-study is interrupted by the old bus full of new students.

Around six months prior, Ervin peeked out from beneath the shadow of the bus door into the light, squinting, with a smile on his face. Squints often come packaged with something that looks like a smile, and Gray was far enough away to be fooled as he watched every new student exit the bus. It's a school bus, just painted white with the prison name branded upon it in maroon, with some extras in the inside to assist in binding humans to its interior. Ervin's eyes had long enough to adjust to the sun. He was smiling. It is not that he was happy to be here; he is of normal intelligence. He was just that young and *innocent* – if that term can be used in this sense, because he was definitely guilty. His innocence was in his not knowing any better, innocent of exposure, like a child. That childlikeness is a handicap, and watching him, others thought that smile might just be the thing to brighten their prison stay. It isn't ill intentioned, but happiness is coveted, and Ervin could be placed in another inmates jar like a lightning bug to marvel at until his shine wears off. Shines always wear off, even more of a reason to covet yet again, new ones, and here Ervin was innocently beaming brightly enough to be recognized in the sunlight.

The crime, he did it and wasn't ashamed to admit it, and once the circumstances of his capture became clearer, Gray understood why.

When the bus arrived, Gray's cellblock was in the yard. It is often timed this way. When Gray arrived, years ago, there were also inmates in the yard, gazing at the new arrivals predatorily like high school seniors staring at a crop of freshmen. There may be no English speaking location on the planet that can better place emphasis on the word freshmen and the two words within it, and do the use of them better justice; it is a language win. Standing no taller than 5'6, Ervin had to be one of the shortest people on the bus, and the bounce in his shackled shuffle only brought his forehead to the shoulder height of some of the others. He stepped off of the bus joking with another new arrival, smiling, with the receiver not nearly as jubilant – understandably, he was heading to prison, and he was returning a loaded gaze to everyone inside the fence locking eyes with him while trying to keep his heart inside his chest. Ervin smiled and didn't even look towards his new schoolmates, and Gray took notice. The others in the yard were taking notice as well, making their picks, new membership and whatnot. The pushups, sit ups, dips, and pull ups stopped; the yard was still as they watched the new group exit the bus.

Gray never joined the exercisers; it was a silent initiation into their click, and he didn't want to adopt any conflict that was not his own. Beyond adding a new conflict to his list of problems that few on the outside understood, and few of the new inmates, most prison sex is consensual and done on a favor basis. One not knowing any better allows himself to become part of a click and taken under another brother's wing, asking too many questions, where they are showing one the game and giving him protection and prison survival tips. Eventually, those favors are called in, in an intimate setting, where the man the one has grown to respect prefaces his request with, *I'm not gay or anything like that, but a man has needs,* before asking for some head. The night he was startled by Gray's exercising, Ervin was worried about Gray taking his ass, all while positioning himself beneath his wing and creating the opportunity to give it away in called in favors. Fortunate for Ervin, that isn't Gray's thing, his sentence wasn't long enough to make it his thing, and besides masturbation, he had sort of an ace in the hole. Gray, himself, decided working out in his cell was best, so he didn't fall into that trap. Exercising also helped him to relieve a lot of his sexual tension. When Ervin arrived, Gray was on his bench, near the game table, chiming in on stories when he could, and watching prison chess - a more aggressive variation where the pawns can capture what's directly in front of them on their initial move. Everything's more aggressive in prison.

The smile wasn't an act, not one of defiance or an act at all. It was authentic, who he was, and the boy could talk like a five year old who'd newly discovered it. With many diligent attempts by Gray, Ervin just couldn't be ignored. Of all possible cellmates, the biggest, the meanest, the baddest and most menacing motherfuckers, Gray ended up with a kid brother this time around. It could have been worse, much worse, as Gray had before experienced and lost blood over, so he welcomed his new cellmate and the laugh that came along with his relief. An empty bunk is an ominous reminder of all of the possibilities prison has to offer, and Ervin being assigned was like winning the lottery. It was kind of like winning for the kid as well. Gray was short time, and doing anything to get any time added to his sentence was the last thing on his mind. While only months away, disrespecting his dead mother was even game – not that anyone did. It was good for them both. Gray just had to get used to the new soundtrack. In a time of overcrowded prisons, that extra bunk had been empty for months.

Only responding in nods mostly, it didn't take long before he knew the kid's life story. Nothing unique, single parent home, barely knew his father, poor, Black, and ambitious enough to do something about it. He had a quick tongue, through apparent practice, and a smile others could trust, basically everything he needed to move up at least one station in life. Gray, too, has some of the same short-comings. They're shortcomings once you get caught. Charm is a free world asset and a prison liability, well, for the most part it is. It can help with getting one his own cell, maybe. The more Gray listened to Ervin, the more he was convinced the kid had no business in prison either, but America swallows her young. He was threatened by society more than he was a threat to it. The boy was just finding his way.

"If it wasn't for fuckin' Jody... Shit. I wouldn't even be here." The kid even said that with a smile, but it was a troubled smile, as fragile as candy glass, but at least his voice didn't crack as he retold Gray how he ended up in the big house.

Ervin and his crew had good plans and great intelligence, the military kind. While everyone else was selling crack, weed, and heroin, they were selling dreams to gullible rich girls, mostly White, that wanted so to be a part of the urban Black experience and also have a little of it *inside* them. In their philosophy, Ervin and his boys, drugs were for doing, not selling, and they were a shortcut in turning these young women out. It was a combination of the lines they were spit and the lines they sniffed that created a euphoric blast of dopamine that their victims called love, relinquishing every inch of their privileged selves to boys not fit to shine their daddys' shoes. The girls often bought the drugs, or rather they financed and encouraged the purchase, while the boys actually completed the transaction in their hood where the products were plentiful. An innocent observer probably couldn't tell who was turning whom out, as one group's excitement in coming up was just as stimulating as the other group's in slumming it.

Robbery wasn't a plan of theirs at the onset. They were just having fun as defined by their age and class. With enough of this fun - sex, drugs, and alcohol, the idea materialized in their conversation while driving back to their side of town one night, from one of the girls' houses. The suburban to urban drive is interesting. It's like wormhole into history, where all the pretty, clean, and new, outside the window, transforms into the ugly, dirty, dilapidated, and old; also, a lot more liquor stores, pawnshops, and cop cars start to spring up, save for the places where gentrification has begun. The moneyed people were coming into the hood and taking whatever they please. It was only right that some from the hood were going to the suburbs and setting the record straight, placing their hands on some of the most prized possessions, like daddy's little girl. It is as if they were game pieces, and their activities guided by the hands of karmic law, all the way down to how they'd stumbled upon the idea that taking more than the imagined innocence and purity of these White girls was fair game.

The spark that led to the conversation was the necklace Ervin had liberated from one of the girls. In their fun, she'd mounted him, and the gold chain kept hitting him in his face. Her stringy hair doing this was bad enough, but he couldn't take that and this necklace that was long enough to be hip. He leaned into the nape of her neck and removed it while kissing her, sliding it in his jacket pocket, a jacket he soon removed, with every intention of returning it. Upon realizing he still had it on the ride back home, the consensus in the car was, *That's yours now. Her rich ass won't miss that shit. Daddy'll just buy 'er another.* All of the fellas chimed in, and that was basically the main idea of what they'd said. Ervin held on to it just in case, saw the girl a couple more times and she never mentioned it, so he sold it to a pawnshop.

The host's parents had gone to a show, so she decided to do some entertaining herself, in the pool house. Their pool had its own house, and it was nicer than Ervin's. She invited some girls and she invited the guys. It wasn't a party; it was more like speed dating, but instead of refreshments they had marijuana and condoms that the guys were expected to roll up and roll on, because of course the girls didn't know how, or pretended not to. It didn't take long at all before everyone was paired up, intimately acquainted and high like a scene out of a Blacksploitation flick. They were just missing velvet paintings and black lights to underlay the tufts of smoke swimming across the room.

The girl couldn't stop talking about France. It was her house and her subject. She even accented her speech with little French phrases as she pranced around topless smoking a joint that Ervin had rolled perfectly her. The family was going to France for two weeks for her Christmas break, a country renowned for its beauty and culture, and out of the four girls there, two of them had already been. Out of the five guys there, not one had even been to the French Quarter in New Orleans, and French fries, French kissing, and Pepé Le Pew was the extent of their knowledge of France. Her vacation was to the other side of the world, and their vacation was to the other side of town, when able. It was just a vacation, this event they engaged in, and the guys knew it. They couldn't even meet the parents of these girls, so each relationship began with an expiration date. Knowing the temporal nature of what they were doing with this initial group of girls, coupled with the ease of taking that necklace, they decided to maximize their profits.

Within months of *dating,* the guys were trading secrets on how to best get the codes to disarm alarms, how to copy keys, and how to gain the trust of the family dog, with the girls' awareness always lost in an intense high, a post orgasmic haze, or preferably both. They would only rob one in a group, in the case of a group, and they would choose which by how much she liked the guy she was seeing, how much she had, and the difficulty of the job. They didn't call it such, but they'd created a risk analysis, and a set of rules to go by – high school kids, and poor students mostly. Robbing more than one in a group of friends would have been stupid and gotten them caught much sooner.

They cased their future scores and found out the schedules of mommy and daddy – they had to learn them initially to date their daughters and to be in their homes in the most intimate ways, anyway. Family vacations were pay dirt. They kept notes on the little details of their relationships that may come in handy in case their girl was to be the lucky girl: grocery shopping on Wednesday morning, family night out on Fridays, Mom cheats on step-dad every other Thursday from roughly 2 - 6pm. The more detailed their intel, the better their chance of a successful heist.

They were at it for well over three years. This became a business. They learned how to pick them; no liberal White families who would accept them were targeted. Secrecy was integral to the score, so Dad couldn't even have a place to start. No matter how liberal they were, that *Black kid* would of course appear in his mental list of suspects. No loner chicks were chosen; they already had trust issues. The extroverted party types, like those living the music video and spring break beach life, are a lot less accountable, with a reality too exciting to worry about putting two and two together. No college girls with their own places unless they were home for the summer. No big brothers, rather no meeting them nor any of their male friends. The males were always suspicious and territorial once they, as Ervin put it, "They were cool until they found out we were fucking them chicks. Then they turned into real assholes. So we cut that. We didn't want a damn thing to do with their friends unless they pissed sitting down. Man... we put this all together just by fucking around and paying attention. Took some notes. Damn I miss that shit. Fuckin' Jody." Ervin ended sentences with *Fuckin' Jody* like the disappointed end theirs with *Jesus Christ*. They whet the appetites of the girls who had no choice but to keep them as their dirty little secret, whose daddies would kill them if they found out. Those families always had more money anyway.

It was brilliant. They made thousands from the resale of easy to move merchandise, mostly jewelry, video games, electronics, and guns, and none of the girls grew suspicious enough to notice the relationship the *break in* had with the *break up*. If love is not blind it definitely has a blinding quality, as those within its rhythms have limited visibility. Love was off limits too. There was too much at stake and Ervin and the crew - of the initial five, one opted out because he was an exceptional athlete, and had options... a smart move in hindsight - had to be able to make a clean break without being all in their feelings after the score was made.

The scores were collective gains, they split the profits equally, but individually, within each relationship, the gang was doing everything they could to break these All-American girls' banks and backs. One got a cash car out of it. Every relationship didn't lead to a score, but a lot of them did. They were careful enough that they were never even under suspicion. It was a good time. Ervin couldn't stop talking about it. Ervin just couldn't stop talking. It was a blindside to Gray to find out that Ervin and all of his talking wasn't the reason they'd gotten caught. They were caught by the Internet.

It took maybe two weeks for Gray to grasp and wrap his mind around the concept of the Internet. It existed before he went in, but it was still in its infancy and it didn't exist at all as far as his routine was concerned. The modern Internet had been around since the mid nineteen nineties, but those in the ghetto either had no access to it or didn't have a use for it like owning a can opener without any cans. The poor are always the last to catch onto a technology as the struggle to survive often gets in the way of learning anything that does not immediately assist in that struggle. It took this same population many years to figure out a use for the personal computer, much less the Internet, and Gray was in harmony. The internet really never became a thing for most of them until they found out bills could be paid with it, which could save them time, and while doing so they were distracted by all of the available sex and sexual engagements and that hooked them. The late nineties and the early two thousands was a fast time for Gray. He liked fast cars, fast money, and faster women. In his teens and twenties, he would go around saying stuff like, "If I can't eat it or beat it (have sex with it), I don't need it... unless it's money." For the Internet, that was a *no*, so it missed him completely.

The best Ervin could explain it was computers and cellphones could now talk to each other, which seemed like a page out of a dystopic science fiction where humanity finds a way to screw itself out of a decent existence with the use of technology. Happens every time, and if Ervin had been up on his fiction, he may have been better prepared to read the events of his impending personal demise. Gray prodded to know more about this Internet thing that had the power remove a person's freedom, or supposed freedom, "Alright, computers talk. So, your talking computer, snitched to the cops? How the fuck your computer know what y'all were up to anyway? And why did it know cops?" Ervin laughed when these questions were posed, but humor was not Gray's intention. Gray really needed to know. Obviously this Internet thing was something to worry about if it's getting kids sent to prison. He needed an understanding to make the proper mental notes because he planned to never return to these bars once he's escaped from behind them.

They were well enough posed questions to lead to an understanding, as they prompted Ervin to explain further. One of the crew members, Jody, began uploading pictures of his money and stolen items in web communities to brag, effectively telling on himself, which told on them all. Comparably, uploading pictures of his conquests was the same as a brother driving down a street at ten miles per hour in his new ride, but this ride is stolen with vanity plates that read another's name with decorations that are culturally inappropriate, with cops walking down the street as well, to complete the metaphor. Maybe they weren't that brilliant after all; cops got talking computers and cellphones too.

The police work couldn't have been easier. Jody faced one hundred and forty two felony counts at age nineteen, and when asked his occupation he reportedly told the cops he was a thief. Gray met that part of the story with a slight smile and a nod because he didn't recognize that answer as dumb, as most probably did, but as Jody going out in a rebellious blaze with one more *Fuck you!* to his captors. He was already caught, the evidence was piled thick, so why not complete the ritual as an inspiration to others, in showing that although his body had been captured, not the rebellion in his soul. While raising Jody upon his cross he spit upon their asses, and would have pissed on them, too, if his hands weren't nailed down. Gray liked that, and for him, in that moment at least, *Fuckin' Jody*, sounded decidedly better than *Jesus Christ*. Unapologetically, Jody was a thief, which explained his garage full of merchandise - not all his, not *at all* his since it was stolen, *and* not *all* his because his crew helped to stock it - that he had not moved yet. Every single item, such as an earring without a match, was another felony. With no photographic evidence, Ervin was hit with considerably less felony counts, the worst of which was organized crime, which has him seeing fifteen years before he is even up for parole.

That's hard time at twenty-one. Even if he gets out when parole comes up the first time, which would be a miracle, he'll be in his late thirties, Gray's age, with no free world skills, wearing the equivalent of the scarlet letter, not an A for adultery, but an F for felon.

Who wouldn't rather receive an A than an F? When they finish with Ervin behind these cold bars, he'll be chiseled into entirely something different. That smile will go, along with what innocence he has left. There is no place for innocence in the pen, even for those who have been wrongly accused or framed. The kid is young and impressionable enough, and weak enough to become whatever they decide he should. He'll change much more than just his name when it is all said and done. His expression, his outlook, his religion, and his sexual orientation are all up for grabs, should he not be careful. They have lots to teach in this school for those willing to learn as well as for those unwilling, but it is best to focus on graduating. If he slips into thinking the temporary is permanent, he'll leave this building as a prisoner still when released, in look and in action, like a school drop out, frozen at a dangerous level of maturity.

Ervin looked up to him, and something in Gray felt sorry for him. This impulse might be attributed to the knot of muscle inside his chest cavity that keeps his blood flowing, mistakenly called his heart, an organ he was branded not to have, before prison, by enough people, and important enough people to make it true. He saw some of himself in the young man, and respected the humanity he'd still possessed because it reminded him of the memory of his own. Ervin was a nice guy. He meant well. He had concern for others. He talked as much in inquiry, trying to find out what the matter was and how he could help, even if just to be an ear to lay an issue on, as he did in exposition. This wasn't prison proper. Inmate talk is the most impersonal grade conversation available, even in personal subjects, their passion is often rubber gloved. Anger is expressed freely, and there is often laughter, but that is about all. Gray never had much to say, and it was his way of leading by example. It is hard to offend with a closed mouth. As Gray's exit date approached, he figured he would do his best to advise Ervin, because his entire world was subject to change. It wasn't that Gray was protecting him, not overtly, but his routine while bunking with Gray was a kind of protection. Ervin was even allowed to hang at the game tables, though he couldn't play chess at all, and didn't have the patience to learn. Gray knew how to stay out of harms way, and he'd known how to long before prison, just like playing chess, because it's just like playing chess; it is thinking faster, moving faster, and outperforming his competition, the hustler's creed.

Ervin had a taste of it on the outside, whether he was aware of it or not. He may not have even called it hustling but that is exactly what his crew engaged in - the negotiating of something of lesser value for something of greater value, and the mouthpiece or skill set to make the transaction possible. It's theft in disguise and the victim will blush and thank his or her perpetrator when it's done correctly, while lost in the high of the experience. They are not even truly victims as the experience is part of the exchange, balancing out the give and the take. As long as there are those that have some things that others do not have and desire, the hustle will endure, even in prison. It's just not as easy to pull as it is on horny teenage girls rebelling against Mom and Dad. Something of that spirit may be Ervin's only hope, identifying who has, who has not, who will, who won't, and what he must do to manipulate these characters to his advantage. It is what Gray had to do to survive, apply his understanding of power dynamics and creating allegiances with it, even when it, at times, made him appear less down or an outright sell out. There was lots of pride swallowing and shallow smiles in the past six years, but the result is his being able to see the other side of this time, and should Ervin want to, he needs to understand that. It is the least Gray can do.

A week out before his release, in the middle of the afternoon, Gray speaks up to Ervin through the bunk, "Yo Erv!" Ervin peeks down from his perch and gives Gray a short, raised brow upnod to let him know he's listening. Gray speaks, "My time is almost up, and I want you to hear me out before I go. You can take this or leave it, but for my own peace I got to say it..." Ervin, reading from the pacing that this isn't one of Gray's normal short and sweets, rolls back up into his cot because hanging over the edge gets quite uncomfortable after a moment. While his change in posture could be seen as blocking and disinterest, Gray understands it is not, and he continues to struggle through the message that isn't coming to him as nearly as clearly as the emotion that accompanies it, "This prison culture, man... It's for them dudes that ain't ever leaving. Don't buy into that shit because you going home one day. Avoid fights the best you can, but don't let these hard heads punk you either. You'll never live that down if someone chooses you and you punk out, and … that will just alert everyone else that you the one to choose. So, yeah, avoid fights, but never if someone is bringing it to you, if that's makes sense… Keep to yourself. Don't talk so much. That's gonna be hard for you, but I'm telling you, it's safer. When you do talk, know who to talk to, and who to listen to. All men aren't created equal. There's a difference between the cat that can do shit *to* you and the one that can do shit *for* you. Respect both, but the latter more, because chances are, anyone that can do shit *for* you, can do shit *to* you too… And tattoos… remember you're getting out one day. It's gonna be hard enough as it is, but if you're walking around with a bunch of tattoos, prison tattoos, and *especially* on your face… Don't do that shit man. You're passing the fuck through, don't become part of this. It's not for you, because you're going home. No one cares that you're a good person while here, not even God. God don't even come here, man, so it's up to you to be smart enough and not become a part of this, because you're going home! Remember that. Make decisions *while* remembering that." There is a pause. Gray yells up once more, "A'ight?" Ervin confirms that he's gotten the message with an affirmative grunting sound; he is growing more nervous by the day and Gray senses it. For one thing, Ervin has a lot less to say, and that partially motivated Gray's little speech.

Gray has run out of stuff to say in his final prison days. The place is becoming a memory faster than the days left can keep up. The people are becoming memories as well. His young celly, Ervin, Ol' John and the players, and the others he knows by name begin fading rapidly in the space they occupy within him, to clear it for something new. The penitentiary is only to be remembered by accident and in bad dreams. Gray starts the process. He is debriefing, releasing it all to leave the majority of it between the walls of his cold cell, and there is no need to unload it all on Ervin who still has fifteen years to go, at least, so Gray just leaves him with what he left him with, some main ideas, a kind of cheat sheet to stop him from being murdered, mentally or physically. Besides, even nearing his release, the rules remain and those in prison don't talk about prison. Silence is better. Talk to him for what? There was nothing left to negotiate for. Ervin's only value had been in helping the time pass. He had given all that he could have about the outside world that Gray hasn't seen in years, and Gray comparably gave him as much information about the inside world that is to be his new home. The cat got the game. The hustle is a stale mate, and it is a convenient place for the older hustler to leave it. Gray's graduating.

*   *   *

They are coworkers who share a mutual friend that takes an interest in them getting along better, so Will accepted the invitation to Robert's small backyard cookout, that Robert probably only extended to show their mutual that he was trying all the while predicting that Will would decline. He always declines anything Robert suggests. It shows how strong their friendships are, or how convincing the mutual is, because Will accepted, reluctantly. The mutual didn't even show. Where the influence should be, properly completing the flow of the trio's energy, discomfort attends instead. Will babysits a cold beer, waiting for the food to finish, listening to a conversation that he finds to be a painful revelation of how much work has to be done before people will be ready to challenge their conditions and their conditioning because they are too busy posturing resistance instead of planning it. The best posturing is before him. None are as loud as the revolutionary gangsters. In Will's eyes they make the coming revolution sound like a pro wrestling bout, and their grandstanding and flexing the camera-candy in the pre-talks.

The topic of discussion is fear, sparked by the recent police shooting, and how everyone, even the so-called revolutionaries are scared to fight back. When asked to share his opinion, Will respectfully declines. Robert didn't appreciate his refusal, knowing it was a subject Will was well versed in. Robert expressed his disappointment in a lip smack and becoming uncomfortably direct with the subject, diving in even deeper. Robert tries using the subject to demand Will's involvement, wanting to impress his friends with the guest none of them know and the information he possesses, but he only serves in making Will, who recognizes his tactic, disappear completely while over in his corner babysitting his beer. Will is left to wonder why he is even there, and the image of their mutual friend who did not attend appears in his mind with a smile as a cunning reminder. Will smiles off the image, and determines he'll not make the situation any more awkward by leaving, and that he'll make it worth his time by making them his study. He studies Robert and his kin as a researcher engaged with a foreign culture, behind a camera, and not in actual attendance.

"Nah. Nobody trying to do nothing. Niggas is scared. They want to protest and shit, march, and others want to debate. You know the drill. Truth be told, they just scared, and I'd respect them more if they just said so. Some just want White folks to feel sorry for 'em, like that done ever worked. That or make them happy. There is a million different excuses not to get out in those streets, and they all are ways around saying, Nigga, I'm scared to… It ain't time." Robert shakes his head in disgust while simulating the masturbation motion with his right hand and arm, while mockingly saying, It ain't time. He glances at Will during his act. "Please…" Robert turns and looks back at his house a moment. "Y'all just be cool. I'll figure something out. Shit, eat this barbeque and drink these drinks and don't even worry about all that. I'll handle the politics. You just be ready when shit pops off. It's gonna pop off, too. Watch what I tell you. Too many are dying for it not to, and even in our backyard."

Robert is surrounded by a group of brothers, clad in black, sitting on lawn furniture on the back porch of his home. There's a small cooler, disposable red plastic cups with a white lip, a smoking barbeque pit within feet of them all, and music blaring out of the house, vibrating the back screen door. They number seven total, including Will who is no longer really there. Robert grabs a pack of cigarettes out of his chest pocket, taps one out, and sticks it in his mouth. He starts patting around his body to find his lighter, even standing to pat his front and back pockets. "You talk to the family?" The man sitting nearest to Robert holding a long neck beer questions him. He disregards Robert's preoccupation with trying to find a light, looking up at him with watery eyes, shaded pink, because of both a good buzz and a high.

Robert nods in affirmation with the dry cigarette hanging from his lips. He responds verbally. "Yeah. Talked to the dude's mother. She's pretty shook up." Robert has returned to his seating position, but he is still scanning the premises for his lighter. "But what do you expect? Her son was just murdered. Good kid, according to her. She's lost a piece of herself. Hurt me just listening. I started thinking about my little man… Yeah. I talked to her. She wants something done, and not no goddamn protest either. I saw it in her eyes. Man, one of y'all got my lighter?" The men grumble in negation.

"Use the grill. You can see the coals glowing in that vent at the bottom. Just stick your square up in there." One of the clan offers a suggestion. Robert follows his instruction with his eyes, spots his lighter on the way, and stands to retrieve it. It's sitting on the shelf of the small barbeque pit. He used it to light the charcoals. He lights his cigarette, places the lighter in his pocket, and checks on the food while standing.

"Oh yeah!! It's about to go down. Beef, yard bird, and even a little swine. Little bit of swine ain't ever hurt nobody. Don't want to hear no preaching either. If you don't eat it, don't eat it. Don't start talking that shit now when my stomach is growling."

Robert jokes and the others laugh, with one responding, "Shit, you the preacher. Was about to say that to you."

"We good then, cause I done blessed it with my holy marinade. A'ight?" Robert laughs while walking up to the house to knock on one of the windows. The curtain opens and a small, feminine face peeks through. "Baby, bring some foil out. It's about done." The curtain closes, and Robert returns to where he was sitting, smoking his cigarette.

"Fellas, I really appreciate you taking a break from your busy schedules to celebrate with me and my queen. Family is everything. Can't rebuild the nation without rebuilding the family first. You know the ladies like to get together and talk shit anyway." He laughs. "And it gives us a chance to build, and our kids get to play together. This is living to me. May not be rich in finance, but we can still live rich. Can't nobody take that from us. Family, friends, love for each other, ourselves, our culture. That's what life is about… Yeah, Freddie, I talked to the boy's mama, and it kind of broke my heart, man. See, some of these dudes ain't out in the community like us. It's like they in a' ivory tower while we in the trenches. When something goes down, they have to hear about it through us, because they not here in it." Again, Robert was trying to poke at Will with the directness of the discussion. "I really think that's the difference. If they were talking to that poor woman, if she had contacted them and not me, if they had to console her, tell her everything was gonna be alright, hug her, and let her cry on them, they might understand a little better how serious this thing is, and how bad it's getting."

Freddie adds, "That's my thing. Those out in these streets talking to the people with us, know how ready we are. Should see how the people receive us. They ready for this knowledge and they ready to fight. Every time something happen they look at me like, what we gonna do? Our face is on this movement man, our temple, and like, the people waiting for us, and we waiting for what, bro? You know we ready."

Robert nods while looking at Freddie out the side of his eye. "I hear you comrade. That's real, but you preaching to the choir, and you right. I got people I talk to though, people I respect. It's not just on me. I didn't get to where I'm at on my own. I was taught by some-body who know his shit, so I'm kind of waiting on them. It won't be long though. Be patient. You wouldn't know a lot of the shit you know if he hadn't showed me and I showed you. So, respect that. I don't like to feel like I ain't about that life either. If they push, we s'posed to push back… I get it. I feel that, but, man, this is Junior's birthday get-together. He just turned twelve. We ain't really get to-gether for all this other stuff. This family time."

Will almost broke character in the last sequence, able to shed light on the situation, but he doesn't. He continues to sip on his drink, pretending he has no interest in the subject. His stomach groans, responding to the signals his nostrils send, in anticipation of the twang and sweet of properly cooked and seasoned barbeque.

"This is about Junior, and all our kids. Junior can be next! Ain't no time out on this revolution shit. This is war." Freddie directs his voice to the others. "This nigga starting to sound just like the shit he just complained about. Calling for time outs and shit." Robert quickly cuts his eyes over to Will. Will turns his bottle up while locked in the stare. Freddie laughs and places his bottle in his mouth. Some beer finds its way beside the lip of the bottle and the lip of Freddie's face, rolls down the side of his mouth and foams in his goatee. The others laugh as well, but Robert doesn't find the comparison funny. He pulls hard on the cigarette and exhales slowly through his nostrils.

"How many of those have you had Freddie?"

Freddie shrugs.

"You a little twisted. I can see that, but this is my last time telling you. We not here for that. You disrespect my son's birthday party one more time, and we gonna let these hands talk my nigg…"

"What?!" Freddie shifts forward.

"Ey, ey, ey!! Y'all quit that shit! Kids and women in the house." The nearest brother intervenes standing between them in the neutral space they were bound to soon be in. "You niggas fight over anything."

"I'm gonna be respected in my own home, even if I got to beat it out of him. I don't care if he drunk. So get your boy and calm him down before I have to."

"Man, ain't nobody…"

"Freddie, Freddie, Freddie…" The interloper grabs Freddie while talking to him. "He right man. This the man's home. It's his kid's birthday. Ain't no place for you to be talking sideways at him. That's uncalled for." Robert is relaxed, reclined in his plastic chair, with the cigarette tip graying between his index and middle finger as if waiting to see the pair's next move, to see whose will is stronger, prepared.

"Listen to him Freddie. He trying to help you. I'm not taking no Ls at my own house, and on my son's born day. Not happening, bruh." The misses walks out of the back door with the foil, fork, and a pan, and the guys all start to play it off, returning to their seats. Robert quickly gets her attention. "There's my queen! Look how cute she is." She smiles and tilts her head to the side while heading to the barbeque pit.

While she collects the meat, the guys just make faces at one another. She speaks, "Y'all ready to eat now, or you want me to put it in the oven?"

"Oven baby. We'll come get some. Kids need to eat first anyway. Ladies too. We'll be in in a little bit. Thank you, though." She smiles again and carries the meat past the men and into the house. The screen door slams. The music that drowned the earlier commotion continues.

Robert addresses Freddie, "You good, nigga?"

Freddie raises his brow with a stare just long enough to be uncomfortable, then slowly begins a nod. "I'm good on your ass, you keep talking that shit."

Before the self-appointed referee could step back between them, Robert takes flight, tipping Freddie backwards out of the lawn chair with a barrage of punches. The comrades close in to break it up, to pull him from on top of Freddie, and stopping Robert from multiple attempts at breaking his face. The music continues to play and Robert's cigarette rests on the concrete smoking after it has fallen and lost its gray head; it's glowing red. Will is not entertained. Somewhere in the shuffle and scuffle his appetite disappears along with his supposed physical presence, and he makes the supposed, actual, by excusing himself around the side of the house without even a statement of departure as simple as, *Peace.*

1:3 *I can't sleep, but I want to sleep. Most are fighting to stay awake, a task that is most difficult when everyone around is sleeping, but some of us desire, secretly, to rejoin the sleepers. They unconsciously float, their beds, woven promises. The conscious are envious. We are, although we will never admit it. The bliss that was exchanged for us to not be ignorant, on the other side, feels like a rip-off. We, reckless in our travel, flashing our lights, blowing our horns at one another and refusing to stop in hopes of encouraging an awakening, are only reminded of the comfort and ease of the sleep of the state of unconsciousness. Our efforts seem fruitless, because besides ourselves, the roads are empty.*

With seemingly little to no friction, one surface glides upon the other like a whip across flesh, rubbing balls of rubber away like strips of skin beneath and before the red lights. The single red light above and the pairs in front, almost kissing a pair, and screeching at the thought - the tires, not the driver. The driver's calm, leaning gently into the leather of the seat like it is the palm of the Creator, watching the show the windshield provides as if television and he hasn't anything to do with the programming; the remote is not the wheel in his palm and the pedals beneath his feet. Changing the channel isn't an option, but he can cut off the television and go to sleep and join the sweet dreams of the rest at rest, permanently possibly. It all depends on his guide above and what He decides, as he glides along, inside His palm, and rides the storm. At rest, his car idles at a red light, merely inches behind the one before it, playing music during this brief intermission, awaiting a green light and being slung back into his insular chaos.

Glory! Won't He do it? Praise His name! He must be *Blessed and highly favored* if he is to survive another late night disco light vehicular slalom on his death-defying back-roads drive returning to his residence. There are less cops on the back-roads, which is the positive, but there is less light too, and without the protection of a median on a two-lane road, every vehicle pass is a near death experience, especially considering he's not the only one driving alcoholi-cally compromised at this hour avoiding the main roads and cops. Some of the roads in his neck of the woods don't even have dotted yellow line centers; they're even worse. The light at the end of his tunnel is mounted upon tons of steel propelled upon rubber wheels and wrapped in plastic, like gifts; it's an oncoming car. Inebriation is his tunnel.

Those in the industry of cleaning up the messes these condi-tions cause, most likely shy away from calling these impacts automo-bile *accidents*. Too much rests on the side of affirmative probability to call it an accident. The math would be better served in saying one, in this condition, makes it home accidentally. Call it a home arrival ac-cident, a miraculous thing indeed, and, again, Will travels as if float-ing within the embrace and upon the wings of a seraph. It must be Grandma's tired, ever-praying, hands still keeping him, because he's becoming more reckless by the year – a recklessness few notice. With the meticulous removal of his defined enemies, he had no choice but to become his own worst, with dry liquors as his accomplice. It's a *miracle* he's able to find his way home in this condition, but a miracle he credits himself for. It takes dedication to learn how to operate a motor vehicle safely in the state that operating one's own legs is a task, but he's dedicated and well practiced.

The screen door is propped open with the resistance of his backside as he leans into the wooden door. The eight step walk across his porch took at least twenty-four steps this time; small, careful, and crooked they were. He can't stand without supporting himself with the door he's trying to open, as soon as he can find that damn key. Adding all of his work keys to the ring with his personal keys wasn't properly thought through, but he likes his keys heavy because they are much more difficult to forget or lose when there is a measurable difference in the weight he feels in his pocket, when with or without them. It's a half pound of fluidly, nearly freely moving pieces of metal in his pocket, weapons if need be, and he feels a janitor or prison guard when he clips them to his belt loop, allowing them to sing as he walks. This is rare. He only does it when wearing small-pocketed pants.

His forehead digs into the grain of the door as he jingles through his many options, trying different ones, even ones that could not possibly fit, different style of key altogether, with the rationalization that he's forgotten what his house key looks like. With the time it is taking, the lean becomes a dependency, and with the finding of the correct key and the knob actually turning, the catch release releases him into his living room and upon the floor like a spilled bag of soil. He almost floats the crash is so smooth. This is the safest of the many crashes he could have been involved in. He rolls to his back and kicks the door closed, neglecting the jingle hidden within the initiating kick and the finishing slam, rises and heads to his bedroom haphazardly. This ends a night of drinking and conversing.

When the conversation is fertile, giving off that reproductive aroma that reaches into that lower, truer, nature, it's rather difficult to break away from, even with work merely a few pie slices removed from the small hand's placement on an analog clock and gaining in pursuit. The drinks kept flowing because The Fifth was in a generous, giving mode. Revolutions were planned in European public houses, and the environment is ripe for another in this nation, a child of Europe. Revolution was not the line of conversation, not on top it wasn't, but maybe a few layers in it was what the strangers were discussing. They didn't even exchange names, and they parted with no intention to see one another again unless they happened upon each other in a way similar to the way they met this evening. They validated one another's anger, and reasoned it as a natural response to an environment that refuses to validate their humanity beyond the lofty ideas in political documentation. They were there to let off steam.

Cops killing people, mostly Black people, some undeniably innocent, and getting away with it, was the spirit of the night. The news stories were taunts, making so many swallow the threats they had offered in the form of, *They bet not or I will,* revealing their manhood as flaccid and ineffective. America didn't *feel* it, laughing asking, "Is it yet?" Even those who didn't make the promises felt the sting of pride with each new, tragic, accidental, justified event that left another Black man or woman dead, that called back to the ritual hangings, community lynchings, and the breaking of slaves like mustangs. Pain, punishment, and murder was a public show. It was good old fashioned theater all were forced to watch as bull whips ripped through the backs of the disobedient, the men and women who had the nerve to think their lives and opinions of what they should do with them mattered as much as master's, the men and women whose arms were ripped from their very sockets and dragged behind horses when quartered, and those men and women of whom ropes were ripped tight by gravity, constricting their wind pipes as those ropes became the stems of the sour, low hanging, strange fruit, these men and women.

Master employed slave breakers, or played one himself. The breakers would publicly beat, torture, degrade, maim, and murder, even raping unruly men. On occasion, they would hang a pregnant wench upside-down and run a blade across her belly to liberate the fetus inside her from the binds of her oppressive abdomen, allow gravity to take it, along with the gel of mother's screams, tears, blood, and afterbirth draining to the ground, only to meet it, its tiny purple face and soft skull, with the heel of his boot, smashing its clay-like skeleton and rubbery flesh back into the clay of the earth that all were once rumored to be made of, liberating it again. Master, the great liberator, the example of what a civilized man was to the encircling savages watching in horror, as he'd then drag, scoot his boots along the grass to remove the gelatin he'd accumulated while stamping a life innocent of everything but its staining, cursed race, away to prove a point, with an expression of disgust gracing his mug as though his temple were the one disrespected. It was all done in public to plant seeds of fear that grew as vines that anchor the feet and climb upwards like spines inside their bodies to tightly wrap their hearts and minds to strangle the thoughts of resistance. The creators of such art took pictures with their *master*pieces smiling, and even mailed postcards of this work of theirs, filled with pride. This was what was supposedly done away with, the ghost of America past, now revisiting, the shake and rattle of its heavy, embattled chains scarring, scaring, and becoming more pronounced the more the populace pretended not to recognize it.

Toni kept the spirits strong though, and the patrons absorbed them like possession. At first they wouldn't acknowledge its presence at all, the growing sound of the shackles rattling upon their wrists and ankles with their every motion. No matter how imposing it was, as the chains materialized upon them and they spoke as if they had the bit in their mouths, they opted not to notice. Its newest expression, this painful memory, unresolved, was too large of a story and all were aware of it, but they just made fools of each other in a game of *pretend it doesn't matter*, pretend the slave breakers of old had not returned with uniforms and badges, and pretend that master was not still on their asses. It was on both of the tips of their tongues and caught deep in the back of their throats like a cough that refuses to arrive that waters the eyes. The more he drank, Will was trying to better negotiate the distance between the phrases *cops killing people* and *cop killing people*, and how easy of a paper edit it is to remove that invasive crooked line between cop and killing, simply known as the letter *s*, and creating a psychic adjustment. A dab of whiteout would do the trick. Surrounded by cowards, he desired to share his pain more materially than they do in group therapy. He fought inside himself, wrestling with the ideas of innocence and guilt while trying to picture a target or an action to relieve this debilitating sting that something had to be done about. His dry liquors agreed.

Of the body count of the innocent and deceased was a twelve year old whose only crime was having no one to play with at the time. Poor baby. He played in a park alone, role-playing with a pellet gun that looked real, pointing it at an imagined enemy occasionally until he tired of doing so. His actual enemy arrived in a squad car and put two holes in his twelve-year-old chest before even verbally engaging him. It was a response to 911 call. The caller thought the gun may have been real, wasn't sure, but also indicated no immediate danger. No one else was in the park, so the kid could have only endangered himself if the gun was, in fact, real. He did endanger himself, unknowingly. In defense of the cop, the cop thought the kid looked twenty. So, a twenty-year-old with what appears to be a real gun in an open carry state is ok to kill before verbal engagement, is the mindfuck of an argument being made, but obviously not as irrational as it seems to be because months prior in the same open carry state the precedent was set.

A twenty-two year old was gunned down for holding a BB gun rifle that the super center he was gunned down within sells, that he had, in fact, picked up from the super center shelf and leisurely walked around with while speaking to his babies' mother on the phone, barrel down, when the slave breakers… cops, rushed into the building simultaneously telling him to drop the gun and gunning him down. His babies' mother heard him silenced because he considered, maybe, buying a toy for their children in the same space as some asshole who decided to call the cops and lie about his activity, effectively arranging his murder, for reasons that no one knows. One being White, the caller, and one being Black, the fallen, and the exceptional health of this country's centuries old racism had not been ruled out as a reason, and Will didn't bite his tongue in stating this to the old detective-like stranger. The cops were White, also. Stories like these, and there were many, all available and being fed like gunpowder to pit bulls, sat like lumps of coal at the back of their throats as they sipped their liquor and struggled to adjust their clenched teeth and jaws from around the imaginary bit, making sticky their spit, and slowly began talking of, not actually of the stories themselves, but instead of the taboo, speaking it and heating it until the first thrusts of steam began engaging the piston. Those events and the many others added to them in such a short time were just the background, the color commentary, of the discussion.

Two Black males, a generation apart, in frustration, shared vivid tales of their own castration, in a fertile conversation bound to produce something between them, even if the offspring is just peace of mind. Conversations at this level of intimacy require alcohol. Toni served drinks, refusing to enter the discourse, yet listening to every word and occasionally making confirmations with eye contact and nods while doing bar business. The conversation ran perfectly like poorly scripted dialogue, with absolutely no friction or building tension between the characters because one disagreed with the other. Their politeness was damning, considering the subject. Manners haven't a place in discussions about the loss of livelihood and the encroaching threat of the loss of life, but it was as if they were sipping tea. Was. There was no disagreement, not in complete or in partial. It was as if they were one, able to complete each other's thoughts, or pulling the conversation from the air, in tandem, like a cellphone signal as they spoke as men pretending to still be men, as if their manhood had not been dropped off in some sad and lonely place that allowed them to make it into this moment. The more they spoke on it, the more they shrank, and in saying nothing, Toni grew, becoming more man than them both.

Their exchange was the unfolding of something so complex it could not be spoken of upon initiation without one thinking the other was crazy or some type of fanatic, and not for disagreement, but for simply being open to saying this thing silently agreed upon without first properly vetting the environment. Someone dangerous or dumb enough to do that needs to be dismissed, disregarded, disagreed with no matter how piercing his or her truth, even in a pub. In apprehension, even with the aid of alcohol they knew their place, and even unconsciously bended their voices more in whisper, the more biting their truth, as if the representative of *the man* was nearby or the old cross leaning against the back wall, in the darkest corner, was mic'd up and God listened. They never truly know whose side He's on. Years of forced obedience in the nurture of children who would not be murdered before their time, created a passivity that was hard to break, openly, but the flames roared violently within the pits of many of their stomachs, especially in the males, as though they housed hell. Black rage has been identified in the facial expressions of boys in years as early as their fifth, and two men-children sat in The Fifth, reducing themselves to a psychological station in life where fear did not have absolute dominion. This night with the bellowing of their liquor fueled, flammable breaths, the discourse turned into fire breathing, and Toni kept feeding the flame with high proof spirits that were easy to set ablaze, also alike hell, making their shot glasses bottomless. A casual discussion accented with the peculiarness of some current events turned into a tribal fire dance and the calling for the falling of blood to stop its burn, once hours in.

They didn't really call for blood, not verbally. It was a symbolic clawing for the manhood they knew was leaking away from them with every new incident that challenged them to do more than weigh in philosophically. Will had been there since leaving work, clothing still as sharp as the morning press made them, wearing a Members Only-like cloth jacket to fight the day's chill. His co-host, the intruder, was a tad overdressed, wearing a thin trench coat and hat like a nineteen forties private eye. Will and Toni had already been tuning the tension in the air to a stressful pitch before he arrived, so his arrival helped but didn't. Conflict was meant to be. There was enough frustration to go around, even between friends.

Toni's statements were littered with sighs. "I'm not insinuating anything. I'm just saying, people are talking."

"My people?" Will inquired.

"You don't have no people, remember?" Toni's eyes sliced across Will like a blade, with enough attitude to fillet him into two, clean, indecisive halves, one a competent and confident leader, and one an exposed consequence composed of what's left when he refuses to be, in an attempt to be all-accommodating. Toni, honestly, finds both equally revolting because Will switches between them like a schizophrenic, allowing no one's palate to adjust. It's the subject of many conversations with Robert. In all his genius, Toni's often frustrated because Will is difficult to work with.

"You know what I mean," Will counters.

"I don't. I used to though, but now I have to ask questions to be sure. Who are these people you passively claim ownership of, so I'll know if we have the same ones in mind. We goin' with Black people today? Poor people? The lumpen? The hoods? Matter fact, let me write this down." Toni reached beneath the bar and resurfaced with a black, leather bound journal with a pen jammed inside its spine that's pulled out and clicked to ready position.

Will tried to explain, "Man…" He sucked his teeth. "Ok, Toni. Are we talking Legion people, or just plain old barber shop talk?"

"People period. I see no need to categorize beyond saying people you identify with." The pen is clicked again and unreadied in disappointing fashion.

Will is blocked as though he'd given the wrong response. Not in the mood to wrestle with Toni, he changed the subject. "Missed you at Robert's shindig. Like, really missed you."

"I actually planned on going, but this woman just couldn't keep her hands off of me that afternoon… Besides, that was more about you two's relationship, not me. Forget that though, back to these people of yours and what we're going to do…" The front door opened and the light shot in like it was tossing Will a lifeline, and the conversation was opportunely closed.

The older gentleman, maybe late in his fifty years or early in his sixty years, skin weathered and bronzed and lips made of jerky tightly pressed together and poking out from behind his salt and pepper beard, interrupted them with his presence. He was clearly holding a lot in, with his lips so tight. He needed a drink, and his timing was perfect for Will because he also wanted to drink, not to argue with Toni, which was exactly what was about to happen. They needed a drink, but more so they needed to release the building pressure tightening them from within across every inch of their cursed black skin. His entry cut Will and Toni's conversation like a tire nipple, the outside light cut into the inside darkness, as he cut across the bar and sat in the stool next to Will without invitation, without acknowledgement, and ordered a drink. Will stared at the man long enough, without flinching, looking to his right, until the man recognized his own rudeness. With a small nod, a wrinkled forehead, and a hanging neck, he apologetically submitted and greeted Will with, "Well, how are you young man?"

Will mockingly responded with, "Absolutely fabulous, old man. Just sitting here drinking scotch and enjoying all of this freedom my people fought for." It was as clear a kick to the gut as Will meant it to be with the overlay of the current political and racial climate making it so breathtaking. Black people are in the streets protesting for the same acknowledgment they were fifty years prior in the old man's generation, yelling that their lives mattered, making their supposed progress from the Civil Rights Movement, if any, quite biodegradable. The old man responded with a nod, and Will was content to leave it at that, one rude gesture for another. The old man let a few minutes pass and decided not the hold his peace, even offering to buy Will his next drink.

That's how they began. It started slowly. They both had lots to say but they just needed a number of drinks to sufficiently lubricate their voices first. Then there was the trust thing they had to worry about. Long gone are the days where someone can be treated as an ally just because they share a similar complexion. Will has never been much for trusting people anyway, as his history showed him not to. With little to no friction, and lots of liquor, they began to test each other's political waters, and used the comfort they encountered as a path to discomfort. Knowing what someone doesn't like is not knowing their politics, but knowing what they are willing to do about those things to change them to what extreme, is. No one likes racism, for example, even the racists, because it is so much easier to just join the general sentiment. If one determines allies by such a thin test, the entire world is his or her ally. They had been propelled by a massive swell of agreements and moving at mach speed, so Will decided to take advantage of their harmony and push a little, wanting to find out no more about what the stranger disliked but what he was willing to do about it, his politics.

The head of steam and the momentum they'd created allowed this strange man to produce the night's most memorable line in his impassioned confusion when his response to what he wanted to do about the feeling he felt turned into an intimate tell-all about his fear of the police, and his admitted fear of White people, in general. Not mach speed, mock speed. The sparks that resulted from his admission, the screech of the dialogue's metal wheels upon the metal tracks were so bright they were blinding to Will, so he balled his face up, leaned back and turned away. This is where the perfection of their connection diverged. The esthetic broke. The backdrop fell. Toni clumsily bumped the bar and the chandelier of clean martini glasses above it rapped against one another in a lighthearted chuckle at the night's punch line. Will couldn't find the humor in ending up in this familiar space yet again, especially when dealing with one from the old man's generation. Just not much fight in them left, and there are those in that generation holding positions of leadership pacifying the lot with their fear. Fear is both highly reactive and unstable; it can bring the strongest of warriors out of ordinary men, or make women of them, as far as the domestic woman is viewed by society at least.

"Man... I'm not scared of other men. We all fall when struck in the right places. Nope, not scared. How could I call myself a man if I was?" Will looked the detective down, refusing to follow with such honesty in his response, while frowning his brow, flexing his distinctive jaws, and negating the man's entire existence with a measured head shake. "It was just a strategy. Non-violence is JUST a fucking strategy. Not to mention a pretty ineffective strategy when your opposition has no conscience, to paraphrase brother Stokely... Kwame Ture. That non-violent shit should've died with King as far as I'm concerned. Was he not the perfect example to how much they truly give a fuck about that strategy? See..."

"Last call!!" Toni finally joins the conversation. It wasn't really closing time, but it was near enough considering the shifting mood. It was either close the bar or Will would, after closing some eyes, old eyes, that honestly didn't deserve being closed, with swelling, any more than they already were. The irresponsible alcoholic releases his frustrations upon his environment, and Will has and Will will, and it's never expected, because he doesn't look like the type, too prim and proper, too straight laced, as if that is any revelation as to what resides beneath a fully buttoned up button-down. Toni was Will-familiar enough to know when to interrupt, being many times an accomplice to the damage he'd cause while drunk and identifying a target and the arguments or fights that would ensue. His cussing was a sign, as he rarely does, so Toni yelled last call, loudly, as if it was a bar full of patrons. Will smiled and backed off, avoided eye contact in slight embarrassment, stirred his drink with his index finger and placed the nail of that finger between the pinch of his biting down teeth and flashed a jaw-flexing smile. Not really a smile at all. Disharmony removed them from the comfort of their pocket, and the one became two, two drunk men speaking at each other in a pub moments before it would close. Will downed the last of his shot, and with difficulty, stood. He rose to leave, placing cash upon the bar, and bracing himself a moment, using that arm as an anchor like a bicycle kickstand.

Will looked at Toni in disappointment, cutting his eyes toward the dick he'd been speaking to all night, while doing his best to not weave from side to side, unsure in his balance. Will was more the detective, even without the man's Dick Tracy fedora and trench, and his investigation ended in disappointing fashion yet again. Toni addressed him, laughing at his wobbling and his trying his best not to, "You're going to kill yourself one day, you know?" A joke is the best approach in telling someone loved dearly, who hates authority and refuses advice, that should they die abruptly, their heart isn't the only one that will stop, because *Will, stop!* doesn't work.

"Probably. Not before you lose your liquor license, though. Besides, it's better I do it rather someone else. Like a fucking cop, or some random racist ass White man, often one in the same, putting a bullet in the back of my head … Until next time." Will solidly slaps his drinking buddy on his back and speaks before making his way out. "Bye old man, stay safe." *Bye* was said in the spirit of a *fuck you,* and *stay safe* in the spirit of *coward,* because that is exactly what Will meant to, wanted to say, save for being raised better. There was no need in standing upon him in this moment after he'd opted to continue shrinking instead of following the natural progression, where the momentum had been taking them, to finding their feet. Will stopped his own shrinking, found his feet, with trouble, and walked out of The Fifth to the danger that was his chariot.

*   *   *

The next morning finds Will through his blurred vision and a headache that pulsed like his heart had moved up to his head to get away from the poison factory his liver had become. His heart and mind share one space, and this explains the pressure. It's early. The light is sharp. It pierces through his vertical blinds, making bars, illuminated strips that crawl across the carpet, stretching up to his bars. They are twins. Buying two small bars was cheaper than one big one, and they are easier to manipulate and maneuver around in his small box of a bedroom. The walls are empty. Blank with potential. The room is nearly empty besides the bars and the bed, and the bars are not even there by plan. Originally, they were bought and assembled in the den, but they slowly made their way back to the room Will spends most of his time in. The only company he ever entertains ends up in the bedroom, naked, laughing, drunk, and interwoven, her body parts with his, so he keeps this location stocked with glasses for emptying and glasses for filling. One of the bars is completely full, cluttered with empty and nearly empty bottles of different colored liquids. The other bar has only a couple of these bottles as if it is used for relieving the first. If only the Alcoholics Anonymous class could see this, Will would surely have some explaining to do. Unless they subscribe to the sinner to saint philosophy, where he or she with the problem knows it most and therefore is the best to challenge it, his lifestyle would be deemed a conflict of interest. That logic makes criminals the best crime fighters. Considering the day's peace officers, maybe there is something to it.

A couple, Will and his girl, sits upon the edge of the bed, admiring one another, one in the other's alternating grasp, gripping, rubbing, releasing, and repeating. They sleep together on different sides of the pillow. Her side remains cool. In mornings she's cool to the touch, and she anticipates his caress as much as he yearns to make contact. Every chilled curve of hers is mastered, and he pulls her until, as the childhood rhyme says, *her backbone slips* and she clicks in submission. Controlled and careful, he places his finger within her, blows, makes sure she's moist, and if not, makes sure she's moist. She's been at his side for nearly two decades and she doesn't look a day older than the day they met. No wrinkles. The story is, Black don't crack, and she's as dark as they come, darker than any would expect to see him with. Her coolness attracted him. His hands warm her, and she responds with the slightest touch if he places his finger in her special spot. She releases the most spine tingling scream when touched correctly, often an index finger pull, like signaling one to come closer, and she'll vibrate in surrender to the deep connection they share because he knows just when she'll climax. She submits. He is in absolute control; he triggers it. Maybe age can be blamed because now he doesn't touch her as often, and it's been a long time since he touched her like that, in the way she'll scream, and they both miss it. He'd stand behind her, with both hands grabbing her hips, finger her just right, and he'd release the banshee, the dream-piercing, life-stripping scream resulting from their lascivious acts. They miss the intimacy they used to share.

Killing never bothered Will much, nor does fighting, as the two share the common thread of the absence of fear. Any behavior once reinforced enough removes fear. It also helps to be pretty efficient at the reinforced behavior. Enjoying it doesn't hurt, a place he found himself in with killing and fighting, an enjoyment he misses dearly with his rejoining the civilized, with common courtesy, laws, and police officers; it is just not what he's used to. One cannot reinforce death, but the experience of almost dying and feeling dead can be reinforced, and this is how he lost his fear. Complete apathy concerning life is the consequence of many calculated choices he's made. He loved so much, manipulating the patch he was in, he might be losing the capacity to love at all. He loves his guns though, and the love they make, but the rest of his reality seems to be fading like his interest in an easy lay after an orgasm and losing color in a routine that at times has had him contemplating kissing her, this gun, upon the lips, but that is not a heroes death. Even with his ending up in this lusterless place in life, caused by his own decisions, the way his mind told the tale he was still nothing short of a hero, and heroes do not die like that, the second act is always a struggle, but heroes persevere.

He rises before the sun, or rather before the Earth rolls toward it each morning. Sometimes he touches her, sometimes he doesn't, but he is always behind the bars, often before his morning piss. The bars are his prison. The counseling of his spirits have a lot to do with how easily he shrugs off the thought of death, whether he is delivering it or receiving it. They are good council, the best, yet part of the living he makes is in telling others that this reality isn't so. He's secure in his lie as long as he doesn't have to become someone's sponsor. If someone called him late at night succumbing to the alcoholic temptation, he'd probably ask where he or she was and what drink was the temptation with aims to join them rather than deter them, especially if it was a woman. There are few things that go as well with sex as alcohol, and he figures that that is not an accident, and surprisingly, there are actually some nice looking women in and out of Harmony every once and a while. The nice looking ones are not the standard though. Most look like addiction, meaning that they've found something more important than life itself, so life and health have taken a back seat. Nearly rubbed out by drug use, teeth rotted, skin blotchy, eyes lost, and the jaw of a cash register, many are drug use domestics. They've a new constitution, a replaced reason for living, and Will would never... Some are pretty though, natural, honest, beauty, because they are not afforded all of the cosmetic advantages of those on the outside, literally putting on a new face. It is a hard time in life when pretty women are doing crime, and most are desperate too, understandably. Will would make a horrible AA sponsor, and they are lucky his composure is such that he refuses to attend the meetings inebriated. He has a position of power and an image to uphold. What would be the use of washing and shaving every morning, ironing his clothes, tucking in his shirt, tying his neck or bowtie, if he was going to allow them to label him an alcoholic? That's why he drinks first thing in the morning before doing all of that. The buzz has time to die and there is no possibility of one of the stronger smells or the liquor itself getting into his clothing in the case of him spilling it.

The House of Harmony is a privately run rehabilitation facility for the newly released from prison, with a special emphasis on nonviolent criminals, mostly drug offenses. Violent offenders are also housed, but they arrive at a much lesser frequency and the programs provided do not really cater to their needs as much as they do for the drug dealer and drug user variety, who are often one and the same. Harmony still receives a good balance. The nature of most drug offense comes with at least a violent disposition, and whether one is locked up for violence or not depends upon the available evidence. There is an entire police unit dedicated to acquiring evidence of intent to distribute or use narcotics and none to keep track of how many metal bats and fists had to be used to keep the business running smoothly, unless the case ends up on one of the desks of homicide unit. There's that violence, and then there is the reality that some enter the prison system without being violent, but very few leave that way - is it rehabilitation or education? Prison has a way of bringing things out of people, a kind of character building in a factory of survival where violent tendencies are encouraged to expose themselves. Few, if any, graduate without this lesson, even those just passing through.

Violent criminals are not afforded the halfway house opportunity as often in sentencing anyway, and many are caught in prison's inviting cycle of endless violence, adding years and years to the time initially given. For those without the correct amount of discipline, sentences become run-on sentences, making a facility suited to specialize in these types of offenders a poor investment, and at the heart of it, it's about money. Anyone with their heart set on working in this type of rehabilitation establishment to make a measurable change is in for a rude heartbreak, especially if they sit high enough within the organization to see the amount of money changing hands. If it is indeed possible to *fix* the clients, it's not as profitable as it is not to, and those on the front lines often wonder if *fixing* them is even the goal. On paper, House of Harmony is not designated as a facility for violent criminals because investors stand to make more this way, but violence still shows its face. Although it isn't often it arrives through his office door, Will knows how to deal with it, and he actually appreciates the break in monotony when a *badass* arrives, mistaking his neatness for weakness.

Disguising and distracting, his eyes are deep, dark, kind, and warm. Not a hair is ever misplaced upon his squared head, keeping the same two to three inches on the top, with his liberal use of pomade in combed through greaser curls that sit like uncooked ramen noodles, a taper fade, and a pencil thin mustache. His neatness is gathered in a tiny enough package where it looks as if at any moment he's prepared to break out into a song and tap dance routine, with this look of his reminiscent of a nineteen-twenties portrait except he is not peeking through a vignette and he's, of course, colored – in color. Negros were very neat back then, and they did lots of singing and dancing. The pictorial history immortalized them with shiny smiles, dances, and jig-ready stances, but the oral history, and the literary history told a tale not nearly as jubilant, making Will's look as disguising as the long lash framing of what he looks through. Camouflage serves a function, and his is more natural. His sideburns grow in a distinctive gray, right by his ears, when he lets them, which is almost never, and the rest of his head is oil black with only a few grays that appear as highlights. His cheeks are gaunt and blemish free except the occasional razor bump, and when he frowns he bites down on nothing, flexing his jaw muscles until they protrude like quarter-sized peanut butter cookies in the corner his jawbone creates. He frowns often. Smiles are rare. Even this frown of his has an allure. It all works in concert and aids in his callousness while outwardly appearing so adorable, mostly compensating for what he lacks in height. His attitude and aggression is compensation for what he lacks in his ability to be visually intimidating. It's difficult to shake nature, and she made him appear the heartbreaker, not the face breaker, but nurture, too, has her say.

His wardrobe is regimented, consisting of solid-color polo cut short-sleeve shirts on days eighty degrees and above, solid-color button-downs when seventy-nine and below, and button-downs covered with a solid-colored sweater when sixty and below, with slacks or khakis with belt no lower than an inch from his navel. He never relaxes his collars and his shirts are always buttoned to the top. Only his most intimate relations can speak of what his collarbone and lower neck look like. He dresses like a Ken doll, and some could joke that he isn't much taller. He keeps his hair short and his face shaved because he is ashamed of his naps the residents say. His hair is actually long enough to nap up on top, but that's not the way it grows. The convicts double as psychologists, and who better to help him to reconnect to his roots than a bunch of unrefined hoods that haven't shown the capacity to plan their own lives much less anyone else's? Somehow his ability to be *down* is tied to appearance, and his appearance is golfer-preppy save the prints – the only print he'll wear is camouflage, and he's retired. He speaks from his nose and pronounces his Rs correctly, which isn't the southern thing to do or the Black thing to do. Their ideas of him are mostly uninformed, but

Will doesn't put much stock into the opinions of human stock; he never told anyone he was from the South in the first place. He has books for them to read, if they would read them, that might change the way they think about these things, but until, he's rather comfortable in the skin that he's in.

Will has spent ten years as the house manager at Harmony, and he's heard every cut-down available about his speech, his posture, the cut of his clothing, his hair, his mustache, his height, and his attention to detail from every disgruntled and every jovially bonding resident. If more of them had ventured outside of the ghetto and watched more than hood fairytales to learn about the world they would have no doubt recognized his style. The cut of his jib was strictly military as he'd been in the Junior Reserve Officers' Training Corps - JROTC - since he was fourteen, and he enlisted in the marines immediately after graduation at eighteen. Higher education wasn't for him, or at least not the reading and writing kind, not then it wasn't. He'd been shaped by his father's lack of experience, and desired experience first hand, and not through text and imagination. He couldn't wait to be taken far away from home, and everyone in it, including and especially his family. He had a hard working father who sacrificed working long hours to provide for his family, but by the age of fifty he hadn't traveled outside of the state, and was too tired to do much after fifty. He struggled to imagine what the rest of the world was like, and did his best to supplement his curiosity with television, but he was bound to a local experience. It made his life compact, Will's mother's as well, and it inspired Will's departure. He didn't want that for himself, so the anchor of family was shifted to future spot on his to do list, and he'd see the world first. The military is how the poor achieve this, unless one is an exceptional athlete and that designation was eliminated by Will's size. He served his twenty and retired after extensive traveling and learning more about life through death than he ever could have without.

Harmony is not quite his dream job, but it serves an important purpose, and it gave him something to do after leaving the military – which he had to do because of the insatiable war appetite of his country. He opted against returning home to New England. He visited immediately after discharge, but he knew he wasn't staying. His parents and all of his friends are dead, in prison, or both, broke and married with children, the same death sentence he refused to inherit from his father. Twenty years is a long time, and he had plenty of time to grow apart from everyone he once loved and defined himself by, and he really just traveled back home to say his final good-byes. It was cold up there, land was cheaper in Texas, and he acquired a taste for Mexican food and Mexican women while in the service. Traveling the world came with the price of pointing his rifle and pulling the trigger at men who were doing nothing but protecting their homes and families, but it didn't bother Will much, not in his early twenties. As a small man, his gun and his proficiency in using one was an equalizer, but he also excelled in hand to hand combat by studying pressure points and learning how to take down men twice his size. Will would get high off of the adrenaline rush of fighting. He was intoxicated by the brotherhood he was sworn to protect, so his targets rarely even appeared human. They were like blips on a video game screen, they never spoke English, they were evil and in the way; it was very easy to distance himself from their humanity, but on his return to the states, he found it difficult to wholly reinstate the humanity of others that he found so easy to strip. He is in practice with this at Harmony, and after ten years it continues to be a daily struggle.

Most of his day is spent sitting behind his desk, sitting in counseling sessions, or sitting in the recreation area bonding, which is like baby-sitting for emotional adults. Will is the eyes for those with vested interests in the facility, actual investors, and his job is to diffuse problems before they even begin, so it is important for him to know his residents well enough to read them. To do this means he has to be around them, and engaging, and this is where his lack of *downness* acts as sort of an Achilles heel. His position hurts his ability to gain their trust, *house manager* is synonymous with *house nigger*, or *boot-licking, sellout, working for the man*, for starters, but his being so square creates an even larger hurdle. He could probably get away with being a *boot-licking, sellout, working for the man* if he spoke more from his chest or maybe grabbed his nuts every once in a while. His conservativeness often gets them laughing though, so a small positive exists. His job is to get them into the facility, acquainted with the rules and regulations, and back out to the streets with the least amount of friction. Seamless is what he prefers, but it is rare that he achieves that. There is a lot of unlearning and relearning that needs to occur before one sheds the callus they build, the institutionalization of the penal system, and is ready to be set free. Infractions happen, but when Will is at his best, he minimizes them, because too many, or problems of a certain magnitude will cause his employers to lose their contract with the state, and him to lose his contract with them.

Will calls back to another time with his look and his consciousness. Being straight-laced, neat, intelligent, proper, and Black was once standard and beautiful, before so many relaxed their standards and allowed Blackness to be defined askew. It wasn't being White or trying to be; it was being proud. There was nothing White about strolling down Lenox Avenue in your Sunday's best in the height of the Harlem culture explosion shortly after the turn of the twentieth century. That time is the arguably the Blackest and most beautiful his people has ever seen on American soil, and there was nothing White about it. It wasn't for Whites, and they did their best to ignore Whites, but Whites could not resist trying to share in the beauty they were able to produce in fashion, dance, the literary, the visual, and the theater arts. They identified with being clean, sharp, straight-laced, intellectual, and challenged others to compare themselves to the standard they were creating. Their role models were creative and intellectual titans, not only defining Black culture but American culture.

It was quite the politically impressive time as well with the brilliance of Garvey and the popularization of PanAfricanism. Will has studied these times extensively and fancies himself to be a part of such a culture. Even if he's nearly alone, he basks in the glow of its zeitgeist. There is no damage in being proud and representing oneself in this way, no matter how many confuse it as a form of denying his Blackness. Will is instead affirming his Blackness, representing it. There is nothing so lacking of Blackness about him that he has to amplify it in his speech, dress, and posture. He found the idea of it redundant and idiotic, and he couldn't help but use such labels for those who practiced these behaviors, often seen as the new expression of Garveyism, the new Garveyites, a candy coating of slogans and liberation colors with none of the filling of Black scholarship and excellence. They are Robert and his ilk.

Pride's being confused with arrogance, and drive is being confused with aggression. To Will, they are nothing but charlatans that divert more away from social consciousness with the thinning incompleteness of their message devoid of direct, attainable, goals, leading to an endgame, than bringing people towards it, at least the intelligent ones. *Acting Black* is a White phenomenon, and *acting White* is a misnomer confused with pride and intelligence from those who do not expect that from Black people, those with very short memories, forgetting when Black and proper was the thing to be. Those who trouble with this association of greatness with Blackness, and not just with antiquity, but in their fellow man who does not fit the new Blackness cutout are instruments in making Whiteness a standard for excellence, like Whites aren't lazy and dumb as well. It tightens Will's jaws because there is indeed nothing pro-Black about that.

Will does his best to represent his people well, when sober at least. He's traveled the world and the halls of Harmony with his head held high, and if that makes some think he's a prude or an asshole, so be it. A gypsy, he aspires to a higher form of excellence, from a lifetime before, because he has found something has been lost in the new translation of Black pride and Black power. He doesn't care what they think, he doesn't care what they say, or he tries not to at least. Although Will doesn't believe in Harmony, he harmonizes, because he is acutely aware that the importance of the music being played is much bigger than his lack of enjoyment in it. So, because the audience demands it, whether he agrees with or enjoys the connections or not, it is like he's of the Harlem Renaissance and still singing and dancing in a way.

1:4

Hate can be motivating, so can be competition, but neither when unrestricted. They need to fall within the tight path of perspective, the track laid by vision, directing them to a certain and specific destination or outcome. Energy is wasted, lost, when not properly directed. The same light bulb that struggles to light a room, once placed into a mirrored concaved pit, can light any point in that same room from any point within it, through this concentrated focus. Instead of wishing for or trying to develop a stronger light, maybe understanding that the entire room doesn't need to be illuminated at once would be just as effective for us. While some wish to take on the entire room, I'll aim at one spot.

"Aww… look who decided to join us this morning. Our fearless leader." The sloppily dressed and similarly stacked groundsman removes his chin from the handle of the rake he's been leaning upon, pulls up the sullied left sleeve of his uniform shirt to expose his wristwatch, which exists not, but he still continues to wrist watch upon its nakedness while yelling across the courtyard, "A little late, but better late than never, huh?" Shots fired. Will hasn't fully gotten out of the car and shut the door before this rude address. He was still grabbing his briefcase from the backseat when he poked his head above the crest of his sedan to find that the enemy had not only spotted him, but also pulled the trigger. Only a windy day and his Panama hat, which he isn't wearing, blowing off of his head as soon as he peeked could have painted the picture of his being targeted better. He lets the shots roll off of him, or miss him rather, tightening his face, flexing his cookie batter jaws into his distinctive baked treats, and only responding with a quick glance as he begins a brisk walk towards the building. Again the groundsman taunts, "We didn't know what to do without you. Without your leadership… I probably shouldn't admit this, but I been leaning on this rake, I mean this doohickey here, for the last forty-five minutes wondering what it's used for, but now that you're here…"

Will shakes his head in blow-off fashion, undeterred from his destination. His shined hard-bottoms, upon the presently filthy and often filthy cement walk, covered in twigs, leaves, grass, needles, a couple of pine cones, and even dirt, the responsibility of the grounds-man, click, when uninhibited and they find cement; they crunch and scratch when they don't. With Will only feet away from the entrance and ready to swipe his badge to deactivate the lock, the groundsman tries a more direct approach, "I'm not sure how to do this! For real, come holler at me Will!"

Just feet away, so close, Will sighs and makes cookies while staring at the door handle. He wipes his hand across his face, from forehead to chin, and shifts into an about-face back towards the groundsman. He drops his briefcase next to the entrance, with the groundsman watching, he makes sure of this, as a signal that this meeting shall not be long. His briefcase will be needing him short-ly. The groundsman smiles as he approaches, and apprehensively scratches at his thighs, dropping the rake. The handle bounces twice and kicks up a couple of old leaves, brown, decayed, and paper thin, for sitting upon the grounds for more than a season. Will pursues, trampling upon more patches of dirt than grass, there was more grass on the cement, in his trail to meet him, and he arrives with, "Okay Tuck, what's up?"

"Ah, ah, ah." The groundsman raises his finger, slightly wag-ging it, then rolls his wrist in display of his stitched nametag. He pinches his nametag, pulling the embroidery away from his chest in emphasis, and says, accusatorily, "I'm Robert Anderson, affection-ately known as Bob… Who the fuck is Tuck?"

More cookies. With a pensive nod, Will responds, "No-body… Nobody to worry about. My mistake Robert… How can I help you? And as you so respectfully pointed out, I happen to be running a little late, so I'm sincerely hoping this is something that couldn't wait."

Tuck responds, "You the boss, nigga. Ain't nobody worried about when you get here. I wouldn't even come if I had your posi-tion. I'm serious. Don't worry about being late either… we used to that." Will tilts his head to the side as if to ask *Huh?* Will is never late. He prides himself on not being late and being removed from the often spoken stereotype about Black people and their lack of respect for starting times. Tuck continues, "The revolution been waiting on your ass years now, but I ain't ..."

Will interrupts, "Really? Man, you need something or not?"

"Yeah. I'm trying to get to it, but you bullshitting and shit. You know how you do... Well, as you know, people pissed. Another cop just got off." *Offed* is how his clumsy tongue makes it sound, but Will knew better as he halfway listens while thinking about his exit strategy. *Offed* would have meant a cop was murdered, and that action itself is rarely heard of, but to modify it with *another* is the stuff of fiction. Without pause, Tuck continues, "Grand jury keep saying niggas cool to kill. Your reading ass probably read about it. I watched it on TV. *Get Out of Jail Free* card keeps popping up in they stack every time black folk get executed. And y'all call it justice... We need to do something man, soon! Tonight. Just so people'll know we out here, and we got they back. A message needs to be sent to these beasts. One everyone can see. Toni won't make a fucking move without your approval, so, I gotta come straight to you, whether I like you or not. See, look what I got set up..."

Will stands, stoic his mask, staring unattentively at the thick tongue writhing and turning like one dying organism trapped inside of a dying other. As soon as he mentioned Legion business, Tuck's signal was lost. Maybe Will is somewhat at fault for confusing the two worlds. He's supposed to be the disciplined one, yet he called the man by his chosen alias. Tuck is no more Tuck here than Will is Will there. It is a rare occasion, but Will even sees that Tuck was right in correcting him on that, but Will could also see, clearly, that he *was* being Tuck. Robert would have been working hard in recognition that, as a felon, there were strings pulled and moves made, high up, just to get him this position that he's performing poorly, embarrassingly bad, and it is reflecting undesirably on the man who bent over backwards to secure him the job. Conversely, Tuck would be leaning upon his rake, cracking jokes, standing in the center of a campus in dire need of keeping, with even the spot he's standing upon unraked. Will's mistake, but he knew with whom he was speaking even before he began to detail this halfcocked idea about sending a message, getting revenge through a planned killing, if Will was willing, that Will wasn't really paying any attention to because Tuck is the king of premature ideas not based on logic but feeling, that never grow legs. Tuning Tuck out beginning at *You the boss, nigga,* and completely blocking him out by, *whether I like you or not,* Will awaited a space to make his exit. Albeit a passionate one, Tuck is a liability, and Will thinks he's incorrigible, not encourageable, but the others think the latter making him a test and testament to Will's discipline. So, instead of listening, Will thinks how a correctly placed up swinging elbow could cause the decapitation of the ghastly flapping organism, making him bite off the tip of his undisciplined tongue. That would permanently shut him up. It was just a thought.

Tuck's unorthodoxy is jarring, and for Will he is a pain to communicate with. He is swine, and throughout the years the Legionnaires, on paper at least, have been embarking upon the recipe for pearls and there is a popular idiom dedicated to casting them before the likes of the uncultured. Will smirks and shakes his head to snap out of the ignorance-induced spell, and pans around the campus before abruptly cutting into Tuck's carelessly thought-out stratagem. "So… right here is where you want to discuss this? Right here, man?! Right now? Damn!" Will adds, under his breath, "Fuck she see in him?" Will calms and points at the building behind him with his thumb, and he rhythmically pumps his wrist with the pauses in his speech like hitchhikers. "Good morning Robert. I'm late and I'm about to go to work now. I doubt this, but I'm hoping your plan for us *doing something* is better put together than your plan for letting me know about it." After one last silently charged batch of cookies as he chews on his own teeth in a serious stare, Will walks away. Tuck smiles Will off, shaking his head, bending down to pick up the rake, and metaphorically his face, to continue the appearance of doing the work he obviously wasn't and hasn't been. Will turns to speak after a little space is between them, loudly enough for anyone listening to hear, "And the yard looks great Robert. You're doing a bang up job!" Tuck responds with a palms-up shoulder shrug and a smirk. Will retrieves his briefcase, scans his badge, and enters the facility.

"Good morning, Mr. Bunting."

"Morning, Ms. Ann. Long night. Longer morning. Had a little trouble finding my keys... Any... problems this morning?" This is Will's way of speaking in code and asking if any issue specifically demanding his presence had gone down before he arrived, a surprise visit from a higher up or a representative of the state, a resident meltdown, an insurrection, or any residents missing between last night's and the morning's count.

"No sir. The uprise hasn't happened just yet, but I think I overheard it being discussed at the juice bar." She whispers, "Kenny's the leader." She kids, and Kenny is the punch line. Kenny has a severe learning disability and an emotional imbalance making him appear as dumb as they come, and with his frailty, poor posture, and his lisp, he is the running joke in the facility and couldn't organize a game of marbles much less a revolt. He'd be dumb enough to spill the beans at the juice bar though, which is another reason he would not be allowed to be involved if the residents were planning such a thing, which they would not, because they are, as the title of the type of facility suggests, halfway home, and at least halfway between discord and harmony. Leaving is as easy as walking out the front door, and they'll be free until the police catch up with them.

There is a disturbing number of inmates that should have, would have been better served in a state hospital if they could have gone, but the state run mental institutions were closed, and there are many Kennys that fell through the cracks as a result, yet another reason the demand for institutions like Harmony is high. Some addicts thought prison too much to handle without the aid of drugs, so the game was to play crazy to force prison to keep them doped up. The joke was on them, because most often, the playing crazy act becomes reality, because mind altering drugs do just that, alter minds. If they only knew what that high they were chasing would cost them. It makes for an interesting mix of clients, both predators and prey, both sane and insane, both sick and healthy, all supposed to be cured or healed by exactly the same counseling methods, behavior-modifying rules, medication, and power of God's mercy. Comically, at least to Will, the residents respond to each other's salutations with, *Blessed*, because if this is the blessed life, he'd hate to see the cursed.

Will responds to Ann, "Oh, ok. Good ol' Kenny. Who'd have thunk it? I'll watch him, alright. I might just have to shut that juice bar down altogether. People get funny ideas at bars, plan revolutions even… I get any calls?"

"Nope. Bob came in looking for you though."

"Looking for me?" Will cracks a half smile and shakes his head softly. "No. He came in here looking for you. He just used me as an excuse."

"Whatever, Mr. Bunting." She looks him away, lips pursed, while her face turns flush. She clicks the mouse and stares at her computer monitor to appear busy all of a sudden. Will stands staring. He likes watching her turn colors.

"Mm hmm. Mr. Bunting sees more than everyone thinks he does. I have eyes everywhere. People are just impressed by the ones behind my head. No lacking in my attention to detail… Well, get to it Ms. Ann. I'm heading back." He bends down to pick up his briefcase and pauses, "Also, I spoke to Robert on the way in, but if I see him again I'll tell him you said Hi, ok?"

"Bye, Mr. Bunting!" Will winks, raises his palms in a *don't shoot* fashion, picks his briefcase up, and heads back to his office.

*　　　*　　　*

Gray doesn't sleep a wink and the night expands lengthwise. He desires to; he just can't. Falling asleep would shorten the length of his night considerably, or at least his conscious experience of it. Staying awake just makes the night longer. The best way to track the length of a minute is NOT watching a clock, because extra seconds are bound to sneak in and make the count inaccurate. This is not scientific fact, because perception is difficult to test, but it is fact, and even though he stares at no clock, Gray has activated this irregularity of time in every minute of this incessant night while he stares at everything but, of what he has available to fix his eyes upon. It is no choice of his. His mind refuses to rest, entering a kind of reverse hibernation, a stimulation that feels like nervousness. Instead of counting sheep, he could possibly count up all of the days he has refused to during his stay, his lists of firsts, new events, scars, inside and outside, that marked up his stay, but that would not be rest inducing. Not the kind he wants. His stint has mostly been rest anyway - rest but not sleep, he never sleeps - and him reacting on mere impulse and doing only what was necessary to survive and preserve his sanity. Now that he is awakening, he finds actual rest eluding. He figures he'll have time to on the morning bus ride out.

The dimensions of the space he has to fill is maddening, the space between his ears. He would have gladly had Ervin talk his ears off to stop his anxiety and give his mind a concern besides walking without a chain of look-alikes ahead of him and behind him, to wherever he chose with no worry about being so damn hardened every moment of every day. A result of both mental and physical exercise, an indelible layer of hardiness is a necessity. Even the queens have it. They soften their voices and lighten their walks, but to mistake them as soft would be just that, a mistake. They'll open up a throat as fast as any other inmate. For some murder is the crime they are serving time for. A little extra hip action is not an advertisement for safety. Prison's a land of wonder, where even punks aren't punks - not punks as in not afraid of fisticuffs, and not punks as in, because they have sex with men, they consider themselves gay. Having sex with a man does not determine one's sexual orientation, but *how* one has sex with a man, who is where and doing what, or rather the orientation, their sexual orientation, as in position, determines their sexual orientation. Many are just gay for the stay. Up is down and down is up in a carnival fun house that few enjoy called the pen, and Gray has spent six years learning its physics, the peculiar laws that regulate this land of wonder, the depths of this rabbit hole, only to soon escape it.

The penitentiary changes all who enter, but few know exactly how they've changed until they exit. Some changes are obvious, like some landed upon these bricks straight and were convinced to bend themselves to its will, a distinct, measurable change, and others arrived in a particular shape, sustained it, but sharpened its edges. Some change is easy to determine, enter as a wad of dough and leave like pumice stone, wholly missing becoming the wholesome loaves some ignorant few imagine of the products of prison; its produce loathsome and never fit for societies bread basket. Not one has left prison better than they entered it, better as in well-adjusted for life after prison, because prison itself is not a microcosm of any free society so it cannot reproduce the values needed in those societies, or create the desired behavior. It teaches a new set of values and new behaviors, and those that appear to be rehabilitated are reaching deep into their coffers of what they recall free world living to be and repressing their newly improved selves. This is the mental augmentation that is often difficult to measure; what has Gray lost, what has he gained, how has he transformed?

The change in the mind is more abstract, revealing itself in different ways, expressions, and reactions. The innocent changes reveal themselves in their own time, then there are the ones that are not so innocent, consciously aware, character adjustments that are purposely hidden when one finds freedom, like the appetite a man builds for the intimate embrace of another man, even when women are available. Only a new environment can properly expose that. On the outside that revelation is often hidden. In the vacuum of incarceration, this desire is excusable so some are open about it while others are silent. The *soft* ones are, of course, the most open about it, but, again, no one in prison is actually soft until their body lays dead and lifeless, and even that softness is only temporary. The softest though, the bowel soft, are almost asking to be fucked, metaphorically. It's just a matter of time and one too many missteps, because they will eventually opt for some kind of protector, and protectors don't take credit cards. It is the massive hand of Big Brother, these prison walls, squeezing them all like pecans, and the weaker the nut, the better chance of it cracking, and the pressure's constant. Gray's mind is filled with thoughts of being outside its encapsulating squeeze. Like a plane in descent or a submarine in ascent, he decompresses in effort to match the normalized pressure of the free world, as free as he's experienced, against his own will, instead of sleeping.

In darkness, he'd be seen if his gray irises were the iridescent, reflective eyes of a feline in waiting. He stares at the walls the entire night listening to Ervin snore, and worrying, wondering if he's too soft, not for the inside but the outside, because up is down and down is up, and he's learned its physics well. If one cannot deconstruct his or her conditioning before exit, or soon after – his halfway house stay should help, one should expect not a release, but a short vacation because they will surely return to prison or meet their end in returning to dust.

The morning transport arrives. Two guards come to retrieve him, and Ervin, still half asleep, balls his face up like he's sick to his stomach, shaking his head *no* a little. A congratulatory sending off would be much more appropriate, but Ervin reacts like Gray is being fitted with shackles in preparation for his execution. He doesn't mean it. He is just honestly expressive. Gray looks back at him, asks if he's ok, and he nods back in confirmation. It's an end scene and both characters know it, and chances are they will never see one another again, not on this side of the gates or this side of the ground, but such is life, and it was really only six months together. Bonds are built rather quickly in the most unpleasant situations though, soldiers and gang members speak of it, being privy to many life-threatening situations makes every moment hypersensitive, and their home fits that description, where a toothbrush can be found in stuck in soft tissue almost as often as stuck in a mouth. Ervin doesn't have any words to say, probably embarrassed his voice will crack as something like his big brother is making his permanent exit. Gray turns to him, giving Ervin more attention than he'd given his own mother within the similar circumstance of uniformed men taking him away, before his arrival, and speaks.

"Get down real quick. Show me some love… I'm out of here man." Gray turns back to the guards, with his wrists outside the bars waiting to be bound and asks, "Can you give me a second, real quick?" He turns again to stare at Ervin. Ervin moves from off the bunk like a child on punishment, too upset to express natural emotion, but he climbs down. "It's going to be a'ight bruh. Come on. Hit me with it." Palms up, shoulders back, chest spread, Gray welcomes him in. Their right hands grasp and he pulls Ervin in tightly, wrapping his left arm around his shoulder and the back of his head like a child into a woman's bosom. His head only reaches to Gray's shoulder. Gray stands at least eight inches taller and outweighs him by 40 pounds, so he completely swallows him in this gesture. Ervin recoils none, because Ervin needs it, and Gray speaks to him in the nest of his grasp. "It's gonna be a'ight. Just remember what I told you. This shit is temporary. A'ight?" Ervin nods. They disembrace with a slight shove and Gray shoots a quick jab at him, to manly up the moment. "Might not hurt you to start doing a little working out yourself. Pop out your bird chest, just in case someone tries to *choose* you."

"Ain't nobody choosing me, Gray!" Ervin punches his own chest twice; he's a taunting twelve year old before a play fight. "But yeah… Good luck to you bro… Write me, man."

"No doubt Erv. Peace, brother." Gray smiles and says, "I'm about to give 'em hell." He raises his brow to signal that he is alluding to the conversation they had weeks prior about the female attention they both missed so. It may have meant even more than that. The *'em* can include so many that are deserving of what he'd locked away for these years and the return of his influence in those places he frequented and nearly controlled at one time. He had hell to give to *'em* all, and not necessarily the negative kind. He was ready to return to his streets, after the completion of this next piece in his state sanctioned punishment.

It is 8am. Gray has been getting processed out since 6am, mostly answering dumb questions from a large torsoed man in a medium sized shirt that breathes like the size of the shirt aversely affects him. It is a seaweed green button-down uniform shirt with buttons on tilt. He looks like a sushi roll, with his rice-colored skin demanding airtime in the crescent shaped spaces the fabric forced together by the buttons makes, and his face even has the sticky rice texture. He prefers pork to sushi though, and lots of it. *Fucking cannibal.* Gray hates this man without even knowing him and fills the spaces of his mind with negative thoughts to which he is the star. Knowing him isn't necessary, just knowing his role is sufficient, and he is doing this shit on purpose, stalling, taking his sweet time just to make Gray's last moments in prison torture. This is the final test, and they haven't broken him yet. Gray is challenging and cursing this man out within his mind, as this obtuse soul is completely unaware and *just doing his*

73

job, the excuse millions have used to claim innocence from the role they played in some human atrocity.

The guard runs down the script with the eloquence of a non-actor who despises acting. He hates his job. They couldn't even give him a proper fitting uniform. He is paid to ask questions with apparent answers, and he has to answer only one: *Why is this taking so long?* Gray has delivered this question at least three times in their engagement, and in his disappointment, he starts half listening and staring at the security camera monitor as it cycles throughout the facility. He's also embarked upon that, *I didn't get any sleep last night,* high, that makes his head feel like an emptied Kleenex box being refilled one disheveled tissue at a time, applying slightly more pressure with each, not pressure like a headache, but a pressurized soft disturbing blankness. He's floating yet flustered, gliding along with the flipping monitor screens with his heart rate speeding up each time one of the cameras cue up that point outside the facility. He's minutes away from seeing the other side, in the flesh. Awakening.

"Yes sir." The guard informs him of where he'll be traveling next and asks him if he understands. The guard reiterates that he is still serving his sentence, just the duration of it will be in a facility geared to reintegrate him into society, but should he not comply with the demands of his sentencing, and the rules of this house, he can be reprimanded and even made to return to prison, if necessary. Does he understand? "Yes sir." It's been hours, with documents being read and documents being signed. The phone rings. The guard answers. The bus has arrived. Gray does his best Ervin impression and lights up the room, involuntarily, like a woman had just caught his eye, and he'd caught hers back. Thoughts of a woman are appropriate; it has been months since he's been with one, and over six years since he's been with one he wanted to be with, something pretty, nicely shaped, that smells good.

It is 9am. He is finally strapped into his cathartic coach set to liberate him from the stockade. The bus that arrived was at the tilt, full of the fruit of society that had *rejected* stamped upon them, and this one leaving had one other passenger besides the driver. It is a White man, dirty blond, shoulder length hair, medium build, with multi-colored tattoo sleeves on each arm, who Gray knows of but doesn't know, so he doesn't even nod at him as he, ironically, despite *all his people been through*, walks to the back of the bus. It is an unwritten rule that everyone sticks to their own kind. Prison is the epicenter of racism, revealing the racist that many never knew they had within them, for the safety of it. There may be no place on Earth as segregated as this American institution. When all of the lulling protections of social existence are removed, kind again matters, more than anything. So, he's seen the man before while in his corner of the yard peering into the blond's corner, but he doesn't know him.

As he sits, he gazes out of the bus window for what he demands to be his last time at the bricks, the fences, the razor wire, the guard towers, the armed guards along the perimeter, and shakes his head. With the turn of the ignition the bus vibrates. His head tilts back with the forward momentum a moment then readjusts. They taxi along the grounds like a commercial airliner, going slowly enough to allow time for the series of gates to open and for the guards to make sure no inmates are anywhere near trying to find an early exit. No inmates are that dumb, besides those that are mentally ill and should not have been sent to prison in the first place, to try an escape during the day. Guards stay alert on their perches, looking for an excuse to use those high power rifles. Striking someone at a hundred and fifty yards would make good bar talk. The land is flat, and there are few trees and for many many miles there is nothing around except more prison units, a creation from the zoning commission, but most wouldn't choose to build near a prison any more than they'd choose to build near a zoo.

Besides, "How much longer is this going to take?," Gray also asked how many hours away the House of Harmony was. It was three hours north, northwest. Early Thursday, after the morning rush, the interstate has little traffic, as far as he remembers. The window of his cell just showed him the wall of the adjacent unit, a beautiful exposure for one wishing not to see beyond his circumstances. Looking out his window was the equivalent of draining every last bit of himself scaling a wall, only to find another, just as tall or taller, from the newly gained vantage point. It's enough to make one turn back around,

75

so he didn't look out of it much, as his only hope in peering through it was catching an occasional bird flying between the buildings. Otherwise, looking out of it and at the wall was a better reminder of his being in prison than his cell. There was no chance of seeing people or traffic. His only escapes were the exhaustion from exercise, the occasional *heavy* conversation, the female guards sprinkled about the place, and reading. There was lots of reading. Gray had a taste for the counterculture, but he'd grab anything he could get his hands on to help pass the time. There were as many handwritten manuscripts floating amongst the cells as there were professionally published and bound works. There is no shortage of reading material behind bars. The prisoners all had something to say and no one to listen, and nothing so effectively breeds writers as reading.

The bus is heading north from the most rural and desert parts of the state back towards where one of its many pulses are. The Lone Star State may have only a single star, but many hearts. It is probably the most diverse and identity free state in the union. It has been propagandized to be the place of southern comforts and the cowboy culture, with ma'ams, sirs, tipped hats, and curtsies, but that narrative doesn't include its Mexican drug cartel run borders, it being assumed as part of Mexico by many, a country of its own illegally seized by the US by many, its horrid race relations, its massive cities and the limitless land between them, the extreme wealth inequality, its being corporate friendly and an overseer to the common man, its fascination with guns, it just recently being surpassed by the good state of Louisiana as the prison capital of the world, or how it is shining example of frequent and efficient use of the death penalty that most of the country has either abolished officially or unofficially through inactivity. Much more than ten-gallon hats, lassos, and tight fitting back pocketless denim jeans on ladies with small asses in Texas.

If one picked up a smooth enough rock and chucked it, nothing, no structure and none of these hollow humans would stop that rock from swinging back around and tagging the tosser in the back of his head. It is miles of baked clay, nappy patches of grass, and graying, leaning structures. Besides the prisons, that is how empty these places are, and there are several in the region, with no shortage of land to build more and Texas with the kind of laws and law enforcement to keep the demand high. Most of the land is not conveniently arable because of both the high clay content of the soil and lacking rainfall, so some genius figured areas like this to be perfect spot for large populations of humans to be broken. Business is booming for the crop called servitude. It grows better than anything else in these conditions.

The prison industry is recession proof, and private corporations are fighting over their chance to get in on it. There is no other way they can pay their *employees* as little as 23 cents an hour on US soil and save a shitload in shipping costs by not paying the same to some Taiwanese. Gray figured this maybe had something to do with why he was so easily added to this labor force. The federal and state minimum wages do not apply to prison, and even the US Constitution only supports prisoners in partial, when it should have been impartial. Investors had to be secure in their investments, so, likewise, prisons had to be filled. A Pennsylvania judge was convicted for accepting kickbacks amounting to more than a million dollars in exchange for assisting the incarcerating of numerous adults and juveniles in a prison facility owned by a developer who was paying him under the table. America eats her young. Why else would a stolen land, colonized by criminals, be so hard on criminals? There is no shortage of criminals, by design. Low wages, high unemployment, and a loss of faith in the job market push people to alternative means to making a living, most of which are illegal. Prison is a great investment and felons are the product. There are always more people going into the factory than leaving, and even those leaving, like Gray and the unnamed blonde, are still a part.

The dirt is rust colored. It stays pretty dry, often moving with the wind with nothing to hold it down but the sparse and yellowed grasses. No hills, not many buildings, all single story, and a couple of paved streets is the basic layout of most prison towns; the prisons are the culture centers, with the best roads flowing to and from them. Gray's bus travels down one for over 20 minutes to get the interstate. The towns in this region are empty and the residents are empty as well. All they do is mate, watch TV and the news, test the limits of toxification with drugs, and fight one another, on the entertainment side of things. On the make a living side, they could become a clerk at one of the dead businesses, a farm or ranch hand, grow drugs, sell drugs, find the nearest recruiting office - which most do, or become a prison guard. Gray learned this from one of the prison guards, lost within the shapes her moving lips would make because keeping his focus tight helped him to skip the rest. Her lips were the wax crayon shaving once pushed through a hand pencil sharpener, different shades for different days. This was her perspective of the locals and her people, and she would give him her all because she kind of took a liking to Gray; he wore his bondage well.

Annabelle was from the town, and the list of recreation there was detailed but short. It was detailed because Gray had her squeezing every bit of it, of her, into his chest, his stash, his mentionables to be retrieved and utilized later. She did so because she was bored, of course, and he encouraged her to because she could not have been anywhere near as bored as he had been. He had other motives as well. She represented power and class within the facility. Outside she was next to nothing, but inside her position compared to his fueled his interest. Being in possession of a vagina, highly coveted, often imitated but never duplicated – some of the contraptions inmates created would make seasoned engineers jealous, and what possibly a third of the inmates are in some way locked up behind, definitely helped her keep his attention. He spent a considerable amount of time, early on, convincing her of her beauty and intelligence, although she was ghastly, and a measure of her intelligence was not only her allowing him to convince her that she was not, but worse, convincing her she was the opposite of. Facts are not important in these cases. Gray's *ghastly* is closer to the average man's *plain*, and it's ghastly to Gray because he's aesthetically above average. She wasn't ugly, but she wasn't pretty, but no one could convince her she wasn't once Gray began to wrap her within the weave of his whispers, making her a wardrobe with his words that made what little she was working with, work. Because he willed it, she wore it. The point is painting a beautiful picture and blocking the ugliness out, just like when Gray would stare only at the lips of his dear, *beautiful*, Annabelle.

The contrast between her story and his had significance to Gray, so he would listen and take mental notes of what excited her, in the interest of getting her talking and keeping her talking. He made talking mostly her job and listening mostly his, an old practice, quite empowering to those skilled in the art. Gray knew a thing or two about wooing a woman, and it was especially easy with the time he had at his disposal to think of what to say the next time she'd stop by his cell that would remind her of the magic she had between her thighs. She'd walk off each time carrying it in her strut like something precious, newly discovered. It was a new high. She eventually began to alter her patrol route to see him more frequently, to get another hit, and every time he'd send something unique her way that would make her blush accent the sway of her hips in a way that was better than words. The heaviness of her steps would become winged, and she'd float when he'd rush to the bars upon hearing her approach, to say, "Hey gorgeous. Been thinking about you all day." It was corny by most standards, at first, but she was country and he was consistent, and that marriage can actually take a couple pretty far. Gray's gray eyes and chiseled features played a part as well.

Those easy on the eyes get bonus points for just being able to speak coherently, and he's only ever been called ugly to address his attitude or behavior. Anna initially spoke very few words. She even exhibited aversion, and displayed a touch of attitude with her facial expressions, but she was building a chemical dependency of Gray's every syllable and he knew it. Her hormones told the tale. She was expressing it in her nonverbal cues. Nature knows no right and wrong; it just is, and it's universal. When one figures out how to properly speak to another's nature, that conversation cannot be ignored, and Gray had done just that. There was only the problem of the bars between them, but Gray knew he had her. She was hooked.

This was in a time before Ervin. Gray's cellie was a certified asshole, a hothead that found pride in making his presence felt by making everyone's life a little more difficult. He was seasoned enough and good enough with his hands to do so without much threat to his own health. He and Gray could not stand one another, and Gray did his best to avoid him, but that just wasn't possible within a small cell. They fought more than once and Gray lost more than once, and settled in his mind that one of the encounters was a draw, but he knows he never pulled out a clear victory. He inspired Gray to create a serious workout for himself. He couldn't be having nobody choosing him and moving around him with the constant silent threat of knowing they can take him. It is a marginalization worse than the marginalization of prison itself, a class lower than what he thought the bottom was. The new bottom was worse. Pat is what he called himself. He had gun wounds, missing teeth, and sandpaper knuckles, and his ugly ass hated every time Gray made Annabelle smile, and his hate and her love of it both proved fruitful in the long run, because Gray was flirting with power.

He knew what he was doing, seeking out a taste of something much greater than pussy. There is a hierarchy to be respected, and she was part of the elites. She was bourgeoisie and he was proletariat, and everything he desired she either had or had access to whether her dumb country sensibilities recognized it or not. It was his job to make sure she didn't recognize it, and be authentic in his courting. It was not a difficult task because he did want her, he hadn't fucked in years and a hand is a poor substitute, but he didn't want her in the degree that he made her feel he did. Annabelle was the only woman on Earth for Gray, and the misfortune of his being in prison turned into fortune because it is where he'd found her; this was his script. Yes, when she started finding the time to stop and listen, Gray milked the moment like he expected the teat to express tight lines of liquid gold. His were lines of gold, and she was a gold digger. Anything she had was possibly his with the exception of her freedom. Prisons aren't set up like that. It takes many guards to free one inmate, and most of the C.O.s were men, and they hated Gray's handsome guts. Gray was short time anyway, but she would have probably tried if he had asked once they'd gotten involved. Gray did have an asshole of a celly that she could help to rid him of though. Power has its perks.

Annabelle did her best to relate to Gray beyond sexual attraction even though she had a man at home. Eventually, she'd approach him with interesting topics in an attempt to move what they were beyond flirting and the occasional, infrequent, when they got lucky and she was able to set it up, romp in the laundry room or some other secluded space. It was more than sex for her. It's what she kept telling herself, and Gray figured that whatever she decided to tell herself to make her feel better was her business, and her business only. Besides, she had some hick of husband at home who probably loved her. Tough chance at getting love from Gray, or even *loving*, the physical kind, if Gray was in an environment where he didn't have to settle. Something in her wiring was willing to give up all she had, which wasn't much, to slum it with a felon. Gray played along, like there was any chance of him getting released and adopting a ball and chain with a woman who was clearly not his equal. She let the bars distort her vision, but still he listened as she attempted to create something like a real relationship with him with interesting tidbits of information that started conversations that had to be partaken periodically, adding upon each other in each subsequent meeting to reach completion.

Her attempts to relate were slightly embarrassing; in trying to challenge the stereotypical picture of the urban Black, she only reinforced it. All she knew of the urban Black experience was from television and the radio, so that is what she had to pull from to connect. She wasn't far off with some things. Gray was indeed in prison for the urban circumstance and his desire to capitalize upon it, but he listened in silent disgust knowing that she thought that all of his people were something like him. He had a mother, had, that didn't even cuss, the best example of Christianity he'd ever met, who was also a part of that urban Black experience. Where would Mom fit in Annabelle's restricted perspective? That all or most were like Gray just wasn't the truth. Honestly, only a small percentage were bold enough to take the road those like him traveled because they wanted to avoid fates like sitting in prison entertaining overweight, liberal, White women who'd like to marry them and have all of their future children. Delusion is real, and Gray got to experience it first hand. For months he endured it, securing his chance to continue to ejaculate with the assistance of her body parts and release himself upon them, and on her work uniform. It was the ultimate disrespect to the state. What better way is there to say, *Fuck the state*, than to fuck it, its representative at least, and send it back on duty with nut in its face and hair like, *Here's your fucking urban experience*. It wasn't her fault, she was a victim of her environment as much as he was, but compassion isn't really Gray's thing.

Annabelle talked about poverty to relate. She talked about drugs and drug use to relate. She talked about racism and how things were so unfair for Blacks and how she only judged people by character to relate. She was trying to use class similarities to erase the natural barrier between the two of them. She'd done what Gray considers real drugs, more than just marijuana, and those stories did more to repel them from each other than to bring them together because Gray refused to touch the stuff outside of selling it. It was for addicts and gangsters. He grew up around street gangsters that developed a culture of smoking heroin before they went out to terrorize a neighboring community by shooting at people. Heroin would make them crazy enough to leave their conscience behind. Anna smoked it too, but just out of curiosity and never advanced to shooting up. Friends of hers would routinely push their limits with new drug and sexual experiences during high school. Fucking an inmate, if it was her first time, as she said it was, was nowhere near the craziest thing she had done sexually. Gray didn't like hearing about her sexual exploits much since he felt he was sharing in it by proxy. The thought of it was less than romantic, and he already had to concentrate harder than normal to reach climax because of her beauty deficiency.

Gray did enjoy the drug talk though, and her illusion that she had become clean, while she breathed in deeply, pulling all of him she could, and inhaling the gray-eyed dragon before her, unconscious of his being in her bloodstream. He was her drug, just another in a long list of; he is a drug, a wiring-changing addiction, and maybe too that plays a part in his never getting into using them. He even get's high off of himself, so he could understand her addiction. While Annabelle has had more drugs in her body than the average person in the ghetto, she'd never be a poster child. Her dealer looked nothing like Gray, and he'd never be a poster child. The dealer's broker looked nothing like Gray, and he'd never be a poster child. The trafficker looked nothing like Gray, and he'd never be a poster child. The buyer and the grower, probably somewhere in Afghanistan, look nothing like Gray, and they will never be the poster child of drug use and distribution in America, because Gray is. It was Anna's conversations that oriented Gray with the idea that everything wasn't as it seemed and that he had possibly been a victim to movements much greater than the decisions he made.

The poppy, in the case of opium and heroin, coming all the way from Afghanistan over eighty percent of the time, clearly paints a more complex system with it making it to the hoods, than the simple supply and demand for smack for some addicts. How far it has traveled to rest upon a spoon, a sheet of foil, or in a syringe, to contaminate blood streams and produce an intense high that strikes within seconds. Gray had never given it much thought before she mentioned it, and he still didn't give it much thought after she mentioned it. It was just one more thing added to the list of blame attributed to the poor and an obstacle already known. It was the game played with the poor and the Black, and he was familiar with it without knowing how complex it really was, because knowing that didn't matter. There was no one to tell. Those in power knew. It was unfair, but it was what he and his kind had to adapt to and get stronger from.

Gray can make the best of a bad situation, and this even worked for him in prison. His knack for finding the path of least resistance is uncanny, and his words, though often unused, are succinct. Gray swears by not being broken, and they tried. A guard broke a rib once – hairline fracture, and he spent some time in solitary confinement, but, by and large, he learned how to shut himself, the malleable, learning, and adaptable portions, off, and do his time. Empathy was a waste, compassion too, and reason was locked far outside the prison walls, all wastes of brainpower, along with the capacity to trust and build sustaining relationships. Nothing much mattered besides respect. All impulses attached themselves to it. An inmate could get his face bashed in for something as simple, yet as disrespectful as reaching over another's lunch tray. Respect, how and how not to show it had to be learned quickly. More than the name that was already inside Gray was revealed while incarcerated, he surprised himself with the self he uncovered, but... the point is to forget that. It is temporary. He has passed through. He'll be able to go home in six more months, and he's presently en route to a home away from home that is much nearer, some could say halfway, to home than this last life-perverting experience had been.

The arriving bus was overflowing with a bunch of, "Pissed off niggas," in Gray's own words, and he was one of them. Judge gave him the shaft and removed him from his place on the streets, a place he'd clawed himself up to, like plucking a tick from behind a dog's ear. According to his, "Punk ass," public defender, he had a really good chance at only getting probation since he hadn't any priors, yet he ended up with 6 ½ years, and a district attorney who might as well have smashed her sweaty nuts in the face of his defense in a slam dunk of a court case, and followed it with a high five and chest bump with the judge. While ignoring the screams of his mother, Gray looked over to his attorney in question, rolling his eyes, like the young girls did in school and the roll came to a tight-eyed halt upon his lawyer. Gray could have kicked his ass right there, but that would have been difficult task in shackles.

In answer, his defense attorney kind of shrugged it off like, *Tough break dude, we'll get 'em next time,* which made it worse.

What next time? This is my life here... Woman stop calling my name, please! Six years??? And where the fuck are my children?, were the thoughts that met the immediacy of the moment, but on the outside he was stone. He showed not a grain of distress. He removed his eyes from his lawyer and back upon the judge, looking his killer in his eyes, ignoring the scene Mother was making behind him. He began shedding compassion in that very moment, because he was going to prison and there was nothing he could do but accept it. Six years later, he doesn't have to accept this style of living while dying, sleeping while awake, or being an animal while human any longer. If there is such a thing as a win with this, he's won, passing through, as far as he knows, unbroken.

1:5

There is no freedom in a system of cages. Escaping one cage only feels like freedom until the boundaries of the new cage are found. The state is a cage collective, most effective when it hides or deters those within the initial cages from venturing to the walls and noticing the bars. The more that know that they are in a cage, or a system of them, the higher the demand that they all be released. The cage cannot sustain itself without the interlocking arms of those of us believing it doesn't exist, binding ourselves in a way that keeps us blind. Those on top, or completely outside the cages, know that we must never realize the reality of our situation, and expend vast amounts of resources so we stay ignorant of it, because the moment we realize the truth, we'll release one another and the cages will disappear.

The bullet, 7.62 x 39 caliber, very popular, very clean, even free of fingerprints, sank into the windshield like it was swallowed with a glass of apple juice. Calming ripples left a small spider web upon its surface as the entire membrane bounced, a tiny microscopic bounce, with the impact, before the glass yielded and peristalsis led it to its final destination. No siren sounded, no slumbers were disturbed, not before the assailant disappeared across the roof, fearing discovery, and not waiting to find out. It's a copper plated capsule, medicine, which is nothing but disciplined drugs, like those designed to enter bodies to make them sleep, yet this one's fired to make bodies awaken… The bus is a capsule as well, traveling across the interstate to one of the state's many hearts, a straight shot, carrying its medicine, as it vibrates, along with carrying Gray's dreams.

The walkways of the cellblock are paced by sentries; the same are the streets of the ghetto, but these sentries don't walk, they drive along assigned pathways that they call beats crisscrossing the pits of the free society in an effort to make sure they stay free. Threatening, interrogating, and posturing peace officers, disturbing the peace and saving the savages from killing themselves, because of course that is what they'd be doing if the light flashers weren't making their rounds all day and night. It's also a way to make sure the residents stay in their cells, so to speak, and do not spill out into the other parts of the city or the suburbs. One would be hard pressed to find a Black man who had not been pulled over by a cop for no reason other than being in a community where he did not belong, cued by the cop asking, "What are you doing on this side of town?" It's an unwritten law that certain people belong in certain places and the police are aptly labeled law enforcement. It is their job to do their best to keep residents comfortably within their cells and away from the temptation of being around those outside of the cells, those who have *cells* and have not *cells*, respectively.

Replace COs, correction officers, with police officers, and convicted criminals with law abiding, tax paying, citizens, and it is easy to see the penitentiary as a fun-sized representation of the inner city and that the people are under occupation. *Police presence* is what they call it, and this by itself is supposed to reduce crime because criminals are so dumb the sight of a police cruiser strikes fear in them and whatever crime they had planned, or better, was about to spontaneously commit exits their mind in a puff of smoke. By this same logic arsonists would set less fires if the fire trucks were constantly circling the areas with a higher frequency of fires, ironically the same places the police haunt, instead of waiting for a dispatcher to send them to a destination because an emergency call had been placed. No. Crime doesn't work like that. It is dumb to believe that the criminal mind is so ridiculously simple that a constant reminder that cops exist will deter most crime, and the result is no more than wasted tax dollars in burned gas unless the police are serving a greater function. They do serve a greater, unspoken of, function in the community, they intimidate and agitate under the guise of offering the residents the service of protecting them from themselves. It is the argument that makes this *protection* for their own good because impoverished communities act as healthy, nurturing, welcoming wombs for society's criminal element. The game of cops and robbers plays out much better with the cops guarding base. The boys in blue are there to snatch these demons from the umbilical chord before they mature beyond the womb, or at the latest snatch these disgusting parasites from the teat of liberty. They do not deserve the freedom they are allowed, so they, criminal and noncriminal alike, are watched from up and down their city blocks, like inmates by guards pacing their cellblocks.

The hood is where the bulk of the arrests are made, so the data supports the procedure, although no mention is made of the correlation between poverty and crime and that higher police presences are indicative of higher arrest quotas more than they are of higher crime and better police work. In the place where crime is supposed to be, police have been known to antagonize, encourage, and flat out fabricate crimes and create criminals. This is how they lost the support of these communities, not because poor people are innately against cops. The aversion of the average urban kid to police and policing is a result of public policy and police being the active tentacles of this racist and classist policy. Too, when the cops are called upon to solve a crime in these areas they rarely do, but they always go above and beyond to create crimes or stop crimes that those in the community have not even requested them to. They do not represent safety and protection, and they instead invoke fear in those that are not even criminals because not doing crime is not enough to not be arrested and convicted for one in such a peculiar place. It's very easy to fit a description, and that is often good enough. Though many lie saying that they did not commit a crime that they are serving time for, as far as those who have been exonerated by new evidence, often DNA, or old evidence that was hidden, decades later, almost all look the same and they hail from the same types of communities.

Gray hated cops before ever encountering one, but he hates authority period, and he's been falling in line only for the convenience of giving himself time to figure out how to subvert it, finding which wheels to grease, if possible. His last six years stand as proof that it isn't always possible. He had much more success back home, the place where the police roam that juncture between those who have and those who have not, where he was caught off guard and outside his cage. When the tensions are high, the cops make targets of these people, only because these people fear them and do not recognize that the routine of encircling their streets is not an advantage for police, but, in fact, the opposite. The same for the known speed trap locations and where officers park to people-watch, the same spots that can become cop traps and places to cop-watch. When some are pushed, some push back, and what better place to do so than in the ghetto? As Gray travels back to the so-called civilized world, tensions are arguably higher than they have been in recent years between the police and the poor. The tensions have been marked by a bullet through the windshield of a parked cop car.

Long stretches of staring at nothing but long stretches of nothing can work miracles for the sleep deprived. The buildup was much stronger than the reward, like many of Gray's first times were throughout his life, at least at the point when he passed out and succumbed to the vibrating vinyl of the tightly wound double seat. The stubborn springs make the seat the pouch of a trebuchet with every bump the bus hits, making the leg chains rattle against the floor and the passengers airborne momentarily. They are not bound to the seats, only to themselves, because they are the only danger, and their being in danger by riding without seatbelts, high speed, in a pill made of metal and glass, is no danger to the people that matter. Besides, this trip has happened many times without a single wreck recorded. The outbound trip is always much more peaceful than the inbound, never any trouble. These inmates don't even need the shackles they're placed in. It's just a formality.

All the excitement of finally being on the outside of the penitentiary walls – an experience like a first kiss, or better the first unrestricted touches, dissipated as portions of the highway were so uniform it could have been a video loop; even an infant eventually tires of the same game of peek-a-boo. His not sleeping the night before did not help his condition. Eyes like lead weights, head full of cotton, limbs numbing and unresponsive, Gray fell under so deeply he lost the sense of where he was, only to wakeup, gain his bearings, and still not know. The bus hit a bump big enough to have him slam his head into the metal guide beneath the window ledge he'd fallen asleep leaning against. That broke the spell, and he woke up lost and in disarray. Being on a major interstate and not behind bars was a pleasant awakening, but he had neither an idea of his location nor the hour; he hadn't a proper setting. It was unsettling as the momentarily joggled snow globe of his mind made fuzz of thoughts that searched for settlement. His right hand reaches up to his temple, the point of impact, with his left hand trailing, guided by the shackles.

The thump didn't break the skin, nor does he feel any swelling. It was just enough of a jolt to disturb his rest and prevent him from spilling anymore of his saliva upon the seat. He recognizes a slight headache, but it seems to be the kind that develops more from interrupted sleep than an impact. In an attempt to move beyond his haze, Gray calls up to the driver, "How long we been on the road?" Feeling out his first taste of his greater degree of freedom by not beginning his question or ending it with *Sir*. Sir wasn't an obligation in prison, but more of a recommendation with consequences when not followed. The path of least resistance when speaking to power is the preferred route, especially to a power biting at the bit to prove itself.

"'Bout an hour thirty minutes. Got at least two to go," the driver gruffly responds like there was splinters churning at the back of his throat. His voice camouflages within the sound of the bus motor and Gray can't make out much.

"What you say?" Gray asks for clarification.

"An hour and a half!"

His repeating it did Gray no justice. It was louder, but not clearer. With the volume of an older diesel engine coupled with how far he'd chosen to sit away from the front, added with the driver's underwater vocals, he had no chance to get the answer he requested, and he wasn't about to ask a third time. He just acts as if he'd heard him, directs his attention out of the window, and massages his temple in an attempt to alleviate the slight headache. They'll get there when they get there, and taking a page from his prison stay, it wasn't like his knowing how much time he had left was going to make it any shorter.

"He said an hour and a half."

Gray hears this response with no trouble, and he looks up to see the dirty blond. He's turned around, hanging over the back of his seat addressing Gray, and Gray meets eyes with him and nods. In six years these two have not spoken more than four words to one another by prison culture dictates, and the dirty blond reaches across the invisible line to answer a question that was not directed at him, not really of much importance, and adds to his answer, "We still got two hours to go, brother."

"Thanks," Gray responds while honestly thinking to himself, *Who in the fuck asked you White boy, and when did I become your damn brother?* They all called each other brother up in the joint, but not in the way the Blacks did. It was a different type of brotherhood, of the Ku Klux variety, taken from the Greek kuklos, and meant for those matching the same phenotype. The dirty blond turns back around as if what he'd done meant nothing, and Gray is left to wonder what it means. Is it disrespect in some weird form? Is he fucking with him? He'd have been disciplined by his own crew if they'd heard him brand one who obviously wasn't as *brother.* Is it maybe just habit? Gray sighed while frozen in puzzlement. He didn't spend all of the time in prison to potentially already have a problem after getting out. He probably was just being nice but while heading to the same destination, Gray couldn't take the chance that this man had a lack of respect for him, because a lack of respect often materializes into the loss of blood in prison culture – a culture of which both men are fluent.

Prior to prison, this would not have been a deal, it would have ended with his, *Thanks,* but the same rules do not apply to ones that have been force-fed a new constitution, and have become acclimated to new ritual. Chances are, something more just happened within that exchange than the exchange itself, and it is better to interrogate it than to dismiss it. Issues have a way of growing if not stopped before they start. Everything has a more aggressive version in prison, even seemingly simple advice. He would have preferred just not knowing the answer, and scenarios like this are exactly why he kept his mouth shut and why Ervin will have a difficult time if he doesn't learn to do the same.

Gray stares at the back of dirty blond's head while balling his own face up trying and make sense of the gesture. His headache is still at an annoying intensity, like a gnat moving in and out of his consciousness, and now he also has this thing to add, along with his lack of quality sleep. It has to be called a good day because he's just gotten out of prison, no matter what happens the following hours with the exception of him dying, it will probably keep the *good* label, but the events thus far seem ready to challenge *how* good. The sooner he finds out what the transgression means, the better, so he decides to move on the impulse. He rises and does the shackle shuffle, jingling his way up the aisle of the moving bus. The bus driver spots him in his mirror, but says nothing – there is never any trouble on the outgoing trips. How much trouble could shackled men get into anyway? Not any trouble that the driver's shotgun can't settle, spraying its sedating mist of settle down that calms on contact. The driver just looks up a moment and returns his eyes to the road.

One good rule break deserves another. Gray slides, uninvited, across from the blond into the adjacent vinyl seat; they are all melting caramel in state change, in several shaded brown expressions. Gray coldly stares at him while, tauntingly, backing in. Gray's response left little to question, while the blond's actions were questionably disrespectful, a member of the Aryan Brotherhood not only speaking to Gray, but calling him brother, which was next to calling him a Tom ... maybe. Gray definitely is not an Uncle Tom, but it also wasn't a secret around the campus that if there was any tension in the yard between the Blacks and the Whites that Gray would refuse to *Get Down* unless it involved a checkered board and chess pieces. He was playing, *Dumb ass games with fucking has-beens,* while a race war was brewing; they'd tell him this, and the residue of his imprecise sell-out labeling causes him to meticulously interrogate being this White man's brother. Being safe, less Black, or diluted is what it could mean, but Gray quarrels with the definition of Black if it means ignorance, questionable decision-making, loud talking, and unchecked aggression. That wasn't and isn't his way; it's quietly calculating, seeking the vulnerable spaces in the cases others make when speaking and in expressions of faces so when he strikes. It's advantageous. This is what he does instead of the constant challenge and threat sending of others, and it's why he keeps his mouth shut and his business hidden like a snake, patient, waiting.

A White boy who made it his business to ignore the humanity of Blacks is not Gray's brother, if any White boy is for that matter. It isn't openly expressed in Gray's behavior, but Whites are not his favorite, he is not a Tom, but they also never directly impact him, as far as he's aware of, in any of his environments. It is an understandable mistake they'd made about Gray, incorrect, but understandable, but the misunderstanding isn't going to follow Gray beyond that prison fence. As Gray told Ervin, he was just passing through and that rumored war was not his to fight, but now that he's passed through, this is something he's demanding not to pass through with him on one side, but on the other, if there is any time to stop acting like a prison inmate, it is staring him in the face now with eyes as cold as his own. The choice is his.

The *Race War* was always ready to spark at any moment as the prison propagandists foretold of it like it was the Rapture, and those that didn't heed and join the appropriate ranks were called out as cowards, Toms, nigger lovers, and the like by the penal system's McCarthys in their version of the Red Scare. That is what all of the working out is for, the war, not Gray's, but those that gathered to do it, in football huddles, designing their next play. Gray found the strategy at the chess table to be much more developed and applicable than the one at the pushup station. The fantasy of the war being won by the superior weaponry of a myriad of sharpened items, shanks, was bad enough, but once that impossibility occurred and they'd killed all the White people, none could imagine what the next step would be for prisoners, in prison, with nothing but trained White guards armed with much more than devices better suited to clean teeth. The shit was stupid, the entire conversation, and the chess table and the old heads made better sense. Gray only had six years to do that he would never think about, so if that meant he lacked love for the melanin in his skin, so be it. What Gray is not going to do, is let a similar disrespect follow him to this new institution, and especially not through the lips of some White boy.

As Gray took his seat, the blond again broke character with a brush of laughter, not the uncomfortable kind, and says, "Guess you're gonna hear him next time."

Gray nods, stone faced, while poking out his chin as if to ask,

What's up?, while bobbing his head. The blond raises his brow in return and returns a stare with the same intensity. "Well since we're on speaking terms now, brother, I figured I'd come up here and speak."

"I got some time. 'Bout two hours for you. Ain't got nothing better to do. What's on your mind? I see your face all tight. You got a bone to pick?"

Biting his lip and holding his stare, Gray slowly begins to shake his head *no.* "Nah… just trying to pass the time. Figured I'd introduce myself. Maybe this portion of our sentences avoiding one another, to stop from killing one another, won't be the play. What do you say?"

"I ain't ever been worried about you killing me… Not you. I figured you were neutral because I ain't ever see you wit' them… Really, that's the only reason I spoke. You got a problem with that, I won't say shit else to you. I'm just trying to get back home, but I ain't nobody's bitch if that's what you came up here checking on. No problem with you, your kind, if y'all ain't got one with me." Gray rubs his hands together slowly. The blond continues, "Don't worry about looking over your shoulder for me unless you've been gunning first. That's all I have to say about that."

Gray tilts his head to the side and lets it hang, gives a partial nod, acknowledging the blond's correctness while alerting that should there have been an issue between them, or should there be one in the future, he has no reservations with rectifying it. It's the, *I don't want to, but I will,* prison respect dance that all the inmates engage in to let one another know, *Don't take my kindness as a weakness, because I won't hesitate to kill you, because I'm guessing you won't hesitate to do the same.* In a potential faceoff, White boy and his kind will play the, *as long as you don't bother me card,* every time, while always the initiators of *bother.* They are fine as long as things stay as they are without threat, but as soon as they feel their advantage, more people, more power, more unity, being challenged, they pull off the liberal, good neighbor mask, and pull out the torches and pitch forks, yelling that group x is trying to take something from them, as if they didn't initially do all of the taking, all over the map. As poor as he is, White boy still has the liberty to pretend it is an even playing field and that the basis of any conflict with the Grays of the world has been because the Grays started it. Not knowing their place is starting it. Demanding the same rights and respect is starting it. Being successful at those things they work hard at, even building a strong community, is starting it. Breathing even, is starting it, so Gray hears him but he isn't listening. White boy started it a long time ago in his insistence that he is a better stock of human than the rest, imposing his culture with the tip of a blade and the nose of a gun, and expecting everyone to forget about it while he pretends to believe in equality. The conqueror and the conquered dynamic doesn't disappear without the wrongs being righted. Foolish Gray is not, *Fuck this White boy,* and the best way to deal with him is to stay away from him so he won't have to kill him. It's always been Gray's way of dealing with White men. He doesn't trust them, and they, historically, haven't given him a reason to. Even the poorest are keepers of the standard, and that standard is based on keeping Gray subjugated. If White, Gray only deals with them if they piss sitting down. Ervin and Gray have many similarities. Gray just didn't make Ervin aware of them.

The air of the entire encounter was as sour as it was in the medium security space they'd just left, where Gray had passed through. At least he didn't escalate the situation. That is a small win, but clearly he is not the Gray he was six short years ago. His change is apparent just an hour away from the high walled, brick and razor wired institution of lower education, with specialization in man's lower nature and self-preservation. It seems that something of it passed through with him. Unlearning is a process. Taking the men out of prison is not the same as taking the prison out of the men. That's Harmony's job, and Will's job, for those willing.

*　　*　　*

Of the several sets of high heels available, one is earnestly clicking its way down Will's woeful wing of the facility, full of framed motivational posters and tacit teamwork jelling expressions, precursors to Internet memes and just as effective, the place where the magic behind the magic happens. It's the white collar wing, the big wigs, the planning committee, those that make the change and take the blame when the program doesn't work in practice like it does on paper, which it never does – they are often mistaken as the upper class, but better they are labeled the buffer class. They are just in the middle, the upper class doesn't work, anyone worth his or her mettle knows that, not suggesting that Will's class works much either, not in comparison to the lower class, but they do work in comparison to the upper class, who only work in comparison to God. That is how hierarchy works.

None of the residents, clients, or inmates even, wear heels, not while in the facility, and few make appearances on this wing unless requested to. As irony has it, the residents dress as though they are still in the penitentiary, exchanging the jumpsuit and sandals for sweats and sandals. The sandal wearing class's walk is more of a shuffle, a scoot as not to raise their feet out of the backless slides. These small steps work well with low hanging, sagging pants, only if the thighs are spread and the clients waddle a bit in this walk as if they are still wearing transport shackles. Old habits are hard to break, conditioning is fact, and freedom from it is fiction. The sandal class has a distinctive sound, like the audio signature of little hope, and beyond them not frequenting this side of the facility, their steps never click, they slap or they grind, so it isn't one of them. The orderlies never wear heels, they wear soft and comfortable shoes because they are on their feet for hours at a time, so the contracts are the only group left, and it is indeed a contract. The heel wearing class gets to do a lot of sitting, just as Will gets to; they get to do a lot of planning and wondering as well, like about what kinds of shoes certain types wear and the sound they make coming down the hall, brain-racking work.

Before Will could finish his game of deduction, a woman, small, dark, bouncy, slightly rotund yet shapely, clicks past his doorway without even peering in. One of his favorites, he knows her well, and today her navy blue heels are on percussion. "Janice!" Will yells out into the hallway still seated behind his desk, but he picks up a stack of paper and quickly places his glasses upon his face to look professional. The clicking stops. It begins again, slow, back towards his door, apparent by the volume of the steps. She peeks her head in, and because fortune is on his side, Will is not reminded of a minstrel show today. Janice is a beautiful woman, with both a complexion and a complex, because she fails the paper bag test. Skin as dark as coffee grounds, smooth as river stones, soft like satin, but she often covers it with powders and pastes to lighten it, and fire-engine red lipstick, the last shade a dark skinned woman should ever be caught in. The vaudevilles ruined that shade of lips for that shade of skin forever. For Will this placing of a bright color upon dark creates the same effect as colored contacts upon dark irises, it either reminds him cheap nineteen eighties horror film transformations, or being at a rave with neon lights and glow sticks. He's not a fan of Janice's proficiency in using makeup, but today she peeks into his office nearly nude. It's both refreshing and slightly arousing. She smiles.

"Yes, Mr. Bunting?"

"Sorry to catch you like this. Hope you weren't mid-task or anything." He straightens his glasses. So professional.

"No." She responds while shaking her head in negation. She taps her fingernails on the doorframe she holds while leaning her head in, waiting for a question or further instruction.

"Well, have a seat, please. Let me talk to you a moment. Close the door behind you."

Janice complies and chooses a spot on the loveseat next to the wall instead of the chair placed directly in front of his desk. The residents facing punishment and discussing possible infractions sit in that chair, and she's another employee, not quite Will's equal, but nowhere near the station of an inmate. Janice works independently of Will, and they have more of partnership aimed at achieving the same goals than an employer and employee relationship. He doesn't employ her. She is under contract same as he, but his position grants him the power to have other contract employees removed that do not fit into the Harmony system.

Janice crosses her legs, like modest ladies do, and leans back into the flesh of the loveseat with both arms lining the top edge of the fabric, comfortable, like his and her relationship. She smirks, waiting for Will to get to the point of his invitation. Janice has been working for Harmony for over seven years. She's a drug counselor transparently aware of her lack of impact in the lives of those she councils, not because she's not good, but because she knows she is just not as good as drugs and that no one is, not for the circumstance of the residents. Will and Janice have had many candid discussions about their supposed impact and actual impact, and this is the basis of their relationship. They've shared many things with each other, as seven years has given plenty of opportunities for developing needs and delivered provisions from them both. Still, the basis of their relationship is their work. They are two people in the cinema watching a book-based movie that actually read the book. From the opening scene they cannot help but to judge it in comparison, and they know how it is going to end, or at least how it's supposed to. The characters in this movie they watch change often, but never really change, like horror movie sequels.

"Sorry I couldn't make to the Family Therapy session yesterday evening. I had a splitting headache and I, honestly, was just tired of being in this place. Learn anything new?" Will left early with a headache, but he was also in quite the drinking mood. He went to The Fifth, not home.

"I emailed my minutes to you."

"I didn't check. I'm sorry. Did anything stand out? Hell, should I even bother to read the email?" The two have been doing this song and dance for seven years; of course he didn't check the minutes. Janice knew this, but she always reaffirms that she did her part. They converse as if they are being watched and recorded while in the office. There are no cameras in the offices though, just across the rest of the facility, with the exception of the dorms and restrooms, but still they act as if. All of the actors are in harmony, in Harmony, including the recurrent roles, but they break character on occasion, especially these two.

Janice shakes her head in a manner that shows her disappointment in not being able to offer him anything more. "Nope. Normal session. You do sound desperate though." She laughs. "No one acted out of the ordinary. Same questions were asked, the same answers were given, same monologues. They could be reading a script. Maybe they are. Like a college fraternity that keeps copies of the tests given yearly by lazy professors… that would be us. So they know exactly what to say. Same stuff no matter the group, just change the main subject. Whether they sold drugs or did them, they're sorry, it ruined their family, their life, their relationship with Jesus or Allah, and then the waterworks are on cue for two, maybe three minutes… It's like they think we haven't seen this act before. If it meant something, the recidivism rate wouldn't be seventy-five percent. To see the same act I've been seeing for the past several years makes me feel as if I'm, if we're, wasting our time, but of course I'm preaching to the choir with you. I figure I'll remind you until you throw your weight around and make the people up top let us do what we're hired to do, problem solve instead of problem maintenance. We either cure them or pull the plug. This in between stuff is maddening enough to drive a drug counselor to drug use." Will coughs and feels a tinge of embarrassment, as his own drug dependency is something he hadn't the guts to share with Janice, while sharing so much else. Something in him thinks she'll just drop character and laugh it off, maybe even admitting to her own similar addictions, but he isn't sure. "This has to be the third group in as many months that I don't see any potential in. Any," Janice continued.

Will responds with, "I know, and I'm working on it. Believe me," followed by a sigh. "I thought I saw something of a rebellious nature in Finley. Tarus, is it?" Janice nods. "Yeah, I was hoping something would spark in him. Hell, you know me. I've even been pushing his buttons, but nothing. The only chance they have is in rebellion, even if it's from us as well. They have to dig down and understand that the system is designed for them to fail and pull away from the comfort of thinking it's not, before they truly have a break through. That's how I see it at least. It's like they're fucking…" he pauses and calms himself, and Janice frowns a little at the out-of-character faux pas. "It's like they've been lobotomized by the time they reach us, numb to the reality they still have to face, and only worried about making it through these last months of their sentence. Exactly why they are back in the system so soon. They aren't even paying us any attention."

"Correct… So yeah, you didn't miss a thing yesterday that you haven't already seen before from this group. This is Collins' last week, along with Johnson, Roberts, Brown, the little one, and Day. All of their requirements have been met, and I don't foresee any issues with either of them, so you might as well start their paperwork, and we got two coming in later today. And we start the process again, crossing our fingers, and Finley? I don't know how you ever saw anything in him. I just see a pervert with disgusting teeth. His brain's fried. That's not rebellion. Every frown isn't proof of a working mind. I was never impressed by him, and I'll be glad when he's gone. Can't walk by those tractor-beam eyes of his without feeling like I need another shower…" Will laughs. Janice's facial expression changes, and she changes the subject along with it. "LaTonya hasn't been around in a while. Have you kept up with her?"

Will is still laughing at the tractor-beam comment upon receiving her question. He shakes his head while letting the laugh die and he speaks, "Nah. I haven't. I feel like I need an excuse to contact her now she's been on the streets so long. She IS our success story. Without her, we have nothing." Will laughs. "So no, I haven't talked to her. I haven't had anything to say… I was hoping you were about to give me something, because I'm tired of checking up on her and others just to do it, while in one sense it's showing I care, or Harmony cares, in another I feel like the Gestapo. Maybe we should put together a project or something with our success stories. That would give us a positive reason to get back in touch without that hungry, desperate look in our eyes."

Janice slaps her knee and points in laughter, "That's you, Bunting!"

Will nods in inaudible laughter with a blushing smile, "We should try something like that, though. How about a calendar?"

"Depends on how low you want to bring the bar, but it's doable. From where I sit, we don't have twelve success stories. We can get fancy and just do one with the seasons. We have at least four, I think." Janice flashes a wide-eyed, wide-mouthed smile, with a shrug and upturned palms.

"Four?!"

"If that." Janice continues. "We look for different things. The drug thing, is my thing. My training. My discipline. What you see sometimes as someone as clean and ready to hit the streets, is often what I see as someone who has staved off their addiction long enough to return to it. It's easy to stay clean here. It's easy to not break laws here. We have people who can't do either of course, making your job necessary, but you have to understand that this environment does not mirror the environment out there. That's why it's important you keep up with them, even our success stories. Relapse happens, all of the damn time, and I'm not just talking about drugs."

"Yeah. I get it. But four? Come on, Janice."

"I ain't budging. We got enough for the seasons and that's it, as far as anyone we'd want to make a positive example of and tell their stories. You'd be surprised what your graduates are out there doing right now as we speak. The world is chewing them up, and they just want to disappear, if just for a moment. Some addicts are quite functional, Mr. Bunting. It takes a well-trained eye to see. I'm seasoned now, and I see a lot that you may not." Janice's eyes are unwavering and locked onto Will's. "You'll never know if you don't know what to look for. All don't have tracks all up and down their arms, letting their hygiene, especially oral, go. It can happen right under your nose, even with those closest to you. I've seen it. Drug use isn't falling. People are just hiding it better, especially outside of the hood." Will feels as if she is talking to and about him, as if his frequency in nursing the bottle shows to someone with her level of training. He listens without trying to somehow give himself away if he isn't the subject, while she speaks. "I refuse to sign off on more than four. How many years are you trying to go back?"

Will shakes his head *no* in thoughtful digression, welcoming the close of that discussion and ready to exit it this time around. "Ok. Yeah, you're right. Would just be more work for us anyway, and what would it accomplish? We have enough chances to fail without adding another…" Will opens his bakery with the flexing of his jaws. "Well, that's why I called you in here, on the off chance that I missed some kind of breakthrough yesterday… but you do look stunning today. I called you in to tell you that as well," Will winks. It goes well with his blushing smile he allowed the return of. Anytime Janice doesn't have a bunch of cosmetics caked upon her face, he makes a point of telling her she looks nice. One day he hopes she'll recognize the pattern and donate her makeup kit to colorfully clad child entertainers in financial trouble or a haunted house. Their relationship is comfortable, but not comfortable enough for him to tell her she appears a clown when made up, or that he drinks enough to make his life a fully functional three-ringed circus, but some things are best kept secrets.

"Why thank you, Mr. Bunting... but nope, you missed nothing at all. Just regular ol' drug addicts and convicted felons ready to rejoin society as the productive members they've always dreamed about being. That's it. A bunch of overgrown babies, ready to rip the next person's head off over stepping on their tennis shoes, but when faced with real world issues, bring out the tissues, because they're just victims and powerless. Even those that don't cry, which is an act anyway, they're worse, sit there frowned up refusing to speak, like Tarus Finley, like that ever solved a problem after the tender age of three... They've put up these walls. All of them. Can't get through to them without a wrecking ball or a pick ax, and I understand it's for protection. I do. But what when what's hurting you is already inside your wall? I can't operate through a suit of armor."

Will shrugs and responds in submission, "Yeah... but they aren't the only ones with walls and the fear of opening up, just to be fair." He was trying to create a type of defense for the recently released, but his protection of them was more like pushing them out of the way of an oncoming bus and standing there himself. Will is the king of walls, a master mason, but sacrificing himself instead was not the intention. Janice didn't quite make that connection, although she knew him well enough to.

"I agree," she nods quickly. "It's not a problem unique to them. It's everybody. Some walls are just thicker than others. The more abuse one has experienced, the thicker the wall, like scar tissue, and you add all of this technology that allows us to so easily stay in touch, yet never touch - make compassionate, caring, empathetic, human connections, and touch becomes a luxury. It easier not to, and ideally safer, but what we do is build up the walls of our tombs that we'll slowly waste away in. This is bare hand, bare skin work that we are trying to do. You can't express love no other way, and if they don't feel love, or open themselves up to that connection, we lose. We lose here. We lose everywhere, and everyone else is losing with us as we all comfortably pull away from each other, but I'm willing to bet we see it best here. Walls, yes. Breakthroughs, no. Not any yesterday, not many ever." Janice pauses while reading the disappointment across Will's face. "But there is always the next group, right?" Janice rises from the loveseat, preparing to exit.

"Yes." Will puts on his team leader costume, woven with optimism. "Always. Won't be a shortage of next groups, and it's going to get better... I'll be there at the one o'clock. You bring your lunch today?" Janice nods affirmatively while walking backward towards the door. "Thank you, Janice... Ey!" Janice stops. "Why do you still call me Mr. Bunting after all of these years? I've never asked you to."

Janice flashes a worrisome smile. "It's professional." Will twists his mouth as if asking her not to bullshit him, and she follows with, "Really want to know?"

"Yeah."

"Because I hate that name. Nothing to do with you though, or anyone really. I just don't think *will* exists, really, and we are all mocked by the idea of it, and every conscious moment seems to prove it more. Maybe I took one too many philosophy courses in college, but as a result I don't really use the word, even in naming. I'll call you William if you'd like or Willie. If it is short for one those, or Bill even, but I much prefer Mr. Bunting to Will."

"William? So you don't even know my name, huh? After all these years." Will is tickled by the thought.

"No. Not unless it's just Will by itself. That's what all the paperwork says and what's here on your plaque, and all your little certificates, awards and stuff around here." She points at his name placard. "It's not like I'm investigating you, you know? I just know what you tell me."

Will nods. "Yeah, it's not William. But that's not important; just keep to what you're comfortable with. I was just curious. It doesn't bother me at all beyond making me feel important, and that's not bad. If it isn't broken, we shouldn't go about trying to repair it. Right?"

Janice shakes her head *no*. "If it AIN'T broke, don't fix it, but I agree. See you at one." She opens the door and bounces out of his office, and the clicks resume their journey echoing down the hallway.

In the darkest corner, with his notepad and pen in hand, propped upon his resting arms, upon a desk, Will has his neck nestled within his cupped shoulders resting. Everyone else calls it sleeping, and he's oblivious that everyone is aware that after twenty minutes or so, his closed eyes are only being hidden behind the glare of his spectacles. It is a remote corner of a room that is poorly lit, most of the facility is poorly lit with bulbs flickering and going out all of the time and the trouble of an unmotivated groundsman, maintenance man blend, and a budget that barely covers bulb replacement. Will rarely asks any questions after maybe the first ten minutes in any afternoon, after lunch session, nor does he take any notes, because he's sleeping.

Janice could have slept as well. The session is another of the uninspiring and uninteresting kind, as many of the inmates have been with them for months and have their act down pat. No one was fooling anyone anymore, so the thrill is gone. The environment is devoid of enthusiasm, thumbs twiddle, gum smacks, and sighs multiply, adding a chorus to the occasional snore by Will as they symbolically pass the mic between one another - they don't use an actual mic, and tell their ad-lib stories with the interchangeable protagonist being themselves in the tale of how narcotics ruined their lives, using and distributing. Tomorrow it will be the same story but the drug will be switched out with alcohol; Mondays the story will be about the cycle of violence they've all been a victim of, Tuesdays the sex abuse, and Wednesdays the family they've been victims to, which is often worse than illicit drug addiction and regularly the gateway way to it, is discussed through counseling with an emphasis on parenting and reconnecting with loved ones with ridiculous role play. It may work better if their family members would visit, which is both an issue of desire and distance. Residents are never local to deter escape. Put them back on their turf and chances are much higher that familiar negative influences, like family and friends, will derail them from the program, mentally, physically, or completely.

"Janice," a voice pours into the room from the back, waking everyone as all were in a sleeplike state; Will was the only one fully dedicated to it. He wasn't even stirred. Janice responds by turning around and raising her brow.

The young lady in the doorway says, "Bus is here."

Janice looks down at her watch. "It's early… Thank you Ann." She turns back towards the clients who are all sitting in a circular formation that she is included in, the only chair outside the formation is Will's, and asks, "So, where were we?"

She is answered with a collective groan as if all were saying, *Who gives a damn?*, a message she readily decoded and expected. "Well, I tell you what," she claps once, "let's call it a day, so Will and I can process the new residents in."

"Somebody cute, I hope." A female client blurts out.

Janice responds with a single raised brow, "That should be the last thing you're worried about, girl." Everyone laughs a little, even the target. Harmony also tries to discourage sexual interaction as best they can. Someone somewhere defined sex as an obstacle between clients and recovery, so the men and women are kept away from each other as often as possible and treated like children. Will has always hated this, and he's made it his point to create situations where both sexes can share the same space because his job is to prepare them for the world beyond Harmony. Janice continues, "Ok then, now you have an extra thirty minutes to work on your projects, and we can talk about them next week. Ok?" The room is rising and gathering their materials before she even finishes her sentence, and no one answers to her *Ok*, beyond finding their belongings and preparing their exit from the conference room.

She's been talking about that project for over a month, an exercise in redefinition, where the clients are supposed to create a timeline starting from when they first engaged with drugs, and the major milestones they hit with them, good or bad, that extends to two years in the future after graduating from Harmony, where they of course no longer have drugs in their life. The point is having them visualize themselves without drugs, and projecting this reality, and putting this energy into the universe. In honesty, if it were not for Harmony's drug policy and their constant testing, many would already have become reacquainted with their crutches, even though they are clean. It is no longer a chemical dependency; prison cleared them all of that. Although drugs are available behind bars, they are not available at the level necessary to sustain a chemical dependency. The emotional and cultural dependency still exists though, and will never leave without a complete shift in their paradigms. What else can they really do besides fade into the obscurity of a high? Face reality? The reality of the struggles of many is much worse than drug addiction.

The group begins filing out of the room, Janice collects her belongings, and Will doesn't move a muscle. "Mr. Bunting... Mr. Bunting!" Janice's calls go unanswered. She places the binder she was working from into her satchel and walks over to his corner post. She watches him sleep momentarily and decides not to call his name again. Instead, she leans into the side of his head and blows into his ear, her bottom lip may have grazed his lobe a tiny bit, knowing that would do a number on his REM state. He doesn't move. She blows again even harder, and he still doesn't. She reneges on calling out his name and does it within an inch of his ear, "Mr. Bunting," startling and waking him.

"Wha... what?"

"You're getting worse. Sleeping at night?"

Will is scratching his scalp and gathering himself.

Janice continues, "The bus is here. Came thirty minutes early. Maybe because it's only two they were able to get through processing much faster. I ended the NA session a little early so we, or you rather, could get to your little orientation."

"Ok. Ok... Thank you. How was the session?"

"Oh wow. The best ever. You missed so much when you went under. Major breakthroughs today. Yesterday, I would've said that

105

what we're doing is hopeless and that Harmony was basically a full of shit way for some disingenuous politician types to appear effective on paper. But oh, not after today my fearless leader. You missed it. We're making a difference!"

Will shakes head, smirks, and responds, "So, again, I didn't miss anything. Understood... but in my dreams though..."

"Literally," Janice adds with a pointed nod.

"Maybe this is the group Janice."

"Yup, Mr. Bunting, maybe. And maybe we'll change the world."

1 : 6 *Our conditioning has disallowed us a proper perspective on who or what our enemy is. There are direct enemies and indirect enemies, I think. Some of our enemies are just us and as unaware that they are our enemies, through working for our enemies, as we are that they are also our enemies. It is a deep confusion, created at such depths that the distortions and the pressures from the currents potentially confuse us all. The sheepdog does not protect the sheep from the wolves for the sheep, it protects the sheep for the shepherd, and will just as soon tear the sheep apart if the shepherd suggests it, so who is the enemy?*

The white and maroon prison school bus pulls into House of Harmony parking lot slowly. It is a small lot, only three riders, pulling into a small lot, unaccommodating, with no spaces big enough for school bus parking unless it's the *short bus*, a colloquialism for the one the *special* or the *slow kids* ride. Oh the irony, considering the mental state of a high percentage of the prison population since Reagan closed the state mental institutions and ramped up the drug war. The state effectively bumped up the flow of drugs, which increased the number of babies and adults mentally, physically, socially, and chemically compromised by drugs, mostly in the poor neighborhoods, the Black neighborhoods, and left them with no place but prison to go. It is ironic that here at Harmony only the short bus that quite often, concerning the condition of many of the riders, *should* park here, could park here.

The success of the drug war has to be measured statistically on a national scale, or else the millions poured into it cannot be justified. Taxpayers are basically investors, and they want to see positive results along with the face of the drug war. The face is the young, Black, enterprising hoodlum, causing the crack epidemic on the corners of urban slums, Gray's, and his victims, those tortured souls reduced to mere shells of their former humanity, complete the picture supporting the demonization of that face. The investors cheer at every engagement of Gray's face meeting the boot of justice. Some also cheer at the destruction, the lifelessness, the addicts, the homeless, and the desperation vacuum left in Gray's wake. It's what they're paying to see, so it filled the camera lenses, the articles, and the stat sheets. The easiest representative statistic for such a war is drug arrests, because the state only *officially* has access to intercepted drug transactions to measure drug usage and flow, but unofficially the state knows much more, as Oliver North's declassified documents disclosed along with Gary Webb's reporting. The state either acted in corroboration and in protection of known drug traffickers or it just turned a blind eye, while certain communities were fingered for this *drug war*. America, she eats her young. This reality is one of the reasons prosecutors stopped giving deals to lower tiered drug dealers, Black kids from the block, to turn in their bosses, because they kept upturning government officials and upstanding, middle class, White citizens.

On the political side, if the line is being tough on drugs, and drugs are no more illegal than they had been and the police are no better equipped to stop them than they had been, the easiest way to create the appearance of a successful crackdown is to increase the flow or access to drugs for the average citizen, in certain communities. Drug arrests increased, in certain communities. It looked great on paper, but off paper, in these certain communities, the policy was ravaging, making new addicts, destroying families, and creating criminals. It was a war on drugs and the hood was suffering and war torn, caught in the cultural crossfire of the accepted drug cultures of the sixties and seventies into the demonization of the same practices in the early eighties. The cultural shift of drug tolerance into strict intolerance hit the ghettos the hardest, and it was even expressed through entertainment, movies, and music, that did nothing but increase drug demand like fattening lambs for the slaughter. And slaughter, they did, so much so with the indoctrination of a portion of the public and criminalization of another, the most popular television show for a long time was about the slaughter and slaughterers, entitled *Cops*. America's prison population climbed from three hundred thousand to two million three hundred thousand in about forty years.

Gray's father, who wasn't consistently there, a father from afar that many hood kids experience and partially a result of such declared wars because family structures were badly damaged, told him a tale once that was a relaxed defense of his condition. Father was an avid marijuana smoker in the early eighties, but he wouldn't touch anything else, and as he told Gray, emaciated yet proud, like a liver of many lives, "One day, we couldn't find it. Nobody could find weed anywhere. For weeks we just wanted to get high, and it was completely dry except for crack cocaine, which was everywhere and being given away so..." Gray watched his pops smoke crack in front of him as a child, making a pipe out of a beer can by dropping the rock through the mouth and lighting the bottom. If this is what they mean by marijuana being a gateway drug, their argument is flawed, but it's the way Father's story explained how many moved from weed to freebase. It was also a way Father apologized for who he'd become, and a segue to borrowing money they both knew he'd never pay back. Gray was already hustling, mostly betting and selling candy, and had his own money by age eleven. Gray is the result, his father is the result, and many destroyed communities moved from the political motivation of self-preservation to self-destruction, and being blamed for the shift, is the social side and the effects of corrupt political policy that the victims unknowingly supported with their tax dollars as they measured out the rope that they'd eventually be hanged with.

Along with all those trapped in the dragnet of drug trafficking, consequently causing the biggest boom ever in the prison industry beginning in the eighties and never stopping, the war on drugs was as much of a joke as the D.A.R.E. program. A young Gray would sit in elementary school classes, led by cops, singing anti-drug songs, winning stickers for answering questions correctly, learning that the drug problem was as easy as *just saying no*, being encouraged not to do drugs because they were very very bad, as well as informing the police about the bad people doing and providing drugs. Children, too young to know any better, were even telling on their parents, wanting to connect personally with the subject just to receive praise and a fucking sticker, because the police were their friends.

A decade later, when young Gray was first hitting the block as an inner city merchant, the number of crack heads dawning black T-shirts that read Drug Abuse Resistance Education in white lettering beneath the solid red letters of the acronym to which they belonged, made plain the success of both the D.A.R.E. program and the war on drugs. They probably still knew the songs, and maybe recited them while getting high for added amusement, *DARE told them so, they had the right to say no.*

The story of how Gray ends up with this charmed life of his is arguably as predictable as the direction a flame will travel when a line of fuel is laid before it and viewed from the advantage of the powerful, and Harmony may just be another stop on that line, if indeed it is in the design, as the bus pulls in. Harmony hasn't parking spaces for full sized busses so the prison busses have to park in the aisle not far form Will's car to release the property. Livestock exchanges have been occurring for centuries. Human livestock built the wall on Wall Street the Dutch settlers used in defense from the British settlers and the Natives in the seventeenth century. Human stock helped to build the business of the stock exchange as well with their sold bodies at the slave auctions at the corner of Wall and Water street, so, many years later the process is now seamless from old slaver to new. Transactions never take long here in the Harmony parking lot, because there aren't many incoming inmates; the trips could be satisfied and better fuel efficient with a taxi.

It happens outside like the open-air markets of the past, where men and women would stand nude or nearly nude, being poked, prodded, having their scars and sores examined, the size of their dick, their breasts, and their teeth checked. How humiliating it must be to be asked to smile so someone can check one's teeth to judge his or her quality, to see if they qualify to be added as property. How humiliating it must be to have one's dick the subject of scrutiny, as it was said to be a determinant in a man's ability to reproduce and create stronger offspring. How humiliating, just like the delousing and cavity searches prisoners receive entering general population. This property exchange is eerily similar, calling back to, or being possessed by the spirit of the original stock exchange. It is basically just the passing of the deed and the keys for those kept in shackles, or the unshackling, and this is the unshackling type. The illusion of freedom must be strong for it to work, or else those in bondage might venture to the walls, notice the bars, and possibly destabilize the entire system, delicately balanced on their belief in the thing.

Gray has been staring at the lay of the land for the past fifteen minutes, since they exited the interstate to enter his new urban home. It's unfamiliar, yet familiar, because Gray knows urban. The hills roll, the grass is green, and the women stand out like long lashes, walking, driving, and engaging in normal life-sustaining activities, striking his optic nerve like they were all dipped in fluorescent ink. They are highlighted, targets, and the men play the background. With a nice outfit and a haircut, he could easily find a corner and resume his old life from a similar place like someone had merely pressed the pause button for the last six years, and he spotted several suitable ones once they entered the east side of town. It's not about who you know but what you know, because what you know gets you in contact with the who, and Gray's convinced that he can find or create that who in any environment similar to his own, any hood would do. Not that that is his plan. He doesn't know his plan yet. It is not beyond the realm of possibility. He just recognizes these places, knowing that he has developed the skill set to capitalize, should he need to, should he decide not to go straight this time. He lost everything from bending, including his family, and he is now trying to start over in his mid-thirties from the bottom with an asterisk beside his name.

The bus stops and idles. The driver yells back, "Ok guys, we're here. Your new home… I'm going to run in and take a quick piss, and I'll be back to take them bracelets from you and hit the road." Although Gray's returned to his previous seat, the driver is much easier to hear with the bus idling, the engine is calm and it is minus the hum of the tires and the expressway wind traveling alongside the carriage. He cuts the engine and exits the bus with a handful of paperwork while the inmates follow him with their eyes like children being abandoned by their father. The driver travels up the untidy cement pathway, smiles and nods at the door window after pushing the buzzer, it unlocks, and he enters. It looked like a human sized birdhouse project that father and son teams put together as a bonding experience. Not an angle was right, and they settled for ninety-two, ninety-one, and eighty-nine degrees instead. It creates the effect of a static structure that dances, the single frame of its actions during a recorded earthquake. It is not state of the art, but appropriately for its least, the felons, and its care for them, it follows the art of the state.

"Home? I think he's throwing around that word a little loose. Damn sure don't look like home to me," the light reflects off of his pale eyes and disheveled strands of yellow and brown hair, looking like dry Texas summer grass, as he looks out the window. The dirty blond turns and leans over the back of the seat to address Gray, he pauses in stare before speaking, looking for clearance in Gray's expression and speaks when he sees a slight brow raise, "We're here, brother. You have any people in these parts?" Gray shakes his head in negation, answering the question and responding to again being this man's so-called brother, clearly a litmus for himself to prove that who he was in prison was just that. Gray would very much prefer not being part of an experiment, the White guilt experience, but he says nothing in direct address. The dirty blond nods and says, "Name's Randy, by the way," before turning his body, sitting again, and directing his focus back upon the front of the Harmony campus.

Without the paperwork, the driver exits the building with his head turned speaking to a trailer, short, sharp, confident, stern faced with a smooth wicker tinted complexion, who responds to the driver's words with short, dictatorial nods, while smoothing his solid knit shirt down his abdomen and tucking the small slack he gathers into his pants and hiking them up by tugging his belt, all in stride. His eyes, beyond the times he rubs them to revive them, never leave the eyes of the driver as they travel up towards the bus as though disinterested in the look of the cargo. They step off of the curb together into the parking lot and travel behind the bus. The bus driver opens the back door, and he can be heard clearly. He's talking about his teenage son and high school football while grabbing Gray's and Randy's boxed belongings from behind the back seats. He sits each box down on the parking lot between the bus and the building with the neatly dressed man walking with him step for step, listening to his story, not looking up at or into the bus even once. The driver finishes unpacking, gestures toward the front of the bus, his audience turns to face the building and clasps his hands behind himself ceremonially, while the driver approaches the front door.

"Okay, this is our stop," the driver says entering the bus with keys in hand to unlock the wire mesh gate between the cockpit and cargo areas. "Come on out and meet Mr. Bunting, the house manager here at Harmony. I can get those shackles off of you and get out of here."

Rubber soles muted, Gray's feet were bare and entering a warm bath when first touching the asphalt that did not belong to the Texas Department of Criminal Justice. His prison issue canvas shoes that only Mexican gangsters and masters of American kung fu wear in the free world, dissolved into thin air with his first freeman steps after the driver kneeled and removed the shackles tethering his feet together, and his hands to his feet. Free from restraints, they walk over to Mr. Bunting, still with his back to them while facing the building. They all stop about five feet behind Will, and the driver cues him with, "Ok." Will nods and turns slowly with a broad smile and frowned brow, giving each inmate a turn of the sadistic enjoyment in his stare. Gray is unimpressed, unintimidated, and unyielding; his first impression of Will is that he's a poser, high off of the smell of his own shit, and bound to be difficult to work with, so one more asshole is added to his *must tolerate* list along with Randy, the dirty blond, White boy.

Finally, Will speaks, "Gentlemen. This is the House of Harmony. Will Bunting. I'm the housing manager here, which basically means the warden in language I'm sure you're familiar with. My assignment is ensuring all here stays in harmony for the final months of your sentences along with everyone else's. If you're easy to work with, I'm easy to work with. If you're not, I'm not. I'm not under state supervision. You want what I have, and it's going to take some commitment on your part. If either of you have served, we employ the KISS principle here. Keep It Simple Stupid, and you're in and out. Simple as that." Will unclasps his hands from behind his back and spreads his arms like he's summoning a hug and ends his spiel with one more smile and, "Welcome!" The school bus growls as it pulls off.

Gray sits in the office, center chair, impatiently rocking and making its springs speak, while waiting for Will to return from getting the dirty blond situated with his new living arrangement. Gray's body language is aggressive. His shoulder blades cut into the cracking leather of the old chair, jutting his pelvis forward in a split thigh dominance projection that taints everything before him, Will's desk and accomplishments, like territorial marking. His fists are balled tightly in a sustained tug at the fabric of the crotch of his sweatpants, and this action keeps his arms flexed, as well as his chest. The language of his body says much, more than his lips usually, and he awaits Mr. Bunting in a display that says he's not only comfortable holding his own nuts, but that they're also so immense, he needs both hands to do so. Will opted to initiate Gray first. Out of the two, the things that influenced his decision most were cultural similarities and judgment of Gray's demeanor – he seems insurrectionary; he keeps a slight smirk and lazy eyelids like one who hasn't any interest in respecting authority. Will always does this one at a time. The physical orientation, or campus tour, is done in a group, but the mental orientation, the rules, regulations, and expectations are done in one on ones. It's not about giving the rules as much as it is about conducting a short psyche evaluation. Will goes through their file with a fine toothed comb asking questions about events while sprinkling the rules in as he sees fit. It isn't like they'd be able to remember the rules anyway, too many. They are printed in a small booklet and given to each resident at orientation's end. The facility rules are important, but not nearly as important as his cross-examination, stare down, intimidation, interrogation, and nut check, appropriately. Gray has begun cleaning his fingernails with his fingernails while still rocking in the seat when Will arrives, legs still spread.

Will walks behind his desk, wheels his chair out, sits, and rolls his knees beneath his desk. He opens his drawer, he rattles around within it looking for something. He displaces items to better search, an unused roll of Scotch tape, some mints, some loose change, and some stray bullets that roll in small arcs once they meet the wood of his desktop. Gray pays particular attention to the bullets, handgun, probably .45 caliber. Gray is no munitions expert by a long shot, but he both knows what .22 caliber looks like and these are bigger, and he knows the nature of smaller men and their compensatory desire to have big guns. *And how much room did removing those bullets clear anyway?*, Gray challenged himself with the thought and concluded that this was all part of his act. Will replaces the items with a jaw-flexing frown, closing the desk without retrieving anything else from it, scanning the top with his eyes pinched. He's yet to look at Gray once. Struck by revelation, he finds what he was in search of, grabbing his glasses. They were in awkward space behind his ears and atop his head, and he laughs at himself while he grabs the file before him with Gray's name upon it. He looks at the name and up at Gray, "Gary Dixon is it?" pronouncing Dixon slowly, like it is two words and an insult to his father in the same manner that son of a bitch would be to his mother, and all from the patient, repulsive way, he let it roll off of his tongue.

"Yeah... I mean, yes sir," Gray responds.

Will shakes his head *no* short and quick, affirming that Gray doesn't have to address him in that manner if he doesn't want to. Will peels open the manila file and asks another question, "First time at a halfway house?"

"Yesss... Yeah."

"Okay," Will stalls while concentrating on Gray's file. "Felony possession with intent to distribute." Will nods slowly while looking above his glasses at Gray. Gray returns a stare, emotionless and motionless. "Well, what happened?"

"I got caught."

"Selling drugs?"

Gray shrugs his shoulders in a, *the file is right in your face,* manner, yet relents and responds, "Yeah."

"What drug or drugs? Weed?"

Gray shakes his head *no.* "Nah. Not so much. I got caught with crack, but..."

Will waits for Gray to continue but he doesn't. Instead, he

just looks off a moment, replaces his hands atop his crotch, and returns his attention to Will like he hadn't been speaking and stopped abruptly a moment earlier. Will tries to assist.

"Crack cocaine. Amazing what that stuff can do to a healthy community." Will opens his drawer, pulls out a mint, and begins unwrapping it. "Candy some call it, but there isn't anything sweet about it. You want a mint?" Gray declines with a head shake. "You ever do drugs, or did you only sell them?"

Gray exhales in an exhausted reply, "Not crack."

"I take it you're not much of a talker?" Gray shakes his head *no*. "Fair enough. Talking is overrated anyway, as long you don't have a problem with listening. That's really what this is about. I'd be lying to you if I told you this institution was about, don't let the name fool you, *creating* harmony. We don't accommodate." Another head shake *no*, the shortest and quickest yet, like a shiver, accents *accommodate*. "Instead, it IS harmony, and the point is for you and the others not to add unto, but to mute yourselves and not disturb the tune. It's not a democracy. Your opinion is not valued outside of counseling sessions, but it's not prison." Will shrugs. Will bends down and opens one of the drawers next to his shin. He rises wagging a small navy blue handbook in the air. "This will be your bible while here, and all sins are listed one by one. There are more rules in here than I care to remember, but a good method to use in figuring out if something you want to do is within the rules while here on campus is just saying no. It's probably not. There was no interest in your comfort when designing this program, and the bulk of your enjoyment will be had off campus. Just make sure you return before curfew. When you get to go off campus, that is. All new residents have a two week probation before you can do that."

Gray nods in understanding.

"This book is yours to read through, but let me hit some major points before sending you on your way." Will gets up, walks around his desk and hands Gray the booklet, forcing him to remove at least one hand from his symbolic gonad clutch. Instead of returning to his chair, he just takes a few steps back and leans against his desk. "Ok, Dixon," he repeats the name with same ugliness that he had initially, and clears his throat, probably of what collected there amidst that horrid pronunciation, with a grunt. He leans in a bit before speaking, staring directly into Gray's grays. "I'm the last thing between you and freedom. And while, ideally, most would sit here and encourage you on your return to society, I don't and I won't. I've had many sit right there where you are, coast through the program, graduate, and end up back in prison in a year's time or dead. That's really not a huge problem for me. It's not like I'm personally invested. You won't break my heart in a newspaper headline. I've just seen too much. But… I do imagine the communities you go back into after refusing the help we offer. What those families experience when you return as worthless as you left, or worse, fueling the ongoing cycle of dysfunction and honestly not giving the honest, hard workers there a chance. They are my interest in not having you just pass through, because when you get back to where you call home, restart your empire, but smarter this time so you don't get caught, because you don't want to go back to prison, I'm responsible. Somebody like you, if you do have the charisma to gain a little power, becomes a tyrant, impacting much more than just the criminals. If a square, that's what you call us right?" Gray doesn't respond but Will is right. He continues. "If a square sees too much and you have to make him disappear, that, THAT blood's on my hands…"

Will grabs the television remote off of his desk and points it at the monitor at the back of his office, and motions for Gray to look. Gray swivels around to view the small wall-mounted television showing different parts of the facility. It's the second time today he gets to watch security camera footage, not the most riveting stuff. Will changes the feed with the click of a button to a twenty-four hour news channel, and as if he's willed it, the current story is about violent crime. Will continues, "You see? This is happening all day, every day in every *hood* in America, and THAT's why society wants to lock you up and throw away the key instead of what we try to do here, and THAT's why I care about what I'm doing here. You can turn back now." Gray complies. "The community you return to is the biggest victim of them all, and it is stained with the inability to heal because of the likes of you. They won't let you live anywhere else. They'll barely let you have a job, and you'll be right back where you started around the same criminal elements and opportunities. It makes the police work easy, too. They figure it's just a matter of time, and they're usually right. True story, by the way, the blood on my hands… a Black man with a wife and three kids was murdered by a graduate from this program who hadn't been home yet for fifteen months, who got strung out and desperate. Now these kids don't have a daddy, and the cycle has a higher probability of repeating itself because somebody who sat where you're sitting decided not to listen to a word I had to say. That's why I'm hard, Dixon. You don't ever have to ask me that question. No, I don't understand you because I'm also Black, and no, I'm not on your team." He leans in even closer to Gray. "I care much more about them kids than I'll ever care about you. Ever. Just know that. The first chance I get to ship you back, I'm taking, as soon as I recognize you're not taking this opportunity seriously. Do you understand me?"

Unmoved, Gray nods and says, "Yes sir…Understood," and an inopportune yawn, full and mature, hitches itself to the back of his short statement. Will leans back to a natural posture while leaning upon a desk like the strength of the yawn blew him there. Cookies of disappointment form along with a couple of tight nods and his attempts to shake them free, while the dramatic news story music accompanies the mood. Gray still has his lack of sleep, emptiness, feeling. He's not at all impressed by Will's attempt to intimidate him, but in a small way he sympathizes with his task of trying to find a method to assert authority and instill some type of fear in those fresh from the penitentiary, the most authoritative and fearful place possible, when they only truly fear going back, if that. Not much fear left in this clan that Will makes his living trying to lead and inspire, so maybe fear isn't the best method of motivation. Gray's listening; he's just not impressed. Gray scratches his brow and looks away from Will for the second time during their engagement, and Will compensates for his apparent loss of interest with refocusing his message.

Will, the rule breaker who enforces the rules, enters his favorite portion of these meetings. He raises his palms and spreads his fingers in a, *hands up, don't shoot* manner, and speaks, "Okay Dixon.

You have Ten Commandments here at Harmony, and a bunch of minor ones that you'll get in your bible there, and no, I'm not God, should you be thinking that along with this metaphor… I'm just the only one God speaks to. I'm going over the ten just so I'll know, you know. " Will pauses, stares at Gray, waiting for some kind of confirmation he understands. Gray gives him a small nod. Will proceeds.

"Thou shalt find a job. And sixty percent of your paycheck belongs to Harmony. Consider it tithing if it makes you feel better. Non-negotiable. If you're making ten dollars an hour, just consider it four dollars an hour when calculating your pay." Will folds in his thumb, and while beginning his next commandment he folds his index finger on top of his thumb, using his fingers as a method of counting like thousands of grade school children do across America.

"Thou shalt attend all counseling sessions until thou finds work, whether you feel the subject concerns you or not. Mondays we have Visions of Nonviolence, which is self explanatory. Tuesdays, Sex Support, which is about sexual abuse. Wednesday is family therapy. Thursday and Friday is Narcotics Anonymous and Alcoholics Anonymous, respectively. I'm sure you can find yourself at home in a couple."

"Thou… Enough of that. I'm just really not in the mood today. Curfew is from 8pm to 8am. Unless otherwise given permission, you must be on the premises during that time. Work is a valid excuse. Oh, and lights out at 11pm." Will thinks that he should have muted the television or switched back to the camera feed, because he cannot stop himself from looking up to match his eyes with the anchor's voice. It's not a major distraction, he's gone over the commandments hundreds of times, but it is a distraction. He also worries if it is creating a disturbance for Gray.

Gray is paying attention to Will just enough for it to matter, and noticing the news stories cycling none at all. There's a couple of women Gray intends to connect with that he saw while on the tour portion of this, if he can hurry and be finished with this orientation.

"No sex. Not here at the facility. This in not a motel, and you have more important things to worry about anyway. Do what you want off campus, but not here. That goes for you with other residents, or with someone off the streets, with a female, or male. None." Gray offers Will a puzzled expression when he mentions *male*. Will shrugs and continues, dropping his next finger down, closing one fist, with his fifth commandment.

"No drugs. Thou shalt not sell them, or do them. This even includes alcohol while on campus. I'd like to include cigarettes, too, but the higher ups think you should be allowed some crutch, so it makes it difficult. Do what you want off campus, as long as it's legal, and we do frequent urinary analysis. "

Will stands with his right fist closed and raised, preparing to start the next rule when he freezes looking back at the screen. The present story captures his attention and his left arm slowly lowers. "…few details have been released but we have confirmed that there has been a police shooting in the Cottonwood district. We haven't received the officer's name, but we have been told his condition is critical but stable, and we'll give you more info as it comes in." Upon receiving the information, Will also lets his fist fall, and he looks at the doorway a moment while wrestling with a thought. Gray watches.

Will addresses Gray again, hastened, lowering the fingers on his left hand with each item, which now hangs next to his thigh. "Alright. No profanity. No gang involvement. No gambling. No stealing. And no fighting, or you get an infraction. Enough infractions, you're headed to county or back to prison, and it's as simple as that Dix… Hold on a minute, will you?" Will swings around his desk and back to his chair, visibly disturbed and his sudden jerkiness and lack of cool has made him more of a subject worth paying attention to for Gray. Gray doesn't understand the change in the demeanor, but he had not listened to the news story, he doesn't understand the climate, nor does he realize that Cottonwood is name of the neighborhood he presently sits in and his new home.

The office phone rings, and Will answers. "Yes Ann… Yeah, I just saw that… Aw hell… Ok. I don't see anything wrong with it. Not really, I guess. Let them celebrate, as long as they stay under control. I mean, we don't have any control over what the residents find happiness in. Tell the staff to stand by, but the official word is I don't have a problem with it… Ok. Thank you." He hangs up. Clearly, the official word and the swing of his emotions are not identical. "We're done here Gary, sorry to have to cut this short." Will rises and starts to gather up his belongings. "I'll be seeing you around campus, and again, welcome to Harmony." Gray stands and heads for the door, as he grabs the knob and twists, Will adds an addendum, "Oh, one of the residents started a small celebration in the lounge area that you're welcome to join. You probably won't be able to get your room assignment until afterwards anyway… A cop got shot this morning." Will flashes a fake smile and returns to his preparation. Gray exits, straight to the lounge to find some woman to whisper to with every intention of breaking the fourth commandment. Shortly after reaching the lounge, and casing the residents, he notices a worried or wounded Will hurriedly exiting Harmony, face focused forward and frowned, like being shot through a barrel.

*   *   *

It's another day with zero patrons at The Fifth. It's still early. The drinkers don't arrive until late usually, but the first regular, seasoned by the many streams of its fountains, arrives. Will storms into the building, yanking open one of the front door and scratching the stucco rocks across the concrete porch nearly with enough force to create a spark, as he split into the darkness contained therein. He speaks into the darkness before his eyes adjust to it, "I told you his ass was a bad idea, Toni!" while closing the distance between himself and the bar. His vision clears upon arriving, and he's staring a wilily smiling Tuck, wearing a bar apron, directly in the face.

"Who, Will? Or am I speaking to Liam now? I get confused. Is this Legion business or some other shit, so I can know whether to say fuck you or not?" Will pauses gaining his bearings as Tuck teases. "Aw whatever, fuck both of you. What you crying about now, huh?"

"Not in the mood, Tuck. Where the fuck is Toni?"

"Not here."

Will grabs his cell phone from his pocket and walks away

dialing. A cell phone rings from behind the bar, and again Tuck responds with, "Not here. Had to make a run and called me to see if I could fill in as soon as my shift at Harmony was done. I didn't ask any questions…" Will ends the call and stands in the remote space he traveled to away from Tuck while Tuck continued. "We have trust, me and Toni. You seem to have something burning to say. The way I see it, anything you can say to Toni, you can say to me if it's Legion business, and I think it is. No hierarchy, right? So who the fuck is the *he* you came in hollering about?"

"Why didn't I hear about the shooting? What The Ears all took a vacation day? We created system for a reason. I log in and I get nothing. Normal fucking day, besides you know…" Will walks back toward the bar. "What dumb nigga decided not to follow protocol and shoot a cop this morning?" Will leans over the bar and presses his face between the space between his and Tuck's.

Tuck leans away. "Nigga? Ok. Now we talking. Thought you was too good for that word." Tuck revels in the building tension. He has a smile hidden behind his every syllable. "Good question though, or is it an accusation? Ain't like I'm the only nigga in the city that knows how to shoot a gun and says fuck the police. I ain't do it. I'd have walked up and blew his fucking brains out. I'm not a sniper. So scratch me off your list. One down, and like one hundred thousand to go." Tuck laughs. "The page ain't mention it, cause nobody knew. You should be happy that someone took the pressure off us."

"Off of us?!" Will looks at Tuck accusatorily. "We did it. I promise. Even if we didn't, *nobody* heard about it? If the evening news gets the drop on anything happening on the eastside before us, we might as well pack up, 'cause we ain't shit. So, I don't know if the *mastermind*," he makes quotes with his fingers, "thought that much into this while trying to make sure I didn't find out, but he in effect told on himself with orchestrating this complete lapse in our system. It's either that or we ain't shit. No gray area."

"Guess we ain't shit then… Whatever Liam. Believe what the fuck you want. I didn't hear about the shooting until an hour ago. One of my members sent me a text, and I been here thinking what to say to my congregation. I figure something about reaping and sowing, and maybe throw a little Maclolm X in there with it. I got to start addressing this. I don't care what you and yours do, but me and mine about to get ready. It's about to be a hot summer."

"Ha! Congregation? At the Tom Center? You need to stop wasting those good people's time, Tuck. You and this building fund that hasn't even upgraded your tent yet. I figure Gawd," will moves his hands behind *Gawd* like he's juggling the testicles of the Divine, "would've made a way by now." He doesn't even laugh at his own jab. He's too upset. "Get Toni to give you that cross back there. At least y'all can have a cross. Spiritual folk love crosses too, and they even say Jesus in bed. I don't mind hearing it there though, to be honest." Will is visibly disturbed, he doesn't even know what to do with his hands while speaking, and they just move like they haven't a clue what point he is trying to convey. He moves back away from the bar area and begins to slowly pace in the space between the tables he was standing in.

Tuck stays patient, deciding to take the high road in his direct response. "What you call that, deflecting right? See, I listen. What'd talking about my church do for you? … I thought so. This is off topic, as you know, but I'm not wasting their time. We're a spiritual people, and have been long before we ever landed on these shores. Africans defined God while Europeans were still in the caves, and now that they running back to godlessness, because God just ain't in them, some of you niggas are running back with them. We wouldn't have gotten this far without God. I'm not wasting their time by doing my best to keep them connected with the Divine. I think you waste people's time by not."

"Keep telling yourself that, Tuck. Maybe once you do it enough your God will stop making you look like a fool and finally answer a prayer for once… but y'all need him."

"You need him!"

"Wrong. I need people. People I can count on, who don't have their heads in the clouds, so afraid of having to go at this life thing alone that they need an imaginary friend that agrees with everything they think, but never matches any of it with action… You and your people need God. I'm good without Him, and while you're busy searching for Him, I'm busy being Him, me and people like me, assuming His duties. Where the fuck is your God at when we need Him?!" Will waves his palms in front of him like creating an imaginary barrier repelling Tuck from answering his question. "Oh, oh, oh, no don't tell me. It's OUR fault right?" He slaps upon his chest. "All of this shit. OUR bad. Because we didn't pray hard enough, because we aren't faithful enough. Fucking babies, BABIES, used as alligator bait would've been OK had they just put their little fat, black, baby hands together and prayed! Follow the logic in that shit! Babies praying, with no concept of language or God... We're their fucking God, and WE let them down, and we still are, waiting for saviors that ain't ever coming and being good niggas, 'cause we're fucking scared to death... of death." Tuck raises his eyebrows and smirks. Will recognizes this, and understands why without inquiry and starts feeling a touch of freefall weightlessness. He continues, with his energy tapering off. "Try praying to your God for liberation and let's see whose God works the hardest. You'll just be praying to people like me, instead."

Tuck shakes his head in negation. "Pray to YOU for liberation? Liberation Liam. I guess we all just see what we want to see in ourselves."

Will slams his hand on the table. "Who put all of this shit together?! You couldn't organize a domino tournament, much less a movement!"

Tuck is calm. "You might be right, and respect to what you've done, Liam. We appreciate you. The people appreciate you. You showed us some shit that we didn't know. You gave us direction we didn't have. Some of that military stuff. That philosophy shit you kick. I ain't making light of none of that, but... if I can use a biblical analogy, Moses couldn't take the people into the promised land. We do appreciate you leading us out the wilderness though, Liam. For real." Tuck sounds sincere. It is if they have begun talking *to* one another and not *at* one another.

"That story's fiction..." Will presses his palms into his eyes in frustration. "And fuck you man, it ain't time yet." His voice has lost all of its aggression as if pleading. "Don't mess this up Tuck. Listen to me?"

"I haven't done anything. Not yet. Just telling you thank you, and judging from your stance, we can take it from here. I'm relieving you of your post, so to speak." Tuck is making a compassionate presentation. "Come on, Liam?"

"Who are you to relieve me of anything? What post do I even occupy?"

"Just go, man. It's about to turn into the shit that you don't like. I got all type of pressure around me. Cops still just shooting niggas. One cop get shot and you pitch a bitch, running up in here like it's the end of the world. Man, maybe you used to be, but I really don't think you built for this no more. Yes, this is all your plan coming to life before you, but on God, I don't think you want it to live. You ain't trying to cross into the promised land with us, and that's OK with me. I take it for what it is."

Will balls both of his fists and shakes them like maracas in frustration, continuing his plea, "Tuck, it's not time yet. How can you follow me so far and all of sudden lose trust? Don't let the enemy dictate this battle. Chill! It's not time yet. Trust what I tell you. Please?"

"Our God is bigger than you Liam, and He say it's time to move. Who am I, you ask? I got more respect than you think I have amongst the membership and out here in these streets. I'm no leader, but shit, you wasn't either. We ain't got one of them, right?... See you feel like you just lost control of shit that you never had control over in the first damn place, and now you got to deal with the thing you've been most scared of, getting out there and fighting, but I'm giving you an out. I'm being your friend right here. I'm glad whoever did it, did it, and I hope it brings the war right to us. You wasn't gonna do shit otherwise, Liam. It's ironic that I'm the preacher, but you the one that act like one. All passive and shit. The flock's getting restless, and it's like YOU suggesting we put our hands together and pray to a God that you don't even believe in before saying, let's fight back. Turn the other cheek... WE let them down. I agree, and it's the end of that. Yeah, your illusion of control is like trying to catch a cup of water and not get wet, nigga. Can't control a drop of it. So, why don't you grab a seat and regroup. Shit, have a drink. Calm down. Make your amends with this shit and plan your exit." Tuck begins pouring a drink. Will doesn't move beyond his pacing trail. "And again, who's the *bad idea* you was talking about when you ran up in here crying, and why? Cut your boy in, won't you?"

"You ..." Will exhales strongly through his nostrils like they were industrial vents releasing steam while pacing his speech through clinched teeth, while trying to process what Tuck has suggested. "Somebody... has possibly messed everything we've been working for up. It wasn't time. It wasn't time. It isn't fucking time yet, dammit! The cops don't even have shit to do with this. Not really, they don't. And what's the result? A dead. A. One! Dead. Cop. That ain't even dead! Fuck ..." Will hangs his head a moment grabbing the back of a chair. He looks up to address Tuck. "Do me a favor, Tuck. Go outside and find a healthy fire ant mound. Shove your hand in it to just grab one. One. Wipe all of the other pissed off ants off of your hand, but that one though, smash the shit out of that one, while tending to the injuries on your hand, a metaphor for the community. Then I want you to think about if killing that one ant was worth it."

Tuck responds, "But it won't be just one! That's what you missing. One is just the start. That same ant bed, in chaos, can't get shit done while worrying about a constant threat caused by two fingers." Tuck places his pinching fingers in front of his face, symbolically crushing the ant. "Two fingers!" He then takes those same fingers, slides his hand back near his shoulder, turns his wrist as if holding a rifle with his index on the trigger, left arm stretching out beneath the barrel in the tenuous space before him. "Pow." His imaginary gun sounds like a dry cough.

Will listens and shakes his head. "Your trigger hand is too deep. Should be higher, nearer and before your jaw. That way your eye travels straight down the barrel, or through the sight." He demonstrates, in statuesque form, making Tuck's look underdeveloped in comparison, and his thumb guides his sight and his imaginary fire-arm right into Tuck's left eye. Their pupils freeze upon each other, and Tuck curls his lip a little. "That's how you use a rifle." He drops his arms without making a discharge sound. "It's amazing you street dudes are able to hit anything that's not point blank range. And no thank you. I'm too fucking upset to be drinking right now." Will acknowledges the drink that has been sitting there for him. "The local PD is on high alert, right in our back yard, Toni disappears, while you stand here telling me I need to leave the shit I started… This can't be life… And you fucking smile about it like it's not a big deal."

Tuck is smiling. "It's not. Not when you prepared, it's not. When you not scared, it's not. When you welcome it, it's not. It's not a big deal to me, Liam, so why is it such a big deal to you?" Tuck grabs the drink he poured, and takes a sip. "I figure now is as good a time as any. The best time to plant a tree is twenty years ago, but next best time is when? Now. And you can't say we ain't got the seed. You believe in what we doing or not? Because, please don't take offense, the longer you wait, the more it looks like you doubt our ability, and how long before everyone begins to doubt it as well and we disband. It ain't ever gonna feel like the right time, that's why, back in the day, me and my crew would set a time, get high off our ass, and just go do the shit! People thought we were crazy, and we were. Crazy is what you need sometimes." Tuck downs the rest of the shot. "We were soldiers too. Nigga ain't got to go to Iraq to know war. Toni knows why I'm here, and I think you do too. How many years you been at this again? But you God though, right?"

Will had started back pacing and punching out cookies again, but Tuck's last statement froze him. He locks in place in connection with Tuck like Tuck had performed his first exorcism as something calmly escapes Will, and he finds acceptance. Life is as much about controlling one's reactions to the things one cannot control as it is about controlling the things that one can control. Will *crying*, as Tuck so eloquently put it, won't stop that ball that has begun to roll and it only serves as a waste of time. Will finally relaxes his face, rolls his shoulders, rocks his neck, to shrug his newly gained stress off. "You're right. Godamn right I'm God, Tuck. If only you would recognize it, but too late for that. No use in crying about it now… We've got a bunch of work to do. The Head needs to meet up soon. I'd like to address the body. Let's give it at least a week, so even some of the out-of-towners can come if they wish, and I gotta go figure some shit out. Put the call out on the site to start, and activate The Spine. You hit The Mouth, The Feet, and I'll contact The Ears and The Hands. Let's let some of this die down first. Hold off on what you got planned, too. Respect me enough to give me this week, no, give me two weeks, so don't be riling the TOMs up either. Shoot for Friday after next around 10pm, ok? And we lay low until then." Will doesn't wait for Tuck's answer and begins heading to the door, with his hand squeezing his forehead. He leaves one last message en route, "And dammit, find Toni!"

BOOK OF SOUND

John 10:34
Jesus answered them, Is it not written in your law,
I said, Ye are gods?

2:1

No matter how well developed they are, a set of wings will never be useful for flight if a person's afraid to remove his feet from the ledge. It is said that birds raised in a cage think flying is a sickness. While it's a beautiful anecdote, I think it is false. Some are created for a specific purpose and even if refused them all of their days, that moment they are free to, they will. Purpose is divine, and we all have one, yet some are hell-bent on denying it. I see it with my own two eyes. There is comfort in a cage, the familiarity of it is an institutionalization more comforting than trusting one's life upon the wind beneath wings that have never before been tested in flight. Beyond the several levels of cages, once one is properly trained, not even a single cage is necessary because the strongest cage exists in one's mind, until one realizes they are meant to fly.

In three and a half years, Gray has not ended a night without his calisthenics, his meditative cross stretch with his head wedged against the iron, and his listening to the ominous prison chatter drift between the cells like canyon echoes. Harmony has provided him that escape. He relaxed his workout, a few push ups here and pull ups there. He relaxed everything in his first weeks. He's relaxed… kind of. The differences in life on the outside, or even halfway outside still keep his head on a swivel and his eyes active. Adjusting is not as easy as he imagined, and he wasn't even gone away for that long. No longer caged, he is still confined to a room with another man - two others actually, the bunk bed isn't much of an upgrade to his cot, and his schedule is still not completely his own; it isn't prison though. Gray keeps telling himself that as an affirmation while often thinking that it is.

The monitor didn't direct him to his room until after the impromptu celebration, just as Will informed Gray would be the case, so Gray was thrust into a social atmosphere immediately. He reacted to it nothing like he imagined he would. Comfort is a difficult state to reach around new people in a new environment, and Gray sank deeply inside his shell, wishing to just have his room and bed available. It was a small gathering of people, but he hadn't any interest in their opinions, perspectives, and ideas, a common position for him, regardless the crowd. Gray was too exhausted to attempt to get to know any of them. He was trying to reacquaint himself with static world changes, the inanimate objects, the sizes and shapes and colors of things first before facing the challenge of people, so he even greeted his roommates coldly. It was probably more anxiety than exhaustion, but exhaustion took the blame when he declined to meet those who were trying to speak... It was a pretty good excuse, considering that Gray was kind of beat... but in addition, it's common, his emotional form of hide and seek... He answered no gazes or welcoming inquiries, and he instead grabbed a fist full of the standard issue, compliant sheets... and stretched them across himself like a giant sheath... Gray said goodbye to the day before the sun did and blocked them all away that first evening and then nightly, to find his sleep... as if chrysalizing in his silent keep... He had to meet change with change, and he was comfortable hiding in preparation. After half a year of bunking with Ervin, Gray returned to the top bunk and avoidance became his norm.

Janice would do her best to get Gray to open up, and Will was almost nonexistent. Gray had Will pegged all wrong. He expected to be watched and micromanaged and Will was barely around, not even in the counseling sessions. He did all that chest thumping in the orientation, keeping his nose at the highest elevation possible for one of his height, then he disappears into the setting. It is nothing that Gray has an issue with, but he had just prepared to bump heads with the man, and as it has turned out, Will could care less about any of them in the facility like he has more important things on his mind. Janice, on the other hand, would not stop poking and prodding in attempt to get Gray to open up because the more he shares, the more she can supposedly help.

Gray cherishes privacy, which is why he is so quiet, and he cherishes it most in places that do not have privacy. The dormitory doors in Harmony don't even have locks. Night monitors pacing the hallways are the locks, living locks that keep residents in their assigned locations. They're kind of like COs; it isn't prison though. Harmony stacks residents four to a room in cubes, walls fifteen feet across with low ceilings that are the numbered squares of roulette table, appropriate for the gamble of reformation, and sanity is the ball bouncing around the wheel of the spinning world. With a small lockable four-drawer dresser, one drawer for each roommate, and mirror, the rooms are only sleeping quarters. There is no room for anything else, like individuality and the personal space it requires, so while Gray hasn't a choice in sharing most things, he does with his thoughts. There are community bathrooms and lockers where belongings are kept, a community recreation room for entertainment, and community conference rooms for counseling sessions. The only spaces that are not community are the offices on the west wing, Will's side of the facility, and the clandestine contents of the guarded minds. Gray's interest is in keeping his and collecting more memories that are no one's business but his own, and his first days, rolling into weeks, are a good start. He kept mostly silent in the counseling sessions, and every engagement discreet, the conversations he's had with a couple of female residents, few and far between, but secretly, the night last had its first smile-making ending. It took him long enough.

Not surprisingly, there is a strong anti-cop culture at Harmony. A bunch of felons disliking cops should not strike anyone as odd, and Will's official stance on the subject doesn't help, so with the news full of police overreactions and acquittals, every time something happens in opposition to the standard narrative, the residents celebrate. They are not big celebrations, but they are morale raising, and Will allows them because they seem to keep everyone happier. He also thinks they assist in the development of the revolutionary spirit. He wishes he could do more to channel it, he even wants to create a class about grassroots organizing, but he risks losing the integrity of his position. While not being for the law, the most he can do is stay neutral, because his work position is pro-law, even if his personal position isn't, so he allows, and silently encourages, the celebrations. In a short two weeks, Gray has already been to two of such celebrations, the first of which was not really his choice but still logged as a relevant memory in his short stay. He's getting a feel for the national climate, at present, as it concerns police brutality and the value of Black lives, Black males particularly, but he honestly doesn't care much. The first he attended was about the cop who was shot while sitting in his car in Cottonwood, and the second was about the indictment of all six cops involved in the death of a Black man in Baltimore, who committed no crime but staring at the officers, and dying with a severed spine while in police custody.

Compliments of Mr. Will Bunting and the good people at Harmony, the juice bar was even opened the evening of the second celebration. The second was more of a big deal than the first as far as the event went, but the first was a bigger deal socially, for them, because it happened in Cottonwood. The first was spontaneous, started by a news story and a resident running through the dorms yelling about it. The indictments were monumental compared to the shooting, nationally, mostly because the local cop didn't even die, and furthermore, because of how the majority of the cases were leaning, but still, Cottonwood made the shooting of utmost importance to those who understood cause and effect. Police on video, acting outside the law, were not even getting indicted, so for all six to get indicted in such a climate, with no video evidence, was a huge deal, so Will allowed some planning to go into the second celebration and even assisted a little.

Harmony's eating and lounge area mimics the continental breakfast set up in small hotels, and the juice bar, usually only available for breakfast, was open. Will supporting their joy, reflected highly upon him and helped with his appearance of being *down*. He'd celebrate too and bring real drinks if he wasn't a symbol of responsibility and restraint. He couldn't even attend for those reasons, but he made provisions available from that background he's been working within for the past weeks. Will provided the open bar, but all other concessions came from vending machines stocked with soft drinks, chips, nuts, pastries, and pastries with nuts. No one was really hungry or thirsty anyway unless they skipped dinner, which had just been wrapping up. Gray passed through the cafeteria, passed on dinner, which they were at the tail end of, and, physically, grabbed nothing besides a seat in the recreation room, but his presence grabbed the attention of many. He hadn't spent any time outside of his room since his arrival except for the counseling sessions, which he abhorred. The men stared at him. The women stared at him. Randy stared at him. Gray hadn't spoken a single word to him since the prison bus. He stared back at the women and considered swallowing his words to Ervin about giving any woman a chance, because many were a sight for sore eyes, for the creation of, painful to look at. Before he spoke a single word, one of the female residents brought him a drink and asked his name, and the moment he smiled and looked up to meet her with his frosted eyes, he was repulsed, noticing the inside of her mouth rotting away where teeth should have been. Self-neglect and self-mutilation create a different type of ugly, one where the compassion Gray gives for poor genetics is non-existent. He accepted the drink and looked away.

The gatherings lacked passion in Gray's opinion. He's seen better in prison, and they didn't have access to women. The first was one was terrible. It was rushed, aimless, and lacked a foundation of supportive information from the event to which it was connected. None bragged, none reenacted, because none knew what had happened besides what was shared by the short news story. Cottonwood is not a huge neighborhood, but none of the residents knew about the shooting either, and all weren't under Gray's form of house arrest. The conversations ran dry of it a couple of sentences deep, and the familiarity with the official subject, the reason they'd all broken their normal routines, created an experience comparably as organic as online dating. The second celebration was both better and more of the same, not because little was known of the event, because more was known, but because an indictment is not a conviction. They couldn't get too happy, while knowing every cop indicted could walk free in a matter of months. Gray only showed up for the second one because he figured it was time to come out of his shell and get to know at least one of these ladies. One brought him a drink as soon as he sat down, but she wasn't the type he had in mind.

Cavalier, Gray watched and Gray listened for an opportunity to present itself, any opportunity. There was no liquor, house rules, the women seemed timid beyond simple introductions, and with lights out being at 11pm, the situation was less than ideal for

Gray to work within, but conditions are met by conditioning. True celebrations didn't even start until midnight in Gray's former life, and the ones that transpired at Harmony were as tame as the timid. And the women, that was the problem! *What the fuck are they scared of?*, flashed across his mind many times throughout the duration of the second occasion. That's what he was there for, reestablishing his dominance in an intense session of secret-making, flesh revelation, and he just needed a partner. Too, he'd reestablish his dominance by being the one they, the women, chose instead of the other available specimens representing manhood with their grooming, features, and forms.

Gray didn't give a damn about the indictments or some cop getting shot. He got the idea from the banter that the others didn't care much either. It was an excuse to gather and step outside of their boxes a moment, with a burst of shared energy that became fleeting because they lacked involvement or a direct connection to those involved. The initial excitement stemmed from the idea that the incidents were somehow payback for all of the bodies the peace officers had been sending to the undertaker, mostly unarmed, committing minor crimes, Black, and male. Many of the residents fit that description. It's a popular description, and they fit it even down to minor crime committing. This made it easy for them to be empathetic to the victims, and then there was that thing about them growing up hating cops anyway, for the most part, and a cop being responsible in some manner beginning the chain of events that culminated in the loss of their lives behind bars and under state supervision. If there was ever a natural audience for the *Fuck The Police* sentiment, it was here, so as obscured as the events were, and lacking in detail, the attempt at putting this small group of many cops in their place was worth celebrating. The announcement of the indictments came over the intercom for the second one, but to signal the first, one resident, Kenny, began yelling, "We got one! We shot a fucking pig y'all!," at the top of his lungs running through the dormitories on the east side of the facility like Paul Revere.

It was *we* like the misery and frustration of *the All*, the disenfranchised, disrespected many, a God in a way, had stopped breathing in one intense moment, squinted its eye along the barrel and through the scope, and pulled the trigger. *The All* would have, no doubt, been a better shot though. In the complexity of many wrongs - an apt definition for the state, what is right disappears, and all is neither right nor wrong, only existing in a state of flux dependent upon future actions and results. It was chessboard politics, and too many black pieces were being captured and a white capture, preferably a major piece but any piece would do, was needed just to show black was still conscious of the game. It worked the same as in prison, the collective identification was just different, and prison got it right with its removal of the gray area that many on the outside are confused by saying things like, "but *that* cop didn't murder anyone," and completely missing the point. When the natives are restless, a sacrifice must be made to the Gods. As bad as it sounds, Gods prefer virgins – the innocent.

If the Gods demand a sacrifice, a sacrifice they will have, and a divine bloodlust began developing with every nationally televised police shooting, paid leave, and eventual acquittal that left another family empty of the promises from American exceptionalism. The United States was supposed to be better than that. In fact, her stump speech to the world says so, and being globally recognized for her bigotry is a public relations nightmare, but still she defaulted on her promises of caring for her least, again and again, a category that should not even exist by her very definition of herself. When the justice system that the many depend upon becomes powerless in support of them, they collectively turn to prayer, and those prayers are sometimes answered in the form of retaliatory gunfire. They were thanking God there in Harmony, and across the country many more were probably engaged in a form of worship of this expression of divine responsiveness. The poor impromptu celebration was nothing but a recognition of the power of God, the God they praised, in hopes that the Almighty would be pleased enough with them to finish the job. That is the long explanation of what was happening in the recreation room while Gray watched the laughs and smiles walk back and forth between the juice bar and the cloth, floral printed, furniture.

Gray wasn't as into being a part of the collective, as being apart from the collective, and picking it apart with his eyes, gender wise. He was very short with the males who thought it proper to introduce themselves; Gray was a *woman's man*, with *no time to talk.* Fresh out of prison, he was only trying to celebrate perfection of human anatomy, how body parts fit together, the magnetism of hormones, the millennia it had taken for the species to reach this level of sophistication through natural selection and attraction, and his being of the premier combination, genetically, to manipulate the system as he saw fit. He did well for himself before going in, his way with words – never talkative, but worth listening to, his complexion, and of course his eyes, but six years in the big house prompted him to develop his physique. He hadn't the smallest doubt about his ability in the arena of wooing a woman as soon as his pecs and delts began to shape the way his T-shirts fit. In prison it was an effect to stop him from being chosen, and on the outside its effect should be opposite; up is down and down is up. He sat there teasing his juice filled paper cup with his mind set on how to get more than his throat wet. Gray was intent on making his official first night out his first night in, and candidates were abound, yet timid, unfamiliar, and unsure. The culture of the place was contrary to human nature, and Gray, out of his shell, began working the crowd like the last human left, overtly making his softly spoken suggestions to any earlobe he could attach himself to and lure their nature into his capture – any piece would do, just about.

"Been gone six years… Not sure I still know how. Suppose it's like riding a bike?"

"Oh, you saw me? Been looking at you all evening."

"Not sure how anything works here, not yet, but I'm sure everything doesn't work the way it's supposed to… You follow the rules?"

"That's a no no, but I'm new, so I don't *really* know yet. You think I'm worth getting in a little trouble for?"

"I'm grown… how 'bout you?"

"Just sitting down here is a waste of a body like that, you know?"

Gray was doing his version of what the pimps called *knocking*, dropping any line that quickly came to his mind to get a read on a woman and break the ice. It works better with questions because they encourage response. It's similar to what the squares do to get a nice lady's attention, but not, because these aren't nice ladies. The ladies accustomed to knocking have been around the block multiple times. They laugh at squares and make tricks of them, while blushing on cue. The women here are not street workers, though some may have been, but they were hoes all the same as far as Gray was concerned because they'd all done prison bids and that squeezes the innocence right out of anyone. He didn't make the good guy appeal because he wasn't a good guy; he'd just done a prison bid, and that squeezes the innocence right out of anyone. Pretending that he saw them as anything more than what they also saw of him was completely square, and basically just a waste of time, so knocking it was. It wasn't much different than what he'd done with Annabelle, except here there was less room for error. Annabelle had to come back around, and these ladies didn't, and it would only take one of them to ruin his chances with them all because word about the new guy or gal always travels fast.

With all of his preparation, the women were acting like it was a middle school dance and not a gala of convicted felons without much to lose. The monitor even got a slight attitude when Gray asked him if they provided residents with condoms, and if not, where he could get some. Gray figured Will had everybody's balls in saline filled jars somewhere at the back of the facility, only returning them at graduation. The culture was consistent, and it did not match the people. A number had been done on them. They'd gathered to celebrate the shooting of a cop, and the arrest of other cops, but the thought of Gray playing between these ladies' legs made them shudder? Gray wasn't buying it, no matter how convincingly they tried to sell it. He was the salesman. Hustling was his trade, and game recognizes game. They wore their scars and tattoos well. They were not demure. The threat of doing something and getting caught indeed loomed, and there was also that slight possibility that they just didn't want to do anything with Gray, but their smiles didn't give off that vibration. Authority depends on fear to work, for there are never enough authority figures to enforce the rules that they create, so fear has to be an active component making up for what authority lacks in numbers. Fear is a character itself, with a bigger job than the authority has.

It was a numbers game. Everything's a numbers game; if a hustler knows anything, it's that. Gray was aggressive, a bit intimidating without saying much, choosing with his eyes and being chosen for single-serve candid discussions while people celebrated over juice, nuts, snack cakes, and crackers. Will had made senior citizens of them all. People were in their pajamas before 9pm. House slippers ruled. Shower caps, hair rollers, wife beaters, and tiny disposable paper cups with colorful congenial designs upon them filled with juice were altogether attempting to mute the keloids, tattoos, missing teeth, and other scars, the mental kind as well. The dirty blond was in attendance and smoothly evaded. Randy nodded at him, but Gray ignored it by looking past at the soft body behind him, too young to be playing along with this geriatric charade. Through his uniquely tented lens, Harmony was a rest home as the attendees, under fifty, most under forty, and some under thirty, prepared for the afterlife. This was completely contrary to Gray's plans. He could have stayed in his shell, instead of leaving it for such a display of conformity. His last six months wasn't going to be spent strangling what life he had inside him left until he was cold and dull.

If there wasn't a resistance already in the political undercurrents of Harmony, Gray would become it, not caring anymore about an infraction than he did in high school. To hell with the damn commandments as well, especially the fourth. If he'd found a way to have sex in prison, Harmony was going to be his brothel and whatever else he needed it to be, all while smiling in pretend obedience. It was all part of the game; the hustle lives where there is something to be lost and something be gained. The initiating power struggle Gray was invited to seemed more worthy of challenge than the one he'd met in prison. He was, quite honestly, bored of adapting, fading, and disappearing for the convenience of another, and his being momentously horny was of little help. Will's speech did not compel one goose bump to rise upon Gray's skin. It was nothing personal against Will or what he was trying to do, but when the will of Will conflicts with the will of Gray, *Fuck Will*, completes this equation satisfactorily. Gray will show him a son of a dick, since Will was so astute in creating its sound with Gray's surname, if Will can even catch him.

Of the men that introduced themselves the night of the second celebration, was Kenny. His spontaneity caused the occasion once Gray had tired and returned to sitting. Weaving between the standing bodies like a pinball between bumpers, Kenny found Gray after a misstep and an objectionable shoulder thrust sent him to fill the space beside him. He sat up, knocked some imaginary dust off of himself, straightened his posture and smiled. Emotional instability was Gray's first impression in measuring Kenny's jumpiness and clawing for acceptance. Kenny was so absolutely unaware that he was even unaware of his lack of awareness. How ironic it was then that Kenny knew exactly who and what Gray was looking for and how to achieve it, and he'd arrived to disclose just that. The more he struggled to make out what Kenny was saying, the more out of shape his eyebrows became, and the more it was all making sense.

"Yeah. Umm. Yeah, she umm. She's waiting." It wasn't a stutter, but it was nearly. *Umm* filled all of Kenny's thinking gaps, which were plentiful when he was nervous or uncomfortable. He'd even reset sometimes and repeat a word, so it could easily be confused with stuttering, but it was his unique way of holding the floor while composing his thoughts just like Ol' John had done back at prison in the yard. "She waiting for you, man. Umm. Yeah."

"Who?" Gray sought clarity. Kenny responded coolly with simply a smirk and a tilted head. He'd done this before. He was an arbitrator, used for his simplicity and how it molds expectations, or was he some kind of special needs pimp? Gray questioned his station because within this answer was an imagined image of the woman he was negotiating to see. A mentally compromised pimp could do no better than have a mentally compromised flock, and physically compromised. It was worth thinking about. If Kenny was only a middle man, his mental state wouldn't mean much. It was clear that he'd done this before, so whichever his position and the cause of his unease, patched with all of the *Umms*, wasn't his involvement in commandment breaking. Gray just dismissed it as his natural expression with nothing to compare it against, having no clue that he himself was the cause.

Surprisingly, there was already an established underground at Harmony and it clumsily stumbled upon Gray, to test him on his own level of desperation – any piece would do, with a smirk and a head tilt responding to his asking *who*. It wasn't like Gray knew any of them by name anyway. He really didn't care who, beyond the revolting or a MHMR client. *Who* was a dumb question, and honestly quite square of him to ask, so he followed up with a much better and more direct one, "Meet her where?"

"Ok. Umm. Let me. Umm. It's. Let me show you…" Kenny began explaining the location of this prepared date, how best Gray should exit to not arouse suspicion, and how the distraction of this event was perfect for rendezvous because everyone's otherwise occupied. The ant bed was stirred, and it bore the print of rebellion's shoe. It was all coincidence possibly, or Kenny may not be as simple as he appears. Gray arose feeling a little like he did so too quickly, leaving his stomach in the chair, nervous about what was next, hoping this she was one that he'd already engaged in an abbreviated conversation there at the celebration of the potential capture of crooked cops, and following his instinct and instructions, he exited the engagement. Like buried treasure, the X her limbs made marked the spot and he found her, found that she was alright, right in the body, right in the mind, and in the exact spot he was instructed to carefully dig. The fourth commandment was pleasurably broken, Gray and his lay had sinned, disrespectfully in the extreme, in the seclusion of an abandoned office on the west wing.

*   *   *

Without a drop of alcohol, it is easy for Will to burn the midnight oil. He's completely placed Harmony business on the back burner, focusing on Legion. He struggles with the idea that Tuck is correct. Again. Tuck's inference is that Will has lost control and the resulting jaw flexing, cookie making sting sustains because he's never meant to have control. As oxymoronic as it seems, the idea pins Will's shoulders beneath him, as he wrestles with passive control and leadership, and being a strong enough example to produce inaction in others. He'd lost control of what he never meant to control. Tuck meant it in address of the unfolding community events, but Will applies it to Legion specifically. Tuck meant that the Legion had no control over the actions of everyone in the community, but Will knows Legion *is* the community, with the ability to control it as they see fit, should they desire to. It has been too long developing to not have that kind of power, but that data is beyond the context of Tuck's experience. He was not there to witness its first breaths, which ironically were not even encouraged by Will, for his fear of failure and lacking preparation… So while Tuck argued the hypothetical, Will argued the specifics, still confident that his group, or at least a faction, had something to do with the shooting. The constipated flow of the information was uncharacteristic, telling the tale, and Tuck's tongue got too thick to speak once Will mentioned that peculiarity. Tuck is right though about Will's control, and Will does not like when Tuck is right. Besides it meaning that Will is wrong, it reinforces Tuck's method, which is best defined as no method at all, no studying, no planning, no manner of execution, or expected result. Tuck being right means that the puppet has found a competent ventriloquist. That is as much credit as Will gives him, but he hasn't a clue who could be speaking for and through him. Well, he has a clue, but not one he is willing to accept.

It's a mistake to feed the fools that do not feed themselves. It only encourages them. Emboldening one who has not done the work to be prepared is dangerous. Like the danger they all now encounter for one who was not prepared to take that shot, and the community unprepared to absorb the consequences. Copycat revolutionaries peek at the papers of those who study to pick up attitude, demeanor, dress, catch phrases, and slogans, but with no foundation in the social sciences, political sciences, and history, they are only able to identify the struggle and where they belong within it, and not diagnose and prescribe anything to progress beyond the stage they entered it in. Many are hung up at the study of persons instead of the study of power, and Will saw every culture, every institution, and every religion as a study in power, simply about who has it, who has it not, and the mechanisms by which this power, knowledge/secret based, allegiance based, or blood based, is accessed or distributed. Study was all about understanding the nature of and decoding power to prepare to break its packaging, the institution or the family it swells within, apart at the seams to release it. This takes discipline. Passion is not a preparer; the love of medicine and a scalpel does not prepare one to perform surgery, no more than a black leather jacket, a beret, and a gun prepares one for revolution. It can be argued, though, that nothing can truly prepare one for the complete reorganization or abolition of static power, or for how exactly society, what's left of it, will resume without an or with a new elite class, but this is the revolution.

It wasn't time, regardless of the solid argument Tuck was able to echo, meant to distinguish that Will hadn't any confidence in the brotherhood. He gave Tuck that argument; it was a gift. Will relented because the ball had already begun rolling and any further discussion about who, why, and how would be fruitless. There was indeed a lack of confidence, for reason. Study had not been taken seriously, and Tuck was the perfect example of this. He was a just-add-water revolutionary, like grow capsules or sea monkeys, only fun to look at. Will has addressed this specifically in documents he's written and disseminated amongst the membership:

> *How to fight is the beginner level, who to fight is moderate, but what to fight for is expert level, and the read on the level someone has achieved easily comes through what their focus is. If it's hand-to-hand combat and going to the gun range, nurture their interest, but understand that they have a lot to learn before becoming useful beyond a foot soldier.*

Someone who's targeted a cop is a moderate revolutionary at best, not understanding the role cops play and who guides their activity. Will's mind never changed in regards to whom he thinks is responsible. This mess is the work of Legion. His child is now walking, it began before he was able to witness it in delight, but it has not yet been potty trained and Will is left to clean up behind it.

"So, how do I clean this shit up… Can I, even?" Will says to himself, pensively stroking his forehead, hunched before the glow of his laptop. He wants a drink, but in this state, one drop of liquid courage touching his tongue would direct him to find Tuck and direct his fist to find his mouth. He hasn't had a taste in over a week. It's why he declined his poured drink at the bar. The more intense his sober anger, the more he folds into himself to hide it, and he was livid, so calmness was his shell, thickening layer by layer the longer he stood and listened to Tuck's incompetence. A drink would not have been a good idea. It's not that he needed the rumored courage, he's confident he can take Tuck, he just needs any excuse to get loose, and that would simply be counter-revolutionary. Tuck is not his enemy. Tuck is not his enemy. Tuck is not his enemy. Will needs to repeat this as a chant, so maybe it will help him understand that Tuck is not his enemy.

It is almost like Toni, who's disappeared without giving anyone the reason why, who wouldn't answer the fucking phone or respond online, was staring at him in stoic disappointment, a look he knows, a look that means, *Don't fuck this up.* Toni is the master of understanding, keeping a diary, preferring the term *journal,* writing in it in emotional blocks that read like scripture, that's black, leather bound, the size and shape of a bible, and even has the classic ribbon bookmark stitched within it. Toni talks things through and sees the bright side, goes with the flow, and redirects energy like life was merely an aikido opponent. It is an artist's way of looking at things, passionate, trained to spin triumph from tragedy, and wellness from wounds, with pens, paints, and a healthy detachment from reality. Throughout the years, Will has learned that it has its use, but it is not his way. Reality is his way, and discipline is his strong point while flipping through the possibilities before him in search of the positive, fully aware that Legion, his child of seven years on paper, that had been organizing six, has been compromised.

The Legion *was* Will's… but it wasn't. He was the only one with the know how to develop such an organization from the ground up, so of course he was left to lead it, but his manner of leadership was in taking everyone's desire to be led and refusing to do so. It was his way of organizing horizontally instead of vertically. They all were to be depended upon as experts, with no one answering to anyone else, bringing out the leader within them all through interdependency. Liberation could only be achieved through a collective, rotating leadership, with and without dependency in the same space like the state of Schrödinger's cat. Will would lead in arms training, but not in negotiations. Speaking to people and gaining their trust was not his strong point, therefore it would not be intelligent for him to perform that position, nor inform or teach it. He was a leader but not. Leadership rotates, and expertise is the guide. There is no leader but all, no followers but all, and there is no head to cut off of the metaphoric snake in hopes that it will die. This is why Tuck is tolerated, and must be, and this is why Legion movements are often not linear and predictable. It lives! Something worth celebrating and worth fearing, because although this isn't the first time it has moved on its own, it is the first time it has with something this major without it first passing among the membership through The Hall. In the designing, Will released his ego to create something bigger than he, and also something that would not place a target upon his back from his involvement. Will was trying to live, not die, and he'd no doubt that his country would kill him. Recruiting fast, being loud, and sloganeering is only a means to be infiltrated or outright stamped out. So, meticulously, Will placed his brainchild together with the precision of a watchmaker, waiting for the moment he'd wind the spring to hear the first ticks of its heart.

It was to function as a body, so he designed it as one. He mapped it out in simplicity in spiral notebook in the moments he was most frustrated with his life and life in general. He had plenty of spaces to plan in, often while behind his desk as the new house manager at Harmony, a job that proved to be much more vile in practice than on paper. From the ad, to the interviews, no one mentioned to Will that he'd be Satan to the believers and a tiny little God to the nonbelievers, with both groups hating him comparably. Sure, his salary was much higher, but his position was emotionally the equivalent of being a bill collector to those well aware of their debt yet claiming it unjust, their supposed debt to society. Their dislike of him encouraged his smiles at first, soft and nervous, with no justification of why lining the insides of his thoughts, but those smiles eventually hardened and baked to the crisps often appearing at the corner of his jaws. He was trying to help them, properly negotiate them outside of the most ghastly place in the system, yet they only looked at him as an agent of, as Satan or a puny God. This inspired his ten commandments spiel during orientation, because if you can't beat them, join them.

Like bodies, it started small and simple, just a cluster of cells, this fertilized idea of his, or one awaiting fertilization, with portions of the collective designated for specific tasks that report back to the source. He wanted the functions away from the source to be self-propelled, involuntary in a manner, like the beating of a heart, both responding to signals yet being active without them like sleeper cells. It wasn't meant to be controlled. The education was to be the control and communication the reinforcement. Trained in the most powerful top-heavy organization in the world, the United States military, Will got a bad taste in his mouth from hierarchy, strict control, lies, secrets, forced obedience, and its culture of increasing ignorance descending the ranks. Legion was his way of liberating himself from that institution through meticulous deconstruction. At his retirement, and the rank he'd acquired, he understood that class was slavery, and information only flowing freely through the channels of privilege, containing life-threatening data concerning those who did not have the clearance to access it was the stuff of the Dark Ages. Will, in the design, cut off the head by not *really* creating one, and a headless snake will never die once one figures out how to make one live. The head had to be important and negligible at once, and removing class was key.

Structurally headless as a function of the most important and designated leader or leaders, there still was a head upon Legion. Will could not complete the design without one. There had to be a vehicle for data creation, collection, and dissemination that all persons could participate in and have access to. The Head functions as the human brain negotiating information from every system, as the muscular system needs to know of the damage incurred to the skeletal system to know to lighten up on particular joints to not damage them more, and instead limp. It facilitates the communication between one system and another, informing without managing. If The Ears know that a certain side of town is swarming with cops, The Body – the entire collective, is encouraged to avoid that part of town by way of The Spine. Legion has five major body parts, whose functions are as follows:

The Ears – The antennae of the organization. They pick up the local news, what has happened, what's happening, and most importantly, what will happen.

The Mouth – The propaganda arm of the organization, both sharing the news and creating it. The most charismatic and artistic members are utilized to sway or create public opinion.

The Feet – The transport operators, motor vehicle drivers, maintainers, and securers of vehicles, and the disposal of them as needed.

The Hands – The engineers and craftsmen of weapons and tools, creating, maintaining, securing, and disposing of as needed.

The Head – The collective presence at a single location, for the purpose of information exchange, and discourse.

The Spine – The collective means of communication digitally and through the calling tree. Data from all parts is stored in the spine, which is a network of websites where the information shared can only be decoded by membership and otherwise looks like the messages shared by nonmembers.

The design was simple, but it promised to be effective. The most complex portion of it was designing the method of communication in a manner that would preserve a level of anonymity to all involved. Without anonymity, recruiting would be hell, even if the bulk of his plan involved those who already had nothing to lose, his felons. Their aggression and their hopelessness was the reason he'd come up with the idea in the first place. Society hadn't a place for them besides the most begrudging of labor, the most stringent of discrimination and inequity, so who better to destroy the system of their involvement? Will figured with their placement being below the lowest, that they'd be easy to organize. One who has anything to lose is much harder to organize than one who has nothing to lose. Destitution is self-replenishing fuel, and Will's connection with Harmony meant he had it on tap.

He had pieced the body together, inspired by his residents, testing portions of its function through them, without their knowledge, through Harmony programming. Will tweaks each system through experimentation, like having residents scavenger hunt, data collect, and learn trades under the guise they are necessary life skills for the newly released. The only barrier he has with this, while they are still residents, is staying within the law, or cleverly hiding that something they are being taught is actually illegal. He catalogs residents by their strengths and weaknesses during reviews. He uses their backgrounds, criminal histories, to assess their threat level – threat to the established society. Gang leaders were natural organizers, drug dealers were great with numbers, thieves were planners, and murderers had little fear and most were good with guns. Those are the dominants. There is also functions for those that weren't so dominant; drug users and the otherwise abused had a talent for milking information and resources from people because they begged compassion and often not seen as threatening. Will found these things out through trial and error by sending residents out to complete tiny missions disguised as errands, and by engaging them, pushing them to discomfort and exposing their honest selves.

The infractions are his net. Those willing to buck his system are granted special treatment, because he figures they too must be willing to buck the greater system. It's an awkward love/hate relationship Will develops with them, because they are still disrespecting him in a manner, but he also knows that spirit is valuable. So when they get in trouble, Will completely gains the upper hand, and he's able to send them through his gauntlet of tasks in an effort to clear their record. He hasn't an honest intention of sending anyone back to prison, but he has to put up a pretty good front to keep a semblance of control. Out of the hundreds that have come through Harmony, there have been less than twenty who Will could absolutely not work with, and they were all from his initial years. Once they are in his clutches, it is an easy task for him to discover what they are made of. For this, the military had prepared him well, and he was effective, charting attributes from information he'd gain from small insignificant operations, but he still was lacking a deeper, more necessary, connection. They already didn't like Will, but once he started these games, they disliked him even more.

Attending counseling sessions isn't even part of Will's contract. Making sure residents got in safely, met their requirements, and got out safety was his job description, and he had control of how he would go about doing that. Further up the food chain, there is more freedom. Professionals are given a problem or a task and they are often allowed to find their own ways to solve them, as opposed to the repetitive, micromanaged, and often mindless, hourly work. He matured into attending the counseling sessions because few residents were forthright with giving him personal information, information he needed to make psychological assessments.

There were professionals there, like Janice, who were much better in provoking their cooperation in the arena that heavily involved emotions. As they slowly began a speaking relationship, Janice would season their conversations with interesting tidbits about inmates in, at first, a, *Well of course you know,* manner, that quickly shifted to an, *I think you should know,* manner, once she realized through his responses that he never knew. He wasn't picking up much information on the personal side, sitting in his office, watching cameras, and occasionally patrolling the facility to start an awkward engagement with someone who had no interest in doing so. He'd long recognized the us vs. them environment, but he had not put much thought into how much of the environment was his fault. They were property, he was basically a security guard, and he was supposed to encourage them to find comfort in that dynamic. They lacked the same reservation with Janice, mostly, because she was not crippled with an ego the size of Will's, and she knew what she was doing.

Conditioning that began as a teenager, through military structure and socialization, an environment that basically did not care about past experiences, present thoughts, or feelings, was exactly not what was best in creating a nature in Will that would easily coax others into opening up. He has his own issues with opening up, so in the interest of gaining a better handle on his profession, he let Janice take the lead, and learned through her how to better exude compassion. The more one senses that their audience doesn't care, the less one will share, especially the abused. Gaining trust is key for organizers with no power. The powerful have other things to offer, power for one, or a connection to it, and material things, but those without power have nothing to offer but dreams.

Will had a dream he could not realize without the help of others, and they had dreams that they too could not realize without his help. He wanted freedom to be a material thing, and no longer the stuff of dreams. Without access to the inner reaches of his clients, there was no possible way he could reveal their dreams and add them with his own, and the Legion would have always stayed on paper. Janice has no idea about the existence of the organization. Will loves her, but he doesn't trust her. There is something too professional about her, and he has never been able to gauge her level of allegiance to the system. She might as well be a cofounder though, playing a very important role in the development of Will's ability to recruit and making available connections with people that he had not seriously considered as potential framers of his planned militia.

Through Janice, Will happened across the genius of LaTonya, a street-smart savant who served a prison sentence for tax fraud, that was sent to Harmony upon her partial release. She was initially underestimated because she was not loud and aggressive, spending more time listening, winning trust, and problem solving. She didn't stand out at all, and didn't want to, preferring the background, which isn't a completely new disposition of most of the residents while engaging with authority, but she did so amongst other residents as well. She had no desire to make a point, make a mark, make a stand, or demand a position in the facility's pecking order like the others. She spent most of her time in her room writing, drawing, or reading when not present in forced group encounters like counseling sessions. She would have to be found, because she wasn't doing the finding, and she was there four months before Will had even gotten to have an exchange with her that lasted longer than five minutes. Being a woman didn't help Will notice her, not for her talents at least. He unconsciously reduced her to her level of sex appeal, unfortunately, because Janice had made her acquaintance during a Thursday narcotics session and noticed that she exhibited an aversion to sexual attraction, but didn't relay that information to Will. LaTonya had nice shape, but she wasn't traditional at all concerning the cultural standards of beauty. She was attractive for the question marks she inspired in him. He spent most of his time noticing her in discovery of if she was noticing him. Was he attracted to her? No, not really, not from looks at least, although she wasn't unattractive. Will's attraction was unconventional, liking her more because she showed little to no interest in him more than anything else.

Once he discovered her, through Janice's diligent assistance, Will would pick on LaTonya to get her attention and get her out of her comfort zone, as he would with most residents he couldn't easily get a read on. The true character was behind the mask, and mask removed moments had to often be drawn out. No matter how much he poked of prodded, he was coolly responded to, and she passed all his tasks in flying colors. Her intelligence and curiosity led her to believe that she was doing more than halfway house business, and she was clever enough to even get Will to admit to it. Will told her exactly what he needed to tell her, wrapping his ideas in hypotheticals, LaTonya was the first to officially hear about Legion, a name he had not referred to it as, and she lit up with excitement at the idea. Will laid his child out in front of her across a gurney, and arguably, although all of the parts were there, logical, stoic, and cold, it was the warm currents of LaTonya's creative spirit that breathed life into it.

2:2 *From my limited experience, some of the best leaders have no desire to do so. Leadership exposes failure, and moves it away from the individual into a collective. In leadership my failure is amplified. The burdens of an entire unit become the responsibility of one, and it is great when there is a win, but not when there's not… Some are comfortable enough with life to avoid such a gamble and risk letting others down as they've many times let down themselves. These leaders will never lead, no matter what is at stake, unless they are pushed into doing so, yet it is an ideal demeanor to lead from because they do not want the power or the responsibility, and those that do not want it are less likely to revel in it and abuse it.*

"Looks like you stayed up talking to God all last night, and like He actually spoke back," Janice laughs at a noticeably disheveled Will, unshaven, and not uniformly neat. His shirt isn't even tucked in. Janice is fully made up without a hair improperly placed like Will would be usually, except for makeup, he's been out of it for weeks, as they approach each other in a west wing hallway like matter and antimatter, indefinably unstable should the two meet; they approach each other carefully as if fully aware. Will makes up most of the instability of the pair by himself this morning. He should have called in. He should've slept. He did speak to God, and he's an atheist, so the conversation was decidedly one sided and only upset him more than he'd already been from the reason they were even in discussion, that whole cop shooting thing. There are some people not answering phones and emails, while there are others basically declaring war by way of the police chief's, *aggression toward police will not be tolerated,* statement in last week's press conference as if speaking at, not to, a city full of unruly children, there's Tuck's challenge, and to top it all off he has a new hothead on campus. These weeks have not only tested Will's cool, they have cracked what holds it, allowing its essence to slowly leak from him, more when the seam is stressed. They are not his weeks, and this is not his morning so his emotional reaction from the harmless jest from his favorite, bouncy, personified expression of self hate, was the thought, *How appropriate, the minstrel jokes.* It makes it easier for him to force the smile that he isn't in the mood to produce as they pass one another without even a *Good morning.* Will enters his office and closes the door.

Will has only been coming into work to abbreviate his responsibilities while concerning himself specifically with Legion business. The discussion he'd been having the entire night has to be finished while he is here on the clock, with complete access to his network, officially through the Harmony database with everyone who has come through the system, their stories and whereabouts, and all of the unofficial information he'd accumulated throughout the years for those included as Legion membership. The Legionnaire call was sent out through The Spine immediately after he left the bar with Tuck. It is the first thing he notices when he logs in to one of the social networks they communicate through. It has been shared and has been spreading along the network for about two weeks. The call is disguised within the biggest sports story of the night, often a shared video, but never associated with anything political. A combination of the wording of the original post, the commentary, and the hashtags give the membership all the information while setting off no red flags for nonmemership. It reads like any other post about a popular subject, and a good percentage of membership follows sports so they even can weigh in intelligently on these special topics although the post is not about the topic at all. Will doesn't. He doesn't care for sports.

Legion business is deciding what to say, what to do, and who to be later in evening of the morrow, while also finding a way to appease the grumble of a growing resistance. The Friday of the planned meeting is almost upon him, and he's down to his last thirty some odd hours to prepare. There has been a considerable amount of investment, labor intense and time intense sweat equity that has been logged into the development of the organization, and from Will's vantage point it appears that some are ready to see a return. How one responds to a threat depends heavily upon whether or not one has anything of value to lose. Though Will is not their leader, he also cannot be. They do not share the same make up. Will knows this. Will knew this from the start, and the organization is a product of what he knows so his insecurities are built within it. Will may have less value for his life and what he's acquired than the average person, but he measures up poorly against his felons. They've been stripped of it all, even their self-respect with the level they've been reduced to *comfortably* engage with society no matter how intelligent or attractive they are. They truly have nothing to lose, including their lives, and the promise that they'd be able to reestablish value within the system that has discarded them as refuse, is the reason their lives have been given to Legion. They were to be born again through it. Redeemed.

Will does not depend upon it as intimately. It's political for him, biological for them. The body he's developed exists outside of him and always will, and it would have eventually even if he'd not designed it to. He's a metaphor, the creator, the vessel the child passed through, but he hasn't the desperation to act as the body needs to function properly. The others, for the most part, have nothing left but the future life they mean to preserve, fighting from the corner, because all else was already lost. Will is Nat Turner speaking from his pulpit, and the rest, they are Nat Turner's Will, the axe-wielding, rumored to be crazy, field slave who eagerly let the blade fall when Turner's rebellion began and Turner hesitated, with a dedication so deep, this Will even returned to the home to rub out Master's forgotten babies, knowing what they'd grow to become.

Reluctantly, Will knows he has to let go. He has to at least enough to understand his place, step away from the canvas to gain perspective, for if he does not, or cannot, the group will splinter from both respect of him and respect of themselves, and it isn't beyond his imagination that some would even suggest his execution if he decides to stand between them and their freedom. As well they should. Trying to see as they see, he respects such a decision, because he knows too much to be neutral. He'd be a willing sacrifice if it came to it, knowing he's the reason they, the Legion, even exist. There is no neutral in chess. Once the pieces begin to move, one can only help or hurt his or her comrades. It is bigger than him, as it was supposed to be, so much so that he'd been placed right in the midst of building conflict and forced to choose which army he'd rather receive blows for or from, because unless he pulls a Toni disappearing act, he's going to feel the pressure from the cops or Legion while trying to sit upon his hands.

His decision is as discomforting as the hairs pushing their way through his face, making it itch, and making him wild. It is too soon for things to fall apart in, not even a difference in strategy, but of the recognition of preparedness, and although Will disagrees with the action, he can draw the conclusion that it was a reaction from inaction, by a culture he strongly influenced the creation of. His child spoke the language he taught it, but nature expands beyond nurture; a master shepherd can never make a sheep of a wolf. How long were they to wait? How many more had to die before the powers promoting, supporting, and encouraging the slaughter were made to feel the fear they so liberally spread? Toni's B.U.M.s, unarmed Black men are falling at the rate of one every two weeks to a cop that fears for his life, and the legal response has been the equivalent of a *Shit Happens* bumper sticker with a man shrugging his shoulders pictured.

It isn't a *small talk* and *get to know people* day for Will. Skipping the counseling sessions is a possibility, like he had been for the last weeks, as this dilemma of his has taken precedence. What he says later will be monumental even in his failure. It shall be life changing, and appropriately, revolutionary. The direction he leans matters not. This will occupy his time while on Harmony's clock. He also has to check his web; he's had a network of temptation-laced traps since he'd caught the first commandment breaker, the first caught after he'd realized what he was building. Most of the commandments are broken now because Will has made Harmony a lair of iniquity with multiple lines of attractive, frowned upon activities, sins, that create an elaborate web of immorality that residents get stuck in. Will places them in sticky situations. Once they vibrate the web, they become parts of it themselves, and part of the same oppressive system that oppresses them. It is nothing short of Will being a tyrant, and he'd not do it if his morality was the measure, but this system is the most important portion of Legion's recruiting, so it is a means to an end that is more positive than negative. Within his orchestrated trouble, in their struggle to save themselves, twisting and turning within the fibers, most are willing to even betray themselves. Then Will can gain the intimacy he never could, that the counseling sessions could only bring him partially into, where he could show them who God is, for lack of a better term. Along with composing a strategy for later, Will also had to check if the night welcomed any new additions to his web.

There is no wakeup call at Harmony, and the increased freedom for Gray has him awaking minutes before eleven a.m., aimless. His roommates are gone. He sits up, hangs his legs over the edge of the bed while scratching his head, and he begins compiling an itinerary for himself for the day. He needs a haircut. He needs a job. He needs to eat. Surely, he's missed breakfast already. He needs to find out the bus system here. He needs some clothes. He needs a city contact, preferably female, that has no connection to Harmony, because his probation period has met its end. He was going to go and look for a job alright: a hand job, a blow job, a rim job, and he was going to get paid to receive them, sooner or later. Not initially and not specifically, but women have always been willing to pay for Gray's time, and finding one or some capable is the first part of his plan to getting back on his feet. If he can catch him a professional one in the suburbs, he'd really be off to a good start but he doesn't yet know where the city stops, the suburbs start, and how to get to them. He has to crawl before he walks. A quick scratch of his crotch reminds him that he most of all needs a shower and to get dressed because his fingernails gathered a scent he'd borrowed in his post-soiree affair. Gray jumps down off of the bunk and begins his day with a stretch down to his toes, and some torso twists to loosen up his back while still yawning. He grabs his shoes and walks over to the dresser placing them on top of it, pausing a second in the mirror trying to recall his drawer lock combination. He rolls the numbers and the lock pops the first time. He grabs his sweats, t-shirt, his shoes, and heads to the shower.

As soon as Gray enters the hallway, he sees Kenny. Kenny smiles uncomfortably and nods. Gray upnods, dismissing him, unaware that for the last fifteen or so minutes he had been the subject of Kenny's entire dialogue. Will, too, had just dismissed Kenny, but in a different manner, not because of his illusion of self-importance and unwillingness to engage with others unless he saw a way to capitalize off of them, not plainly, at least. They'd met to discuss a task, a small assigned mission. Kenny owed Will a favor and was in the *Getting to know you* process and working off his sins. Will takes Kenny's condition into consideration, and he's been very apprehensive throughout this process, but he is anchored by the idea that everyone has a use. Kenny's simplicity, his lack of intelligence, may in fact be exactly what gets him through doors that others can't. He is the perfect example of someone falling through the cracks. While he needs state supervision, it is basically just to keep his medication ordered and taken on schedule, and not because he is a danger to society, at least when properly medicated. He's mildly schizophrenic, hearing voices; they keep him company at times, yet at other times they make demands of him.

The system is full of cracks, if they can even be called that and not something more intentional, and Will's web is cast wide to catch as many of those falling through as possible. When the fibers of his efforts become strong enough or numerous enough, the cracks will disappear. In the complexity of many wrongs, what is right disappears, and all is neither right nor wrong, only existing in a state of flux dependent upon future actions and results. Otherwise, baiting them like he does would be a disgusting display of his lack of compassion and respect for their humanity – an apt description of the state. This means to an end is not their reduction to a deeper position of servitude at the disposal of the elites. Will imagines them disposing of the elites. This embarrassment is only temporary and it assists them in getting past their emotion-driven reflexes by having to face the consequences with a guide this time who intends to train them beyond them, something the state has no interest in doing as it is counterintuitive to its goals with them. To be defeated, helpless, and malleable, and angry is their use, but Will is changing that. His is a therapy in itself, getting to places that even Janice and the group therapists cannot. Janice is correct about the state or even Harmony having no interest in rehabilitating the residents. It's not profitable, but cleverly, Will has the state sponsoring true rehabilitation, unknowingly, signing the check made out to Harmony, a private institution, and with the unending chain of new recruits it sends.

Too much thought and planning has gone into this for Will to allow it to fall through his fingers now. Tuck has to be addressed. He has a starring role in Will's growing discomfort about Legion's future, but Tuck also has a good point, or the person he's probably listening to does. Tuck is a strong recruiter. Impressively, he was able to build a church, and although he lacks culture, while ironically drawing on African culture, his charisma has gotten him far in the organization as far as general respect is concerned. His lack of discipline is a rallying point for others, and it isn't a good thing because he represents the same emotional place that Will has been trying to move people away from and into the realm of calculated intellectualism. Tuck counters with, "Revolutions are fought with guns, not books nigga." While Will is forced to agree with such a simple argument, his point is to point him beyond the physical fight and toward what will be built after victory, if even a proper target can be identified without a firm philosophy in place, which will never come from guns, but Will can never break through Tuck's emotionalism. They are water and oil, and then there's Toni the creative, always finding ways to make two rights or two wrongs out of their perspectives, who has so conveniently decided to disappear at present, but not before checking in with Tuck first… These have not been Will's weeks.

"Ms. Janice, and I take responsibility for what I did, hell, I've done the time for it. Still doing it. Know what I mean? But, for months we sit here and talk about drugs, whether we hooked on 'em, or got other people hooked on 'em…" The mask pauses while properly formulating his thoughts, like he was deviating a bit from the script he'd personally prepared. Janice leans in with interest, lips parted and moistened to have him. Short and course, his hair frames his face abruptly with an intrusive wedge at the center. He has beady eyes, and the surrounding skin's blackened bags pressed flat, depressed like released blisters, with all of the familiar ticks and the posture of an addict. Gray recognizes this in him, and he was as sure of his orientation with narcotics as he was of his widow's peak.

Gray spends every group counseling session staring, trying to understand the meaning of the activities, and where they will lead. To guilt and shaming? Gray hasn't found employment yet, or even started looking, so the meetings are mandatory, they keep the state's checks coming, but he has found an interest in being able to hear the stories of others, assess them, and returning little of his own. The wiry man with the raccoon eyes, resumed as if pleading, "but it's like some of the story missing. Cocaine don't grow nowhere 'round these parts, Ms. Janice."

Stretching into chin-folding, long-faced, surprise, Janice sweeps her hair behind her shoulder and ear in one smooth stroke of her left hand, as she instinctually looks back towards Will's usual seating, while nodding. Will isn't in attendance, and his corner chair is empty. Janice, a Mrs., clearly by the diamond wrapping her ring finger, takes no offense to the many that refer to her as Ms. It is sort of a country comfort, and it makes her feel young and attractive. "Ok, James. I think that's an honest concern, and while I'm willing to facilitate such a discussion, I have two… let's call them issues." She raises her peace sign in illustration. "First, I don't have all of the answers and our discussion will stay at the level of speculation, and second, I have reservation concerning what use this line of conversation will have for you all besides possibly upsetting you… but if it's something you would like to do," she shrugs and nods as if convincing herself, "we can." Head nods and affirming grunts color the crowd. Randy is there. Gray doesn't respond. He just adjusts himself in his seat while watching the others. Part of his interest was hopefully seeing the nameless woman who shared herself with him the night before. Not that it meant anything more than what it was, but he just wanted to see her again, in a normal, well-lit environment, curious as to whether he'd even recognize her because her tone was masked in shadows and her voice masked in whispers. He's pretty sure she's not in attendance, nor is Kenny, the special needs pimp, who Gray will probably have to reconnect with should he desire to reconnect with her.

Janice completes her visual survey and shrugs with her decision to move forward. Janice smiles. It is as if she welcomes the direction. If her sit-downs with Will have exposed anything, it is her exhaustion with doing things the way they've been done, but things can't properly change without Will's willingness to completely throw out the old way and chance losing his position. He won't because he's afraid, or he won't because he's comfortable would be the perspective of anyone in Janice's position who has no idea about the real Will. If Will was in attendance, or rather Liam, as there are underlying behavioral differences between the two, he would now have the perfect opportunity to add to the conversation that all in attendance were not victims of bad luck and poor choices but systemic oppression. The story goes much deeper than a person committing a crime and getting caught; economic and racial disparity are codefendants. The bad guys in real life aren't nearly as easily distinguishable as they are in spaghetti westerns, and for Will, everything is material, boiling down to property and resources.

An olive complexioned woman wearing a do rag fed the discussion, "I just don't understand how getting high got me in prison. I ain't hurt nobody but me, and if the people had a problem with that, how's sending me prison s'posed to help. I was hurt more there than I've ever been."

Janice nods in reception and responds, "Yes. That's called a victimless crime, and many have argued the usefulness of prison in cases such as yours, but please, let's not stray away from James's point. I think he's pointing at the obvious victims of the drug war, mostly looking like us and often in the same income bracket. Stop me if I'm wrong." She looks over at James, and he signals for her to continue. "So, how do we, who own no ships, no planes, without the chemistry knowledge to create most of the drugs we see in our communities, end up being the ones imprisoned for their existence?" While Janice is talking Will enters the conference room, but he hangs back by the door as to not disturb anyone by crossing the room. "Now as I said this is only speculation, but some have said that removing drugs has never been the intention. How many years have they been trying, and still how easy is it to still go get a hit of whatever you desire? They've removed the drugs from not one city block, but instead they've just been removing people. Particular people, to keep this paired with

James's question, people who do not have the resources or know-how to get the drugs to these communities in the first place."

"Yeah, it's like a trick," James adds. Will begins making his way across the room. He smiles at Janice as he passes. He stands a moment before his seat looking at who's all in attendance, and when his eyes meet Gray's, he appears satisfied enough to take his seat.

"Glad you could join us, Mr. Bunting." Janice acknowledges him.

"Likewise. Already an interesting discussion, I see."

"Would you like to add to it?"

Will frowns a little and shakes his head in negation slowly. He can add of course, but his mind is still quite occupied with his troubles. He only came to the session to find Gray, as he's ready to have a follow-up meeting after the news he's received from Kenny. "I'm not sure I really can add, but you know what I would like? To hear from one of the new guys, especially Dixon," he says it like he says it, dragging it along the gutter of his throat, like pulling up phlegm, "I'm sure he can add his personal experience from supply side."

Gray looks over at Will then back at Janice and shakes his head with a dismissive smirk. Janice takes the feed. "Dixon?" She looks down at her roster. "Gary Dixon. Ok Gary, it is about time you really joined us. Surely you know that these sessions are part of your contract with your state mandated rehabilitation. It's uncomfortable at first, but be assured that you are not being asked do anything that the rest have not. What are you thinking?"

After a sign of frustration, Gray speaks, "I don't talk a lot. You and Mr. Bunting are aware of this." He cuts his eyes over to a stoically staring Will and continues, "And I ain't even a drug dealer, so I can't help with what you talking about."

"Felony possession, intent to distribute, and serving six years for it tells a different story. You're innocent now?" Will taunts. Gray doesn't respond. Janice, unsure of where Will is going with this, decides to stay out of it and allows the empty space to just expand, increasing the discomfort of everyone it touches. Gray patiently looks back and forth between Janice and Will. He finally decides to break the silence.

"So, Bunting directs one question at me, and now this is all about me?" Gray laughs softly. "I don't deal drugs. I hustle." He looks over at Will. "I'm not a liar either. Getting caught with drugs was just dumb luck." Dumb luck is Gray's way of shutting that portion of the discussion down, but he is sure his being arrested was a product of planning and someone tipping off the cops, a set up, but that is not the business of anyone in this room besides Gray.

"Ok. How about we come back to you?" Janice suggests then looks at Will to see if it is Ok. He clears it. "How about you Randy? You're new as well. Would you like to add?"

Randy clears his throat. "Well. I've done my share of drugs. Sold a few, too. Sounds like I shouldn't be here though, since I don't look nothing like you. Or maybe I heard that wrong."

"You shouldn't." James juts in. "Some White boys got to be locked up just so things look fair."

Will stands and speaks, and like the center of James' hairline he's a wedge into the budding discussion. "Please excuse me. I really just came here to grab Dixon." Gray shakes his head, sighs, and slumps into his seat. Will notices. "Come on, man. This shouldn't take long." Gray reluctantly rises and follows Will out of the room.

Will leads the walk to the west wing without speaking a word. Gray walks behind him with a strong desire to put his foot through his back, but he has the idea that he's already in trouble, and he has only been there two weeks. If he could though, he would. Gray never considered himself a violent person, but the authoritative types bring it out of him. They reach Will's office, and Gray takes the seat he was in the day of his orientation.

"So Dixon... We meet again. And so soon. You know why you're here?"

Gray shakes his head, but humors Will with an answer. "Because thou shalt not bear false witness, or some shit like that."

"Lying. No. You're not here for lying, Dixon. It is about a commandment though." Will leans back and swivels in his chair. "Tell me something. What do you think we're trying to do here?"

"Honestly?" Will grunts in affirmation. "Turn chicken shit into chicken salad, or shit into sugar. Make us all nice and sweet so society love us again."

Will lowers his brow and tightens his jaws, and he'd be turning out another batch in a record-breaking peanut butter cookie day if it weren't for his whiskers. He'd been frowning all morning wrestling with his conundrum, so much so, his jaws were sore. He leans forward. "That's a way of looking at it. You really have no idea what you're up against once you get out of here, if you get out of here, do you? Once you're outside of these doors, you think life was hard for you before you went in, being poor and Black, wait until you see how it is with your updated status. It will be almost impossible to hold onto even a bad job, and everything out there will work at directing you back into the penitentiary, living on the streets, or dead. What we're doing here is helping you avoid those three things. That's what I'm paid to do. But I'm only going to be able to do my job if you're doing yours, which is right now, following the rules. That's not hard to do."

Gray responds, "I agree, but… how 'bout I save you the all of the trouble."

"What?" Will is surprised.

"This your job. And I figure watching one less person'll make it easier. You'll still get the same pay, right?" This was a situation with a gain or a loss, so, naturally, Gray is negotiating. It is what he does. Will is caught off guard. "Right? And you don't have to worry about those good people you told me you were doing this for a couple of weeks ago. I don't murder. I just hustle."

For interest in the direction this is going, Will begins to take the bait. "So, what you're telling me is, with you, I don't have to do my job, and not only will I free myself up a tad, but once you're released, it's going to be just like I'd done my job because you'll not be a danger to society or yourself. Interesting proposition, Dixon."

"It's Dixon," Gray attempts to correct Will's pacing, "or just call me Gray. What do you have to lose?" Gray is already closing, and the only thing he'd offered was Will the time he'd have to spend trying to keep up with and train Gray, back to him. Gray could laugh at the idea, Will could laugh at the idea, but neither even cracks a smile. "You don't want to chase me around this place, man."

"Chase you? I don't have to chase you." Will postures arrogantly. "I see everything in this place. I saw you last night, and I wasn't even here. What does that tell you? And while I'm on the subject, did you enjoy yourself?"

Gray tilts his head in a palms-up side nod. "How could I not? Been like six years." He lies, excluding his prison affair, because it is none of Will's business.

"That's a major infraction. Two more in a month's time, and it's time to consider whether you're better off here or back in prison." Will has begun to close, directing Gray to the corner he'd prepared for him since initiating the discussion.

"Yeah, but you not. That's what we been discussing. No consequence for you. Them good people on the outside gonna be fine. Cause I'mma be."

"Ha! Not that I have a reason to believe you anyway, but you were safer in prison. You thinking you'll be safe out there, in itself, shows you need me more than you think you do. I admire your confidence, I admit, but you'll be fitted with a body bag in no time, imagining it's safe in those streets. Oh the PD has an overflow of bullets with your name on it, son. What are you about 6'3, muscular, and an ex-con too, you can have your hands up and they'll still fear for their lives. You can be running away, they'll still fear for their lives. Your size by itself gives them a good chance of killing you and getting off. They can do it with an illegal chokehold and on camera, but add to that that you're a recently released felon. Your illusion of safety and control will only aid in getting you killed. This cockiness is familiar though, with new recruits. Your friend Randy's got the same edge."

"Man, you got predators and you got prey. I think you're confusing me for one and not the other, and… that White boy ain't my fucking friend," snaps Gray.

Will smiles at getting a small rise out of Gray, and a complementary read. "What are your plans? No one will hire you. How will you make money?"

"Don't know."

"See?! That's the beginning of the end right there."

Gray shakes his head in negation. "I don't know while sitting here in front of you. Put me out in them streets and I'll know."

"What, drugs?"

"No. Told you I ain't no drug dealer. I hustle. I sell whatever I get my hands on that I can make a profit from. Hell, I've even hustled hustlers… Pimping women. You name it. If it's done out there on those streets, I've done it. Drugs too. But the return is horrible, and you can get six years for nothing. Give me two women and a nice corner instead. Money won't be problem…" Will is losing ground. For a man who chooses not to talk much, Gray spends his words wisely, and he keeps placing Will on the defensive, making what he wants to be as his concern for Gray and others look completely selfish and ego-driven, should he go through with assigning Gray his first infraction. Will had no intention of going through with it in the first place, but he intended to gain the upper hand from this exchange, but he has not done that decidedly and an infraction may be necessary. "So, what do you say Bunting? What you need from me?"

With the last question, Will is released, covered in calm, and allowed to save face. Negotiations are back open, and he can move to where he needs to without appearing to have an authority complex or a bruised ego. Gray has impressed him, challenged him, and even offered him a reprieve, probably knowingly, all in this short disciplinary meeting, and with Gray's final question, his concession to play ball, Will doesn't even have to go into the barbarism of blackmail. It was not Gray's intention, but no resident made such an impression upon Will in so short a time. If Will was challenged to confirm, he'd answer that, *Yes, Gray is a hustler, indeed,* just from the shapes he'd been forced into while Gray really hadn't anything of value to offer. "What do I need from you Gray?" Will even calls him by his chosen name, "I'm glad you've asked…"

*　　*　　*

Membership from many walks, but not every walk of life, start filing into the clearing of felled trees that they've designated their meeting hall. It's not far from the unfinished concrete structures that were meant to be a shopping center. A small line of trees, mostly deciduous but a few pines have integrated that keep the resistance walking on needles, stand tall in remembrance of their fallen. Many have fallen in the war of capitalism and the advancement of *progress*, and many more shall if a greater consciousness does not intervene. On the civilized side, they are forty meters thick, on the wild side the trees stretch back for miles, and in the center, The Hall, is a space that appears as if it had been engaged intimately with a massive ice cream scoop. The Legionnaires travel on the tight track that lay between The Hall and the concrete wasteland, all maybe a mile out from The Fifth, which is at present, closed and locked, with Toni not answering the call, online, and nowhere to be found.

This space was chosen as The Hall because the trees act as a wall; the concrete areas are just too open, too inorganic and cold, and even in the darkness of the twenty-second hour, they might command attention from someone traveling the nearby road; a directive for the membership has them cutting off their own headlights when within a mile of their meeting destinations if it's dark outside. It assists in their disappearance, along with the cell phone ban, because smart phones track their every movement. Encouraged instead is leaving phones at the places they'd usually be at the hour, like home, a mate's house, or even a bar, and some members, intelligently, travel to these places prior to meetings, leave their phone, and travel back to retrieve them at the meeting's end, even if it's out of the way. They cannot run the risk of the entire collective's location appearing at the same place on some GPS map, if some organization does have the power and access to such data, as it would arouse suspicion.

The collective has not developed this long by being uncalculating and reactionary, they pay attention to detail, all of the details they have access to through the disciplines and industries of various members. The system by which they stay off of the radar goes far beyond the choosing of four-letter nicknames, which itself is one security measure wrapped in another because those names become four digit numbers that plug into nearly impossible to decode number sequences that store information, track membership, and instruct. The names seem silly and cumbersome to those who know each other's government or Christian names, and to this Tuck is the most vocal opponent, but that percentage is extremely small, and some members were much more creative than others with coming up with theirs, like a measure of their dedication to the idea. Will knows more of the real names, because he is, by far, the best recruiter, and many know his name for the same reason, but many don't know each other in that way, and they are cautioned against sharing that information mainly because it isn't important as far as the collective's goals are concerned. Safety is paramount. They've been trained to know, and are under no illusion that their government will not hesitate to kill them. The precedent has been set, and the pattern is so consistent, it's predictive.

All organisms that have reached the complexity necessary to become self-aware, dedicate resources to self-preserve, and the state falls within this category. Of course it will kill to protect itself. It is both discomforting and reassuring that Legion has also reached that level of complexity. When all of the pieces are self-aware, how can the collective not be? How does one address or direct such a collective? It is not often that Will is apprehensive, but beneath the blanket of stars this night, he is still having this same conversation with God in hopes he can be insulated from destroying one of the few things left that has his dedicated love, maybe loving them, or their potential, more than he loves himself. This is why it stresses him so. If he could, he would, because he wanted to, for his own peace, but he couldn't care less.

Tuck came through Harmony, Toni came through Harmony, and many others, so Will is known and respected by a large portion of the membership and could be confused as the leader, but that position does not exist. Because so many are acquainted with him, he has gained a particular advantage in trust and acceptance by being a stranger to few, but that advantage is offset by so many being able to positively ID him in the case of trouble. Also, many know him as an asshole through Harmony, and the jury is out on whether or not that is just a character he plays. There are many in leadership capacities defined by their skill set, but no static leader. Just as Will uses Harmony to recruit, Toni uses The Fifth, and Tuck uses his Temple of

Morality, that Will only refers to acronymically as the T.O.M. Center, calling all of the membership Toms and their leader the *Grand* or *Uncle Tom*, affectionately, of course. Tuck's recruits are mostly products of the street, Toni's recruits are a mix of street and suburbia, and Will's, through Harmony, are mostly from a level more street than street even, so the joke of Will calling anyone outside of himself a Tom is only considered an expression of self hate. Maybe if someone outside of Will had read Uncle Tom's Cabin, they would understand that even in his jest that being called an Uncle Tom isn't an insult at all, because the character wasn't a sellout. He actually died from not selling out, refusing to disclose where his comrades had gone, and that is no sellout unless they have a problem with his Christianity, which they don't. Many are Christians, and if not, something similar. Will teases with the title in hopes of eventually exposing the stupidity that makes it an insult, in the same way *house nigger* is an insult, when none of the enslaved chose their conditions and sellouts were not created through condition; some in the house were the most dedicated to liberation, and some in the field were conversely the least dedicated.

The Hall is dark, with not even lamplight. The clearing is already littered with the spirits of deceased trees, dying for an idea that never came into fruition, and the organizers long ago decided against adding firelight or electronic light to this holy space. The stars paint the night sky and put out ample light as long as one is willing to let their eyes adjust to it, and they just plan away from the cloudy nights. The darkness adds to the mood, the secrecy, and the anonymity as well. The enslaved ancestors of many of the attendees planned in similar conditions, crying out to preserve their humanity beneath the intimate lens of the cosmos. All can speak and all are respectful of each other's turns, and their ideas wrestle amongst themselves on occasion, like thoughts within a immense mind. It's a séance, but every word counts creating a relevance that chants only used to have. The one who calls the meeting starts it, but after he or she opens the rest of the session is organized through hand claps, standing, sitting, coded language, and sometimes laughter that determine whether a topic should be built upon, destroyed, or further interrogated – no names, no egos, just ideas, a burning cauldron of ideation. The same voices do the speeches, the same voices ask the questions, and when the newer ones get comfortable they add unto.

As the bodies filter in between different trees, Will waits until the majority find a place to seat themselves in the grass, so he can then sit amongst them, before standing to start. At exactly ten, Will leaves the tree line steps into the bowl, beside and around those sitting and seated and finds himself a suitable space. All sit, except those few still scampering in. Will, never one to wait or give those tardy any more respect than they've shown those who were not tardy, stands and begins his speech. The stars are bright enough to show the faces of those gathered and gathering, and the sky is clear.

"We Are Many!... Surely if you're here, you know the news, at least in some capacity. I called this meeting. We need to talk. Things are changing around us, and I fear within us, and I'm offering this thought to the body concerning... It seems people are thinking we're not about what we're about, and I challenge that, respectfully. We've developed as much as we've allowed ourselves to. If you don't like where we are and what we are doing as a response to certain events, please don't forget to look in the mirror first, and at what you've done to develop yourself, and at what you've done to develop the collective. The Legion will be as strong as our weakest member, because not only are we many, we are also one. Let's leave that for a second though, and let's get to work...

"To get power, we must challenge power, and contrary to how it appears, the police do not have any power. They are highly organized extensions of power granted. It's power's illusion, as they act as a buffer between the powerful and the powerless, but do not be confused. They *are* in the way, but they *are not* our targets. They are us, and just asleep, like a lot of the people out here in these streets. You don't get in the seat of power with any post that you can fill out an application for, comrades. Not true power, and true power is what we seek. Their threat will need to be neutralized though, to get us there. No denying that. But do not allow them to be your target. We must aim past them, and through them only if need be. As supposed public servants, they share a unique relationship with the public, and our point is to win the public over, not to intimidate them or anyone closely associated with them...

"As I'm sure you've heard, and I'd venture that some in attendance know more than others," he clears his throat conspicuously, and continues, "a cop was shot some weeks back. And where did they shoot him, you ask? On the eastside, in Cottonwood, right in our own backyard... Oh, that's not what you meant by where? I understand... In the fucking shoulder is where. There is presently a citywide manhunt, and except for, his ass can't shoot that well, nothing's known about the perpetrator. You noticed how many cops are riding up and down the streets now? That's just the start. They got military grade weapons and vehicles. Some towns got fucking tanks, and someone wants to shoot a cop, and basically miss, at that. They are looking for you, and it makes trouble for us all, and this is the reason I suggested everyone lay low for the last couple of weeks. Thank you all for that...

"We needed this meeting to realign ourselves, because I feel like we've lost our direction. Hell, Legion didn't even know about the shooting, which I find a little suspect because news like that spreads fast. Ears, we lost a day's time since many of us didn't know of this before the evening news reported it. One of our brothers could've been jacked up over this, and if one of ours is in custody, it is a threat to us all. We leverage the information for everyone's safety, so if The Ears know, The Head should know. I cannot stress that enough. Our effectiveness is only as strong as our communication. Sound communication and direction allows the small army to outmaneuver the large. The who, the what, and the why don't even matter anymore. It's happened. We just have to prepare for the consequences, which are already expressing themselves on our streets.

"There is a higher police presence. Warrant roundups. More police intimidation. There have been more contacts with the law on our people. There's been some rough handling but nothing more serious, fortunately, in the last few weeks than we've had in the last few months. We push, the people push, and the state pushes backs twice as hard. The cops are on full alert over a... over a football injury. The cop can go back to work and do desk duty with a sling on for crying out loud, but the cops are working on clearance to walk around our hood like it is Beirut, flack vests, helmets, the big guns, military issue, having our streets under occupation with permission to treat us like combatants. This is why we must be careful, unless you want that, because that's next. Nothing new really if you're poor and Black, or poor period, but it will get even more aggressive. It'll take as little as one more event. The aggression now is a test, and if we allow it, they'll have nothing to compel them to let up. They're trying to break our spirits to get us back under control. They want us in complete submission, sending a message to never test their authority.

"This... this is why we're here. Everything can be back to a new, more aggressive normal in a month's time if we stay in our homes and shut our mouths, but personally, and I've thought about this for the past two weeks with little sleep, I'm tired of normal. If normal means our babies can be shot down in the streets like animals and we can't say or do anything in response, fuck normal! Shit, the ant bed is already stirred up now," Will identifies Tuck 's unmistakable supportive chuckle in the crowd. "And while they spread themselves thin in a ceremonial show of force, it's the perfect opportunity to hit them where it hurts. So, what do we want? Are we going to tuck our tails and return to normal, or will we recognize their aggression as a declaration of war and take power right from beneath their noses and create a new normal that we desire? Because if that's what we really want, that's what we can have. But, and understand me here, it's going to take a whole lo of sacrifice to get there. It's going to be uncomfortable, painful. It will be war, because I don't expect nothing less from that side. Too much time and energy has been invested in keeping us asleep to think they're just going to allow us to wake up without a considerable amount of blood spilling. A direct challenge to their supposed ownership of us all shall not be tolerated, or addressed at the level of debate because they stand to lose too much, the entire world is in the balance and your lives on the dotted line... Yeah. Let's just keep that in mind." Will's energy tapers off while making a case for how difficult the challenge would be because Tuck's statements, *convince people that we got no chance to be free*, and, *no building up the enemy on my watch*, became a reminder challenging his own efficacy.

Will stands there, suddenly embarrassed, with more questions than he has answers, not poised to finish strongly, so he jumps to the standard closing, "Many, we are." With the last three words, Will signals the others that he is finished and he takes his seat.

There is a small commotion, a grumble amongst the membership, as Will's message receives mixed emotions. Inspiration isn't his strong point. He's better at just providing information and offering challenges to his audience. He could never be a preacher, speaking to the positives in people and ignoring the negative as encouragement. It's coddling, and it only reinforces negative behaviors by tolerating them through kindness, and that isn't what he wants from the others or from himself. He didn't excite them. He stirred them, but he also spent time acknowledging their failures, which is not energy to easily build upon. He gave them things to think on, but simply building up their spirit may have been the better move. No one offered a direct challenge, but also no one clearly cosigned in the way they are trained to do so. The wind does all of the talking and only the sky listens, waiting as well for the signal for them to continue.

"Indeed!" A familiar voice calls from the crowd. Arguably as familiar, as respected, and as anticipated as Will's, though she rarely speaks at these gatherings. Will is probably the most surprised to hear her, pleasantly. Slowly she rises, small frame, proportionally curved, short curly head of hair, the glint of her jewelry, which she only wears on occasions, catches the light every so often, on her arms, her ears and her face, and regal posture against the darkness of the tree lines with the stars cutting her away, as she takes the floor. The crowd stays silent, awaiting the movement that assembling the collective promises. Her voice is shallow but her passion is always deep, and every word is worth listening to, as she's been lending her poetic command of the language to them for years. The cold frame of the body may never have moved without the essence of a creative as an animating force, and that is the position LaTonya played. She's soft-spoken, but exacting and a smith of composition. Following her *Indeed*, which signaled acceptance of all that Will had said without challenge, she stands to address the crowd, and Toni opens with, "We Are Many!"

2:3 *As much as I want to, I cannot deny that there is a divine presence. Only so much of existence and all its interconnectedness can be left up to coincidence before the idea becomes ridiculously silly. I don't care how we got here anyway. I just care about how we move forward. I see divinity as collective awareness, not control. Awareness is guidance for those who respect the balance of things, which in itself is accepting that there is no balance based on respect, morality, or righteousness. That's where religion gets it wrong. The only true balance is power, actual power and the threat of. The man will stop hitting you once you hit him back as hard as or harder, or you break his hands, not because of compassion. If he truly had compassion, he would have never started striking you in the first place. Even the Christian God chooses to rule with consequence over compassion, because man is stubborn, and he requires an 'or else.'*

Harmony and Legion are all-consuming for Will. Everyone and everything is viewed through the perspective of one or the other or both, because one was reduced to being the recruitment arm of the other as soon as the other began developing. Harmony became an extension, like an umbilical chord or a blank check by which Legion is fed. As long as the numbers look right, it serves as government funding for government's own destruction, the rope it will hang itself with. The ticks at the top, or pigs rather, bloodsuckers, are so fat that they're blocking the sun from the rest, and the every twenty-year rebellion suggested by Thomas Jefferson is long overdue. Government should fund it, since government, the state, enables the destruction of the poor by the rich. *Enables* is a nice way of putting it, *facilitates* fits better, but some recognition has to be given to the voters, dumb as they may be, in a representative democracy that does not represent them, and has never, and they're aware of it. Some of the Legion membership feel comparably unrepresented, and without periodic elections to pacify them, pressure will only build and revolt is imminent.

How irresponsible of Will to try to keep them from being

murdered on one side, and keep their efforts financed on the other. Will must keep the appearance that what he is doing, in the small space that he is allowed to move within at the halfway house, is useful, so he has to run a tight ship, because should he fail, so shall Legion. It keeps him occupied, manipulating the strings of his contract puppets and his resident puppets, playing God, and creating programs that appear to do one thing in the paperwork but do something completely different for the training of his urban militia. He also has to be clever enough in his creation to fool those he works with such as Janice. One can never be too safe around the petite bourgeoisie; they hold onto their positions for dear life for fear of joining the ranks of the poor and powerless. Will is not sure that this is the opinion of Janice and the others, but he designed his programs as if it is.

The adornments that make life worth living for most do not decorate Will's. He's reduced living to satisfying impulses, an efficiency shared only by the extremely poor and soldiers in combat zones. He's imagined what having a steady woman would be like or maybe children in fleeting glimpses that would be smudged out by some reminder about the decay of the world and the terrain his family, Black and poor, would have to navigate. Many would measure his status as middle class, but Will only believes in two classes, clearly making him poor and not rich. He couldn't trust his own behavior had something existed that he loved more than life itself, especially an innocent something, like a child. His time spent in the army, in capitalist turf wars that were dubbed humanitarian, supposedly saving people from themselves, showed him the worst of mankind from the inside out. He didn't watch it; he became it. He trained it. It was a cure for psychological obesity, quickly making one lean in concern of only what matters - eating, drinking, fighting, and fucking. No time to stop and smell the flowers, unless one wants to lie beneath them and assist their rise, as in pushing up daisies.

Will has always been a loner, but his ability to form strong social bonds may have increasingly suffered during the military crossfire. Maybe it was struck by one of the bullets that came so close he thought he was hit, and instead it ripped this enveloping, aura-like desire to bond with people, causing it to fall away from him and die. Soldiers make brothers of each other, with their lives depending upon one another normally, but not Will Bunting. He didn't bond in the military either. Just finding a few people he could tolerate was a miracle. He enlisted as poor teenager with a desire to escape the wretched claws of his community and the mediocre living it promised. That was really as far as he'd thought it through, and while there were some like him, there were many more boys dedicated to the popularized idea, actual patriots, buying every bit of the stories they were told, crying during the national anthem, and speaking of being willing to die for their country and meaning it. That was psychosis to Will. There wasn't much worth dying for, especially not a body of land and some unrealized promises that has done more spilling of the blood of people that looked like him than of any place they'd invaded. He also encountered his fair share of racism while in the Army, and although it did not shape it, it was the kiln that hardened his revolutionary nature. He learned a lot, but it was not an easy time for him. He climbed the ranks slowly, fought a lot – whipped three White men at once, once, went AWOL a number of times, and was even pulled to the side and told in confidence that if he wasn't careful that, "Bunting, they will kill you." The *they* wasn't the enemy, well not the established enemy, but an admission that friendly fire is not always accidental, and they'd just lie to his family or anyone that asked. Power warned him and it wasn't a bluff, or if it was Will was not willing to try to call it. His rebellion as a result became a study of weapons, military and political science, and power, with the interest of creating the conditions where friendly fire could, too, be his excuse, all while making no friends.

People were just tools. Will used them as needed, and he was humbled by the idea that he was also a tool for others. It didn't bother him one bit, as long as together they were building. So, Will hasn't any friends, not really. His family, blood relatives, is lost somewhere in New England. He hasn't a steady woman, only needing them for one thing, and needing all as tools are needed. Oddly though, in an awkward space in his mind, Toni satisfies all three vacancies, becoming something more. Will's filter is professional grade in keeping the, *he doesn't need people, socially,* message away from people. When it fails, the result is, *he's an asshole*, and it has failed more than it has succeeded, and it's addressed on each occasion with his shrugging shoulders. He has to stay thin and neat. His meticulous dress is a reflection of his disciplined mind. Ordered. Streamlined. Compact. Only what matters.

The past couple of years drained his social life down to a mere ring around the basin – eating, drinking, fighting, and fucking. It doesn't take much to satisfy his list, and it is done so through a tiny battery of people and places, with *fucking* most often demanding his routine change slightly, because most women tend to desire a little more than what he's willing to provide. They have to be replaced frequently as a result, and he's not able to stretch a traditional sexual relationship much longer than a couple of months. Will's not a smooth talker. He's a charmer, but not through his wording. He has a full wallet and no reservations about opening it, wide if need be. A hustler's dream catch, a victim to the right victimizer, he could be, but Will is no fool. Men end up paying one way or another anyway, and not having the stress of trying to please a set of conditions as complicated as what a sexual relationship brings is worth every penny of the cost. Still, even with the x-factor of women, Will's movements stay reasonably predictable. It is as simple as a game of rock, paper, scissors. If Will is not at Harmony, he is at home, if he is not home, he is at The Fifth.

Conveniently, The Fifth is especially where Will would be on a Friday night; it has proven successful in the *fucking* portion of his itinerary. It's never crowded so it keeps the competition low, and having an intimately known bartender who hasn't a problem with tossing him a bone is always a plus. Toni plays a great wingman. So with the night's meeting, it is both where Will parked and left his phone. The convenience doubles because now with Toni reappearing, he cannot see himself closing out this marathon of a day – he has now been up roughly forty-five hours straight, without speaking with her first. His world is starting to look like a 3-D movie without the glasses. Sleep deprivation itself is an altered state comparable to many produced by strong narcotics. It's like an extreme high, and it has to be slept off. It was two a.m. before the session at The Hall began to die down, and audacity held his puppet strings disallowing him to sink right into the ground he sat upon. Instead, his fatigued mind was stretched, torturously, across question after question like each speaker was trying to outdo the previous with a better manner to arrange words where they would project a particular spirit, while materially meaning nothing at all. Even the intelligent members were doing it, which was further proof that they were all full of terror, yet pushing through it. It is human reflex to address fear with hyperbole, an aggression that promises more than what's available, that calls on God.

It was not strategy session. The spirit acknowledged the seriousness of their suggestions, and alike those in Jonestown, they were all drinking from the kettle. They were high on it. Those less prepared strategically or politically, but still wanting to add to the energy, brought just that. Materially useful it was not, but maybe upon some spiritual level people were growing from it. Will toyed with the idea as part of his own growth, but it was like arguing that the cheerleaders had as much impact on a sports competition as the countless hours of practice the players endured. He knew they weren't ready, and they admitted it themselves without doing so. The first shot had already been taken and the protective seal broken, and likely by someone in attendance. People were exhausted by such an emotional and consequence-laden topic turned pep rally, but the night ended at a surprisingly clear consensus; one Will wasn't sure he agreed with, but sure he was not going to fight, even if he had had the energy to. He was letting go, loosening his grip with every new idea that seemed beneath him and ill prepared, with his psychic adjustment making it beyond him and his taking ownership of their lack of preparation. This is the game he played.

The discussion was nothing about what he'd introduced in the idea of should they or should they not respond to the coming aggression with aggression, but only about how hard they'd respond. Not responding was not an option. They'd been not responding all of their lives for the most part, and with no positive results. Tuck was not alone in his desire to strike back, and the expressed energy of the discussion took on a bullying tone, idealistically shoving Will to the dirt and asking, *What took you so fucking long?* He tip toed out with the subject, speaking it softly, thinking that any more than a hint would possibly scare them, but the fear was only his own. It was apparent. This is why he shut up and let the sweep of energy stirring within the bowl move about him yet without him; he had held them back long enough. He was convinced. If there was no better example of this, Toni rising behind him and accentuating his suggestion without question, with exclamation, saying more with less, obviously a message prepared and not intended to hitch to the back of his, was the vote that they were moving on with or without him. That is the way his doubled vision, straining through the stress of lack of sleep and low light saw it.

Toni's departure and return, with no mention of anything to Will, but at least some mention to Tuck, and her making an address at The Hall which she rarely does was a strategic military coup. The energy shifted from protective to aggressive, and Will can no longer properly carry it without first releasing it, distancing himself, protecting himself, only, and not limiting the rest by keeping them in his protective embrace. Liberty and security are opposites, so how secure should the seekers of liberation actually be? Their hubris lit the darkness, and Will was dim, thinking about how pride comes before the fall, like an enemy to them all, and he could not help it. He imagined the first deaths, felt it; the warm handshakes went cold right there within his palm as they greeted each other in departure. "Yes, yes brother. We are many," was repeated ad nauseam, as Will parted his way through the exiting membership opposite the general direction. His energy was not needed, not the energy he's dragging. He exited forest-side instead of street-side to deter anyone latching onto him and trying to talk. He didn't have a social impulse left in his body, and he'd rather cut through the forest and take the long way back to the street and to The Fifth to avoid contact. Surely, if someone saw him walking on the street they would offer him a ride. The Fifth was only a mile out, and he'd much rather walk beneath the suburban and urban cusp's celestial exposure, alone.

Will disappears into the thick. Every step away from the clearing, the more he disappears. The thickening canopy limits his visibility, and the tips of his fingers are the first to smudge out as the starlight struggles to reach them. Next comes, or goes, his hands, then his arms, his legs already, as they succumbed quickly to the darkness rubbing his body parts away the farther within it he walks. His body's gone. Without it, he's lost. His sense of direction is fine. He mapped the sky, staring at it all the while in The Hall listening to his heart's reaction to the loss of his body, part by part. He clearly knows where he is at, but he's still lost because hasn't an idea of where he's going. There was an overwhelming sense of pride pouring out, cockiness even, emanating from their supposed preparedness. God was mentioned, more than once, as backing, as proof that the time, their time, had come. Most can't even close their eyes to picture God without envisioning a robed White man who belongs at Woodstock, or his afro or dreadlock counterpart, still in a robe and belonging at Woodstock, but they feel they are ready to challenge the system that placed the image there, that created their definitions, that told them what wrong and right was, and gave them God. If this God is necessary to make any argument compelling, the argument is not compelling. If this God of theirs has been consistent in doing anything, it is in doing nothing at all. He does not intervene, and Will fears that they may actually need Him to. They have no idea what they are up against, and emotion carries them. They've been long in the depths of a world that has bound and abused them, and they've been waiting for their hands to be freed. They are free now. Will walks away. Will lets go.

Will cannot safely move forward without floating his invisible palms in front of him like one who has lost his sight once twenty or so meters away from the tree line, using his sense of touch as his guide. The sounds of night surround him. The nocturnals scurry about and beat their wings, the insects buzz around him, bounce against him, and crawl upon him as he travels deeper into unfamiliar territory, where placing himself becomes difficult. He leans upon a nearby trunk, deterred by the idea of walking in any deeper. All is black except for the occasional glimpse of the moon peaking through the leaves. All is lost besides what's left of his consciousness. He slides down against the tree to meet the ground and loses his head, by losing his consciousness too.

Multiple legs, miniscule and moving across one's cheek is the best alarm clock. Will sweeps whatever it is off of him so quickly, he hasn't the time to discover what it is. His eyes open slowly to make out the unfamiliar backdrop, trees and leaves in every direction and a soft morning breeze. The morning sun finds him beside the tree he fell asleep leaning against. His desire to sleep overpowered his desire for safety and comfort. The parts of his body in contact with the ground feel tender, and there is no telling the number of little bites he's accumulated throughout the night. Will stands and rewards the tree for watching over him with a watering. He's living the aftershocks of a drunkard. It as if this night and morning were a reenactment, yet he hasn't had a drop to drink in about two weeks. His face itches. His beard grows. When his spray upon the bark becomes a dribble, he shakes it, zips up his pants, gauges his location, and begins his walk back toward the hum of civilization to hopefully catch Toni.

Her car is in the parking lot, along with his own. He enters his car to grab his phone and straightens himself up the best he can using the rearview mirror. He's missed calls. Toni has called multiple times and left messages that he doesn't check. He leaves his car and knocks upon The Fifth's front door. A moment passes. Will yawns while staring at the archangel and his sword, thinking that if there is anytime for him to protect them, it is approaching.

"Who is it?"

"It's Liam, Toni." The bolt slides, Toni pushes the door open slowly and peeks her head out. Her face lightens as soon as it meets his.

"Liam!! We were worried about you." She walks out and hugs him around his neck. She wears a t-shirt, pajama bottoms, and no shoes, and with her tiptoed hug was either a gun in her waistband or she was very happy to see him. Something hard pressed into his abdomen during. She punches him in his shoulder, as strong as a love tap, when they disembrace. "What happened to you last night? I saw your car here."

"I went for a walk and…"

"Wait." Toni cuts him off. "Come in. I feel awkward standing out here talking like you're not welcome." They enter the pub. "Excuse the mess. Some of the members came by here before going their separate ways. Waiting for you, I think. I know I wasn't the only one." Several shot glasses are on the bar and on a couple of the tables, and some chairs need to be pushed in, but it is hardly what anyone would consider a mess. Toni walks behind the bar, removes her handgun and places it beneath upon one of the shelves. "One thing I hate about those doors is no peep hole, but why would a church need a peep hole though, right? God got this." Toni winks in tease. "So, yeah, what happened to you?"

Will takes a chair away from the bar, at one of the tables. "I called myself going for a walk in the woods behind The Hall, but it turned into me setting up camp for the night… I was exhausted. Still am. Been talking to God, as Janice put it."

"Janice. How is she doing? Still wearing that god-awful makeup?"

"Of course. She's well, though. Asks about you often. Wonders why you don't visit like you used to. I have her thinking that we rarely communicate. I figure it's better than telling her that you own a bar now and that I'm your most stable patron. She doesn't even know I drink." Will laughs.

Toni leans against the bar upon her elbows and wrists. "She knows, Liam. You'd be surprised who knows. It shows." Toni struggles to compose her face muscles, while a smirk forces its way out. "Crackheads, meth heads, and heroin addicts all think no one knows." She completes her smile. "She knows though. Trust me. Maybe not about the bar, but definitely about you."

"I don't think so." Will disagrees.

"It's what she does for a living, Liam. She knows the signs. Give her that much respect. Play dumb with smart people and they'll just play along. No telling how much more she knows about you after recognizing you trying to hide that."

Will dismisses her point. He scratches his cheek. "Maybe. Well, you say you were worried about me. I was just missing a couple of hours. It's been weeks for you, dear. Think how I felt. A lot of the sleep I've been missing, you owe me back. I thought you'd left us and run away." Toni sucks her cheeks in and rolls her eyes away innocently. It is just precious. "What happened to you?"

"Well…" her face loses all expressiveness as it becomes lost in thought. She stares at Will, but through him, not at him. She rolls her bottom lip beneath the pinch of her teeth while in thought, then Toni unhinges herself from her elbows, walks from behind the bar and takes the seat across from Will. She places both of her hands upon the table flat, she then clasps them together, then she places one beneath her chin, all with a pensive innocence while finding comfort. She settles on the hand beneath position and answers Will's question, "I was out of state."

Out of state. Simple words, all single syllable and common, but when placed together in that order they cast a spell. It is witchcraft, and it causes Will's jaw to drop and breath to stop, placing his palm upon his chest like he needed to brace it and ensure its contents stayed put. He shut his eyes, shook his head, closed his mouth and tightened his jaws, but the new layer upon his face, his unshaven brush, hid the signature trouble indicators. The bakery is closed. His eyes reopen, set upon Toni, full of questions that his mouth knows not to ask. His self-talk is calming, everything he wants to say can be taken in a negative manner, and he possibly means them to be negative. He isn't sure. It's a lot at once. The terrible streak of news he'd rather not hear, events he'd rather not take responsibility of, and face consequences to, continues. Toni is considerably matter of fact for the weight the announcement, and placidly, she continues to advance, "I got back yesterday night. Not long before the meeting. I saw the call online, but of course I could not reply to it without chancing giving away my location. I'll spare you the details, of course… Aw look at you." Will is still frozen; Toni effortlessly glides upon him like skating blades, effortless for her, but they cleanly dig into Will's flesh like razors. "You were worried about me, Liam?" She places her free hand on top of his and gives it a pretentious squeeze of support. "I'm flattered, but I handle myself as well as the rest you, if not better."

Will breaks his silence, "But… why? And why you?"

"Because it needed to be done. And why not me? And that

question is exactly why me, Liam. I have your answer. I am your answer to why. It needed to be done and I did it. So, no more question marks concerning preparedness. Hell, I even removed them from myself."

Will is still frozen, eyes accusing, pressing heavily upon her, in a space where encouragement would have better fit. Toni reacts in defense.

"Why? Hell, you're the reason why. That's why."

Will shakes his head no, still speechless, still puzzled.

"We're moving into escalation, Liam. Whether you're ready or not. Be honest, who was less ready than me? So now we're all out of excuses." The sentence didn't come out nearly as confidently as the wording demanded. Will was unmoved by it. He didn't bite and Toni continued.

"Remember sitting down in here that night, pissed, trying to address our struggle when yet another unarmed Black man got murdered by the cops, this time right in our back yard? Dude in the truck?" She is looking for his co-signature, but he doesn't even offer it in a glance. "And I said that, *maybe it's not time*, to calm Tuck, but I also said, *but maybe the time is near*?" Still nothing. It is as if Will isn't listening. "I was terrified that night, Liam, and just doing my best to hold it together in front of you two. Surely, this latest shooting, right in our back yard, was going to be the start of active operations, the end of the life I'd grown accustomed to, possibly life itself, and I wasn't ready. If you would've cut me deep, right then and there, my blood would have sat at the wound's edge, shivering, afraid to come out. It was that thick in fear, but Liam, I noticed something that night, and forgive me for saying this, but you were just as scared. You were just cooler about it. Still are." Toni twists her mouth at Will's unwillingness to respond to her jabs and shakes her head.

"I was looking to be inspired, reassured, guided by you. That's who you've been for me since forever, and here you were pulling back harder than I was. We'd talked about this Liam, before Tuck came around even, and the way you deflected, challenging his inexperience, is the same you did me years back. I know it makes sense in a way, I know but... Well, I was so scared then, I welcomed your apprehension. I also determined that if you were as scared as me, maybe I needed to seek inspiration elsewhere... I'm not scared anymore, Liam... You know, that wasn't the first time we had that discussion. We just switch out the victims, say we not ready and talk about recruiting. For someone who don't believe in God, in Her infinite wisdom, you sound just like one who does, waiting on a sign or some kind of savior. I mean, what's happened in all these years besides bodies falling more and you drinking more?"

Will is still searching for words, stuck on, and wanting to question further into what Toni has just done, but *out of state* trumps all. He hears her indictment of his leadership, or lack thereof, but out of the convenience of the moment, what she's possibly done is much more important. She hasn't said anything he wasn't already aware of anyway. Had he not just come to a similar realization in the forest the night before, and had he not heard the same from Tuck, she would have made a stronger impact, but as it was, Toni's message was weak and weeks late. His point was not to be a leader anyway, and it appears that he's been doing that brilliantly, even better than he imagined he would, to the point of disappointment. That's not what he wants to address.

Instead, he's unsure and torn between the safety of a future idea and the safety of one he loves. Toni could never fall into the hands of the law again, and still she'd not be safe from what she's done, if she has, in fact, done anything. This wasn't for Toni, and of course she'll think he doesn't approve particularly because she's a woman, a barrier she's run into her entire life. It has something to do with it, but Will's feelings are anchored more deeply than that. He stands, still completely disregarding her last question and the direction she's taking the discussion. He paces around The Fifth like a disappointed father with a pregnant daughter, who happens to be adult, hands completely tied by a rebellion that he'd created. How many living room carpets had been trampled with dismay with a comparable conversation and the thoughts, *she has her father's stubborn resolve*? This is similar, but Toni is not Will's daughter, not even of blood relation, and only young enough to be if Will had started reproducing really early. But like Legion, she was his, and he'd intended to protect her, and had outright done so many times in the form of fisticuffs when any attempted making a spectacle of her and her lifestyle choices and thought it OK to give her less respect than a woman deserved, a man deserved, or a human deserved. Maybe he could quell this overbearing paternal instinct if he had children of his own, even though he did not view her as a child or his child. He wished Toni would have borrowed from the pubs name, one she decided upon for its relation to both, a *fifth,* popular measure of alcohol, and covertly for *the fifth* of November and anarchist ties and class clashes being made in the visage of Guy Fawkes of the failed British Gunpowder Plot to assassinate a group of notable elites, including a king, which is also, conveniently, the date Nat Turner was tried and convicted, but Will saw a third connection. She could have pleaded *the fifth,* even if it would have settled nothing but his insides.

Out of state means murder. It is not spoken of beyond those who plan it. It is between members of different locales, travel is done by highway, and it is not for Toni. The hit on the local police officer could have even been an *out of state,* as often the negotiations are one for one, but the officer was not notable in any way, not that Will was aware of, so it was probably not. *Out of state* hits are meant for somebodies, people who are clear enemies or traitors to the people, to the movement, or a representative of imperialism whose removal will assist the jelling of the urban milieu, as they have been killing thousands indirectly for years with their decisions. Those of representative level do not even need listing, they are always watched, and they exist under the category of *money shot,* for the satisfaction they will create, but there has yet to be one removed.

The list is full of people with local significance, not national, or international. If it went as planned, Toni went to a place she's never been, killed a person she's never met, and returned immediately, leaving their local PD with a case that will always remain unless they frame someone, or force someone with no connections to confess to it. Even the negotiators of these hits are unknown to each other by name, by location, and even the time the contract will close is not shared. Toni could have picked that contract up a day before or a year before, and closed it yesterday. The time isn't important, only the deed. No money changes hands, and the communication between the opener of the contract is indirect so nothing ties back to the closer. Nothing. They are just assumed names on a private message board with addresses across the country, enemies to the cause, being added and subtracted with a simple edit feature that has grown past one hundred names. Will refuses to confirm if any names have been removed from the list and from the planet; he's more comfortable not knowing and looking at it like an inactive idea or a bad one. His humanity demands it. Although he's killed, he is not a killer, and he wishes that feeling upon no one, especially not Toni. Yet another reason Will does not want to lead. He no longer has the heart for murder, desperately hoping for another way. The only stipulation of *out of state* is one cannot add a name to the list without accepting a contract to remove at least one. Toni has just confirmed for Will that it is a bad idea, and there have been many throughout the duration of the militia.

"You're clearly disturbed, but I don't see what the problem is, Liam. I'm fine. Look?" She stands, spreads her arms in attempt to get him to look at her, to give her the kind eyes he has many times. He doesn't and damaged, Toni returns to her seat. "I'm sorry you worried, but you know the rules. Hell, you wrote them." She is right. She did nothing wrong. She completely followed protocol, told no one she was going, took her car which cannot be tracked as long as she used cash with every stop she made for gas or food purchases and even lodging, left her phone – because smart phones track movements, and returned safely. She only apologized, not for a misstep, but out of respect for her mentor who has been negatively affected by her decisions. Will finally responds.

"So you're a soldier now? No! What's getting into everybody?"

She sought embrace and his words were dismissive, pushing her away. Toni's eyes blacken. She lashes back with, "I'm whatever the people need me to be, dammit!" a statement more revelatory than she meant it to be. "What do you see me as is the question? Can I not do what you do because I'm a woman? What should I be instead? A lady in waiting? Just trying to sort a couple things out before

Prince Charming comes, I pop out some future revolutionaries, and we live happily ever after? Saving myself for my very own, in house oppressor, who has the man bearing down on him all day, while he holds his tongue and his fists to keep his job and support his family, but comes home and releases the built up pressure, his tongue, or his fists on me and the kids? Negative. That's kind of not my thing, if you haven't noticed, or do you think this is just a phase I'm going through?" Toni's eyes begin to well up with emotion as she explains. "No. I think I'd have trouble finding a man I respect enough to share myself with anyway, even if the attraction were there. Cowards. I'm more man than most of you…" A tear falls. She lets it with no attempt at wiping it. "Another reason I did what I did. Where is any of this going anyway, huh? While you and Tuck debate, and make enemies of one another, completely ignoring the real enemy, I figure why not? Sometimes you need a woman to do a man's job, and damn you, Liam! I'm invested into the liberation of my people just as much as you. That's not contingent upon having a dick!"

Those aware of their oppression in a display to be recognized as an equal to their oppressor, or a representative of, tend to overcompensate their own value or reduce the value of the oppressor, or a representative of, to a level beneath their own. Will knew this was coming, and he will not allow the complexity of his argument against Toni's participation in that level of their liberation to become a dick measuring competition, which he would win, naturally. The rules are in his favor, human value is measured with manhood's ruler, which is one of many expressions of the problem and what she, sloppy with emotion, is trying to get across to the person she's discussed power dynamics with most and not her enemy. This is why Will was apprehensive in questioning her decision in the first place; the chance it would be received as a personal attack and as a divisive maneuver instead of an inclusive one, was high and amplified through their oppression. Hurt people hurt people. They began with a hug, and now she could choke him without apology, because he knew better and was supposed to understand, making his jabs more precise – but he wasn't even punching. He was the one dodging jabs as he heard her, and still he'd hurt her. Love and hate are next-door neighbors in row housing, they stay on speaking terms, and sometimes one is confused for the other.

Will grabs the back of the nearest chair, locks his elbows upon it, wears his shoulders like ear muffs, and offers a flippant reply. "Yeah, that's it." He needs to draw all of the venom out the wound before attempting the closing of it. She needs to say this, and he needs to listen, but he needs to listen without further aggravating the injury. Not an easy task, but, fortunately, discipline is Will's thing.

"I know it's it! But having a dick doesn't mean you have nuts, Liam." She pinches her lips and tightens her face like she just swallowed some bad food, not proud of what she's become. Tears follow suit, and Toni's voice begins suffering from the flow. She's upset at her tears and becoming so emotional. How woman of her... It is a discrediting inconvenience in a world of logic. She aggressively shoves the small round table before her, sending its contents, and, unbalanced, it rocks back and begins a spindle top twist and wobble instead of tipping. An empty shot glass from the night before dives and spreads itself across the floor. Toni rises, ignoring the danger she'd created for her bare feet like being hurt more was impossible, and walks hard back behind the safety of her bar, her sanctuary, where she keeps her bible-like diary and her handgun, the pulpit where she is king. While Will traced her movement, he noticed that the old signature cross, back in the shadows of the bar, had been turned upon its head and into a sword. Appropriate. Even if its orientation was only changed for something as simple as a cleaning, it was appropriate, symbolically, for the collective transformation being experienced. They are wrought iron to some universal blacksmith.

"Exactly Toni... LaTanya," he breaks character. "It's because you're a girl, or maybe..." Will is calm and measured, trying to get a handle on the situation. "Maybe it's because you're not expendable. That's a thought. Hold a gun because you can do nothing but, but if we need you to do more, which you've proven to be very capable of, I'd hate not to have you over some stupid ego bullshit. Ego! It's all ego around here! Myself included. I hope you proved whatever point you were trying to for yourself, because you didn't prove anything to me. I never thought you were unprepared or scared. Tuck is unprepared, and a bunch of others. I never thought that of you. Anyone can hold a gun and pull a trigger. Kids do it. It may be part, but that is not what this is about, and I'd hate to see you lost, your mind in another space, from a move that doesn't much matter. You're too damn important for that! We got killers to kill, and you're one of our brightest minds, if not *the* brightest," it was like Will bowed before her majesty, but she probably didn't even notice the humbling he allowed in following *if not,* and he closes it with, "…not a grunt."

Her tears gradually begin to dry, the few rebellious ones that flowed without her invitation, and Toni calms herself through busying herself. She wipes down the bar in a single spot, like the wood itself is a stain, nodding and listening with lips tight. A tense moment passes between Will's words and her response, as if she was making sure he was finished. "Well, I didn't do it for your agreement, and I didn't expect you to say you were proud of me, but know, honestly, that you're the reason I did it. It's time, Liam. You said it in your own speech… You don't have the time you think you have, meaning we don't have the time you think we have, because we need you. Just like you think Janice doesn't notice you drink, you probably don't think I notice you falling apart, your self-destruction, and it's more than just the drinking. The drinking just gives me a front row seat and makes me an enabler. You're going to kill yourself one day, you know?" She reminds him of the closing of his last bar visit with her. "I'm watching it! Helpless to do anything because I love you, and I can't help you without hurting you and vice versa, so fuck you for giving me that burden. And it's not about the drinking. That's just what you hide behind. I know, Will." She breaks character. "You will kill yourself, you will, trying to passively play this struggle, rationalizing it, and timing when to jump in like it's fucking double-dutch. That repeating sound is not ropes slapping the pavement, but gunfire, and your people are slapping the pavement. Why build a damn army if you're not going to use it? You needed that first connecting gunshot more than everybody, to give you a reason to live, to make you necessary. It should've been you behind the trigger, though… and you know it."

*   *   *

There are no group sessions on Saturday, and Gray got zero items crossed off of his Friday to-do list, so he rose early with that in his plans. He's accustomed to being told what to do, and whether he likes it or not, it's what he responds to best. He has to change that to function as a free man. He chalked his Friday up to free world jitters, or his institutionalization cool down lap. His meeting Will upset him a bit and he went back to his room and just came out to eat the rest of the day, but this time he has every intention of getting into the community and away from Harmony. He's off probation. At lights out he'd successfully completed another day of ignoring his roommates, and he exited this morning in quiet reaffirmation that they had no value to him. They are already starting to get the point. The people are weird to him here, cult-like. Surely, it's because of the little general. Not that Gray would have been much for conversation had it not been a culture ruled by fear and control, but since it is, he definitely passes on getting to know any of them. He left that culture in the pen, and didn't intend on continuing it through the psychological bars created by a group of nursing home cowards.

One can't be afraid of death without being afraid of life, and these junior citizens, not old enough to be senior, took the path of least resistance, just lying down and playing dead until their time is served. Somebody had to tell Will about Gray's nights before dealings, meaning they all were potentially backstabbing snitches. Gray needs to find his dance partner to find out what trouble it caused her, among other things. She may be one of the few warm-blooded residents left; there was nothing scared about her from their initial embrace until his final release. She finds her way into his thoughts, and he hasn't even a name to assign her to. The facility is not big enough keep them apart for long, and he'll find her when he has the time. If for nothing else, to confirm that it was not a dream. Will's disciplinary meeting and Gray's *assignment*, which he has yet to decide whether to go through with, is pretty solid proof of that it was not, though. First on his agenda is leaving campus, and he won't even ask any of the Harmony minions the way around the city, although they'd be the most convenient. He's also considering leaving all of this questionable ass at the facility on the table. He can run through the ladies on the streets with less consequence, plus the residents are all broke and powerless, and many hideous. He needs more than a nut, and he refuses to be the other half of a ghetto fairytale where love conquers all. When it works, it isn't love's conquest, but delusion's. There was just more to lose than gain in his doing anything other than sleeping at Harmony, and only that because of the curfew. The harmony in Harmony and the trouble it would take to disturb it, since so many appear to be in accord, was too much, and only someone of less than normal intelligence would risk it, which explains Kenny. Gray's departing as soon as he finishes breakfast.

"Ooh, what makes me so lucky? I almost didn't come in today, too, and here's my reward. You're never here on Saturday." Ann blushes uncontrollably as Tuck leans against her desk. Gray can see and hear them through the cafeteria door, while quickly downing the minor meal.

"Been begging for months for some extra hours, and they finally approved me coming in on some weekends."

Tuck nods. "Get your paper, because I know there ain't much official business happening, as you can see. Easy money."

Ann bucks her eyes as if to say, *Shut up, don't blow this for me.* Tuck catches it and laughs. "We good. I want you here whenever I'm here, and…" He leans in to whisper, "Fuck them. Break they greedy asses. I be damned if I ain't trying to. I worked sixty hours last week, and ain't a damn thing clean around here that I'm supposed to clean, or working around here that I'm supposed to fix. So, more overtime this week."

"Hush!" Ann bursts out laughing. Tuck smiles and shrugs his shoulders, impressed with himself. Gray exits the cafeteria, folding what little money he's accumulated in prison he has left and sticking it into his back pocket. He starts to pass behind Tuck at the receptionist's desk, and Ann stops him. Tuck looks over his shoulder. "Excuse me, sir?" Ann speaks.

Gray points to himself.

"Yes, you. Did you sign out?"

"I gotta sign out? No, I didn't. This is my first time leaving."

"Yes. Anytime a resident leaves you have to sign out, telling what time you depart and destination. You also have to sign back in when you return. It helps us keep account of where everyone is and when. There's a clipboard attached to the wall next to the bulletin board." Ann points the direction of the clipboard.

"You thought you was free, my nigga?" Tuck turns the rest of the way around to address Gray. Gray crunches his face. "No sir. They just removed the bars, bro."

"I see." Gray leans around Tuck and addresses Ann. "I have to tell where I'm going?"

Ann nods *yes* with both brows raised.

"You know, just in case an old lady gets knocked upside the head somewhere near where you're supposed to be and around the time you were supposed to be there, it cuts down on the police work. I'm not kidding either. The police come and get copies of these logs when there's a crime and they have nothing to go on, and they've even come and conducted investigations, holding interrogations right here." Tuck shakes his head in sad disagreement.

"I don't know where I'm going. I haven't been out into the city yet. Just off probation. Don't know anything about it. I planned to get out and learning something."

"That's not how it works. I can't believe Mr. Bunting didn't mention that to you." Will's spiel was interrupted by an inconvenient news story. "You're property, and potentially dangerous. For the safety of the people out there, they got to keep tabs on the people in here. So, no, you can't just go for a walk, sight see, or nothing like that. You're no tourist."

Gray nods. "Sounds like you know what's up. Where should I tell them I'm going, and how do I get there?"

"The library. There's one up the block, maybe three miles. That way you ain't got to spend no money, and you can start learning these streets. They also ask for a reason on that sheet. Just put job hunting. You can use the computers and the internet up at the library for up to two hours straight."

The Internet. There was that word again, but this time Gray

has some context about what it means because of his talks with Er-vin. "You'll tell me where?"

Tuck nods. "Yeah. I'm coming out right behind you. I got work to pretend to do out there." He turns and winks at Ann. "Sign out and I'll give you directions... What's your name, bro?"

"Call me Gray. Cool." Gray goes to the hanging clipboard with a ballpoint pin attached by a soiled string and begins to fill out the form. Tuck turns back to Ann, speaking through a smile, with her speaking through the same.

Tuck synchronizes the closing of his flirting session with Gray's return. "Ok, Ann. Talk to you later. And Gray, yo man, don't know if you're keeping up, but ain't nothing safe about these streets right now. Brother got gunned down by the pigs not too long ago. Then a cop got shot. Right around here, so they mad, and the streets being terrorized by the same people s'posed to be keeping them safe. Bastards. Been going crazy all over the country, shooting niggas for little or nothing. Biggest gang in America. Cops make us hate cops, just like White folks make us hate White folks. We the monsters they created us to be. Better keep your head moving and watching. As a matter of fact, what you got up tomorrow? I know a spot speaking on just that. On what we got to do to protect ourselves."

"We?" Gray seeks clarity, fearing he already knew the answer. Clicks in prison always spoke in assumed *wes*, solely making their judgment on the phenotypical, and it was seen as typical to Gray for each organization that automatically saw him as their type without hearing a single thought of his, completely unaware of his philosophy. It's an easy way to get infiltrated, for sure.

"Yes, we, my ni... African, the people of the sun, creators of civilization, Black folks. They trying to wipe us out, and they will if we don't organize." Tuck turns to Ann. "Sorry, I don't mean to get all political in front of you."

Ann is eating it up and beaming, "No problem here." Gray figured he'd be apologizing for something else.

"I think you'd like it Gray, we..."

"Wait..." Gray interrupts Tuck's pitch. "Gonna be any wom-en there?"

Tuck nods with a pinched-eyed smile in response while giving a head nod, encouraging Gray to exit out the door with him. Ann buzzes them out as Tuck's pitch resumes, "Yeah, you should come out tomorrow... It will get you out of being up here, and I'll pick you up." Gray partially shrugs in agreement. Tuck continues to talk as they disappear out of the door. "The spot is called the Temple Of Morality, and we meet at the corner of..."

2:4 *The ego makes us all feel like there is something to gain and something to lose. It takes a static life that connects us all, and individualizes it, breaks it into a bunch of tiny demanding pieces. One organism becomes many that decide to jockey for position to be at the best spot. We feel entitled to the best spots. We deserve them because we feel like we deserve them, and the others don't because… I can't have it all if they are having their share. Many argue that this kind of competitiveness is in our nature, arguing that nature can't be wrong. I argue that we're wrong about nature, and this life is not in accordance with it. Actually, it's anti-nature, and the decay of the world proves it.*

Cottonwood is typically *urban*, making Gray feel at home with his familiarity negotiating within such environments. The larger the city, the larger its underlying disenfranchised class, defining it in manner, is. They are the victims, the foundation that determines how tall the pyramid can rise. Urban used to mean those things related to cities or large towns, but the word is now also used as an acceptable label for a place or a thing having a high percentage of Black people or Black influence. Not just any Black people, specifically the poor and Black, characterized by a high level of expressiveness and creativity, along with a low level of education and discipline. It is no compliment. Urban is the label for the lowlifes and the desperate. On the social scale, suburban is more preferred. Urban houses are small, urban neighborhood blocks are small, and so are the urban opportunities. The most notable urban characteristic is its ghettos, where everything is extra small, compact, and stressful except the unrealistic goals set by the population. It's rare for a halfway house to be found outside of a ghetto.

Gray cuts through the feebly manicured campus following the fingertip of the one responsible for its condition, Tuck, who he knows as Robert, and who he is already a tad bit suspicious of from his level of enthusiasm in trying to procure portions of Gray's personal narrative. Most of his questions were answered with looks. Tuck embarrassingly smiled off his prying in unanswered questions by asking more. Gray only endured them long enough to get directions to the library. What did he want to know Gray's gang affiliation for, was he Crip, Blood, Black Guerilla Family, other, or none? Where was his family? Where was he from? How much time did he do? How much time does he have left at Harmony? What did he get locked up for? Was he on medication? Can he read? All of the questions were none of his business, and Gray felt like he was being interviewed for a position he hadn't applied for and had no interest in. *Gay* is the first thought when Gray encounters guys who want to know his life story upon meeting. He has been wrong many times about this, but the idea remains steadfast. There is no reason a man should desire to know so much about another man, and it's disconcerting. It was unrefined and awkward, and as far as introductions are concerned, for Tuck's to be any less smooth, he would have had to ask Gray for a full body, double arm embracing, hug.

A couple more questions, two more, and Gray was going to return to the building and just ask Ann for directions, and while doing so challenge some of that raggedy game Tuck had been laying down to her, just to spite him. She looks like a nice shot. Nice breasts, clear skin, and she doesn't look run through. Gray just might see about her. He knows her type, knows Tuck's type too, and while Tuck will probably have little trouble getting her to open her legs, Gray's aim would be having her surrender her mind, not just having her. An open mind leads to more places than open legs, like open pocketbooks, open cars, and open homes, but often the legs lead to the mind. Tuck was trying to appeal to her conscious self, but her conscious self doesn't fuel her interests. Her subconscious is why she smiles and changes colors, why she can't help but to, and what the intelligent man would target. Knowing what not to say is as important as knowing what to say. Saying nothing is a road less chosen, yet rather effective. Eyes can cut through the majority of the lip service. Often eyes yearn for something to do, to follow, to chase, and words just get in the way of this game where eyes play hide and seek. Gray can get further attentively ignoring than Tuck can adoring, giving her his undivided attention, as long as he's grinning and saying limp lines like, *I don't mean to get all political in front of you.* Plus Gray looks better. Much better. Ann noticed, and Gray noticed she noticed. Impressed by Tuck, Gray is not, and he faintly sensed that beneath that layer of apparent Black Nationalism, what truly impressed Tuck about Ann was her complexion, and the nerve of him to throw the word *nigger* around in front of a White chick.

The streets are small, the blocks, the homes, everything is small but the dreams; dreams are grand in the ghetto. Every child walking the streets dreams of playing in the NBA or NFL, putting out a hit hip-hop or R&B album, acting, or otherwise becoming rich and famous. That is it; those are the goals, no matter how low the odds of achieving them are. Entertainers are loved. They are the center of attention. This is extremely attractive to those who are not loved and forgotten about, unless given attention for their collective negativity. The negatives are sensationalized. They are tightly defined and rightly defiant in attempts to move beyond such a constricting space, physically and mentally. Their souls cry out for something more, and aims are set higher, always, than the place where they inevitably end up. There are negative results. The residents are reflexively trained to dream and defy the odds in their schools and homes.

Gray came through these schools and communities to receive the treatment. His corner told him his opponent was weak, scared, and nowhere near as talented as he, but after each round his cutman had his job cut out for him. When his father left his mother, left the planet actually, by a gunshot to the face, his corner said, "Good round champ. You're slowing him down." When the newly acquired stress of the home life affected his school life, his corner said, "You got this." Gray's father didn't live with them, his mother and his brother, but he was still there. His feelings or lack of feelings for the mother of his sons contaminated his love for his sons none. He picked them up often and did his best to instruct them about life. When he died it created a vacuum in Gray's life that nothing could fill. His mother, in her own pain, thought it best for her sons not to see their father like that, refusing to let her teenage boys attend his funeral to protect them. They never got to say goodbye, but it would have only been symbolic anyway because the dead cannot hear. Their father would promise them that they'd stay with him one day, and it was something Gray secretly wished for, while at the same time not wanting to hurt his mother's feelings. This was in the time before Father got heavy into drugs. Life pushed him to them, and everything just seemed to attack him at once, so he opted for an early exit. With the loss of his father as an anchor, as an example, Gray rapidly began sliding downhill himself, resenting his mother in the part she played in limiting his exposure to his father and equating his own manhood with his lessening obedience. When Gray was expelled from school, his corner said, "Ok. We're way behind on the cards, but you can still win this with a knockout." Upon going to prison, he still needed that knockout, and now, upon returning from prison, he is still looking for it.

The weather is nice, so the locals are out. Gray lets his grimace fall away, relaxing his jaw muscles and up nodding at those he passes. It's good to be out and unwatched. The desire to be hard drops, the colored shell begins to crack and fall away to reveal the sweetness of his particular shade of chocolate. He smiles. The sun is shining upon him, he is shining back, and he walks upon the air. It's his first time in an open space in six years. He can walk in any direction he chooses. He can even run if he wants, or do cartwheels, and no authority can question him because of it. The eyebrows of those watching will surely question if he assumes a sprint or starts turning flips, because it's just not what adults do, but he can if he chooses. Only thieves and children run in the hood. Children are often sheltered enough from the reality they face to find enjoyment, and some still feel free, some. This is the freest Gray's felt since leaving the pen, and since being a very young child, enamored by the world around him and loved for his long lashes and eyes the shade of ashes. The openness of the streets and people without direct agendas and the deepest of social scars is liberating. Harmony has revealed itself to be just a different kind of prison. It's run under warden Will, a different kind of warden, who's made the threat of the return to behind bars and the paranoia of everyone, one against another, his bars. Harmony is the small prison in the middle of Cottonwood, one of the ghettos of the east side.

The children play, unmindful that they're neighbors with

child molesters, child abusers, sex offenders, thieves, drug dealers, and murderers. The adults know, but still most wave and speak, resulting from a mix of genuine kindness and a little bit of fear. They are not much higher than felons on the social scale; many are probably felons themselves, and their kids, future felons, so they are markedly less pompous and more human in their interactions with the likes of Gray. A third of Black men, statistically, will see the inside a jail or prison cell, compared to one in six Hispanics, and one in seventeen White men, so when three Black children play innocently in a park, all should cherish their innocence and each other because one is scheduled to lose both. Gray lost his friends, his innocence, and the ability to even appear that he had not with the label *felon* following him like the reaper for the rest of his days, and to think some will get a teardrop tattooed upon their face to announce that they've done prison time. It's nothing Gray intends to broadcast, even if the places he'll most likely be allowed to live will be full of those with the same distinction. He feels insecure that his standard issue, newly released convict clothing will give him away, his sweats, his t-shirt, and his canvass shoes, but he's presently left without an option of wearing anything but. Still the people wave, and still the kids play; it is a good day.

The ghetto is a hotbed of crime and a hotbed of criminalization. It's by design. Discrimination and unfair housing practices got them there, and discrimination and biased law enforcement keeps them there like the latches along the lips of a pressure cooker. These people, stuck in a way, are underpaid, yet they have to pay more for properties and services, like with realtor blockbusting. They do less crime, yet they serve more time, like the nineteen eighty-six Anti-Drug Abuse Act making being caught with *five* grams of crack, a Black drug, a five year minimum sentence, and comparably, being caught with *five hundred* grams of cocaine, a White drug, a five year minimum, when it's basically the same drug. The nineties delivered more of the same with Violent Crime Control and Law Enforcement Act making it easier to get in and stay in prison and more difficult to get out; prison populations rose by sixty percent by the end of the Clinton presidency, filled by the residents of communities like Cottonwood. The heat and the pressure these beautiful people face daily from the contradiction in the freedom narrative and the hypocrisy of the American value system make it difficult for those who do not understand their conditions to recognize their beauty, and that they have been *made* ugly, while others, many understanding their impossible struggle, just refuse to recognize their beauty.

Gray recognizes their beauty like he recognizes his own in expressed vanity. He still has a ways to go before he respects it in others like he respects it in himself, through no fault of his own. Gray has been properly programmed. He is exactly who he was designed to be by the external pressures, the manipulating forces pushing against him, shaping him, his entire life. He's factory fresh and stamped, *Made in the USA.* Event after negative event, act as resistance, shaping the putty of his mind until it rocks up like his arms and chest after years of his lights out work out. The brain is the strongest muscle in the human body, and most dangerous when flexed. Gray is trained as well as Will is, but he's an X factor because he's not nearly as disciplined. He has no code and honors nothing above himself. His is not a story of adaptation and ingenuity, but one of streamlined process and design, like most in and from the ghetto but for some the conditioning takes better. They have been created to serve a purpose to no benefit of their own, responsive to the instructive tugs and pulls, yet oblivious to the strings.

Is the joke on the puppet or the puppet master when the puppet stands and proclaims that he's a real boy, a real man, or a real nigga? Is the joke on the puppets or the puppet masters when the puppets erupt, destroying properties and each other in demand that they are real, actual, flesh and blood humans that deserve the same respect as the puppet masters? How dare they act like what they have been conditioned and string-trained to? How dare Gray walk around armed, as a bomb unaware, awaiting his signal to detonate? How dare these people, ungrateful with all of their eruptions? Twenty-teens America looks like the nineteen-sixties, with the police aggression again being the spark. Whomever the joke is on, it is indeed a joke when puppets pretend to not know their composition, all while fully aware of their place. They know what stage to protest or riot upon, as if the locations were sanctioned, marked off, like cancer clusters. The programming is strong. The strings are tight. They know their place.

Knowing their place isn't the problem. They are well aware of it, humbled by it, even when they don't accept it. The problem is misunderstanding its permanence. The ghetto inhabitants think it's only temporary, a stage they must pass through before they become great because a popularized handful has accomplished this before them. They all believe they'll be rich and famous. This belief is being reinforced daily, as they are propagandized to by family, friends, teachers, preachers, and popular entertainment, all making them confident in their potential. This message is not harmless; it removes their collective identity, their connection with God, actual, and their power. This dissociation with the ghetto, those within it feeling beyond it, is one of its biggest issues, because the residents cannot care for what they do not truly identify with. The poor man who aspires to be rich will not waste time concerning himself with the struggles of the poor and the worry of removing them for the collective. He's just passing through. He'll never identify with the collective struggle of the poor and assist in the fight. Just as Gray was telling Ervin not to identify with being in prison, many in the hood view their station as temporary, not a part of who they are, so they neglect fighting back against the enemies who conversely see them exactly as the identity they refuse, and use it against them. Even Gray believes there is a chance he can salvage his life because he can talk just about talk any woman out of her panties, he fears no man, and he's clever and quick witted, as if many with that formula are not destitute, depressed, and still trapped in the hood. At least Gray takes ownership of the streets, seeing his eventual success through them and not away from them. None are more street than he. It's honed his craft and his craftiness, and he wears it in his strut and his smirk, redemptive, and where many have failed, he's confident he can make the hood work.

Gray was trained to believe he could win, instead of trained to win. The trainers weren't even winners themselves, so they were ill equipped to impart such knowledge. They still spoke in inspirational tones. What loving adult is going to give it to them straight? Who's going to tell them that, *You can be whatever you want to be*, is a sick, twisted lie that works better as a punch-line to a joke than encouraging advice? So, their guides lie to them to keep them in love with life, a love that fades, immediately for some, and never for others. They lie to them because they love them and they figure, *What hurt can it cause to make them think things in the world work by desire and passion?* There are consequences to the lies. They damage the collective identity, and collective identity is God, and those without it will never witness God's power; it's harnessed through religious and political associations and able to be molded by he or she that controls it. Being absent of a self-serving collective identity makes them all easier to manipulate by those who deal with them as a collective as they try to behave as individuals above or apart from the collective. If one does not identify himself to a struggle beyond himself, he is no help to anyone but himself, and conversely, no one else can be help to him, defined through the same framework, and he, himself, is not strong enough to improve his condition, no matter how much he's been taught to believe it, mostly because he is constantly challenged by other collectives, not individuals. Those without grounding in a collective consciousness are easier to manipulate, single out, and destroy. The people in the hood do not identify with anything but rugged individualism. They are just as soon to hurt one another, as they will anyone else, becoming enemies to themselves, along with being enemies to everyone outside of the ghetto. The conditions they must agree upon, in this challenge of theirs, make succeeding nearly impossible.

Nearly impossible, yet possible, or else Will would be wasting his time. He has binders full of lessons for those like Gray, and he's mapped out strategy sessions, Legion specific, telling them not only who or what they are against, but who they are. Those who could see themselves without seeing the collective, the poor and disenfranchised, were defective, and they needed the most work. Will would have them in field operations teaching them battle strategy, while staying in their ear for the most important part of the training, which was collective identification, to which Tuck became a master. They had to know who they were before they could know who or what they were fighting, so Will had the task of reeducating the miseducated, taught to hate their people, their places, their behaviors, which is only a clever and indirect way to teach them to hate themselves and keep them unstable. They had to relearn who they were, culturally, racially, but for the most part and Will's emphasis, classically, so it is this he taught.

The hood is a pool of the lowest class of workers on the legal side and the illegal. It is the bottom rung on the social ladder, with the exception of felons. It's a plantation for the future prisoners of America, a containment zone, and a place for the untouchables. It's more accidental to not end up in a low wage depressing job or serving a prison sentence, than it is to be successful by capitalist standards. The life that's advertised is never the life received once they get their order, an identical occurrence happens millions of times a day at fast food restaurants. They have been fooled by the menu picture or the TV commercial, but their actual meal looks and tastes like shit. Many aimed for the stars and didn't even make it off of the block but the thirty-six or so inches of their vertical jump – NBA hopefuls. It is not a painless failure. The hood environment does a number to the self-esteem, and those with unfulfilled dreams, most, degenerate to both predators and prey – capitalism in the extreme. The rhetoric says that an incentive-based economic system that rewards hard work will create initiative and create a drive for innovation and progress. None work harder than the poor. The reality of the competition is not people pushing ahead and outdoing one another, advancing society, but instead a perverted struggle where the competency of the majority is subverted in favor of creating privilege and entitlement for a few. It's a foot race full of cripples, and society celebrates the healthy, White male who finishes first and calls it the result of hard work and dedication, maybe even invoking God's favor as a reason. The lower one falls on the social scale, the more their position is cemented as who and what they are. The poor, the disenfranchised, the felons, the minorities, the Blacks, like Gray, are all prey, refusing to recognize the hungry eyes in the bushes and the glint of society's teeth. When one truly recognizes his or her circumstance though, from prey to predator can be a small adjustment. This is where Will's interests lie, because he, too, is a product of the ghetto.

For the privileged class, the game is as easy as shooting fish in a barrel. The ghetto is the barrel and the people are the fish, or some would call them crabs to borrow the popularized nature of the crustacean while neglecting to recognize that a barrel is not their natural habitat. The game is easy for the elites for the arguments often mentioned, things like poor schooling, the preschool to prison pipeline, racism, lack of nutrition in a food desert, low wages, high crime, overaggressive policing and harassment, which all have an effect on rate of success, but rarely are things like redlining, generational wealth, discriminatory government programs, and prejudiced banks mentioned. These are also pieces of the capitalist puzzle. They control one's ability to move vertically within the system through wealth generation. Wealth has a myriad of advantages that the poor cannot access, like not paying late fees or worrying about interest on loans they do not need, or cheaper prices for the ability to buy immediately or items in bulk, to name a few, or even buying a politician.

Land appreciates in value, most resources are found within or upon land, and entire segments of the population were kept from owning land while others were given it freely by government to encourage settlement. Cottonwood, like most ghetto communities, is full of those excluded from programs such as Headrights – a seventeenth century program that gave White males from England fifty to one hundred acres of land and the tool to work it, The Homestead Act – a nineteenth century program that gave away over two hundred and forty million acres of land, and the Federal Housing Administration and Veteran Affairs loans – twentieth century low interest loan programs that were, for a time, offered exclusively to Whites. Generational wealth begins there, and the beneficiaries and their descendents, since capital can be passed down, are the main arguers for small government and that the poor should pick themselves up through hard work as if that's what they did.

Capital can be collected and passed along to offspring, so what happened yesterday matters today and tomorrow. The residents of Cottonwood are descendents of those who were not afforded opportunities such as free land. They are still expected to compete on the same level as those who were, and labeled as lazy and dumb when they cannot. The enslaved were labeled as lazy and dumb also, while doing nearly all of the labor. Without any of this *government assistance,* much more assisting than food stamps and public housing like the projects, the Dixons and the Buntings are expected to prevail in a competition based on wealth accumulation, without any wealth, and the added inconvenience of the other hurdles people of color face. Alongside systematic discrimination, there is also individual discrimination. The land and the business owners have the choice of who to hire, who to sell to, and who to buy from, and Blacks often make the *Do Not* list. Being Black has never been easy in America. Through no choice of those born with this affliction, an extra set of tests rests between them and ideal success, and these tests have kept them at the bottom for centuries as the most resilient underclass. The only group with less opportunity is the felons, and at least they have some choice in the matter. No one is born a felon, but where one is born, the color of their skin, and the quality of their schooling does grant access to the state of the art preschool to prison pipeline, along with foster care and mental illness, all conditions ripe in the hood. Then there are the thousands like Gray, both Black and felons, hoping to somehow make something of these disadvantages, wanting to build something besides mounting frustration, set to blow, and people in place like Will trying to assist them.

The game of Monopoly started before a majority of the players were able to sit down. The board was set for a privileged few, with rules written for them to maintain their advantage. When the others were finally invited to the table, the properties were already owned, and they found out the banker was an asshole. A game of Monopoly to those who own nothing is only about taking chances, collecting debt, and trying to avoid jail; there is no better description of life in the ghetto. When the enslaved Africans were freed, there was no sufficient attempt to place them on an even keel with their former masters – forty acres and mule went unrealized because the state emphasized wage labor instead of land ownership for Blacks, conveniently. The only reparations that were passed out were to the White slave owners for their loss of property. With no ownership and only skills, the former slaves were forced to go back to work for those same masters, the landowners, often for less pay than they received as free laborers, once overpaying for lodging and food is taken into consideration. If equality was the goal of emancipation, it would have been handled differently. Slavery, instead, just took a new shape. Wage slavery works on similar principles, but the labor is rented instead of owned. Powerless people who own nothing can only be liberated through their labor, which isn't much liberation at all depending on the rules of the game.

It is not about labor, but the level of compensation for labor. The basis of capitalism, the capitalist incentive, is surplus value, which is the added value retained over the wages paid. An extreme example is slavery, extreme in its degree of dehumanization, and also extreme in the ratio of labor versus pay. Slavery is unpaid labor, but a portion of the labor is always unpaid to the laborer in capitalism with a percentage retained by the owner. Harmony takes sixty percent of the resident's paychecks, and the residents are already getting screwed by their employer and only receiving a fraction of the value of their labor, so they are only allowed to keep a little bit of a little bit of the total value their labor creates. For example, they may be getting paid for performing a fifty-dollar an hour service, getting paid ten dollars an hour to do it after the owner's cut, and making four dollars an hour in compensation after Harmony's cut. Making four dollars in compensation out of every fifty dollars of labor is still better than third world or prison wages, but the point is not to make a comparison, but to challenge the principle of surplus value in itself as wrong. If it's wrong at one hundred percent of value kept by the owner, slavery, at what percentage is it not wrong? Is not ten percent still wrong? If one were to throw the phrase *surplus value* around in a conversation with Gray, he'd have no idea what they were talking about, but he actually knows more about it than most through practice.

Surplus value is also the basis of hustling, but it's just called *getting over*. Hustling is capitalism in its purest state, with every transaction about someone gaining and someone losing, or *getting fucked* - literally, if it's the pimping and prostitution hustle. The hustler is the shining example of the application of capitalist principles, yet most will turn their noses up at Gray, tell him to get a *real* job, meaning one where he's getting fucked and not the fucker. He'll pass on that surely, as he always has. He's never had a nine to five, not even at a supermarket. Gray has been pointed the right direction his entire life, and refused it because there was no reward in it. He didn't buy the line about there being a reward in hard work and perseverance upon the offered path. There were two many examples right there in his community of squares who did everything by the book and had nothing to show for it but gray hairs and the respect of future squares. His father was one. The hustlers didn't respect them. They were wastes of life and the reason the hustlers existed, from the example of what not to become and from their patronage. The squares were the customers, with their steady jobs and miserable lives, crushed when the hustler ends up fucking their wives. They did it all correct though, and most could not make it out of the hood. They were harassed as badly by the cops as the criminal elements because, in the hood, everyone is guilty and it's just a question of when they get caught. There was no reward in that, so Gray opted out of the safe road and would rather risk death or prison to live like the hustlers lived. They were loved and respected in a land of no love and respect. The same lack of love and respect caused the questionable death of his favorite square, his father, who most have settled upon what Gray continues to challenge, that he committed suicide. It was his gun, his fingerprints, and his terrible life, but Gray refuses to accept that his father would leave him, even ignoring the example he'd set with leaving his mother, or being left by, no one really knows which.

Gray was loved. Gray was hated. The women were the drug that dragged him away from the proper path, but he did not go kicking and screaming. Their inviting caresses were guides along a trail he'd wanted to travel anyway. His cold stare, symmetrical features, and his words, few but confident, just assisted them in assisting him. The more he veered, the more he was revered, so there was no changing him from the direction he steered. He was already viewed as the bad guy before prison. His blood relatives, Mom and big brother, thought him a waste of so much potential, while Gray saw the waste would be becoming as them, hard workers with little to show for it, along with the stress of trying to stay straight and raise a family that crushed his father. As irony has it, as he walks these streets only owning the clothes on his back, he, too, has little to show for the work he's put in. Even when he returns home, or if, he'll have nothing because the streets don't give one the ability to start back from where they left off. Whoever his snitch was is still there anyway, and there would be no reason for his old contacts to trust him any longer now that the police know him. A felon can be picked up by the police at any time just because they are a felon, and they are always watched because they haven't many options besides resuming a life of crime.

The industrialist is worshipped for his ability to generate profit, move pieces around, making and breaking deals, screwing others over, often ruining the lives of tens of thousands, but the low class hustler, such as a pimp or a drug dealer, is despised for doing the same, who'd be hard pressed to even ruin the lives of one hundred, most of whose lives were already ruined and chose to play the game of chance. Pimps, drug dealers, and other salesman are disgusting individuals for how they use and abuse people, but no, not the business leader. The reality is that not only are they identical and just at different levels of influence, they also work hand in hand because most of those destroyed by legal and acceptable forms capitalism, end up in the gallows and in the desperation of the capitalist underworld. Society breaks them first. They fall once they find out they can't fly. The greater system destroys the self-esteem and feeds its victims to people like Gray, who are also creations of the system, who have the charisma to take them deeper and further take advantage of them, all while unconscious of being taken themselves. It's the American way. All are victims except those at the very top; Gray walks the blocks feeling freer than he has almost ever with countless strings attached to him along with his leash.

Those outside, accenting his walk, are all different shades of brown, the darker shades, Blacks, and the lighter shades different mixes including Hispanics, or Mexicans specifically. Poor Whites avoid the ghetto, programmed to think they are better than it, preferring the trailer parks and White ghettos that aren't called ghettos because they aren't Black. The ones who stay in the accepted ghettos are often drug addicts or in love. Many a White woman has rode into the ghetto upon a Black man's… hips, disowned by family, rejected by friends, never finding their way back out. The entry is much easier than the exit, like the roach motel. It is home of the rude awakening. The American dream is not really for these people. It's fine for them to believe that it is; in fact, it's encouraged. It's a pacification as strong as church. Gray walked past at least ten churches en route to the library. One intersection had three and the fourth corner had a liquor store. He also walked past several slowly patrolling police cars, one of which had a driver with a staring problem, who Gray just ignored. They, the people, know nothing about how the system of their involvement works, neither does Gray, and they collectively blame their failures upon themselves when it is not really failure but a well executed plan.

Gray has walked these blocks before, although it is his first time in this city. Every ghetto is basically the same, plantations for the new slaves, laborers for the elite class, and the place where people either fall completely apart or the adversity chisels them into Gods. Gray isn't the falling apart type. Gray has fallen, not apart, but from his original place of worship as one able to create something out of nothing and life out of death. They've tried to break him. Forces have been trying to break them, these people, for centuries, and while most are less than favorable, mentally, and drones for the establishment, others have derived power from the powerless and thrived in a circumstance meant to ruin them. The falling hammer that collapses many just rattles some and sharpens their edges, and if they are made conscious of their divinity, they're dangerous. Should something or someone make the unconscious conscious, the sleeping giant awakens. They have much more power than they realize. Gods, they are. One cannot become hard without hardship. Liberators are forged in the flames of their oppression. The slaver trains his slayer, protected only by a thinning layer of fear and prayer. The poor, these residents have constantly been preparing for war, unconsciously, just through the mental and physical training of their condition. Conversely, the elites have been growing softer through lack of labor and loss of touch with the rest of humanity, as engagement with them has become a luxury. The poor have but to be made conscious and defeat the poor between them and the elites, like the police, or to win the gatekeepers over, including the many that are too old and too conservative to continue the fight.

Gray's pleasant walk concludes at the library. It is exactly where it was told it would be, on the corner of a side street of a major thoroughfare, for the size of the community, across the street from a carwash. The carwash is teaming with people, it is Saturday morning, and the library has the activity of an antique shop. The librarian is an antique herself, old, out of touch, and she holds a smile that promises to assist her balancing her shaking head. She's a Black woman, Civil Rights era, which is a proper excuse for how tired she appears to be. She greets Gray upon entry and asks if he wanted an open computer. It must be the popular thing. Gray looks over at the computers a moment, at the people sitting upon them, and politely declines. They are squares, unquestionably. Gray utilizes the men's room, mostly for the mirror, and exits the library to cross the street where the hustle is alive.

*   *   *

It took over an hour to calm Toni down, or rather over an hour of patiently listening to her and listening for her in the long spells in between her spells. She cast them in verse. They were extensions of her poetry, spoken words and body language. She spoke scripture, and wrote across the air with degradable strokes, delicate, insecurity-drawn, graphitic pictures about the shape of her, that resulted from the shape of the world. Each block of speech would blossom, swell in a physical push and shrink away, clearing the way for the next like they were but beats of her heart. Were she rehearsed, she could not have put on a better performance than speaking through the rawness of her pain, and placing it all before Will as if he'd caused it. The display placed Will in a state of paralysis as Toni purged and dictated to him from her little black leather bound bible without even removing it from the shelf. It was her diary, her journal, brought to life.

Will listened. He could only vandalize such a beautiful display of spirit, a connection he'd argue against the existence of, but without the use of her hands, she had clearly taken a hold of him. Whatever it was to be called, it could not be called material. Her tears were dry but she seethed with anger, and her outcry of emotion was proof for Will that she did in fact kill someone, and her *out of town* excuse was not a fabrication. She was too passionate to not have done something. If one is not truly prepared to take a life, the new folds it makes in one's mind are worse than being caught by the authorities. She needed this space to release, and she needed someone she respected to listen. Will didn't say another word. He could only make it worse at that point. Emotion was the conductor. He just listened, even when she stopped talking like some mystical presence would pick up where she left off. Will paced himself slowly, as not to disturb the moment, and began to make his presence productive as a gesture of good will. He crept around the bar, calmly pushing the chairs back beneath their tables while listening. He grabbed the broom and dustpan and began carefully sweeping the bar, paying particularly close attention to the broken shot glass, while listening. He cautiously picked up the remaining glasses on the tables from the night before, took them behind the bar and washed them, while listening. He took the rag from behind the bar, wiped it and all of the tables down, while listening.

Toni wasn't even quite thirty years old yet, and she'd experienced the pain of many people twice her age. Prison was her blessing, not that it was an experience she enjoyed, but she'd surely be dead if it had not intervened as a space saver in her life. Toni is smart, but Toni is impressionable, and always has been. If Will had to diagnose the cause of her troubles, it would be her feelings of inadequacy stemming from her childhood. She had a mother who valued attention from men more than spending time with her daughter, and naturally, Toni watched and learned and felt that was what life was about. Value was never instilled within her beyond how she could make another feel, and what they conversely make her feel by telling her nice things and touching her in nice ways. She could not exist alone. Those that loved her, or those who told her they did had her on a string since thirteen years old, because of course, her mother never gave much of a damn about her. Every crime Toni committed, a pretty long list, but only caught for a few – she's smart, was at the request of some man in her life. She only knew getting used, and grew to appreciate it and define it as love, following directly in her mother's footsteps. Her experience with people, with men especially, caused her to build walls to protect herself from them, which were really walls to protect her from herself because she desired the attention, and she eventually left men alone altogether. They were too much for her and her desire to be dominated, to her own detriment. She hasn't let a man get as close to her as Will has in a decade, and that only happened because he convinced her that he had no interest in her body, but only her mind.

Those who loved her most, hurt her most, at least the conditioning that defined what love was for her. Love was pain. Love was an extension of the desires of the person that loves, and the tasks they require. Toni developed an emptiness inside of herself that only could be filled by the affection of others to make her feel as though she was worthwhile and belonged on the planet because of the failure of her mother. Her father failed too, but he wasn't around enough in her life to be mentioned. She was beautiful, intelligent, talented, and lacking self-awareness, which is really the source of her talent, as she developed the ability to gain the trust of others and draw them in to keep her from having to face the deficiencies in herself. The best artists are owners of the most decay, and Toni's decay is so bad she hates love, and matured to a state where she refused to acknowledge it or even think she was deserving of it, so those closest to her get hurt the most. Will knew his position. He's known her long enough and loves her enough to be the punching bag she requires. It is part of the rent he pays to share in her brilliance. It isn't her fault; she is just a victim of many victims, as many from the hood are. For Will, Toni is worth every bit of the required struggle of being next to her. With genius comes madness.

Toni requires a stabilizer, and Will is it, or she'll do ill advised things like going *out of town*, anything to prove her own worth to herself to try reduce gaining that definition from someone else, who'd only use her in return. As an expression of this desire, she'd covered herself in multiple tattoos, cut off her hair, and plays up her masculinity to avoid the trap that has hurt her most, a man's love, or supposed love. Still pretty, her body read nothing but hurt and pain, and she lashed out to the word in beautiful verse that once decoded tells of how much she is unloved and desires to be, and it has been that way since her mother first abandoned her for the supposed love of some man. Toni was saying this. Toni was speaking this in her spaces of speech, this pain of being alone and unwanted her entire existence, no matter what she has done for others, and even her latest task, going *out of town*, admittedly done for Will, the person she probably loves most, went unappreciated. She'd kill for him, and he'd find something wrong with it. Will understood the mistake in his reaction, but it was honest, and him catering to her psychosis would not aid her in getting beyond it, so if the sacrifice was that he had to be another in a long line of men that weren't worth much, misusing her gift or gifts, he'd just be that. Will did not agree with her decision, and he doesn't agree with her need to be accepted so, and he wishes she would just snap out of it. The worst of her pain is self-inflicted, and Will hates to see her suffer, but, patiently, he listened.

Toni stood in the pulpit and preached this sermon riddled with long pauses the entire time. She asked Will no questions. She just questioned him rhetorically as one questions life. She told him several times to stop cleaning the bar, but he ignored her. When the bar was clean, when her conscience was clean, and she hadn't much else to say, Will approached. Heavily guarded, Toni pinched her eyes, but Will ignored this too. He grabbed her, hugged her, and the way she stiffened it could have been classified as rape. Will embraced her until she softened, and after a moment, her essence returned, and she returned the embrace while digging her cheek into his chest. After over an hour of being mute, Will said, "We got work to do," released her from his clutch, turned and left. He needed a shower and a shave desperately. He'd just slept outside. He probably looked and smelled like a Neanderthal, possibly adding to the reason his hug was initially resisted.

Will was at the end of a couple of weeks from hell. Each new day added a new conflict and by the end he had not figured his way through any of it, and had only added upon his pile of work. He may not even have the capacity to answer the questions before him. He's considered such. He knows he has to step away from Legion, but at the same time he realizes how much he is needed to stop his people from being slaughtered. He wouldn't be able to live with himself if they are not prepared the best they can possibly be this late into this turn of events. They are not doomed. The police don't even know they exist, so the impending community lock down, which can be no more than one event away, with the kid in the truck being shot, then the police officer being shot setting the stage, will only mean less flexibility. As long as they have no lead, they cannot direct their aggression enough to be effective and their lack of direction with increased presence can even be used against them. These are the thoughts that wrestle within Will's mind, along with who can he now utilize, who can he now trust, and who he should trust no longer. He doesn't even know what to make of Toni and his relationship. Losing her, if he has, would be like cutting off his right hand. The stress of these increasingly complicating matters is too much for even the most calculating, coolest head. Will needs a high intensity release, and he knows just where to find her. He checks his wallet to see how much cash he has, starts his car, and departs.

The day is sunny, and there's a nice breeze, so many are out. The guys have taken out their toys, their weekend cars, the ladies have put on their most revealing outfits, and they meet at the same spot. Will slowly pulls off the street onto the lot and up into the only open stall. It's the eastside's most active carwash. There is a lot of activity there, legal and illegal, and it's avoided by those who don't know how to take care of themselves. Will can take care of himself, and he keeps his forty five year old, black beauty of a girlfriend with him should he need assistance. He's never had an issue at the carwash though; he always knows at least ten percent of those in there. Harmony is a popular place, a school many have come through, and a good number of graduates choose to not leave the city to stay away from the failure of their former lives. Will frequents car washes and barber shops because they are great places to read the pulse of the people, so even if not from Harmony, the people know him. As soon as Will pulls in a man with a hand full of rags and a spray bottle approaches.

"Mr. Will, what's up man? Want me to help you out?"

Will responds while stepping out of his car, "Hook me up or help me out? I know the difference now. Last time I thought I was getting a free wash, because all of the favors I've given you over the years, then you stuck your hand out when I was ready to leave."

"Aww man." The man sounds disappointed. Will laughs.

"Just messing with you, Ray. Yes. Help me out. Who been around here today?"

"Everybody been through. Still coming and going."

"Ladies?"

Ray pushes out a tough exhale. "Man. If I had your kind of money, wouldn't be these rags in my hand, with the kind of ass I seen advertising today."

"Alright." Will leans down into his driver side mirror to check if he looks presentable. He doesn't. He showered but he didn't shave. It's not a look he prefers, but it has its own allure. "Yeah, take care of me. I'm about to walk around a little bit and see what I can find." Will begins to walk off and stops. "Now, Ray. If I get a catch, I'm not trying to walk her back to no dirty car. I'm counting on you now."

Ray laughs. "Yessir. Don't worry 'bout that. I got you covered."

Will puts on his best cool act when he's around urban Blacks in a social atmosphere. He's cool-headed, but not actually cool, but it helps that he originated in the hood, so he does have a working understanding of what's going on. He just can't move within as seamlessly as Tuck or Gray can, especially Gray.

Gray entered the same parking lot thirty minutes prior, and he already has people calling him by his chosen name, and ladies calling him their new boyfriend in tease. For a man who doesn't say much, he knows just what to say. Gray sits upon the brick base of one of the vacuum units, teasing the strings on the front of a young lady's wind shorts, feeding her lines that make her movements the gestures of a twelve year old. She isn't even aware she's in public any longer, and if Gray pulled that shoestring knot right out, she'd just smile harder. The sunlight is hitting his eyes perfectly for someone watching, but they are slightly sensitive to light so he squints. As soon as Will walks out of the stall, he sees Gray. His attention was actually captured by the lady Gray is talking to, but he notices Gray as well. After a moment, Gray notices him back, and Will just stands there smiling. From the distance, Gray could not tell if he was taunting him or smiling in support. Gray doesn't make much of it, and he continues to do what he is doing so well. Will resumes walking around the lot, full of potential candidates, to see if he could be so lucky. He will deal with Gray and why he's there at another time, as he is presently trying to relieve stress, not add more.

2:5 *An idea whose time has come is powered by many components, pieces, simple machines, forced into position because they hadn't anywhere else they could retreat to. Machinery works on precision, every piece in its place and in its pace, or the mechanisms, dependent upon one another, will shut down the entire system. I have a job to do and I've been groomed to do it, and it has nothing to do with whether I want to or not. I have ways of making myself do what I won't. People can be those components, forced into the proper places that best utilize the talents their conditions have shaped and forced them to have, and people can be those components, forced out of those proper places, or both in concert. The idea whose time has come might be the destruction of one thing to create another.*

Sometimes it takes spending a little money to feel loved, and when the ratio of disgust versus appreciation reaches that bitter, swollen sap of a cherry tree, thickness, Will willingly cracks his wallet. None can completely ignore their environment, even masters of meditation. Separating oneself from ones environment is separation from the animating force of the motivated life itself. The unmotivated life is not nearly as sharp and responsive, only challenged by adversarial ideals instead of conditions. The challenges of ideas are fattening, and the challenge of conditions burn fat; who Will has become and who Gray or Tuck or the others still neck deep in the struggle to survive, are, is well defined in such a statement. One is better positioned, knowing and angling, but one is better conditioned, unknowing and training. They need each other. Nat Turner was a house slave, and his Will was a field slave. The bitters and sours make men appreciate the sweet and seek them out, like oppressors are the makers of freedom fighters. Comfort moves no one, and neither does near comfort, the station Will has climbed to which defines the convenience of his life. The predictability of his routine had been stripped, and he's been forced to bite down and chew on the lemon peels of the fruit he's sowed. It hurt his jaws and pinched his face until sweet was becoming a memory, to which he had a remedy.

He needed something sweet to taste, an antidote, and doting's the language his handsome spoke.

Will found a woman to role-play with him for a price he was willing to pay at the carwash. His roles are quite demanding, requiring more than just the proper plumbing; they need to know their lines. So, while the young actresses, with a face of a child of God and a body fresh out of the Devil's workshop, capture the eyes, Will has found their performance to be lacking once *action* is yelled. He values experience and the dramatic pauses of the seasoned actress, who not only knows her lines, but knows all of the accompanying body language, and can smoothly sail into improvisation when the flexing of Will's body calls for a plot twist. Still, the young ones capture his attention, and he cannot completely avoid the handiwork of both God and the Devil, the best of both worlds. He knows some have to be able to act, and for him to dismiss them all, in all of their beauty, in one definitive pass, would be discriminatory. It's very hard not to like them; his like of them makes *it* very hard - to which the dirty old man thinks, *Better to love you with, my dear*. What does a forty something year old man need with a twenty something year old woman beyond some kind of exploitation, from both sides of the exchange?

It's an adrenaline shot straight to the heart, and it breaks the paralysis from an overdose of the drug, common life, that builds a chemical dependency with the comfortable. Will blames his addiction to young ones, and the charm he needs to secure them on his grandfather. It is there when he desires to tap into it. He wears different hats, and the Harmony Will stays in his office and traveling those halls, because the hood closes itself to it like suspicious drug dealers to unfamiliar White men. His Boston, inner city, upbringing rises to the occasion to do what it can to give the women something to want. There is a cool to his corniness and twang when he concentrates it, plus he has money. Charm fills in where his looks make a soft sell, a charm generations deep that skipped his father, or maybe his father just didn't need it because he was tall and handsome and not on the compact and cute side like Will and Granddad. Dad is over six feet tall, imposing and rebellious, not clever and charming. Stature often helps determine what tools one is forced to hone. Dad didn't need charm as much, he was more like Gray, just imposing his aesthetic will upon women, so he didn't develop charm, but young Will, never growing like he'd wished to, often disturbed by the hardening reality that he wasn't going to be tall as each year passed, needed a counterbalance. He needed charm, the charm that lay dormant in the recesses of his mind, inactive until stimulated by the spark of necessity. Granddad called on his well into his seventies. Will has twin aunts that are half his age as a result of it. They were born when their mother was twenty-one and Will's grandfather, in his early seventies. That takes charm, because Granddad hadn't and hasn't a dime to his name to make up the fifty year age difference. It was charm, simply, that got that young one out of her panties.

That young one ended up breaking Granddad's heart though and hurting him pretty badly. No one is sure what he expected from her, being fifty years her senior. Maybe he thought that her having his babies meant something more than her having his babies. It hasn't meant, *We've started a family and we'll be together*, since back in his day, and the nerve of him to even consider it meaning that when his familial legacy is having more kids than anyone could keep up with along with abusing and leaving Grandma, his wife, with the ones he'd made with her. The deterioration of family values all over could have started with him. Well, not actually. Slave masters had been breaking apart families for centuries by the time Granddad came along, through forced separation, murder, and rape, and the she shame the memory of it all caused. Will's father recalled a family reunion as a child where he was sure, as clear as day, there were White people in attendance, but his grandfather refuses to confirm that he is of mixed blood because it's nothing he's proud of. No matter how light his skin, he refused to be identified as anything but Black, a ride in his race that many from his generation hold, knowing that the miscegenation was rarely a product of love. It was also the generation of reparation of what was so badly damaged, the Black family, and Granddad gave it a good shot.

He left North Carolina in the early fifty to find work up north and send for his wife, two children and one on the way, once employment was secured. By the time he was able to send for his family, they were four. His wife had delivered a third boy, which made two born in the calendar year nineteen-fifty, one in January and the other, Will's father, in December of that year. In their new home in New England, the couple would have five more accounted for children, and Granddad stayed around long enough to see his oldest sons enter high school. His oldest son, reaching manhood and the physical competence to defend his mother from his father's abuse, most likely had much to do with Granddad's final departure, because protect his mother is exactly what his son did. There were other kids concurrently being made alongside these eight; no one knows how many exactly, but the last two were twin girls seventy years younger than he, delivered from a woman bold enough to break the heartbreaker's heart, by not wanting to create a family with him. Charm can only get one so far. Will wasn't looking for a family with his charm anyway, and unlike his poor grandfather, Will has a little money.

This connection he desires has more to do with the physical expression of love and feeling adored than reaching climax, because in the latter case his hand would be sufficient. Many women, long legged and well proportioned, were cast as milking agents, pullers of his love, making him feel loved, in love, and a part of the universal interchange and currents of belonging. Will, because of his arrogance, because of his east coast conditioning, because of his intelligence, and because of his position at Harmony, receives a lot of negative attention. It is impossible to ignore it all. At his best, he just hides that other's treatment of him has an effect. Who he is is a character, and it serves a greater purpose that many aren't aware of. The charming version of himself is actually closer to the real Will than the strict and square version he portrays at Harmony. He's not the typical asshole because he enjoys creating discomfort in others; the greater good is always in his target. He needs to be a certain way to learn what he needs to know about the possible usefulness of these people society has discarded. Their treatment by society makes of them a composition tough and durable, which can be useful, but constant contact with the unloved can be chafing with the abrasiveness of their manner. After so much, Will is drained of the idea that he is doing good work and that there is any love left in the world allotted for him.

He buys that feeling, and he uses the money that would have otherwise been spent on the nuclear family he passed on having, that should have been filling that recess. Whether it is a prostitute or a woman willing to play a prostitute for a couple of hours or maybe overnight, depending upon the aperture he's willing to stretch his wallet to, he doesn't care. His care is that she makes him feel like their connection is a product of and the physical expression of the most aggressive love, and that the monetary exchange is just a formality. He talks a lot, he touches a lot, he kisses a lot, long before he ever decides to moisten his fingertips and stir inside her and remove his briefs. It's too sensual to be sex for hire. Will desires something more, and it is a complicated thing. He chose not to start a family so he wouldn't be tied down by a family like his father was. Will didn't see any advantage in bringing more Black people into a world that hated them, and he feared that kind of commitment being aware of his growing desire to sacrifice himself to the liberation of his people. He married the struggle. He is one of the few that bought that lie wholeheartedly, and now with his world crumbling, and his struggle losing integrity, he is compelled to buy pussy that whispers into his ears the things that only a loving wife could and mean it.

His time in the military made it easy for him to start viewing women as objects. It's not an accomplishment he's proud of. He respects women beyond what's between their legs and the capacity most have to create interplay between reason, emotion, and intuition. He's met more intelligent women that have made life long impressions upon him than he has men, so the sexual object thing is not a reduction of their intellectual capacity, but more so a reduction of his. He doesn't need them for more, although many have more they can offer. It's difficult to offer something to someone not accepting it; he'd only one cylindrical hole he wanted to fill so all of the other shapes spaces they tried to offer his person were kindly rejected. The shape he'd a vacancy for defined his revolution, not his love life. When Will talks money up front, he usually has less trouble shaking them and feeling like a horrible human being for not wanting to see them two hours out of a day, possibly twice a week, and talk to them nightly. Ironically, his big head ran the show, and it's where he likes to keep the priority of his blood rushing. Maybe achieving an assisted orgasm was just too easy for him to desire to have one in house, or maybe he just hadn't met the right woman. Women often told him that he hadn't yet met the right woman and that was his problem, insinuating that they were in fact her, and he imagines that they felt pretty funny once he stopped calling them as well.

With every deployment, he was leaving a lady or ladies behind with the intention of finding another. He's slept wit multiple women of every hue, size, shape, and many couldn't speak more than ten English phrases. That is how base sexual intercourse became to him, as he traveled the world in the name of imperialism. He was desensitized and this conditioning changed his chemical composition, making him desire to have a life partner, someone to share himself and grow old with, about as long as it takes to reach an orgasm each time the desire returns. Will has never been a deep feeling man anyway. The love feeling was fleeting, and for him to stay in it longer than a commercial break, he felt like he was catching the Holy Ghost or speaking in tongues, both quite orgasmic in behavior, ironically, and like he was doing it to please the other parishioners and not God.

Many reach strongly for a love that Will isn't convinced exists. He is sure that it is just a product of cultural classical conditioning. They don't want to appear failures in life and approach death alone, but they will arrive at death alone regardless. Maybe Will's loss of the fear of death impacts his love life. One can't really live until he's accepted his death, and Will has accepted his own many times over. If he had not, there definitely wouldn't be a Legion. The existence of the organization is an expression of his suicide, the sacrifice of his personal life, as it lives off of his blood, and the intravenous connection is bound to kill him. It has already killed the kids and the wife he would have or should have had and his chance at a normal life. The killing him process, as he's been recently informed, has moved into escalation.

Will put his thoughts and energy into killing something else, with measured strokes, in single-serve simulated romance. Maybe she's good for more than a single. He won't send her on her way without getting her phone number. She performed well enough, smelled and tasted clean enough, and they fit together. It doesn't take an engineering degree to know what works and what doesn't, and she, Erica's her name, works. She actually approached Will with a joke containing a punch-line that inferred that he was out of his element. "You look lost, old man," is how she put it before breaking into a small laugh. Will was twice the age of most of the people gathered at the carwash, including her, with the exception of the drug addicts, and he was also twice the sophistication. It was a fair observation by Erica. It wasn't an honest taunt because she didn't say it then continue on her way. She, instead, waited for Will to respond, and respond he did.

"No. I'm not lost. I'm getting my car washed. I figure a carwash is a good place to get that done. But umm, if you're not getting your car washed..." Will, clearly noticed she was without car in her approach, when she broke away from a group of friends, "or washing a car, maybe it's you that's lost... young lady." She smiled and the ice was mutually broken, and from there he had only to get her to his car through the expected three or so *nos*, stop to pick up something to eat, and go back to his place. It worked exactly as planned. She had to say *no* to not look like a hoe. Modesty must be projected at least a little because it adds to the attraction. The man must feel like a hunter, and a woman his prey. If it's too easy, the man is left questioning why he should even want it, so although Erica said she wasn't a pro, a prostitute, she knew something about the hustle on how to keep a guy engaged and drive up the price. Her apprehension was laced in pretension the entire engagement though. Her sensuality, if it was all an act, was A list quality, and it even had Will feeling in love for that tiny moment between the beginning of intimacy and orgasm. She wasn't old enough, exposed enough to carry a heavy conversation, but Will forced her to talk as part of his fee while he prodded and listened. She could teach him plenty just by talking about what she knew. Her story was the typical, down on her luck, urban narrative, but with the more she opened up the less Will felt like some dirty old man out to take advantage of a helpless young woman. He didn't rush. They sat upon his bed eating fajitas and drinking the spirits upon his bar in his empty room. He was so attentive in the moments building up, when he finally leaned into her slightly quivering lips, it was as if she'd been pulling him.

Young Erica was a welcomed distraction of Latin and African persuasion. She helped him get the sleep he needed, and as a bonus she also helped him awaken, but still she was only a distraction. Sunday morning finds him back upon the subject needing his desperate attention, Legion. So the way Will sees it, through what he'd taken from his talk with Toni, his talk with Tuck, and the general feel with the talks at The Hall, a small contingency has decided it is time to move into escalation and that Will has basically outlived his usefulness. This decision was made before the meeting at The Hall, because Toni was prepared to speak on it at The Hall, directly after returning back from *out of town*, where she had no contact with other local members. This has been in motion at least for weeks and possibly months, this plan of moving into escalation without him, but out of respect for him, they are either moving in secret, like with the wounded officer, or waiting for his clearance, which was basically what the meeting at The Hall was, a ceremonial passing of the torch to the younger, more aggressive talent.

Will has put more organized thought into this than the entire collective outside of himself. It is his blueprint, and he knows that the structure is incomplete; the shape of it isn't right yet, but his struggle to properly articulate it in a system with little to no control has made others lose faith in his planning ability and has instead made him look like an incompetent coward. The numbers are available, and if they are judging him as stalling because of the numbers, he could understand their argument. The numbers are sufficient, quantity is fine to destabilize the local power structure, but quality is not. Another piece is missing, and Will viewed it as sort of a counterbalance, an anti-Will so to speak, with a use both internally, for the Legion, and externally, for social impact. In the classic game of good cop, bad cop, Will projected his qualities as most efficient, so naturally, he'd appear the good cop, because of his education, calm demeanor, and his culture, but the reality would be bad cop, worse cop; he only needed a bad cop.

Tuck evokes the proper amount of fear. He has all of the thug qualities that the average person is revolted by and afraid of. He's arrogant, loud, obnoxious, uncouth, and disrespectful, all while claiming to be aware of a greater good and grounded in the greatness of the ancestors. He means well, but his execution is sloppy, often making more noise than he is able to back up. He is just not intelligent enough for the job, and Toni is wrong in thinking they could move on with him as one of the recognizable faces of the movement. He can attract the streets; he doesn't intimidate them with his commonness, but as easily as he's read in his comforting of others, he is also potentially read with the same ease by enemies of the cause. There's that and Tuck cannot recruit the professional class, those with skills and money, necessary tools for any movement. He turns them away as quickly as he turns away White people. He is not the man for the job, if it even requires a man. Tuck is more dangerous than helpful, and he's too damned excited about the prospect of physical a engagement, showing he has not studied and has no idea what the Legion is up against. Will's convinced that an undying faith in God causes such foolish behavior and fault filled projections. Tuck would be better as decoy. He would be marvelous as a decoy, especially if he has no clue he is being used as one, but Will has to do some heavy planning to make that possible, while continuing the search for the person they need, and hoping time is on his side.

A car horn honks twice and breaks Will away from his thought-induced trance. He turns and looks at his guest, now in his living room having coffee, and smiles. She returns a naked smile. There is a sweet innocence about her, especially with no makeup. She'd showered and cleaned herself up, Will even has extra toothbrushes for company, and with her hair still moist she looks like she lives there. Tenuous and unassuming, and young for her age, she could've been somebody had she not fallen through the massive cracks in society that she was designed to fall though, and she probably still can be with either lots of luck or a complete social overhaul. Will is working on that. Being pretty and young is all she has going for herself, and she has to race against father time to try to secure something of value with those things before they fade. She grabs her clutch purse and rises. Will follows, while standing he unties and reties his bathrobe for a more snug fit. Erica, in a fleeting moment, probably thought something else when he first untied and briefly exposed himself and his paper-like boxers, worn slightly high upon his waist, in the vertical seam. He reties, follows her to the door, reaches into his pocket and hands her a tightly rolled wad of money for her services and the cab ride back to the eastside. The departure is always the most unpleasant part for both parties, as the chariot becomes a pumpkin, the gallant equestrians become mice, the gown into rags, and the princess into a struggling maid, overworked and down on her luck. Will escorts her out of the door, stopping at the threshold with one foot upon the porch. Unexpectedly, Erica turns, kisses him like a fairytale, cascading glitter and all, and walks out of their happily ever after.

Will watches the taxi pull out of his driveway then returns to his cup of coffee, hoping it will reactivate his buzz from the night before. It was the perfect insulation, along with her soft body parts from the impact of his tough decisions. Will's crisis is as simple to solve as buying a plane ticket, or packing some belongings into the back seat of his car and heading back to the east coast before things around him explode. It is a thought that has crossed his mind, in a, *my way, or the highway,* fashion, literally. He isn't at Harmony for the money. The money isn't much. He is retired military, twenty years in; he can live off of that money easily without needing to dip into his savings, which is six figures. He's been frugal all of his life, and soldiers do nothing but save money when deployed. Money is not a problem for Will. From where he came from, he is successful. Any stint in the military without losing your mind, mentally, or having it blown out of your skull, is success. He sold his soul to the Devil and the Devil has allowed him enough to be comfortable for the rest of his days. Comfort is alluring. His team doing whatever they feel is necessary is not comfortable. Will can do without police kicking in his door, or worse, opening fire through his door because of his involvement in an insurrection that he has not even planned. Yes, Erica's soft, sweet smelling body, along with the liquor was insulation.

If his coffee can't reactivate his buzz, he'll have to remedy the clearness in his head with something sure to cloud it. His mind is telling him to run. He's in over his head. He'll have the threat of death from both sides waiting for the slightest slip or buckle along this tightrope to an envisioned liberation. Freedom fighting is feeling like cage fighting because he knows too much to relax and allow the situation to develop without him. It will be sabotage, or seen as. He's in it for life like an idiot teenage gangbanger allowing his peers to beat the hell out of him for the privilege to never again be able to define himself away from those who gladly made him bleed. It is an awkward love. Like always, Toni is in the middle, arms stretched doing her best to pull both sides together. She wants what both sides want, she wants escalation, *and* she wants Will to lead the charge, while others would rather he just disappeared. Toni was informing him of his necessity, knowing the design called for no leader, but at the same time crowning him as the needed position that didn't exist. She was not only willing, she sacrificed her own innocence to prove her loyalty to the king, who had all along refused the crown because that was not the shape of things. Had Will not sacrificed enough? Does he have to sacrifice his life too? Must it be liberation or death, especially when he designed it specifically beyond such a decision? Will is still not ready to face the new set of circumstances and accept the role he is being pushed into, as he attempts to yank away, so he considers disappearing. Toni did it. He can do it too, just better. The new set of life distorting circumstances all matured within the last weeks. A couple of weeks prior, Will was fine besides the scheduled cookies he'd bake upon his face, but no real danger approached him. He was only uncomfortable from living in the predictability of the environment that he'd meticulously set up.

The Lord rested on the Sabbath. It's early Sunday, not the Sabbath, but some argue that Jesus' resurrection created a new covenant, some kind of worship audible, so Will can pretend and give himself one more day of rest, even though he believes none of that nonsense. It may be considered a knock on his discipline, but when Will feels overwhelmed, he often does nothing. Like a child, he hides from his problems rather than face them, and here he doesn't even know what to face first.

Direction has to be created without him telegraphing his intentions, and Will is at the moment trying to figure out how with the use of as few resources as possible. His play has to work without the conscious aid of Legion. He could plan, in confidence, as well, and he had to direct them away from being destroyed. Decades of active military duty showed him the ease it was to neutralize a static target. The example of this also exists on American soil, although omitted from the history books. Being seen and heard, while great for recruiting, is nothing but a homing device for those who aim the missiles. Superior power cannot be challenged directly, even in ideology, because it is the attaching of a target upon the challenger, a victim or victims will be created, the organization will be infiltrated to find out its vulnerabilities, the propaganda machine will demonize, and the police, local, national, or international will neutralize. This is the story of the Universal Negro Improvement Association, The Nation of Islam, The Black Panther Party, MOVE, and even communities like Oklahoma's Black Wall Street, anything with the expressed intention or that functioned as a means to garner power for the powerless without the consent of the government.

The Legion is fluid. Being static and able to be located is a death sentence, sometimes fast, other times slow, and the state will break its own laws to rub these threats out and punish no one when the illegal activities are exposed. Power doesn't apologize or negotiate with the powerless; it only responds to threats of equal or greater power or smaller threats that it cannot find to impose its will upon, therefore projecting themselves as comparably powerful. This is the design of Legion, an outfit to create chaos using guerilla strategy in an urban environment, not drawing a line in the sand and challenging power to a duel, which is clearly suicide. Tuck is suicidal, yelling *Black Power* at the TOM Center every week, talking about what little culture jelling, motivational, and mobilizational history he knows to rally his flock, only creating profiles for them to be, eventually, infiltrated, demonized, and destroyed. This is the main reason Will refuses to attend, and denies any connection to them. Besides, the program runs a lot like a high school pep rally and not a strategy session. They're just targets awaiting bullets, like the black silhouettes at the gun range.

It is also Will's opinion that Black Nationalism and Black capitalism have yet to prove themselves powerful, post segregation, which changed the dynamic of both. Capitalism doesn't change in essence when it becomes color-coded. Selective capitalism is still capitalism. The Black dollar can flip one hundred times within the Black community and still some in that community will be getting richer while others are getting poorer. The successes of the model communities were the existence of multiple producers and creators of products that even those outside the community desired causing the collective wealth of the community to build. That cannot happen intra-community with the same money turning over; it will never grow, but they can self sustain if that is the goal. If growth is the goal, a product must be produced that other communities desire, created by someone who is willing to stay in the community and build it, turning the profit into other producers of products drawing more money from other communities, so on and so forth. The only product the Black community has produced with that kind of potential is art, especially music, particularly hip-hop, as other races don't seem to buy anything else Black, but those artists disappear as soon as they get their first big check. That is the only way it would work, in theory, and the reason why it does not in practice, yet the *feel good* of it remains attractive. Attractiveness is not effectiveness, not necessarily. Will has once supported it and thought it through thoroughly. Capitalism has run into the extreme where sixty-seven people own as much wealth as the bottom three and a half billion people on the planet, while millions starve, die of curable diseases, have no shelter, or clean water, and there is nothing getting Black people to buy from Black people can do to change that or to stop the trend from growing worse. Profits are higher than ever, yet wages have been falling since the late seventies. The elites and their greed, pigs, are also destroying the habitability of the planet. It's class war, and it's too late to do anything but make the poor conscious enough and bold enough to take their share of resources back from the rich.

There isn't much use in having a bunch of like-minded individuals, sitting around agreeing with one another. Instead of walking around, wearing red, black, and green, they would be more effective with tattered clothing and tracks along their arms. The truest revolutionaries must be able to disappear and go undercover as well as the police. Will in his polo and khakis, will never be suspected, giving him a distinctive advantage to he or she who dresses in the traditional revolutionary garb and colors. Will knows their kind, and allies with them from afar when he can. They will prove valuable in misdirecting the authorities when tempers begin to flare. It's expected to come from them, with their tactless rants and irresponsible Internet postings. Tuck and the TOMS are the perfect diversion, should things reach that intensity. The cops, for example, would never suspect Will, and would probably seek out his advice to help control the natives. Will is a gatekeeper; his position at Harmony makes this apparent. His team, on the surface, is not the disenfranchised, and his bank account supports that statement. Who better to lead the questioners in the wrong direction, with his neat clothing, cropped hair, and well-spoken words? Infiltration can work from either side, yet liberation groups constantly get infiltrated and rarely infiltrate, as huge and as porous as the system is. The larger the organization or institution, the easier it is to infiltrate.

This is what The Legion was set up to do, have people in places, prepared, even while unaware, staying fluid and diverse, but Will is lost with how exactly to pull the pieces back together when they need to strike. Maybe that is what appeared to be stalling. It wasn't. It isn't. It just isn't finished. Now they've, in their impatience, pushed Will between a rock and a hard place, and they have him contemplating deserting this beautiful piece of clockwork that he's been instrumental in having work correctly, even without being a leader. This is what the watchmaker was up to, making sure all of the parts fit, and were ready for when the time would come. Parts were in place that did not even quite know their function, and the strained relationship Will has with these members are part of them playing their position correctly. If only they would be more patient. The watchmaker isn't stalling. It just isn't time yet. It just isn't time yet. There is another important piece, a spring that needs to be placed and engaged before the clock officially can begin ticking. Rome wasn't built in a day, but the wrong leadership in place can lock its gates and burn in down in about a day. Some have the potential to leave what has been so meticulously built, in ruins. Will, doing his best not to let such thoughts ruin his Sabbath, decides more drinking is in order, in his bedroom. He's greeted by his ringing phone.

"Hey Toni. Goodmorning. Feeling better?"

"Cut on the news." Toni sounds like stretched elastic, calmly vibrating but bound to snap if the stress pulls upon her too much more. "And morning to you too, dear."

"Which station?"

"Any of them, or hell check the front page on any Internet search engine. Can't miss it. It just happened again… They're fucking laughing at us."

*   *   *

To say the TOM center is underwhelming is an understatement. Once setting his eyes upon the layout, Gray could kick himself for accepting the invitation. Tuck didn't make it sound like what it looked like or sound like what it sounded like. It was a refresher in the rules of a hustler: *Someone is always making a sell. If not the initiator, the receiver can becomes the hustler by making the salesman buy something of little use, a lie.* Gray knew better, and he should've told Tuck that he didn't really believe in that Black stuff and that Black people were their own worst enemies. Not that Gray had an affinity for White people, Randy and his entire clan could fall off the face of the Earth and not inspire a single tear, but every enemy of his looked just like himself. Black is not nearly as beautiful as Black folks have tried to make it seem to him, and he should've just given it to Tuck straight. That would've worked. Gray would never say that in front of a White woman though. There is no need to throw his people under the bus in the company of others just because he had better things to do than go to this… church in blackface, his best description of it while sitting beneath a loosely erected vinyl tint, flapping with the day's wind. Gray hadn't fully defined it before completely dismissing it, but he was uncomfortable, sitting hot and sweaty and wishing he had transportation back to Harmony, or at least knew which direction to walk to get back, awaiting the sermon.

He should've said *no*, but he left it in the air while ignoring all of the other questions being fired his way, and once he saw Tuck there at Harmony, early this morning and not in his uniform, he could only think, *Damn*. Tuck offered to pick him up yesterday, and there he was. Their eyes met when Tuck entered the building, and Gray sat reading the day's paper in the lounge, on the surface, but he was honestly thinking about his next life move. Seeds were planted on his first day out, good seeds, at the carwash. In about two hours, he found himself becoming knowledgeable of the local who's who, and even rubbing shoulders amongst some. Also, *The best looking chick there was all on his dick*, is how he'd put it in explaining that she was showing him a lot of attention, if he had someone to explain it to. This occurrence, in turn, made everyone else, guys and girls, show him lots of attention. Who is the new guy, and look who's standing beside him? These planted seeds can grow into much more than a set of split thighs and some moans – which are on his mind as well. Thinking how to nourish this small plot of his was front and center, not Tuck and his Black stuff. After a pretty good Saturday, his Sunday began horribly. He should've *Just said no*, and treated Tuck and his solutions he'd soon propose to the Black problem centuries in the making like the escapist drug that it is. D.A.R.E. taught him better.

"'Sup my nigga? I see you. Ol' Gray… Just give me a sec and we can go. I gotta grab something right quick… Don't forget to sign out." How inconsiderate. Tuck didn't even think to ask if Gray was still planning to attend, a classic hustler maneuver: *Never give an out from a sell that's already been made*. Gray twisted his face at the idea that prison had both hardened him and softened him, because he clearly felt like the one being manipulated in this situation. At least women were promised to be in attendance; that was salve to his developing wound. It also would get him out of Harmony and away from so many who'd already collectively lost his trust. Gray was determined to make as many outside contacts as possible, so possibly, in this Tuck could assist. There was only one person in Harmony that he truly desired to see any more of, and with every hour he adds to his stay at Harmony, the more it seems like she is just a figment of his imagination. Sure, it had only been a couple of days, but these are twenty-four hour days with a pretty intimate group who share eating and recreation facilities with each other. He saw others enough to ID them, like Kenny, even ones he didn't want to, like Randy, and mostly saw them at least twice a day, but never her. Maybe she works, or maybe she graduated and wanted a little fun before doing so. There is little evidence that his dance partner even exists. If he'd open his mouth about it and ask about her it would help, but what happened had to have happened since he's been reprimanded for it and set up to a task that he's intentionally neglected. Besides her though, all of Harmony can go to hell, and if she's like the rest, she can go with them.

It was a short but uncomfortable trip. Metal folding chairs, the real reason Tuck was there at Harmony and was going to be there whether Gray agreed to attend or not, rattled in the bed of the truck across the pot holed roads the entire way. Also, Tuck is a talker. He is one of those types that can't let a space exist without vandalizing it with his verbal graffiti. He's uncomfortable in a space without speaking, while Gray is often uncomfortable in a space with it, two peas in a pod, or in an old raggedy short bed truck with chairs rattling in the back. There are no counseling sessions on the weekend, so Will allows Tuck to use the facility's chairs for his service. Tuck didn't need the chairs for extra seating; they were the seating. If not for Will's generosity, the concrete would be seating them in the vacant parking lot that used to connect to a strip mall they meet at, beneath a tent. Down the line of the sun, thousands of pieces of broken glass scatter across the lot and shine like reflecting waves across the ocean the sun walks upon at rise and set. The area where the tent was being set was barren, the result of the man sweeping it as Tuck's truck pulled in.

The location suffers from economic depression. There are no prescribable pills to assist this kind of depression. Locations die or money has to come back to rescue them like white blood cells or antibodies, and ironically, the money is often White. Businesses that can not turn a profit close, and buildings that can not host businesses that turn a profit get old and unstable, and are either burned down for insurance money, torn down, or they fall down. This is how parking lots with no buildings are created, especially in communities where Blacks are the majority. If not this way, the parking lot is built first and developers change their minds like in the area around The Fifth. Capitalism is extremely wasteful. Good buildings and good land go to waste instead of providing use for those who can use them yet not afford them. There are more vacant homes in the U.S. than there are homeless people. The same waste happens with products through planned obsolescence, creating a constant demand and a wealth vortex that sweeps money up from the working poor and delivers it to the nonworking rich. All through the eastside there are places like this, dilapidated and only good places to sell drugs and do drugs, sell hoes and do hoes.

Nearby, there are two very cheap motels, a bus stop, a carwash, a barbershop, a beauty shop, a huge abandoned apartment complex two blocks away, and a gas station that makes most of its money, outside of gas, selling liquor and drug paraphernalia. The area can be called downtown Cottonwood. It's one of the few places that has a nightlife because of the cheap motels and the streetwalker populated strip. The carwash also stays fairly active, yet not as active as the one Gray graced with his presence, on the other side of the neighborhood. The seedy motels, both with burgular barred windows, probably make more money than the big hotels in the city's official downtown, with the traffic they receive. One is a motel so classy the entrance to the drive has a wood plank fence topped with barbed wire, and the other, directly across from Tuck's lot, called Park Row, should be called skid row. The streetwalkers are called Park Row hoes by the locals, and the law abiding citizens, squares, waiting at the bus stop are disgusted by them. As much as the squares are disgusted by them, the hustlers at the carwash and the gas station cheer them on, and patronize them occasionally. Other buildings are vacant as well, along with those that are still active. There are people around and illegal activity, but there wasn't enough to keep the shopping center open, or there just wasn't to right kind of traffic to keep it. It is now the location for the Temple of Morality.

The number of vacant properties and lots make great hiding

spaces. For a citywide game of hide-and-seek, the eastside is prime real estate, but that is the only time the real estate is prime, unless someone is buying it up cheap for gentrification purposes, to demolish it and build something the locals can't afford, push up the property taxes and push the locals out. These communities are both crime infested and cop infested. Like a tree falling in a forest with no one there to hear it that does not make a sound, a community without cops there to define it through law enforcement, has no crime. It has survival behaviors, not crime. The crime is the environment forcing them to be highly reactive elements, taking for survival, there at the pressurized bottom of it all. The strongest animal is at the bottom of the totem pole, not the top, because the rest ride upon its shoulders – the top is pampered, weak, and out of touch. Wealthy muscles atrophy, while poor muscles build. Of course there is crime where it is designed to be. The police presence makes victims of those that are already victims of conditions that give them few options to live comfortably. Beyond those who *have* not needing anything to survive, the lack of police presence assists in defining the lack of crime on the west side, unless an east-sider is caught there.

It only took around twenty minutes for the tent and the chairs to be set up. The 9 a.m. service still hadn't started by 9:45, but around twenty people, possibly whom Tuck was waiting for, had gathered by that time. There were women there, a couple Gray recognized from the carwash, one for sure, but they weren't Gray's type. The guys weren't his type either, and both were in his face trying to be welcoming. When Gray was on the streets and running his unrespectable business, it was their type, calling themselves trying to clean up the community by running people like him out of it, by the authority of Black Jesus, Black Allah, and something old and African, all stirred up really well in the ancestral spirits and topped with a little hot sauce and served upon a Kente cloth printed table mat. Their types were full of pretension and just another of many ways failures could be born again, have a spiritual makeover by which things they lost respect for were forgotten in their new enlightenment. These women were the same hoes every dude had run through, and the men, the same thugs and squares that couldn't quite get it together, that through some intervention, gave their lives to Mother Africa. Liberation was as simple as learning some indisputable facts hidden by Europe, adding them to the current narrative, going natural, talking Black shit, and wearing an ankh. Someone trying to get their life together is fine until they cross the line by trying to get Gray's together too. It was comical. He knew them. He knew their history, and all the damage they'd caused, and thought that it took a lot of nerve for them to instruct him on how to behave in his hood. He didn't quite make Tuck out as the type, he's more thug than cultural, or he definitely wouldn't have come. Here he was, Tuck, tucking his head in a dashiki, preparing to lead this charade, another bit of information he conveniently left out in his advertising of it, made it seem like it was a function he sometimes attended, not one he'd created and leads. The street hustle is definitely in his blood.

Religion is another expression of the hustle. Tuck grabbed the microphone sitting atop his portable speaker, tapped it and blew into it for a simple sound check to start. Tuck opened by making a connection between the practice of libation, a ceremonial acknowledgment of the constant ancestral presence by the calling of their names and pouring water, and what the streets call *pouring out a little liquor*, often done in remembrance of deceased friends. Making connections between the past and the present is his thing, and the character he assumes in presentation is much stronger than his social persona, rather convincing, and attention capturing. Gray, who'd been thinking of finding a way to leave the entire time, is captivated. The subject was right. He was speaking on what he promoted, how Blacks could best combat the overaggressive police and protect themselves from the global system of White supremacy. Although not directly solution oriented, he was engaging and his delivery was such that it seemed the solution or solutions were sure to come up soon. Tuck is a God in his element, delivering blessings with who he became through the splashes of water upon the asphalt and with who Gray became through his instruction as if both resulted from the pouring of the libation and the presence of the ancestors.

Tuck was good, or Brother Robert as he goes by, his stage name, but he wasn't saying anything that Gray hadn't heard before, some of which he also read about while in prison. Gray appreciated Tuck's ability to talk big and bad about police and about White people. For one that didn't know any better, Tuck sounded like he was even willing to do something, but Gray knew better. Tuck was skilled in the art of rhetorical regurgitation, and his ability to spout it is the most impressive thing in his organizer arsenal. Gray knew the type. Beyond his threats, it was the common narrative about the greatness of Africa and African people throughout the African diaspora, which often had to draw on the strength of ancient African civilizations to complete the argument.

If an argument needs a proof that is four thousand years old, it is not a strong argument, as far as Gray is concerned, and it was nothing against his people and their potential, he loved them, but they were not the Gods and Goddesses they assumed they were, even the ones heavily involved in such engagements. It was just ritual, and it is reinforced when they convene, and it is removed like makeup when they depart. Power is not in symbols but in the practices that challenge and take power from those who have it. Tuck, for example, speaks of the Godliness of his Black people, but is there a better opposite of such a sentiment as referring to them as *niggas* when away from the stage? And the women, every one that Gray has laid his eyes upon are just women, and he'd have them drop all of that spiritual stuff just like the dropping of their draws. He's done it before, exposed the act in others, pulled the curtains on the grandest stages, and no one has impressed him, none authentic. As a result, he's entertained, but the Temple Of Morality is just another show.

2:6 *We romanticize the revolution like we romanticize romance. I don't romanticize romance. I don't envision one special person in the world that is perfect for me, and I do not wait or even look for this person. There is no one. There is instead many that have been groomed for the position, and thinking that there is only one, a perfect fit, is the reason many have none. The revolution is a whore, she needs to be engaged, entered, and directed by many. Anyone will not do, but also one will not do. Each John stimulates her differently. She is a whore, so she is easy to bore for the many positions she's been in before, making her desire dedicated attention all the more. It's not easy to make her come, and she refuses to fake it.*

Toni's phone call could not have been timed more perfectly, catching Will before his version of libation took place. There wasn't much time between when the two, Will and Tuck, viewing the world through slightly different perspectives, would have been engaging in the same ritual. When Will thanks the ancestors, he does it nothing like Tuck, but his is libation all the same. His spiritual is just material with his understanding of the *ritual* part of the word and the *why* behind those things attributed to powers outside of the material reality and anchoring them to reason. When the alcohol touches the tip of his tongue, he is thanking all ancestry who had anything to do with the discovery of such an amazing elixir, directly and indirectly. He believes in man in the way others believe in God. Man is both God and the Devil, and a man that forgets he is God hasn't a choice but to become the Devil. There are devils running all around who lost their touch and balance with creation, and it is up to the gods to dispose of them. With the complexity of Will's web of influence, consequence and reward based, mobilizing those who society had completely given up on into disciplined potential, how could he not see himself as God? He was godlike in his practice in the things he was able to materialize, as if creating something out of nothing, like he's created of himself, and he was definitely created from the dirt.

Toni set a small fire beneath him with the pain and anger

in her voice, a reminder of everything he's been trying to forget recently, escape mentally and possibly physically. Yet again, America the beautiful pulled a nut check as she spread her pretty legs with yet another acquittal for the murder of an unarmed Black by police. This one was a two for one deal, one hundred and thirty seven shots fired, one officer charged, the officer who stood upon the hood of the car and fired the last fifteen rounds through the couple's windshield, and he was acquitted. The chase began when the couple's car back-fired, and the police thought they were shot at, so they gave chase, they caught them, and they fired back one hundred and thirty-seven times at people who hadn't fired once, besides the car's backfire. Justifiable homicide. Like a broken record, the people will protest, the media will demonize them for doing so, and the police will get lots of overtime and a bunch of easy arrests. Killer cops that aren't prosecuted are putting money back into the local economies, and save for a little property damage in specified containment areas, where it's expected, nothing is really lost besides the initial life or lives taken by the *terrified* officer or officers. Insurance companies have to foot the bill for the property damage even, so it is win win all around, except for the dead, and all those who match them phenotypically being painted as animals. Even the dead get a small bump in popularity. Their names get mentioned in Internet hashtags, telling that they should be remembered and that they matter, their faces may make a t-shirt, and their families may receive a cash settlement. They are, of course, a worthwhile sacrifice; the jury and judge verdicts reinforce this fact. Their lives don't matter much beyond fertilizing the urban economies with the drops of their blood.

Will can't even stomach the response, this is not revolution, and it isn't even the beginnings of it. It's a distraction at best, if he can properly utilize it as such, or his projected result is a massive desensitization coming of it all. While people should be in the back rooms planning, like they've done in The Fifth, they are instead out in the streets revealing their hand. Only empty hands resort to protest, and the idiocy of so many, doing the same and expecting different results is not only insanity, but counterrevolutionary and disrespectful to the race as a whole, as everyone gets judged, as the *dumb niggas* argument gets strengthened. They might as well paint their faces. They are being laughed at, and Will doesn't appreciate getting dragged into being the butt of a national joke through his racial identification, and the genuine White guilt and compassion makes it worse. Any man who cannot get it up before a sexual performance knows that how understanding she is of it just makes it worse. A moment ago she was asking for it, and now she… understands. America the beautiful, keeps asking for it, and part of her is understanding of the poor or nonperformance and part of her laughs. Redemption only comes through masterful performance not understanding, so the only recourse is to prepare to do some serious fucking, when the power structure is its softest and wettest. The Legion is hardened, a portion of the membership fully erect, ready before Will, who can easily be defined as the head, fearing premature ejaculation. Like Huey P. Newton's spear metaphor, the head can only be as strong as the shaft that follows it, and everyone is proving ready to sink deeply into the dark and moist depths of the life-producing struggle and engage, even without protection, to see what can be born of it, get sick, or die trying.

The American law enforcement rap sheet is filled with similar incidents with unjustified uses of violence and very few prosecutions, with the victims often being poor and Black. Toni's B.U.M.s. The shootings themselves are upsetting, but the lack of prosecution is what infuriates the urban centers that protest and riot, because they have set a dangerous precedent that is holding firm. Cops can kill Blacks with the only repercussion often being a paid vacation while they investigate themselves and find that they did nothing wrong. As a bonus, they can potentially receive hundreds of thousands in donations thanking them for removing another thug off of the street and similar pay for television interviews as if what they did was an act of heroism. While the general population conviction rate is almost seventy percent, the conviction rate of law enforcement hovers around thirty percent, and it's probably even lower when the victim is Black. The message being delivered is the victims, along with those who look like the victims, do not have enough value in this society for their murderers to be prosecuted, especially when the murderer is a police officer. There are also examples of the same happening when the murderer is not a cop, there are also examples of the same happening when the victim is White, but there are no examples with a victim being both White and wealthy. The discrepancy between the successful Black and White *stand your ground* and *castle doctrine* cases is telling. The difference in value has become so painfully apparent, Blacks see no other response but to beg to be recognized as human and equals with protests and popularized slogans such as *Black lives matter* like a repeat of the Civil Rights Movement of the nineteen sixties or the Abolitionist Movement of the late nineteenth century. How resilient they are in begging to be accepted as equals, and the groveling tightens Will's jaws in that signature cookie fashion as he watches their constant pleas denied. It's embarrassing. It's soft shoe, big smile, minstrel show, embarrassing. How simple they are in their argument, how obtuse, how unrefined and self-defeating; they make Will's job more difficult.

This is truly the root of Will's disgust of Tuck. It's more than his intellectual clumsiness. He's not dumb by a long shot, just clumsy, and easy to take advantage of and made to look dumb by those who gain from the exposure. He represents a large segment of the population that serves in making the entire collective look bad because he doesn't know what to say, when to say it, and when to shut up. If Will subscribed to such a backwards philosophy, Will would represent the black man and Tuck the nigga. There is no separation though. They are one in how Will sees it. He sees it more than Tuck sees it. One is just consumed by the American illusion of equality. Will, on the surface, has the appearance of that one, but it is actually the opposite. His behavior displays his respect for a system that will remove him from the face of the planet in the blink of an eye, and while Tuck will openly rebuke this system, that behavior is actually fueled by him thinking they will respect his civil rights when push comes to shove. Tuck speaks of events to create engaging arguments about the wickedness of this nation to gain membership, at the same time neglecting to take heed of the lessons he espouses to his flock, exposing his lack of faith in his own teachings. Will dismisses the activity as some southern country bumpkin, geechee shit, that his New

England upbringing would never allow him to understand.

Will still never sees himself as better than Tuck or anyone else for that matter. He's better at planning and being careful maybe, but not better in composition. Will's better at being realistic while the Tucks find comfort in overcompensatory stimulation of the downtrodden by telling them they are smarter, more beautiful and powerful than they are, and than their enemy is. They eat it up like manna from Heaven, but it doesn't prepare them to fight, making this expression of self-love, self-hate in disguise because self-preservation must be first. Tuck's manner is offensive to Will, and it makes a caricature of Black Nationalism and African history by reducing it to sound bites and placing it in an aggressively framed message that he hasn't the power to back up. Since he hasn't the power, he comforts them with God talk, filling in the nervous spaces within them all… nothing fills the gaps quite like God. To Will it is still begging, just flagrant, dangerous, and divinely insured begging that will place targets upon Tuck and those near him. Aggressive and unrefined begging is still begging.

With the amount of time that has passed, it is safe to say that either they don't know how to ask, or respect is not something that can't be kindly or aggressively requested. Power concedes nothing unless directly threatened. Will's study has proven this. His military years have reinforced it, as sometimes going toe to toe was the only way to really resolve an issue between the enlisted. As barbaric as it sounds, the language of violence is one that all are fluent in, some just let their cowardice convince them it is foreign. Power respects the threat of power, and negotiates only when the possibility of power changing hands exists, not because of morality, God, and an inherent oneness that runs throughout mankind. They are spiritual fictions and not material facts and shall not become material until Will finds an opposing expression in the world that makes them true besides in pacifying, feel good, fairytales. Love conquers all in fiction; fear conquers all in fact, and power is all about fear. The fear must be present because the scientific reality is that no man is better than another, by any broad classification, be it race, culture, or sex. The propaganda tells a different tale, breaking some men down and pulling them away from their potential greatness not long after they leave their mother's womb. Caged birds may sing intoxicating songs, but an untold part of the story of its song, its crying, its creating beauty in the ugliest of conditions to be recognized as beautiful and having a life that matters, is its singing compares poorly to flight. The caged bird would much rather fly, and maybe its song is a derivative of the bars that prevent it and all of the conditioning that tells it it cannot and it accepting it as truth.

Will couldn't just leave; it would be like leaving his children. He wouldn't be able to live with himself if he found Toni, for example, headlining the front page of the local paper in handcuffs or worse. Cops shoot women too. Toni is wrong, but Toni is right. That is how complex this thing is. In all of his sacrificing, Will has also been failing them, albeit accidentally. The flower bloomed before the garden was ready, and something or someone important is still missing. If pulling them away is no longer an option, which it is not, he must snap out of his haze and make sure they are able to do this thing correctly or to the best of their ability with the resources available, one of which is Will himself. Outnumbered and outgunned, the least they can do is be burned into the American psyche, like Denmark Vesey and his clan, another house slave, as a possible reaction any time the disenfranchised, the working class, the laborers, the minorities, especially the Blacks, are pushed face first this deeply into the excrement of American entitlement, where breathing is not only difficult, but sordid and revolting.

Will needs access to his network, his physical one, the wonderful web he's weaved, and the digital one, Harmony's database. He only has partial access at home, and the added security of a multimillion-dollar company, their firewalls and updated software and equipment makes for better storage of necessary information. They created a hell of a Trojan horse for him and his to organize within and pour out of when that quickly nearing time is right. He has some access at home, but it's nowhere near as detailed, should someone hack his system, the four letter names and codes would read like gibberish. Will, driven by absolute fear of his government, meticulously burrowed himself deeply within layer after layer of insulation so bullets would find it difficult to pierce his skull. He is under no illusion that his government will not hesitate to kill him, should they find him or them to be a threat, and they'll utilize the cops, the first line of defense, and progress from there. Will knows this, and this knowledge exposes some of his missteps that have slowed the development of his organization along the way. They have no ties to the police, and six years has been ample time to create it. No one coming through Harmony would be allowed to be a police officer, as well as any other professional position, so it was the duty of Will to go out a create such a friendship himself. An officer as a connect would have been invaluable. He's supposed to keep his enemies closer than his friends, and he only resembles this lesson with his relationship with Tuck, who isn't really his enemy, although he often feels like he is. There are very few professionals in membership, all recruited by Will, and too, Will has done a horrendous job of recruiting Whites, even with the many who have come through Harmony.

With the professional class mostly omitted as a possibility, from those that come through Harmony, a major piece of his projected struggle is missing. Felons are barely hired at low-tiered jobs, so surely the human resource worker laughs when they see the *Do you have a felony* box checked, *Yes*, on applications for a professional position. It's a bigger laugh than Black sounding names, which have been shown to reduce the chance of one getting an interview by over fifty percent. So Legion hasn't a lot of professionals, and this is bad for three reasons: they have money and influence over their peers, they have a mid grade level of power in their jobs, and they are gears in the functioning system. The burger flipper at the local restaurant, no matter how revolutionary, cannot do much more than spit in or poison the food of the establishment, but conversely the manager, the professional, can hire, can fire, can access the till, doctor the books, and also spit in or poison the food if he or she chooses. There is power in the professional class. They must be paid more because their position, defined by those three reasons, makes them more of a threat. Influence comes with success. Will, as a professional, is the perfect example of this. He's paid well enough to be comfortable, so why should he be a threat to the system that pampers him? He's paid enough to be comfortable, so why should they limit his access to important information in this company and industry? This gives the professional class leverage with information that the labor class will never be trusted with. The labor class, along with the unemployed, is expected to be upset and disloyal, so society keeps a tight watch of them; the police dip in and out of their communities like needle and thread through fabric, making a nice tight hem.

The same way that argument works for class, it works for race. He or she is White enough, so why should they, the elite class, limit their access and ability to maneuver through a system that has been created with their advantage in mind? They make pretend allies of them instead. Will's personal bias hurt his recruiting of Whites. He couldn't swallow his pride enough to withstand their level of entitlement, behaving like they were better than he was, even with a felony, and rationalizing their arrogance with behavioral equivalent of, *atleast I'm not Black... or a nigger.* They probably thought *nigger.* But just like the professionals, the Whites would be able to gain access to what most of the membership could not. This was a big mistake that Will could only blame himself for, and he works tirelessly to make up for it in his plan. The point of getting Gray in his web is to trap Randy as well, and although Gray quickly made it clear that Randy is no friend of his, he has a task set before him, and it's not about what he likes. The struggle is much bigger than him, but his rebelliousness and intelligence, no doubt, sets off red flags for Will, and he's unsure whether his plan will be properly executed or executed at all. He adds, *checking on Gray,* to his to-do list for this Sunday morning's trip to Harmony.

The Legion is in at least seven major US cities, and in more minor. No significant numbers in any other city unless recruiting is going better than Will imagines, but the way things are organized, one disciplined soldier can have the presence of a terror cell. It is all in the organizing and strategy. The extended networks need not be activated until the central cluster sets the stage by pushing the panic button. That's all Toni is asking for. That's all Tuck is asking for. They want a distress signal sent out in representation of the pain the people are collectively in, and a response, symbolic for most, but slumber-waking for those in the know, that creates a tremor big enough to awake the sleeping giant with activity that only an organized, revolutionary, presence can produce, and not another protest, something with complex reasoning and a pulse. The people deserve as much, and so does the nation that has been so bold as to ignore any other means of communication, so it must come to this. It would increase the resistance by inspiring some of the many who identify with revolution, yet see no one leading the way. The copycats could be inspired and create blips all over the radar, alongside the many places that The Legion can have lit. It's a fair request, and Will knows it. Giving the people something to do, something to see, is in order. As the oppositional presence builds, it only creates a stronger cloak for The Legion to hide behind. The cops are doing their job for them. With every new acquittal, a new revolutionary that would have never been one springs up anonymously, and the inhuman push is even hardening and preparing those in the professional class and Whites too, a negative byproduct of extreme levels of hypocrisy, and these people are looking for a signal, a direction, a connection, and they are an unaccounted for potential, which could number in the thousands, that Will is neglecting. America liberally tosses out tons of rugged rope, it laps against the concrete in heavy thrusts, completely unaware at what point it will be enough to hang herself with as she continues to obey the command of the oligarchs as if they are not absurdly outnumbered.

Toni called. Will didn't drink. Will didn't hide. Will answered.

Will stares at himself in the mirror while the hot water runs creating the constant hum of white noise and a rising fog. He has shaving cream in his hand and a razor before him on the sink. The revelation of how rough and mentally stressing the past weeks have been is all over his face. He hasn't gone this long without shaving since the time before hair grew on his face in a respect-worthy number and pace, except the couple of times when he intentionally tried growing his beard. He doesn't look nearly as conservative, nearly as unthreatening, as castrated and safe, as like one who should be unaffected by the news that people just like him are being victimized and demonized, as long as they are only like him and not him. It's how many in similar positions rationalize it. It is not their problem because it is not them, their kids, or their parents, who suffer. It is the logic of cowardice, but it's sufficient, and some even go deeper into the why it wasn't them, the fit of their clothes, the properness of their speech, the respectfulness of their behavior, and even the location of their presence. Will knows it all, and can use the arguments the same, and has before in his coward days, but that was many moons ago and those arguments drive his choices in look and behavior none at all. That is not his reflection.

Presently, Will looks a lot closer to how he sees himself, how he feels layers beneath with maybe his hair a tad nappier, his beard a tad heavier, his lips a tad thicker, his skin a tad darker even, his eyes redder with him standing a good five or six inches taller for good measure. He sees himself as America's Whitest, most racist, bigot sees him, or how the cop that fears for his life sees him. The face he has been wearing nearly his entire life is just a mask that is applied with the blades of a razor, to make him appear of the acceptable stock. If a Black just has to be tolerated, it will be one like Will. It's just a tiny shade of entitlement, but it's enough to be sought after and have those with the distinction, the empty achievement of acquiring pet Negro status, creating an extra level of skin based, behavior based, education based, discrimination intraracially. Colorism is racisms ugly little brother. They even use labels stating that the desirables, or rather the tolerables, are Blacks, and the undesirables are niggas. Everyone only saw Will's mask; his true self was the meanest, Blackest, most animalistic, untrained, uneducated, and craziest nigga achievable, triggered by the wicked depths of the American psyche. He lathers his face. He becomes White. He shaves. He stays White, or as White as he can possibly be. Whiteface is his character, his costume, his Trojan horse for his infiltration, and he has been wearing it since the advantages of it became apparent in his later teenage years.

It is rare that Will goes in on weekends, but today he must, to take an honest inventory by sending some messages and making some phone calls. Keeping in touch with former residents is part of his duties, his insistence in mostly contacting those that have been trained as insurgents and placed in key places across the map is merely coincidence, and still fulfilling his job description. Will will set off no red flags, and this is why he's so necessary to the movement. He bathes his cheeks in aftershave, flexes his jaws with the burn, and stares himself down in the mirror as if one version was able to cower from the intensity of the other. Neither bucked or buckled. He was ready to go back undercover, and ready to return to a life that he hated as much as he loved, pretending to be the same person he'd just as soon choke out if he had met them on the streets, not understanding the context from which he needed to be viewed. Those without anchorage in Black excellence, driven by high expectations of the race, will never understand. His first stop was Harmony and checking his precious web. It needed to be shaken, all needed to be awakened.

After over an hour of intense, closed-office, work, Will emerges to scour the halls, specifically to find Gray. The task he'd been set up to had to be addressed, and also some sort of explanation was in order for why he was up there at the carwash. He wasn't in his dorm room and his roommate present hadn't a clue of his whereabouts, seasoning his response with the inclusion that Gray doesn't speak to him or the other roommate, so they'd be last to know. Will made a lap around the entire facility with no luck, when he happened upon Kenny.

"Kenny. Have you seen Gray?"

Kenny shakes his head *no* in his normal nervousness. "No. No. I haven't seen him. Not this morning, I haven't seen him."

"Ok. Kenny. Thank you. You taking your medicine, right?" Kenny nods in affirmation. "That stuff's important. Remember to take it. It keeps you out of trouble. I'll talk to you later, and if you see him, let me know. I'll be back in my office."

"Yessir, Mr. Bunting." Will begins back toward his office when the thought strikes him to check the sign out log. It was a pinch to see Gary Dixon scribbled at the top of the list for Sunday, and an aggressive twist of that pinch to see the TOM Center as his destination. It was written, Temple Of Morality, but it is only known, affectionately, as the TOM Center to Will. Tuck, in his ignorance, and his growth in cockiness, was becoming a major problem, and he definitely wasn't enough in Will's grace to be trusted with a potential new recruit. Tuck would have Gray hating White people in a week's time, if Gray is weak enough to listen. Will cannot properly utilize him if he's programmed with such simplicity. It is one thing for him to arrive at that conclusion himself, which many have, and he already could have, but through indoctrination that serves no strategic purpose but to have a focus to concentrate negative energy upon is just a wasted energy. Gray deserved a chance to develop before automatically joining the ranks of the grunts, and Will opts to rescue him while potentially endangering himself by deciding to take a trip to the TOM Center. He imagines Tuck has made enough noise to be watched, and Will does his best to avoid being associated with them for that very reason, but this day he's compelled to do so.

*   *   *

"I just don't understand what you still get upset about. I think getting mad means you surprised, and if you surprised, I mean if you STILL surprised after all the times this done happened, it might be time for you to trade that brain of yours in for a new one, 'cause it ain't working good no more. Cops can kill you, and it's cool. You got to get over that shit. We need to worry about what WE need to do to create consequences for them shooting us, because the American justice system ain't worried about it. You not important to them! Black lives matter. What… ever. Don't talk about it, be about it. Hell they shooting White boys and getting away with it, and you think they care about you? This pig hopped on the hood and dumped fifteen shots into 'em, into two unarmed civilians, our brother and our sister, and the judge say it's cool. It's cool ya'll! It's been cool. White folks looking at ya'll like, fuck you expect? And I look at you thinking the same. It's been pretty consistent.

"Black lives matter, my ass. You ever noticed how many of these White people online talk that shit, but it's only a handful of them out there in those protests. Watch it. We're thirteen percent according to census data, which I think shorts us every four years, but regardless, there is no way we should be the majority at any of these protests if White folks thought Black lives mattered... If they were really serious they'd be out there thick. Too many to count. They don't really care to do nothing but pacify you, so they can get back to business as usual so you can stop interrupting their shows with news updates, and standing in the street making it hard for them to get home to them shows. Cops don't beat the shit out of them like they do us, so their presence *would* actually matter. White lives matter. If a bunch of White people came out, showing they gave a damn, maybe things would change, cops don't beat the shit out of them the same, but I wouldn't hold my breath for nothing like that.

"Your main concern should be not ending up on this list." Tuck taps on his pocket where the folded paper full of the names of the murdered rests. He read off some notables among them at the end of libation. Everyone called out their favorite ancestors by name, some famous and some family, and Tuck summoned the names on the list to also lend their presence to the occasion and watch over them. He read some of the paper, folded it back up and placed it back in the pocket he removed it from, and he was referring to that list. "Pigs killed one hundred and eleven people in March, and I don't see them slowing up because we're at war. We just didn't get the memo. I read somewhere that laws ain't killed nothing but like fifty people in the UK since year nineteen hundred. Nineteen hundred! Wasn't even airplanes yet back then, and they cops killed like fifty two people since then, and our cops done dropped a buck eleven in one month.

"It's going to be a hot summer y'all. The hottest on record, I promise, and not because of some damn global warming. I'm tired of it. You tired of it. The Creator's tired of it. Who else do we need on our side to stop this beast? By my count, he's outnumbered. Man... fuck the police, and the system of global white supremacy they protect." Tuck has a mobile microphone and speaker set up in the middle of popular intersecting streets on the eastside, and he begins hurtling obscenities. This is not his norm, not on the microphone, it's not, and this is not the same as those who talk Jesus in the same manner. Those names in his pocket give him charge, recent additions to the ancestral body who are quite sensitive to the subject of police, so they attend and lend generously to the energy. As their flesh sours and dries beneath the soil, their spirits answer to Tuck's call. Consciously or subconsciously, Tuck is the lead as they move into escalation.

"They JUST killed one of our own! Rest his soul. This ain't just about New York, Los Angeles, Ferguson, and Cleveland. It's happening all over and we got big red targets on our back." Truck speaks a truth more relevant than he is conscious of, like the spirits are speaking through him. A patrol car rounds the corner on cue as Tuck encourages his audience through hand motions to add chorus to his declaration in yelling, "Fuck the police!"

Gray, while enjoying the show and the subject, has never jumped at being part of a crowd and that includes choruses, so his voice is not among those chanting. He's more entertained by watching them all, and he quickly notices a drop in enthusiasm along with head turns. Gray's eyes follow the eyes of other audience members as they rubberneck, their necks stressed in twist and facing behind themselves. They lead him to a police car stopped in the middle of the lane nearest to the curb on a four-lane street, with heavy tinted windows rolled all of the way up. The audience gets restless, shifting and making the folding chairs squeak. Tuck capitalizes on the nervous energy by pushing the issue. "Fuck the police! Yeah, I said it, and I mean it. Fuck the police! Fuck the police! Fuck the police!!"

Only a handful of people join him with his latest chant. Tuck picks up the friction in the energy and moves on. "They ain't nothing but slave catchers. There ain't no pride in that job. They don't stop crime. They work for the biggest criminals in the world, yet they patrol around nothing but the poor communities, the ghettos. Try to keep us scared, shoot us down like dogs if we ain't, but I say fuck 'em!!" Tuck paces to the side of the audience, so there is a clear view of the cop or cops and a clear view of himself for them, him or her, behind the tinted window. "Errand boys for the elite class, that's all they are, and they're not even paid well. If you gonna be a bitch at least the pay should be worth it. Be a high priced hoe at least. Stop believing the lies. They ass don't protect us. They protect property and those who have lots of it, keeping us from them. They only terrorize us, and dammit we're tired of it! And I'm here to tell you slave catchers that ain't no slaves here. Not anymore. We're Gods! We're kings and queens, creators of civilizations. So, wrong niggas, nigga!"

Tuck walks back to where the audience is between him and the patrol car. The police officer quickly flashes the lights and siren, like a hiccup, and pulls off. "Cowards!" Tuck wins the battle, along with the hearts of his membership. He made an impressive stand before his congregation. The heart rates of them all, Tuck's included, decrease back down to normal. Not even five minutes after, Will pulls into the adjacent parking lot. Tuck and other former Harmony residents recognize him by his car. The only current Harmony resident, Gray, recognizes him as soon as he steps out. Again Will finds him; Gray feels as if he's being stalked. Will exits his car and walks smoothing his clothes, looking at everyone but at no one until he gets close. Will smiles and nods at those who recognize him and cocks his head in question when seeing Toni, as Tuck continues his sermon. Will rounds the back, walks up the aisle, and takes the seat right next to Gray. Gray shakes his head, leans away, and makes it obvious.

Tuck interrupts himself with Will's arrival, "Welcome to the Temple of Morality, Mr. Bunting, or the TOM center as you like to call it..." Tuck pauses and smiles. He appears to be considering placing the pressure upon Will to define his nickname of his church to the church, but he does not. Tuck leaves it at a welcome and continues, but his pause was used as a shoulder tap reminder to Will to alert him to where he'd walked, what line he'd crossed, and where the power lies across it; it is Tuck's environment and Tuck's people. Will picked up the vibration and anticipated it, along with shrugging it off, knowing Tuck's people wouldn't even have a chair to sit in nor Tuck a philosophy to bastardize, mutilate, and make incomplete if not for Will and his assistance. This is the church that Will allowed them to have, Will provided, and again the Godless Will, becomes God in a way. They can't worship Tuck, without worshipping Will, who Tuck worships. Will knows that Tuck doesn't really want to go there, not seriously he doesn't, not with Will he doesn't.

Will only knew a handful of the membership, and he was honestly surprised to see Toni in attendance. They'd sat down and discussed Tuck on numerous occasions, in the negative, and in frame of mind that they'd wished, because of his potential, he would update both his methods and message. Maybe it was Will's imagination that she agreed, or maybe she agreed then but does no longer. Here she was, dressed in black like it was someone's funeral. She wore black cuffed slacks, brown leather sandals, some copper toe rings and bracelets on her wrists and upper arm, and a short sleeve black poet's shirt with a brown leather string lacing up the front of it. Her style is militant couture, revolutionary but artsy, and a physical manifestation of her conflict as a conscious artist. At one point, displays like this weren't her thing, she'd thought it posturing, and this is more evidence of the apparent shift within the organization. She looks at Will and smiles. Will smiles back. Toni probably thinks that this gesture is Will symbolically passing the olive branch, Tuck too for that matter, when the reality is he is only there to make a claim on his property. Will is content with letting them believe what they believed. They've become no more privy to his thoughts and plans than he has recently become to theirs.

Tuck has been speaking for about two hours and he's wrapping his sermon up by the time Will arrives. The sun is telling him it is time. The adrenaline from the police encounter and the heat has him dripping with sweat, and he turns the outward aggression of his message into inward compassion about black people and all they have been through and how Blacks should deal with one another with soft hands to close. The sun heats the day quickly in Texas, and people can only take too much sitting out in it, even with the tent. It is a little after noon, and ten minutes after Will's arrival, when the service adjourns. The crowd begins to speak to one another, rising, gathering their belongings and catching up. Gray begins to rise, and, immediately, Will taps his arm to get his attention before he gets away into the aisle. Gray wants to punch him. Gray didn't acknowledge his arrival, didn't appreciate him seating himself right next to him, and now he is being forced to address him with this unwanted physical contact. Gray has been free to leave Harmony all of three days, and here Will has been in the same location with him both times he's left. The first time was completely coincidence, but Gray has no way of knowing that, and he feels that Will's checking the sign out sheet and seeking him out, specifically. Gray doesn't like the idea of being micromanaged when he leaves campus, and it makes him want to punch Will, multiple times. Walking away is the best option and when he tries to, here Will is tapping him. Gray presses his weight back into the seat, turns, and looks at Will.

"So, what did you think?"

Gray responds with little energy in turned up palms, a raised brow, and a shoulder shrug. "Fantastic…" His energy doesn't match up with his words. "I want to…" He waves his finger around, "speak to some of these people before they go, if that's ok? We can catch up back at the… you know."

Toni walks over to greet Will, before he gets to respond to Gray. "Hey Will. Pleasure seeing you here. How is everything at Harmony?" She directs her attention to Gray who was again trying to rise out of his chair, but she has pinned him in. "And you are?" He tightens his lips and sits. Gray looks at Toni then over at Will for his response, since he was questioned first.

Will looks at Gray and back up at Toni who is standing in the aisle, hanging above Gray like a buzzard, and answers, "Harmony's fine, LaTonya," while tilting his head in revelation that Gray was part of Harmony's business. Toni nods quickly as if disinterested, refocusing on Gray's turn to answer his question.

"Gray." His response is flat, and he leans back in his chair, slumps his posture, and stares ahead using his body language to ignore them both.

Toni smiles uncomfortably at the amount of warmth he's giving her. "Ok. Nice to meet you Gray. Glad you could come out. I hope our first time meeting won't be our last… Glad you could make it out as well, Will. I just wanted to come by and speak before I left. Tell the Harmony family I said hi. Ok?" Without changing his posture, and with Toni looking above him at Will, Gray begins inspecting her from head to toe to try to get a read, and he pays particular attention to the tattoos up and down her forearms.

"Will do. I'll let them know. They'll be happy to hear from you, I'm sure." The entire exchange moves between them like they didn't know if their act was in fooling Gray or each other. Something in the way of trust was being lost between them, and Will struggles to find Toni while looking directly into the eyes that he's been staring into for years. "You should stop by sometime."

Toni nods, quickly and falsely, again. "Maybe I'll just do that. Well, let me get out of here. Again, a pleasure seeing you." Toni walks off. Will turns and follows her with his eyes, unsure, as if watching her walk away would give him an answer. Gray stares at Will. Tuck is wrapping up his equipment. Members are gathering and folding the chairs. Gray is awaiting the return of Will's attention. Will turns back to face Gray. Gray speaks.

"I'm about to go."

Will nods, lost, zapped of the energy that brought him to his decision to return himself to this struggle. "Yeah, me too. I'll catch up with you later, Gray." The entire world continues to spin without him. Will's never felt so out of tune, out of step, out of harmony, with the events happening around him and right in front of his face. The chairs around him fold up, the tent above his head folds up, both along with his own body. Will declines to speak to anyone else. He just shakes his head quietly with eyes as vacant as many of the nearby business properties, including the nearby apartments. He shakes his head even when Tuck walks up asking about the chair he's holding hostage, and speaks not a word. It's more Will's chair than Tuck's anyway, so Tuck just left him there in it.

Tuck wasn't sure what his issue was, but he wasn't concerned enough to wait around until he was ready to talk about it. Tuck mentioned this to Gray on the talkative way back to Harmony. Will just sat there in the sun thinking, while everything, the chairs, the equipment, the tent, and everyone, the people in attendance, continued without him. Everyone left him behind. "I don't know what's wrong with his ass. He can sit there forever for all I care. He see my movement's growing. Last he came it was probably five people, and it was close to thirty today. That bothers him I bet, to know people listening to me." The chairs chatted behind Tuck and Gray along the bumpy trail back, where Tuck has been talking the entire time.

Gray cuts in, "What's up with LaTonya, Robert?"

"What do you mean what's up with her? I was surprised to see her, actually. She doesn't usually come out, but what you asking?" Tuck is slightly defensive, and Gray picks up on it, and he decides to explore it.

"Now you know I came out looking for women, and now you playing."

"You feeling LaTonya? Is that it?" Tuck is amused by the thought. "Nah Gray. I don't think that's for you. I don't think you're her type. She not really into dudes. Not sure how you couldn't see that. Maybe you just been locked up too long." Tuck laughs.

Gray continues to pry. "Oh really? That's just a phase, man. I've turned out plenty chicks that like chicks. They didn't want nothing to do with a woman no more after me. I've done the opposite too, turning them onto women. Don't tell me you ain't done that before?"

"I don't think she'll work for you, my nigga. You should hear me out on that."

That quickly, Gray gets a read on Tuck's and Toni's relationship. He's protecting her, or doing his best to. Gray's interest in her has nothing to do with attraction. She's the only name he was able to pick up because she introduced herself while speaking to Will, so, naturally, she was the easiest woman to inquire about. Either Tuck feels this way about all his membership, or Gray has struck an intimate nerve, which makes his secondary reasoning for asking about her, and the tertiary even better. Gray smiles with his thoughts and at Tuck's vulnerability, with intention to exploit it. The thinness of his skin makes it almost translucent, and Gray is in the mood to even the score between them. Tuck had one-upped him with his invitation out to his *church*. Gray couldn't think of anything else to call it.

"So, she came through Harmony too, huh?" Gray did not leave the subject of Toni, even though he was kindly advised to.

Tuck shakes his head slowly in negation. "Who told you that?"

"Is that a no?" Gray challenges his shaking head, wanting to know whether to apply it to his persistence in discussing Toni or if it is a lying response to his question.

Tuck repeats the question. "Who told you that?"

"Who said anybody told me that? I just asked a question... my nigga... I figured it would be a yes or no answer." Gray is not telling him what he knows. He'd much rather measure Tuck's propensity to block and lie. He's also interested in keeping Tuck on the defensive, so, no answering Tuck's questions, especially while Gray's unanswered question is still on the table.

"Yeah. She did." Tuck relents and answers the question, an intelligent move considering Gray already knew the answer, and his integrity was the only thing being questioned. Gray takes note of how long it took him, though. This is a short ride, but informative. They pull into Hamony's parking lot, driving around to the back of the facility where the chairs are taken in, and Gray is still asking questions.

"Same time as you?" Gray didn't even know if Tuck came through Harmony. He knew Tuck was informed about it, but that could come through being an employee. When Tuck initially stalled to answer the earlier Harmony question, Tuck left the opening for this follow up. Gray asked if Toni was at Harmony *too,* while not being asked to clarify to whom that *too* was attached, Gray, Tuck, or even Will. Gray decided to run with Tuck as if he'd already admitted his attendance.

"Nah. She was there long before I got there..." It is like taking candy from a baby. It's always easy with people who talk a lot, because they rarely listen a lot. Tuck continues, "I think our graduations were like four years apart. She was a senior and me a freshman, or something." Tuck coughs out a laugh while backing the truck up to the building.

"What she get locked up for?" Gray is relentless. He's found out how close Tuck is to Toni, her preferred sexual orientation, that she's a felon that came through Harmony, and that Tuck is a felon that came through Harmony four years afterwards, all in a ten minute ride because Tuck doesn't know how to shut his mouth, and he's not yet satisfied.

"Man, why are you asking all these questions about her? Damn." Tuck plays frustrated.

"I told you that already. You asked earlier." Gray address-es and dismisses in the same breath. "Was it drugs? She do drugs, right?" Gray enters the third segment of his interrogation. The truck is parked and idling. Tuck turns and looks at Gray with the kind of expression that is an answer in itself, whether he wants to answer or not. Tuck should never play poker.

"What?!" His questioning face is genuine.

Gray repeats himself. "Drugs, she's on drugs. Am I correct?"

"No! She wasn't locked up for anything to do with drugs... Where you get that one from, because of her tattoos?" It didn't have anything to do with her tattoos, although lots of tattoos are good for covering the track marks of needle users. Gray is the authority here. He knows something that Tuck knows not about someone he sup-posedly knows so well. There is a slight chance that Gray is wrong, but still he pushed forward to make his argument.

"May not be what she got locked up for, but if that's one of your people you plan on organizing with, it's good you had me come out today. I just stopped in at the library for a second yesterday. I wasn't really feeling it, so I went to the carwash across the street. She probably didn't see me, but I saw LaTonya yesterday. I remember her tattoos, and I remember who she was talking to... And my-man don't sell no fucking weed, because I talked to him and he can't make enough from it, and if I ain't her type, the point you keep making, I'm sure she wasn't in his face trying to fuck him either... If I had to take a guess..." Gray took time to study Toni, especially her arms in search of track marks, "I'd say don't be surprised to find out your girl's chasing dragons."

Tuck smiles and shakes his head until his smile begins to melt away from his face with his thoughts. When the last drop of smile falls, he's wearing a grimace with his eyes cutting into Gray like he could cauterize his blasphemous lips for what they spoke, but his challenge of the information melted right along with his smile. Tuck grunts in frustration and slams his forearm into the truck's steering wheel, causing the horn to sound. "Fuck!!!" Tuck really likes Toni. He's auditioning for the scene when his best friend is diagnosed with cancer, and Gray's willing to give him the part, especially knowing it isn't an act, as Tuck tightens with aggression and asks, "Who is this nigga? I want his fucking name."

BOOK OF SPEECH

Luke 17:21

Neither shall they say, Lo here! or, lo there! for, behold, the kingdom of God is within you.

3:1 *He must increase, but I must decrease. I had thoughts that would not silence, interfering with what I needed to become. Thoughts telling me what I wasn't, when I knew what I was. Some of us lose before we ever pick up a gun. Some of us lose because we've been conditioned not to believe in ourselves, so we never test our own greatness, preferring the safety of mediocrity instead. I've no devil and angel on my shoulders, but a hero and a coward. I shall feed one and become it, while starving the other until it dies. Just a little taste doesn't hurt. It's like steroids, but for the mind. It mutes the negative self-talk and allows me to do those things, make those necessary self-sacrifices for the greater good. Just a taste is all I need. It was all I needed so I could disappear.*

It was like he'd been kindly asked to slip his head beneath the waterline and to hold it there. He made pouches of his cheeks in mockery and laughed it off at first, only to be asked to do so again, more sternly. From those that love him, if they love him, being asked multiple times is not just an experiment to test the discipline of his respiratory system but instead a warning that the waters, cold, dark, and deep, are coming to sweep him away, with a current so massive that holding his breath is the only way he can survive. Even if he can hold it long enough, being slammed around by the surf with bone-breaking and lung-bursting force is a distinct possibility, and trying to swim is useless. Will cannot swim through this. His limbs would be thrown like a ragdoll's, so it is best he conserves the energy that would be fruitlessly burned in strokes, and follow instruction, holding his breath, trying not to choke. He'll need that energy to make it back to shore. Their request hit him exactly as a wall of water would have. *Hold your breath and float away, peaceful like, Liam,* but Will initially challenged and thrashed against the idea as if water is not indifferent.

Toni sent him away by telling him she wanted him to stay. Confusing, but such a duality is an ever-present part of her personality. Toni wants to please all those that have shown the capacity to love her, anchored by their good intentions, no one that loves her can truly be wrong. Tuck was right and Will was right, and she loved them both, just like the night at the bar when they conversed about their next move one of the many times, Tuck was saying, *go*, Liam was saying, *no*, and Toni was saying, *maybe*, agreeing with both. It was as if her face rested in between them both, one sitting on each shoulder. It looks good to the undisciplined mind, which desires to see problems solved amicably and friendships strengthened, but it is not a sought after leadership quality. Indecision is frowned upon, and wrong is wrong no matter whose lips it projects from. It also reveals an emptiness where she should be anchored by her own philosophy, and choosing the side which mirrors hers best or offering her own, instead of trying to adopt and create a synergy of both. She was too smart to be doing that, and that is Will's biggest argument against her, not her willingness to pick up a firearm and pull the trigger, but her willingness to pull the trigger on the ideas she has loaded within her with no regard to who may get shot. He or she who sacrifices the most to be liked, does not like themselves, because they truly haven't a self to be besides the one they sacrifice over and over again for others.

So, Toni told Will that she wanted him to stay and take a stronger leadership role, but her actions showed otherwise. She had to say what she thought he wanted to hear, but her tears were fueled by the decision she'd made within herself. It must have been a difficult decision for her; Will pondered over it more than he desired to. She gave up one God for another, and denied the option of becoming one herself. Tuck talks a good game, but he is no leader. He attracts people with his energy, not his information. Some mistake excitement for preparedness. Will was trained to be more afraid of the silent type than the loud mouth. The elite mercenaries in his military unit were always the silent type and the most likely to return from missions. Those who were overly animated, psyching themselves up for the fight, yelling, cussing, and waving their weapons, were projecting because they were cowards, terrified, hoping others believed the act enough so they could believe it themselves, and were the most likely not to return. Will is not sure that Tuck is a coward, he's done his share of terrorizing people that just like him, living in the same communities, but that is no measure of how prepared he is to fight those that will welcome it. Will wouldn't follow Tuck to a location that Tuck only knew the existence of, and the thought that Toni is willing to is the strongest part of the current of that slapping wall of a wave, that pushes him into this cold, breathless, white sound, daze. As a result, Will is still no good, adding to the weeks, just holding his breath and trying not to drown. Will's routine is strictly, go to work, go home, and go back to work, not his normal, and no one even checks in on him. He's ready to leave it all behind him.

When the cat's away, the mice will play. Will had not departed, but he had; his physical presence traveled in his place like a body devoid of a soul. Everything demanding his constant supervision to run smoothly began to suffer because his attention had been divided for weeks. As if a keystone shifted, everything that depended upon the stability of the structure became unsteady. Legion is his keystone. Will and his engagements have become shaky and unstable as a result. He could not get beyond the idea that it was time for him to move on. The pharaohs the pyramids were built for were never alive to see them finished, and his self-talk was a constant reinforcement that the others were right. He imagined finding a nice woman, a young one, and possibly starting a family. He sent his mind away to other possibilities for his life and dropped all of his micromanagement practices in Legion and Harmony letting his beautiful web, meticulously woven, fiber by fiber, fall into disrepair. In a months time, there was not a single strong strand of his web left in the health that its vibrating could mean something to Will.

The lives of those that Will would usually be hunkered over, developed well in the light that reached them without his shadow blocking it. They grew like vines, wild and revolutionary. Decisions were being made without his input, strategies were being created, and plans being made to destabilize the power structure just as they'd been made to destabilize Will himself, a microcosm of the power structure. Tuck took an unnatural lead because he desired it, and Toni preferred staying in her role of support. It wasn't an aggressive leadership, Legion has no place for that in the design, but many, a better qualified many, did not want the responsibility of passive leadership so they fell in line. Tuck kept Toni close while penning his designs, and she wasn't going to let him stray too far from Will's philosophy. He also kept her close to watch her, popping up on her at the pub at all hours hoping, while not hoping, to catch her self medicating. The Legion was moving forward without its creator. Harmony also ran smoothly with Will only floating along the halls without much to say like a haunting specter. He'd become true management, just there in the flesh, doing what he was paid to do and not a smidgeon more. The veteran residents, conditioned to his rule, didn't change their routines any, but all of the newly enrolled, from Gray's class and those following, lived like commandment-free heathens. The God no longer had any power, he'd fallen, he was amongst them and vulnerable, and all who recognized took advantage.

While Will decreased, Gray increased. Gray had no job and wasn't looking, he was skipping counseling sessions like he had a job, and he was departing Harmony daily by at least 2pm. Some days he walked right past Will, Will didn't say a word, and wasn't inspired enough to give him a questioning gaze. His name stayed on the sign out sheet with the destination daily being the library for his supposed job search. It was a half-truth. He'd stop in the library any time he had to use the bathroom because the carwash didn't have one, but he didn't touch any books or any computers there. The carwash was often just the spot he'd meet with his ride, once he got acquainted enough with people to have one available. He already had a job as far as he was concerned, and he'd already thought up an excuse for the day Will decided to challenge him about it. Gray was making money daily, and he was willing to even give Will a cut if he'd just leave him be. One doesn't have to fill out an application to have a job. One with skills creates his own, and God blesses the child that's got his own.

Gray gained the trust of the low level hustlers in a matter of weeks. A month out of prison he was already doing better than some of the squares around town and the pathetic hustlers who would've been better off as squares. He was even making transactions of his own. Small deals. Some illegal, some not, but all necessary to help him work within the trust of the other hustlers so he could learn the structure of their business. Drugs are the sacrifice to find the bigger games in town because drugs are so easy to find, but drugs have never been Gray's thing. The entire underworld is connected though, and drugs are the easiest access to it. It was stupid, and Gray was well aware what volunteering to again stand upon the wrong side of the law meant for his future, but his bitterness with the system, and the rush the hustle gave him convinced him that it would work better this time around. Once his six months at Harmony is up, he won't have to worry about this city any longer anyway. His hustle is abbreviated, and just a means to an end. He needed the respect it provided more than the money. He wasn't making much money, but the money he makes matches his effort, unlike it would if he'd found a job and gave the owner his cut and Harmony sixty percent of his pay.

Gray is building a system of trust between himself and low-level criminals. They are the people that can get things done for a fraction of the cost, and they respect skills and one's ability to produce in the way the greater society respects degrees. In his late thirties, Gray doesn't have time to start again from the bottom that going straight provides, because it gives no credit for time served. No matter how many times he plays the scenario of what he'll do once he's free, he never pictures himself holding a steady job with a nametag and a smile. He's never even had a normal job. He doesn't want to go back to prison, but he's intelligent enough to recognize that going straight is prison as well. A middle-aged man with nothing to his name has no choice but to gamble what little he has, which is his life, in hopes he can establish something before old age sets in. If not Gray will still be working at seventy trying to make ends meet in a system designed for them not to. His present safety has to be sacrificed for his future safety. There is no way around it, and he finds Harmony's denial of that fact with their programs dismissive and impractical, so he stays away. They know less about the real world than the people they are guiding. Squares can't tell nonsquares how to navigate the nonsquare world, and the best most of the counselors could suggest was *faith in God,* and some even had the nerve to have the residents reciting the serenity prayer. Meaningless chants are the easiest path to keeping him thoroughly repulsed, so Gray chose to just stay away.

Part of Gray's away from Harmony time is spent with street dealers, and the rest of it is spent with women, particularly the lady he met at the carwash, a street-smart chick named Lena. Gray left the carwash with her phone number and a promise that she would see him again. He told her his situation immediately, along with telling her what he would do to her and for her if he wasn't in his situation, and promising that the situation was only temporary. A woman needs to have something to believe in along with the raw material attraction is made from. If Gray hadn't the raw materials, she would not have approached him and stayed there in his face while he offered her the intrigue to keep her. Intrigue is all that's needed to hook them, later they'll desire stability but intrigue is the bait. Lena wanted to know what he was and what he had the potential to become, and he had but to sell her that while at the lowest place he's ever been. The rise he told her about isn't game that he used to catch her. Gray means it. He isn't staying much longer at the bottom of anything. He is too smart for that. It is a genuine promise added to the all of the false promises he's whispered to her about him needing somebody like her in his corner. Gray told Lena this within ten minutes of their meeting. Time wasn't on his side, and if it ran her away, so be it. It was worth taking the chance to see where her head was at. She smiled, walked closer, and listened to him more intensely.

Lying to her was not the play. It wouldn't have taken long for her to find out he was broke and living in a halfway house, and he only served to ruin his chances by pretending that wasn't the case. Lairs only win for so long. The man that can get the woman to buy his story, even if it's a tragedy, wins in the end. Gray has always easily gotten a feel for women, plenty of experience, because of his natural advantages. Lena wasn't so hard up that she wouldn't give him a shot, so his being honest paid off. He was tying up the Harmony hallway pay phone, evening after evening, that first week in getting to know her. She did a great job of helping him forget the woman he had the rendezvous with, that he never again seen in the facility. Gray had set up a date with her by midweek, and had her giving some of what little hustle money she had, to invest in him, in a week's time because he proved his physical worth in a manner that made him memorable and special as soon as he had the chance. He still knew his way around the bedroom, and prison increased his appetite, aggression, and appeal – admitting that he'd just gotten out was game in itself; women wanted to reintroduce him to what he's so long been missing. No women complained; their spines were sugar monuments touched by the rain, as they lost all of their regal arcs to bow to his will. Lena also helped him get a cellphone through a free program that gave users so many minutes per month. Lena is offering tangible assistance, while Harmony is playing mind games. A woman willing to incorporate him into her dreams, Gray has found him one.

Lena is a native, from the city and from the eastside, and she knows all of the hustle spots and many of the hustlers. Gray knows why, but he refuses to ask her to confirm it. Her beauty and her savvy tells him all he needs to know. She doesn't have a job because she doesn't need one. She hustles as well, and her body is the product, but not like the whores of old, or the old whores. There are levels to everything. The best in the skin hustle don't pace the streets in skimpy outfits anymore, and they don't require pimps. It shows how far reaching the Women Rights Movement has been, as even down at street level, most still don't need a man. Only the drug addicts continue that tradition. They meet people, exchange information, and set up dates just like a square does but the date never means anything more than a date, unlike with the squares. This was something that Gray neither wanted to talk about or think about. He just knows she likes him, and she has the kind of connections around the eastside he can use. There are always multiple games in town, she is his connection to them all, and he doesn't have to worry about her hustling him because he owns nothing but his thoughts. She doesn't have to hustle to get those. They are the reason she likes him like she does; they are his hustle. His body is just a bonus.

Gray was building relationships he could benefit from, ignoring nearly everyone at Harmony, including Tuck. Tuck tried to get Gray to return to The Temple, but Gray respectfully declined. It's just church with a new skin on it. Gray enjoyed it for what it was but he had no interest in emphasizing his Blackness anymore than his skin does. His run in with the Black Nationalists or Black culturalists, spiritualist, Africa is this and that, type, before he got locked up were never positive, and he opted out of getting that old feeling around this new group. No matter how much their intentions are to assist him, Gray likes no one telling him what to do with his life. And they were felons, at least two were for sure, and he had his suspicions about others, not exactly who to listen to about liberation when what freedom they have is a gift from the very system Tuck speaks against, who keeps track of them, as they must register and admit this status no matter where they travel within the states. That's not freedom, and Tuck talking to that cop like that also repelled him. It all looked like an easy way to end up back in prison or dead, trying to reenact the David versus Goliath tale without a sling, a rock, or a God to assist them. Tuck not recognizing Toni's addiction also didn't help. Their struggle is full of red flags, and dressing up God as Black and calling on Africa and some ancestors isn't enough to get Gray under the spell. He needs practical moves, not spiritual, to find his liberation, and the streets are the best place to find them.

Tuck wanting to know the drug dealer's name was also disturbing. Gray honestly has had nothing but negative thoughts about Tuck besides his stage presence. How was learning the drug dealer's name supposed to help him? To blame him would be like blaming the lion for the death of the hyena. It is the natural order of things for things to act within their nature. More of the focus should be placed upon his injured hyena, with decorative spots all up and down her arms and keeping her away from the plains. There are levels to everything, and as far as the street was concerned Tuck didn't strike Gray as someone who could get stuff done. He saw him as a better follower than a leader and, if he had others following him, that entire outfit was doomed. Will wouldn't follow Tuck to a location that Tuck only knew the existence of, and he was curious why anyone else would, and it seems Gray agrees. Gray did give Tuck the dealer's name though since he brought up the subject, but at the same time he decided that was the last he'd honestly engage with Tuck. The rest of their exchanges would only be about Gray gaining and Tuck losing.

*   *   *

The blue paint flaked away from the impact, leaving tiny chrome cone piercings in the car door like ant-lion pitfalls. The gunshot sounds chinked and echoed throughout the deserted complex. They were the voices of residents past, from before the apartment complex got sick and eventually died from the sickness. Drugs are a sickness, they often enter the body, the desire to have them there never leaves, and such an addiction can destroy healthy multilevel apartments. They are the modern equivalent of ancient ruins, with scattered belongings, old dolls, socks, panties, and syringes, that tell of the people who once lived there. The coupe has seen better days, and the new holes will raise no brows. Its metal frame sits upon two structurally sound cinder blocks and a third in the process of disintegrating, crushed under the weight of the engine upon the axle on the driver's side, and a flat tire with the roughened reddened rim peeking through on the passenger's side. No windows are left, lots of the paint is gone, and it rests rusting on one of the streets within the complex. The young man made good use of his one hundred dollar hoop shoes while holding his pants up and running away from the main street, through an alley, and through the split fence of the apartments, vacated by city mandate because of the poor living conditions and the drugs and crime.

"There the motherfucker is right there!" was yelled to the heavens to assist in not to giving away his location, same for the gunshot following that Tuck fired into the sky. Gunshots and police sirens scatter the criminal element in the inner city like the light does roaches. They scatter the noncriminal as well, so at times it is hard to know who is who. The people have been programmed to trust that a bullet has no name upon it and that, likewise, the innocent often fit the description enough to become guilty. Many an innocent man has been locked up, some even forced to confess for crimes they didn't commit. Of all those in prison that claim innocent, some are telling the truth, and DNA evidence has proven it. Running is best. At the sound of the first wind-ripping shot, the small collective darted like a sunburst, but only one ray, the target, was followed by eyes that had been watching them the entire time. It is not the first time they've heard shots that were possibly directed at them, and their plan of escape may be as methodical as a school's fire drill. It may just look like chaos, and each has a designated direction and destination to confound those in pursuit, so all can never be apprehended or murdered. This way one out of the group will be able to secure the stash. Tuck fired before they were aware of his presence, too busy running their mouths to one another, one led an animated tale, apparent from his hand motions and body gestures, and the others listened and laughed until the shot rang out. They broke into sprinting, clutching their loose fitting shorts and pants, before even attempting to find Tuck's vantage point. One even ran Tuck's direction, but the paralysis of fear arrested his peripheral vision and froze him into the tunnel of only envisioning his destination. He wasn't Tuck's target; Tuck's target pushed beside curbside shrubs, hopped a recycle bin, and darted into the alley.

The target knew exactly where the split in the fence would be at the opposite end of the alley because his customers frequent the place, preferring to get high away from sober eyes. They get high in secret, and come out and display their high, the amazing way they keep their balance while leaning upon nothing, or how they manage to stay awake while appearing asleep, to the world. Many times he had to walk through that fence with his goons, find someone and straighten them out for somehow disrespecting his business. He'd chased customers there, intimidated competition there, and even received sexual favors in some of the buildings there, where the boards have been pried away from the window or doorframes. Irony has him seeking refuge, running through the twilight to the same place where others sought refuge in trying to escape him. He galloped, long legged, weaving anticipatorily from expected gunshots that Tuck was firing into the air, and then he ducked behind the car. Once hidden behind the car, he drew his own weapon and fired back. Subsequently, as the threat level increased, Tuck started aiming, lodging three bullets into the door of the midnight blue coupe, probably at least as old as the young man taking cover behind it. The young man darted away again.

Tuck was in pursuit, steady, slow pursuit, but pursuit all the same. He had to be cool about when to initiate chase, giving a head start like British foxhunters or Negro lynching parties, not knowing what eyes were still watching. He didn't need any eyes seeing him. He walked toward the alley leisurely, crossing the street looking around like a nosy bystander, before he entered the alley and started running. If either or both would have had their pants pulled up to the recommended height, their speed could have been increased. Tuck wasn't in the shape to chase after a man no older than his early twenties and in decent shape, considering the amount of weed he's smoked and liquor he's consumed, with Tuck over thirty and not in shape. The young man was too busy with anticipatory dodging to reach top speed, and he was holding his pants up. Tuck intended for his handgun to make up the distance, with its ability to shoot projectiles faster than them both. It was his plan to scare the kid, and maybe clip him if necessary; a direct shot would slow him down. Tuck parked blocks away from the exact corner he told the kid weeks earlier he bet not see him on again, and decided to make a go of it alone because of the nature of what he was doing. He was there to protect Toni, her health and her story. What she was going through was no one else's business, and if he'd recruited the assistance of others, it would have to become their business as well. Tuck would have had to disclose why he'd targeted this drug dealer, whose Christian name is Chad, and whose street name's, conveniently, Chase.

The news of Toni's self medication rattled Tuck and sent him into a controlled rage, one he planned his way out of. By his calculation, he could be most effective, both helping Toni and others like her, by removing the dealer from the picture, and eventually others like him. He'd long prided himself on the Black community and dedicating himself to rescue it because he used to be a part of the problem. It was not the success of Harmony programming that helped him see a different potential, but Will and his web. Tuck has an aggressive nature that has shaped his language. It appears as strength and it attracts others who are in search of that quality, but it also upsets the strong. At Harmony, Tuck was always fighting or about to fight, and if it were not for Will's seeing something redeemable in him, he would not have made it through the program. Tuck needed to be humbled, and infraction after infraction wasn't going to do it.

The eastside is a hotbed for gang activity, and Tuck was a gangster. Many will say he still is, just trading in a single color rag for one with the three African liberation colors. The trouble he would cause stemmed from that persona. Will saw the neighborhood territory wars as similar to the global turf wars between nations, and the ease of those involved to stay sane was their being able to remove themselves from the suffering of the victims. The majority of gangsters got intoxicated, shot with their fingers crossed and ran, never waiting to see the aftermath. It insulated them from the emotional and psychological effects of their deeds. Many soldiers have the same liberty. They are the ones able to return home with their mind in tact because they didn't have to watch their enemies and friends bleed out before them calling for their God to save them. Guiding a drone, firing a mortar, or shooting from a cockpit was much easier. Tuck was the toughest man in the world behind his insulation, never having to face up to the damage he'd caused, so Will prepared a space for him where his padding could be removed. Tuck secured a job at a dollar store but Will found him something better making twice the pay for his last three months at Harmony, in the space that he'd prepared.

"Aw, nigga naw," were Tuck's words when Will pulled into the space's parking lot. "What is this shit?"

"This, Robert, is your last chance to stay out of prison while under the supervision of Harmony. I've already started your paperwork to send you back. I've talked to your parole officer and all my staff, and everyone is ready to sign off on your trip back. We're convinced you're just a troublemaker and this here is your chance to show us, show me really, that you're worth anymore of our time." Will sold this opportunity to Tuck as if it were his last, so Tuck didn't have a choice but to accept the job. Will walked in with him to introduce him to his new boss, the mortician. The mortician met them in the lobby, smiled, shook their hands and invited them back to his body in progress. A sixteen-year-old kid lay on the gurney with half

274

of his face removed by a shotgun blast. He was also in a gang, and he was perfect. Tuck spent most of his time looking away until the mortician called him over to assist in draining the teen's blood. The mortician was callous, handling the boy's body like a side of pork in a butcher's shop. He'd seen it too much to care, but Tuck had not seen it any. This sixteen-year-old was the first of many humbling experiences Tuck would have upon that gurney, and Will's showing him the other side of the terror he participated in worked well.

It was humbling, spirit challenging, reminding of God, and maturing for his hate of Will. It is complicated, a love hate, instead of pure hate, and for Will the feeling's mutual. The younger the victim, the more painful Tuck found it, and his loud mouth went silent. Thirty speeches Will, Janice, and the other staff about the importance of community and the respect for the common man would have never made the impact of the over thirty dead bodies, the violent deaths especially, Tuck had to spend hours with, making them presentable for their last day on the top side of the dirt, and to best look like themselves, like they were living for their loved ones who'd over their favorite pictures of them, alive, happy, and handsome. People tend to value life more when they become intimately acquainted with the loss of it, and the same would work for incarceration and the appreciation of freedom if there were actually freedom outside the cells for those in the ghetto, especially felons, and not just a different kind of cell. Children are born behind the bars of the ghetto, few are able to get out, and many don't reach adulthood, like the kid on the gurney with half a face.

They die from gang violence and drugs. They die trying to be somebody in a place full of nobodies. No one joins the gangs because they find the ideas of fighting, shooting, and getting shot at, fun. They do it to gain status and respect, same for drug selling. There is nothing to lose at the bottom, so those with the guts, bet all, their life, to advance. They've been convinced that their lives have no value so it is an easy decision to try and trade that valueless life up. They are not taught to love and value themselves. Instead they are taught to love God, their country, and the material things that they can acquire should they sacrifice themselves to become important enough to matter. Being respected, admired, and feared by those in their immediate environment is the easiest path away from nobo-dyness, so their actions are more of a reaction to where they are in life rather than behaviors absolutely tied to them. The ghetto lies to them, perverts them, converts them, with its song that makes many fight away the death of nonrecognition or surrender to it with their silence or drug use. There are so many traps there, and they make the bad situation worse, magnifying it.

Tuck didn't have the heart to approach and accuse Toni of illicit drug use, so he opted just watching her closely and destroy-ing her network should the story be true. Destroying the network was worthwhile even if it wasn't true, but he leaned towards think-ing it was true as soon as Gray mentioned it. It wasn't that Tuck had noticed anything about her behavior that tipped him off; he hadn't. His pessimism took charge in the confirmation. Things had been go-ing as planned, including the beginnings of pushing Will out of his nonleadership-leadership role, and just too well without a massive snag. Tuck informed Will of this all, straight-faced, as he sat in his office after being summoned. Someone with the ability to ID Tuck, saw him, and saw him before he entered the alley and covered his face with a bandana, because The Ears informed Will of a shootout between Tuck and a local drug dealer. Legion has eyes everywhere. Will, at his wits end, having the worst weeks of his life back to back to back, got Tuck to tell all, waving his job security above his head in a threat that appeared to be much more of a promise. Will is tired of Tuck. He is a thorn in his side, the rock in his shoe, the cramp in his stomach, annoying, and the perfect person to blame for any missteps he may have made in the organizing of Legion. Tuck was cornered and Will deserved to know, so he started at the beginning to tell him why, starting with what Gray had told him that Sunday after leaving his temple. When Toni's name came up in the capacity it came up in, Will responded, "What?!" in complete disbelief, and loud enough to wake a sleeping giant.

"So you attack supply side, and hell the lowest peon on the supply side link like someone else won't fill his spot? He's like a bag of chips in a vending machine? Strategy, Robert! The same point I was trying to make about the police and the people, in general, works for drug dealers in the hood. As backwards as it may appear, you might just be making an enemy of the people's hero. They grew up with him, seen where he came from, what he's been through, where he's gotten to. They know his mama. Hell, he may not even be a bad person, and you're a transplant, not even from here, man. Really?"

Tuck just wanted to teach young Chase a lesson, scare him, until he started shooting back and was close enough to making contact to cause the retreat of all rationale. Chase started it then and at the very beginning as far as the way Tuck told the tale. Tuck tried to be reasonable. Of course Will was judging Tuck's idea of reasonable, and measuring it against Tuck's ability to reason. Tuck first approached the dealer at the carwash. He spoke to him as a brother, sharing information about their common goals and common enemy because they were both Black, long before he even brought up the subject of drugs. Chase listened and nodded as if he was following, but his nods were accompanied by the glazed over expression indicative of his undedicated level of involvement. His nods were just a way to get Tuck to shut up and out of his face, because he did not give a damn about what he was talking about.

"What did you expect from him? Damn man. I thought you were street? You can't communicate with your people better than that? I could have told you he wasn't trying to hear that shit. When's the last time you did something for the brother? Does he even know you? Who's going to feed his kids when he decides to listen to this stranger about what he needs to do with his life?" Will becomes see no evil and begins rubbing his eyes. "I take it he got away?"

"Yeah. He ran up into the complex. I didn't follow him any further. He had the advantage. Could've run twenty paces and turned and waited for me to appear. The light was in the front of me too. It was too risky. Plus there was no telling when his crew would come back looking for him and then I'd be surrounded. I scared him. That's all I wanted."

"I see you learned something in tactical training. Good. So, umm, you think he knows who you are?"

"Not sure, but I don't think so. I had a rag on my face. He'll probably just think I'm some pissed off gangster. Ain't nothing to tie it back to us. Don't worry about that. And I'll just have to finish the job if it do. Either way, you don't need to worry about it. Toni is the real problem."

Will shakes his head, *no.* "Let me decide what I need to worry about. I just need you for the facts. I'll do the rationalizing. And I don't buy that about Toni. Nah. You said you started watching her, right? Seen anything?" Tuck shakes his head. "Well, I don't see no reason to pursue it then. I'm desperately trying to get settled myself, and trying to resettle the organization. Look at us. You just picked a fight with a drug dealer, and Toni just took an ill advised tripped out of town. Both of you could be dead or locked up right now with one tiny adjustment in the chain of events. You make the readiness argument *for* me, to be honest, but suggest my departure."

"I'm here because you called me in here. I'm talking to you because you threatening my job. Don't get it wrong; I didn't come here for your advice or leadership. Done with that. Ain't shit changed but the date, Will. Not sure how you're doing, but the rest of us doing fine. You'll see."

"You just had a shoot out, and Toni's on drugs, but…"

Tuck interrupts. "You just said you didn't believe she was. See how you are? Always mind games with you. Yeah, we're fine. Like a said."

"Ok. What time is it?" Will looks up at the clock on his wall. "It's a little after two. She opens at four or five. Lets go have a drink… She gave you the key when she went out of town, right? Still have it?"

Tuck nods yes, and follows it with shaking head. "Nah. Can't go by there like that, without calling or nothing."

"You've been calling before you see her?"

"Yeah. She ain't my daughter. I can't run up on her like that."

Will responds matter-of-factly, "And you expected to find something when you got there?" Will pensively stares at Tuck in smirking disappointment. Will is gaining perspective and viewing Tuck, the rest who agree with him, and possibly Toni, like rebellious teens that don't truly know what it is that they want. It's not that they don't need him as much as it is they cannot truly test and reveal who exactly they are without him. Tuck does not have things figured out, and the freedom to make his own choices without any scrutiny has revealed the immaturity that Will suspected was there. As soon as he veers off from the proper path, the place Will has carved through the brush, Tuck's behavior becomes that of the lost, and any dedicated followers will be lost as well, a lost tribe, confused yet full of pride. Will stands, "Yeah, let's go check on her. Come on. And if there's nothing, we can talk like old times."

"I'm not a drug dealer!" Gray pleads with his palms up. "But yes, I've sold drugs, and no, I don't regret it. I've sold a couple of cars before too. Does that make me a car salesman? I don't like that classification. This is the life I was given. Unless you go and start blaming wolves, lions, and bears for what they do, don't come shaming me for being a predator... I'm not a bad person. I made some bad decisions, but who hasn't? You have too Ms. Janice, I'm sure. Right? So, which meeting exactly do we start to place the blame where it belongs? They all seem to be the same to me, different ways to tell me how I fucked up, like all this shit is my fault. When do we get to blame God for this fucked up world? I'd be much more interested in that session." Gray finally shows up to a session, and he really shows up, instead of holding his tongue.

Janice is surprised by Gray's response. "Dixon in the five weeks you've been here, I don't think I've ever heard you say as many words at once. Thanks you. You should speak more often. I want to hear that. If you feel we're unjustly targeting you, or that the emphasis in our programs is all wrong, we need to hear that. I'm not sure how blaming God would help, though."

"Better than blaming me. That's all I'm saying."

"Understood. Well, Dixon, why do you say it is your nature. In essence, are you saying no matter where you were born, let's say you were born wealthy instead, you would still have the same nature. You'd still be a predator with all of your financial needs met?"

"Hell, they the worse ones ain't they?" Gray's response hits like a punch line and the group laughs. "Yes. It's who I am. I can't help it. I don't think being rich would change anything. Wouldn't mind finding out though."

"Mr. Bunting!" Janice notices Will at the door. "Glad you're joining us. I've been missing your input in our sessions."

Will smiles, waves, and bobs his head a bit, all uncomfortably, because he hasn't come to stay. "I'm sorry, Janice. I just came to take Dixon off of your hands." Upon hearing his name, Gray slaps his thigh. Leans back, and looks up in exasperation.

"Ok. We miss you, though." Janice doesn't hide her concern while addressing Will. She's recognized, as everyone else has, his drop in enthusiasm and productivity in the passing weeks. "Ok, Dixon. You're dismissed. Thank you for sharing today." Gray nods at Janice, rises, and exits by cutting through the circle of desks. Will smiles as Gray approaches. Gray does not.

As soon as they reach the hallway Gray speaks. "What I do now?" Tuck is leaning on the wall waiting for them both as they approach, with Gray following Will.

Will baits him with, "I don't know. You tell me."

Gray doesn't bite. "Nothing. I ain't done nothing."

"I seriously doubt that Dixon, but you're not in any trouble. I just want you to take a ride with me and Robert." Tuck is in the hallway near the exit talking to Ann, smiling. Gray thought nothing of the sight until Will mentioned Robert as being part of the party. It gets his mind moving, not knowing the extent of Will and Robert's relationship beyond employer and employee, and Robert being a former resident. Gray isn't curious enough to want to know more, but he doesn't want any parts of this outing.

"What? Nah man. I got some shit to go do today." Gray stops with his statement. Will just looks back and nods him along with body language that shows that this action is not up for debate. The little general is again in charge. Gray picks up the vibration and returns to walking.

They reach Tuck, stop, and Will then resumes the conversation. "What, you got a job now?"

"I'm looking for one. That's what I been doing."

"Sure you have... Dixon, but don't worry about that today.

What's one more day unemployed, huh? Or better, consider this a job, and hopefully you can handle it better than the last I gave you... What ever happened with that anyway?"

"Well, I'll go sign out then." Gray ignores the subject of the assignment.

"Don't worry about that either. You're with me. Ms. Ann won't get too bent out of shape. I don't think." Ann looks up and smiles. Tuck stopped his conversation as soon as Will and Gray joined him. Will looks him down. "You ready?"

"Yeah man." Tuck's energy is low. He's being led. He's being led against his will and against his wishes. He was sure he had broken away from the very web that he is presently stuck in, and Will is using his discomfort as fuel to further anger him. Puppets do not cut their own strings. They only can be released when the puppet master chooses to release them, and Will realizes he made no such decision and the power that those organizing with him had was the power that he had given. If they were choosing to misuse the power he'd allowed them to have, he reserved the right to take it back. This was a new rule, made on the fly, while processing the present recklessness of power players in the organization and presently being implemented. Will cares not how it makes Tuck feel. As a matter of fact, he is at the point of daring Tuck to get mad. Maybe they can give Gray a show, or maybe Gray will make it interesting by choosing sides and helping one or the other. Will processes the thought, always thinking ahead, while determining how exactly he'll push Tuck's buttons in return for trying to freeze him out of his own dream being actualized.

"Well, let's go... You're in charge, Ann. If I come back and the place is burned down, I'm blaming you." Will doesn't turn to wink, smile, or indicate in any way that he is joking, as he is first to exit the door.

Ann says, "Ok. Mr. Bunting," while watching Gray follow and Tuck trailing behind them both with his shoulders slumped.

"Robert, you got shotgun." Will presses the button on his keychain to unlock the doors.

"Looks like you need to go back to the carwash again, Mr. Bunting." Gray teases while ducking his head and sliding into the backseat behind Tuck. "Nice ride though. Even got the leather guts. You know, you're pretty smooth to be so damn square."

"I don't even know if that's a compliment, so I'm just going to pretend it's not… Seatbelts. Let's try not to give the cops a reason to stop us. It's not like felons get preferential treatment." Will starts his car and places his own seat belt on.

"I mean, we just gonna go like this? You don't want to think this through first?"

"No. And since when are you a fan of thinking things through? You mean like doing research, planning, waiting for the best opportunity? You and I both know that that's not how you work. Stop playing." Will turns to look over his shoulder and begins backing out of his parking space. "We running up in there on sheer emotion with the ancestors, God or whatever, watching our backs, like you do. You going in first matter fact. Hell, you got the key."

"What? Will you tripping. She keep a gun on her," Tuck protests. Will ignores him, instead paying attention to the road that he is pulling out of the parking lot onto.

Gray has no clue what is going on, but he's picked up on the tension between the two and has surmised that its root is deeper than what he knows of their relationship. Gray is in the back seat watching the energy travel between them like it was a tennis match. His biggest issue is not their issue, whatever it may be, but why he has been drafted to accompany them. Hearing that a gun may be involved unsettles him, but he tries keeping his cool. He decides to question, still with the thin veneer of cool he's keeping, "Anybody want to tell me what the fuck is going on? … And what I got to do with it?"

Will answers with his eyes fixed to the road, "You got everything to do with it, Gray. You're the reason we're doing this. Seeing if your story checks out?"

"What story? Man, I was supposed to hanging with my girl about now, and y'all done put me in some shit I ain't got nothing to do with?"

Tuck turns to reassure Gray, "The story about seeing Toni with that drug dealer."

"What you tell him for? That was me and you. So, you the

reason I'm involved in this? What the fuck else do you tell him? I knew it was snitches all around that damn place that's why I don't like to be there." Tuck turns back around in frustration from the position Will has placed him in already, and it can only get worse once they reach their destination. "Well, Robert, my nigga, I sure do appreciate this. Lord knows I'd rather be here than ..."

"Job hunting?" Will interrupts. "With your girl right? That's what I heard. I'm familiar with the type of jobs a woman can help with, but I'm not sure how Harmony can get its sixty percent out of that?" Gray blows Will off releasing air from his lips like steam.

"Really, what is he gonna do, though? Besides learn about shit he ain't supposed to know about? What's your plan with that?"

Will laughs and shakes his head. "You just fucking told him. Right there is your fucking problem. You talk too goddamn much. You just made him aware that there was something working here that he isn't aware of and only an idiot won't start to piece that together. And I'll give you this, in case you haven't noticed, Gray's no idiot, so here we are ... What else you got to say ... Tuck?" Will called him by his alias with the intention of being disrespectful.

"Man, fuck you? ... Fuck all this shit." Will smiles. "You wasn't doing shit. You wasn't gonna do shit but keep wasting our time, and now you mad 'cause we moving without yo' ass. Want to go cry to Toni or some shit, and bring this nigga along to spectate, I guess. Well, fuck playing your games, Liam." Tuck mirrors the same disrespect in revealing Will's organizing name. "Tell us when to walk, when to run, and how high to jump, all while pretending not to, and consider this my resignation letter." Tuck sticks his middle finger up, floats it for a second, then thrusts it into Will's cheek pushing his head to the side and the car swerves with it. Will's right forearm flexes like the muscle wanted to break out of the skin, and he prepares a batch of cookies so hard they appear overcooked and inedible. Will just nods, tightly bouncing the cookies before his neck, continuing to drive. Gary is silent and watching, Robert doesn't say another word, neither does Will. Gray is watching, Tuck doesn't say another word, neither does Liam.

3:2 *If one refuses to accept the existence of a problem, the problem doesn't exist. This truth is the basis of social engineering and the driving force behind the increasing availability of mental, physical, spiritual, and chemical distractions for those who would otherwise demand a change in the social order, those at the bottom of it. The task is to raise their consciousness, by raising the contradictions in their lives that prove that they are not living the lives they think they are, earning what they think they're earning, or doing what they think they're doing. The task itself is made more difficult when the leaders are contradictions themselves.*

There was ten minutes of uncomfortable silence before the trio approached The Fifth. The car became a childhood hiding place where no one would speak because it would possibly alert the searcher. Will hid from Tuck and Gray. Will had lost feeling in his right hand from gripping the wheel so tightly that blood struggled to circulate within it. He wanted to kill Tuck. One pedal press and tight jerk into the nearest broad trunked tree would do the job, but that wouldn't be fair to Gray or himself. He honestly wanted to before Tuck crossed the line and touched his face, but the middle finger, punch, or shove thing is what gave his mind reason to let the thoughts free. Every problem Will has had, even the unrelated, like the occasional erectile dysfunction, wears Tuck's undisciplined, smiling mug. Tuck was probably hiding mostly from Will. He had said more than enough, even going as far as to add a disrespectful touch to the mix, but Will placing him on display and exposing him as untrustworthy was worth staying hidden from Gray as well. Gray hid from both Will and Tuck. They are, or at least they were a team, and he doesn't trust or like either one of them. Tuck had the potential to be liked if not for his pretentiousness, and Will, there just wasn't much hope for Will because of his position. Gray hates authority figures, always has, always will. Gray sits in the back of the car waiting to get this thing that they are doing over with so he can further remove himself from the presence of them both. The car isn't large enough for the three of them, so it only holds one with two hidden regardless from which perspective it's being viewed.

If not for this kidnapping, Gray would be hiding in his lady's insides right about now, if she can be called his lady, she's definitely his something, or definitely his. The question arises as to whether or not he's hers. It's complicated, and Gray is content with the purpose they serve for one another without interrogating it further. Lena is young, sexy, sassy, street smart, and she has the libido of a teenage male. If the universe were responsive to the innermost desires of its inhabitants, Lena would be an example of just that for Gray. Or maybe it would be the universe responding to the desires of them both, judging from her level of adoration, but the universe doesn't work like that. Gray has always had a way with women. His appearance opens the door of interest, but he hasn't any trouble holding it once they enter. He has them doing all of the things that they promise not to as if he consciously set out to do so, but there is nothing conscious about it on his end. It happens independent of his desires. The women betray themselves, the ultimate sacrifice, to lay it all at his feet to show a level of dedication that he's never requested or required. The rhetoric is so loudly reinforced, it's deafening, but these women not wanting to take care of a man have always been proven untrue. The irony is that Gray has never wanted to be taken care of, but the nurturing nature of his suitors, because he's been pursued by women in the way men do women, has always been overwhelming.

Women want to take care of some men. Some go as far to protect them, residue from how they were conditioned to raise their boys to increase the chances of them not being murdered. Gray didn't even want that type of care from his mother. He was completely out of her pocketbook by age thirteen, and the women that he would take money from, he considered it for services rendered. He never felt great about it; he was indifferent. His love for Black women, particularly, was his hustler's soft spot. His mother didn't do a perfect job in raising him, but he could not help but see her and how hard she'd tried in the struggle of every Black woman he'd met. Gray was often still cold to them, but not nearly as cold as he would have been if not for his mother's influence. He was much colder to

White women; he only felt like a trophy to them anyway, because many would seek out and only date Blacks. They were still sneaking to the slave quarters to fulfill their fantasies by fucking the help and yelling rape should they get caught, same as their husbands, just a different time on the calendar. A White lie, a woman's, has caused thousands of Black men to die, lynched for a forbidden, often one sided, love that they really had little choice in. It's how Gray saw it with every White lay he's had, even Anna. Was he correct every time? Probably not. Did he care? No. Matters of the heart are rarely his concern, especially those matters when seasoned with White guilt. He related with Ervin's stories so well for a reason, but Gray worked alone while introducing these women to his coldest self.

His mother honestly raised him better, showing him how to treat people period, but he chose to only apply it to the group Mom most intimately belonged to. None have worked harder than the Black woman to hold the entire world together, all while being told by the entire world that it was not hers to hold. When possible, Gray refused to add to their oppression, although many men were not so kind. Pimping could only exist from such a woman's existence, the standard of beauty and the exemplar of social rejection, with even the Black male often taking advantage because abuse travels downward not upward. With all these women have been subject to, they were still willing to stretch themselves to accommodate Gray. Gray was mostly raised by a woman, and there are problems with that. Many argue that it increases the propensity of homosexuality in men, but Gray thinks the result is a higher sensitivity to women, that creates a more emotionally expressive, manipulative man. Black women aren't raising homosexuals as much as they are raising men that understand them so much they do not offer a counterbalance, but instead a handicap. They are raising the men that will best destroy them. It's really not the woman's fault, but the boys that grew up learning how to manipulate Mom grow to become men that learn how to manipulate women, especially in a dog eat dog, manipulative, society. Gray knows exactly where he'd gotten it from, and it wasn't from his father.

It isn't a lack of love and respect. Gray loved and respected his mother, but he still manipulated and used her until he graduated to bigger arenas. He also resented her for his father not being there. She owed him everything she'd taken from him with the absence of his father, because she was the only one he could take it out on. He couldn't take it out on Dad, even though he was available at times. He couldn't chance pushing Dad away any further than he'd already been pushed, possibly by Mom, or possibly by society. Dad also didn't speak Mom language, so getting over on him was something different altogether, if it would have been possible. He owned nothing of value besides his thoughts and he shared them freely with Gray and his brother. So, Gray can love and respect women, and still drag them through the mud, not because he wants to, but because society has dragged him through the mud so much that he cannot help but drag a woman along as well, behind him, of course. He tried not to with Black women, for Mom, but Black women loved him. If Gray was willing to be a kept man, he probably could have kept himself out of prison, but the idea interfered with his idea of manhood. He had to find and have his own, and this truth still remains, but he has no problem accepting the occasional spoiling. Lena hinted at being willing to take care of him. She spends her time using other guys, and she's hinted at, more than once, desiring to be used by Gray, in a relationship barely three weeks old. He has that affect on women, and he should be somewhere reinforcing that affect right now, but instead he's quietly riding along with two men acting like women to go do God knows what.

It is sweltering in the heat of the day in North Texas. The days reach their hottest between two and three p.m. The car is cool. Leather seats respond well to cold air, and the air conditioner is on high while the three sit quietly in frozen silence, all looking out windows. Toni's car can be seen radiating heat in the parking lot of The Fifth as they approach the building coasting down the only road that leads to it. No other cars are within eyeshot. The area always looks deserted. It *was* deserted - the developers changed their minds, causing a failed church at the edge of the city, and property cheap enough for Toni to get her hands on. Will drives past their assumed destination. Tuck looks over at him but says nothing. Will breaks the silence.

"I don't want to alert her. She might hear the car pull into the parking lot. I'd rather park a ways up and walk." Will pulls off the street a quarter of a mile away from The Fifth, and the wheels grind in the sandy gravel making a rising haze of smoke. "Ok. This is our stop. Parking here also gives us more space just in case you got more you want to get off your chest, Tuck." The space immediately becomes a stuffy, airless vacuum with Will's last words, and the air vents were still spilling cool air, unnoticed. Will cuts the engine and all of the car doors unlock with the press of a button.

Gray cracks a smile while watching, excited, as Will and Tuck exited the front of the vehicle. This kind of tension reminds him of prison, and it's like a homecoming. Harmony is full of cowards and maybe Will is about to show him why they are so afraid of him, maybe it was more than just his ink pen. Guys fought all of the time in prison. Fights happened fast, starting fast, and finishing fast, an efficiency that kept the guards unaware of most of them. Gray avoided his fair share by hanging with the old players and not saying much, but he's always enjoyed watching others get into fisticuffs. Will has surprised him with the amount of heart he's presently displaying. With the same situation, Gray would have reacted the same, and he'd written Will off to be a punk that hid behind a position of power. Here he was, a boss, standing outside of his car and untucking his shirt after politely asking Tuck if he wanted to square up. Gray gets out behind Tuck. Tuck is looking at Will across the hood of the car with a slight scowl. Will pulls up the hem of his polo, showing Tuck his waistline in the front and the back. "As you can see, I'm unarmed. Hell, I'll even take this shirt off. Do like we used to when enlisted. Some people..." Will begins pulling the shirt over his head and stops talking until his head peaks back out. "You can't reach by talking. I learned that a long time ago, and that's why I learned how to fight." Will tosses his shirt upon the hood of the car and begins to empty his pockets. His cellphone comes out, then his wallet. They are also placed on the hood of his car. Last he extracts his ball of keys from his packet. He tosses them into the dirt; they roll and kick up dust like a spider falling over itself or a tiny Texas tumbleweed.

Tuck laughs and looks back to address Gray. "Man, you see

this shit?" Gray just shrugs, offering him no energy. Will stands in his wife beater, small framed but toned with a patch of coiled hairs center-chest in direct rebellion to the rest of his grooming, waiting for a response from Tuck.

"I mean, ain't no steering wheel in my hand right now. Now's the best time to touch my face." Will begins cracking his knuckles. "Fuck me, right? Well come get you some. You taller than me. You outweigh me. You a gangster. You been to prison. The way I see it, you should come and whoop my ass. Make short work of me. I figure you've imagined doing as much. Well, here's your chance, Tuck. You want to run shit? Come whoop my ass and take the respect I've earned… You ain't smarter than me, so I figure you must think you tougher. So, right here, right now, one of us can shut the other up once and for all… I know you can't whoop me. You ain't in the shape to whoop me. Probably punch about as well as you shoot."

"Put your shirt on nigga. You done, man! Me whooping your little ass ain't gonna change that. That would just add insult to injury. Put your shirt on and let's do this shit. You can say goodbye the right way." Tuck speaks through a smile, holding a character that reads he is not taking Will's invitation seriously.

"I'm not saying goodbye to shit. Didn't you just resign or something? You're about to say goodbye if you stop being a bitch and walk around this car. Come on Tuck. Come get you some free therapy, and maybe even a nap."

Gray leans against the car, bored from the lack of action. Prison fights start fast. It would've been over by now if this were prison. Gray sees no fight in Tuck, so he's not surprised by his inaction. His bark is worse than his bite. He's verbally aggressive to decrease the chances of him having to become physically aggressive. On the contrary, Gray doesn't talk much, and would rather use his hands; it just wasn't the right call in prison, too much to lose. Gray speaks in hopes he can stop the charade. "Man, what we supposed to be doing? I really got some other plans."

"This is what we're supposed to be doing? Right, Tuck? You take me out, and I'm done, but if you don't, if you can't, you're done. You fall the fuck back in line or get the fuck out of the organization.

Go focus on your bullshit church, but leave my people alone."

"Your people? Man, you so fucking delusional. One day there's no leader, next day you're the leader. You ever stop to think that maybe they want a leader, and you ain't the one they want? That'll keep you up at night better than any ass whooping I can give you. Put your shirt on and let's go. I don't have to take your wager. You can't give me power I already have. Whooping your ass is only going to make Toni feel sorry for you, get mad at me, and ask a lot of questions I won't feel like answering. Bet you won't take your shirt off when them rednecks and them cops come around... Put your shirt on, and let's go."

Will taps on the top of car to get Gray's attention, and Gray twists his neck while still leaning against the car to listen. "You see? He talks real tough, but that's about it. You ain't got me fooled Tuck. Bet not ever touch my face again. I'm not giving you an option next time." Will grabs his belongings off of the hood of his car and walks over to scoop up his keys.

"Whatever Will. Doing yo' ass a favor right now. Put your shirt on and come on." Tuck begins walking toward The Fifth. Gray looks at Tuck and back at Will. Will begins placing his shirt back on. He smiles when he catches Gray looking his way. Will knows Tuck better than Tuck knows himself, knowing the difference between confidence and cockiness and of which Tuck was composed, at least in the highest concentration. That was a loss that Tuck couldn't take the chance on enduring with the image that he'd built for himself, and if he would have accepted the challenge and won, which he would not have, he would have only beat up an older, smaller man, who had not made his name on the premise of being tough, and Tuck was correct about him having to next face Toni. It was a lose lose, and he was going to receive lowest side of that loss with Will breaking his face, after several measured shots to the soggy, powdered filled sack he calls his stomach. He hides it well but there's not a tight muscle in his body and his big talk, his numerous peers, and his carefully selected targets are the only reason he hasn't been tested and publicly exposed as the act he is as far as physical threat is concerned. Will is no fool. It was a game of tic-tac-toe, and he had Tuck three ways, regardless of where he moved. Tuck has already fallen a few notches, whether he wants to or not. He is back upon Will's leash, or caught in his web, through all fault of his own. Conversely, while Tuck leads the group with his walk of shame, Gray has pulls up to walk beside Will with a newly earned respect. Any respect Gray had left for Tuck has just been stolen by the little general with the precision of a pick-pocket.

"So what are we doing here?" Gray engages Will while Will tucks his shirt back in during the walk. The sun is so high and intense the world looks orange. They are walking the desert sands. The Fifth beacons before them like an oasis.

"We're separating fact from fiction, and the process has already begun. The sun doesn't revolve around the Earth, but some people don't study physics. And you're here because of what you know, or what you think you know, and how that compares with what others know. This has nothing to do with Harmony. It has everything to do with disharmony, actually." Will made a joke. He doesn't laugh. Beads of sweat begin to bubble upon Will's forehead as he makes his point and Gray watches them grow, like the sun was mining them from his skin. Gray's t-shirt begins sticking to his back from the same extraction process. Gray has no more words to add, although he still isn't confident as to what is transpiring. Their feet stop making the scratching sound of walking on the dirt and fine gravel and start making the patter sound of landing upon the asphalt. They cross onto The Fifth's parking lot.

"This is stupid." Tuck stops. "I'm not just going to walk in there. It ain't right."

Will and Gray catch up and Will responds, "What're you scared of? Consider this your final lesson, our final operation together, your test before venturing out on your own. You've been watching her for weeks and haven't found out anything concerning a pretty serious charge. Either you don't believe it, or you just don't want to so much you're afraid to confirm it. Both are selfish. I don't believe it, and I'm not worried about what we'll find in there, but it's worth a look. There's a lot riding on her, and we... well, I, I just received your resignation." Will taps himself on the cheek that Tuck stamped with his middle finger. "I don't need her compromised … We're here now. Let's finish it." Will means more with *finish it* than just finding out about Toni. He's not worried about Toni. She's a big girl, and she takes care of herself well. The purpose of this entire trip was to make Tuck uncomfortable enough to buckle under the pressure, and separate the fact from the fiction as he told Gray.

Will had plenty of time to think about his personal predicament and the predicament of the entire organization. It may have appeared as though he was just feeling sorry for himself, but what he was actually doing was much more strategic. He turned the volume down on his influence, which could easily be seen as him giving up, which he considered. He wanted to, but never wanted to. If he was the problem, if he was the scapegoat, all he had to do was step back, not leave, to prove that the incompetence was not at all his. In three short weeks, Tuck gets into a gunfight with a meaningless target, and that is just what Will's gotten wind of. There is no telling what else he has set in motion in all of the time Will has given him space to make a fool of himself. What Will decided during his sabbatical was that he could not, no matter how he tried, work side by side with Tuck. Tuck has to go. His aggressiveness will be better utilized outside of the system that Will's created, so Will intends to assist his removal from the system. Learning about the shootout was perfect. Toni is an afterthought. The shootout matched expectations and confirmed his apprehensions of why Tuck was not a good fit, so Will had to run with it, and here he is still running, and standing in front of the The Fifth. Tuck has to go and Will wants Gray to replace him in some capacity. This is why he had to come along.

Will knew what Gray was up to. The streets talk, especially when there is money involved. Will has been going to that carwash for years and many know and trust him there. Seeing Gray there was a good thing, and recognizing on the sign out sheet that Gray was returning, or returning to the library, officially, was also good. The Legion has ears everywhere about and so does Will, with the connections he has been able to form throughout the years. He's not down and accepted as *street*, which he doesn't want to be because it would inhibit his ability to communicate with all those who do not identify with the streets, but he's acceptable to the streets. They know he means them no harm, and he holds almost an ambassador position in some pockets of the eastside. The ones that have been around for a while know him, and Will has hired many to perform odd jobs at and away from Harmony, even some of the women. The carwash is one of his pockets. He knows the older hustlers there, and women. Those he doesn't know are only a couple of questions away from being known because he knows who to ask. Knowing everything about what Gray was doing and with whom was only a couple of crispy twenty dollar bills away, that Will had no problem spending.

News travels fast about the new guy, especial by way of the blushing cheeks and batting lashes of hustling women. There is no honor amongst hustlers because money is their god, and Will offers the blessings of disposable income. Similar to what he is able to do at Harmony, he doesn't have to be in the streets to watch people in the streets, because he can pay people already in the streets to watch people in the streets. Just like in a game of craps, that man with the deepest pockets is the biggest threat because they don't depend on luck when they have probability on their side in the game of chance. Will is nowhere near rich, but it is an easy game to play amongst the poor, and his ability to play it has just a fraction of the impact the wealthy have in the ones they play with the poor. Will has the metaphoric ability to wait everyone else out, but in issues of the street, it is never much of a gamble. He always bets on the women. They know everything. Men, on average, are much more guarded with what they know, unless they've vetted the seeker of information or unless they are like Tuck.

According to Will's sources, Erica and Ray mostly, Gray hit the ground running in developing a local network once granted the ability to leave Harmony. People know his name, and he is quickly gaining trust with different pockets of influential individuals, intelligently, not placing his eggs in a single basket. He doesn't have his hands on any real money, nor is he engaging in anything seriously illegal, nothing that has gotten back to Will, because that is what Will was looking for, but Gray is setting up a network of respect that he will be able to easily maneuver within and broker negotiations. His

Harmony urinary analyses have come back clean every time, with alcohol not even showing up. There unfortunately isn't a way to detect illegal activity outside of drug use with a piss test. On one occasion, Gray returned to the facility with bruises and abrasions, especially upon his knuckles, and a slightly swollen lip where he told the night monitor, "You should see the other guy," while smiling. Fighting off campus isn't against the rules, and it comes with his chosen territory, as he had to climb the ranks and that was not going to happen with him avoiding direct challenges.

Gray was maneuvering quite responsibly for one that didn't know he was being watched, besides the choice of company he was keeping, which wasn't much of a choice. It isn't like he could go to the west side of town and mix in with them. They wouldn't have it, Black folks and White folks alike. Race matters and class matters, and he's a poor, Black felon. On the eastside though, he was weaving his web, and it was being built for the occasion that something will eventually fall into it, solely on character and composition, the power of his personality, his looks, and his information, because he hasn't anything else to offer. Uninhibited, Gray's name could be buzzing in these streets in as little as six months, people are naturally drawn to the glow his charisma creates, and he does it without excessive talking and projection, and that's power. Will admired him from afar while creating his strategy to regain the integrity of Legion's local chapter, and he decided that Gray should be a part of it. Will is desperate.

What Will saw in his simplification, his stepping away was about simplification, reducing everything in his reach to black and white, removing the grays, was two strategies at work, intimidation and assimilation, in assessing the ways the people could be reached. Will used intimidation. It made reaching the people already in the system easy, but the risk was high that many would respect, but not like him. Many graduated Harmony, returned to their respective cities and never spoke to Will again. That was the failure of his approach. The felons were already destitute and disillusioned with the system. It didn't take much to reach them using Will's approach, which is basically blackmail, Tuck's approach, which is embellishment, or Toni's approach, understanding. The felons were easy. Will tricks them into building trust by threatening their freedom. Tuck gains their trust by telling them about a greatness within them that does not really exist, not to the extent that he says it does. Toni, who is by far the worst recruiter of the three, uses empathy, expressing her honest fear and apprehension and some relate.

By the blueprint, recruiting felons was the goal, but the shape of the organization is telling that a greater segment of the working class is going to be needed, and they are not equipped to grab them, not with what they've been doing, not without some big event. Tuck's approach is the best for recruiting those that are not already tied up in the system, but Tuck is the problem, not his approach, when he's talking to anyone that is not street. People spent years getting away from his sound and style, and he only reminded them of what they were ashamed of or opposed to. Will has nothing to sell anyone that is not already under his authority. He's honest and a realist, and telling people that the foundation to their liberation may take generations to build compares poorly to Tuck's just add water version of revolution. Many of this same class of people do not even recognize that they're oppressed. That is a strength of the oppressor, hiding the oppression of the moderately oppressed behind the oppression of the extremely oppressed. Each level of class views the class below it as the oppressed while ignoring their own oppression. Much of the middle class is oblivious to its oppression because it only identifies oppression as what the poor goes through, and their lack of drive makes them deserving of it. Will has thought long and hard about this, and the shift in the power was a result in alternative philosophies, one was the tortoise and the other, the hare. The larger the organization grows, the more traction Will was going to lose, as most people, conditioned through patriotism and religion, are dream driven by the programming of fantasy. Will couldn't sell them a dream, but maybe, he figures, Gray can, in no way sure if he'll even be willing to. Will concluded that, on the design side, he was revolutionary enough for the whole of Legion, and what he needed, what Legion needed, was a salesman.

Their shadows stretched before them, pointing at The Fifth, as they huddled and regrouped once more, with beads of sweat forming and running down them all. Will locks his eyes upon Tuck, whose his face is a thousand wet valleys. Sweat travels a myriad of channels, the folds he holds to make sure his disgust showed. He might as well relax his face and let the water roll because Will is not concerned. He doesn't care if Tuck likes the mission. He honestly likes that he does not like it. It's amusing. Tuck is losing his cool in a low stress situation because he's such the disciplined soldier. "Come on. You got the key, right?"

"No, man. No." Tuck shakes his head.

"You don't have the key?"

"I got it, but no. Shit ain't right."

"What you scared of, the gun? You mentioned that in the car ride. Yeah she got a gun. She keeps it on her, but it's a little bitty gun Tuck, and she probably don't shoot no better than you. Arms training never got to where I was satisfied. And I think there's only a slight possibility she'll be willing to shoot the gun. Not really her character. It's a better chance of us catching her shooting up dope. Right? That's why we're here."

"Nah, she smokes it. No tracks." Gray interrupts.

"Whatever. Yeah, it wasn't no tracks, 'cause she's not a junkie..."

"Nah." Gray interrupts again, amused by Will's denial. "Your girl's on that boy... and it's the only kind of boy she fucks with from what I hear."

Will frowns and looks from Gray and back to Tuck with his head tilted as if asking *why*. "Damn you talk a lot... Grab the key and let's go. You scared to walk in on your fucking comrade, who you know, who cares for you, who has one small handgun and you talk that armed revolution shit. You pump up a whole crowd talking about arm yourselves, train, and the police ain't shit, and you scared to walk up on one woman with a small handgun, in there?" Will points at The Fifth. He's proud of himself. He's been able to take a loose idea, just a framework of what he needed to accomplish in this mission, and he's filled in the details superbly. Tuck has been meticulously picked apart, and by the time he enters The Fifth there won't be much of him left.

"I ain't scared of shit, nigga. It's about respect."

"Is it respect when you tell this man Toni's business?" Will gestures towards Gray; Will is working on all cylinders. "Is it respect when I'm apprehensive about making a move against the best killing machine of a government known to man, so you pull a coup? Don't even answer that… Once we get in there, and everything's cool, just blame me. You blame me for everything any damn way. Just do it in my face this time, 'cause we going in there. I didn't come out here for nothing… Last operation Tuck, then you can go do things the way they're supposed to be done, without me holding you back."

Tuck curls his lip, makes an about face and begins marching toward the building. If The Fifth had normal windows and not stained glass, Toni would have seen them standing there huddled in the parking lot like street football players, or saw them approaching. The windows only show changes in light, like a cloth covered canary cage. It's great for blocking out the outside world, but not so great should the outside world approach. It's a tactical nightmare, and the archangel Michael would be the only hope for anyone holed up within.

Will gives orders. "And Gray, once we're in, I need you to survey, look around for drug paraphernalia, the smell of the stuff or whatever indicators there are."

"Ain't no one smell. By time stuff reaches street level it's been stepped on and cut so many times, there ain't a indentifying smell. You'd be smelling all the chemicals they added to stretch it so the dealer can make a profit. I'm sure pure has a smell, but you'll never find that around here, or any other ghetto, with boy or girl."

"Sure do know a lot about drugs to not be a dealer."

"I know a lot about cars too. Sell yours back to you for a good price, if I got my hands on it, but you don't call me a car dealer. Women too. Know a whole lot about them, but I ain't no pimp, not now at least. I'm a hustler. I sell shit. The more I know about a product, the easier it is to move."

"Shhh." Will quiets Gray as they approach the porch. He doesn't want Toni to be alerted by talking, should she be out in the bar area. Gray studies the building. The massive stained glass window in the front with the White man dressed in white, commands his attention. He recognizes it as a church. Only the sign above offers argument, labeling it a public house and having alcoholic beverages, fifths of alcohol, of course, pictured. Everything else screams church though. Gray even views the scratches the doors and the fragments of stucco make upon the concrete as a large minimalistic dove representing the Savior. While entering the dove is on its back, but it regains the proper orientation upon exit. The building gives Gray that old church feel that he's never been fond of. The deeper he gets involved with what's going on, the less he seems to know, and the lesser his comfort.

Tuck stands before the double doors. He shakes his head slowly while reaching into his pocket. He grabs his keys and searches for the correct one for the single bolt lock. He turns to look at Will for reassurance that this is really what he wants to do, and Will's return gaze says nothing to the contrary. Silently, Tuck slides the key in, softly turning it to pull back the bolt ever so slightly as not to cause a click. The lock is disengaged. Tuck removes his keys and places them back in his pocket. He inhales deeply while grabbing the door handle, his back can be seen swelling, and he slowly begins to pull it open, stretching the crack of blackness before them all.

*   *   *

"Ok. Ok. Ok...There's a trick to this and you know it. The trick is to fall out of love as easily as you fall into it." This she'd tell herself, but usually if she had to say it, it was too late. To feel deeply, immediately, while totally immersed in an all sensation consuming emotional swell, is such the dreadful experience when the feeling is not returned, or when it is returned but one's own apprehension, from the many times it had not been returned, blocks the view of it. Those that are hardwired to finding a qualifying connection, a partner with comparable handicapping intensity when concerning love, are often left loveless and desperately searching like souls in out-of-body experiences. It's much easier to just not deal with it, take up a hobby instead, love something intangible that has no choice but to return the love as unconditionally as it is given. Toni chose to love her people. Toni loves her people as an abstract collective, because individual by individual, her people continuously fail the love test, men and women, young and old. As far back as she could remember, Toni had always been looking to be loved, looking to fill the vacuum her hard life left behind her breasts.

Toni's ugly. Toni's ugly because she says she is. She's quick to deny her beauty, and quick to reach frustration from the attention she receives from a beauty she swears she does not possess. Toni has even gone as far as to ugly herself up, doing things to remove her from the ranks of conventional beauty, covering her arms in large, boldly colored tattoos and hand modeled copper wire jewelry, a brow piercing, a septum piercing, cutting off her shoulder length locks, and often wearing a grill upon her lower incisors, also fashioned from polished copper that appear as decay in the shadows of her mouth. Nothing worked. With the tone of her skin and the color of her copper adornments, she appeared metallic in the proper lighting, bronzed, and the jewelry, carvings within her person that strike the light differently. She only accomplished distorting her beauty, like viewing it through a prism. She enhanced it, made it stand out, cutting herself away from the common, although pretty is not the look she's ever going for. Warrior is more what she is going for, a rebel against everything standardized, bitter with the world, bitter with herself, cute as a plum with the heart of an anarchist. She'd never admit it, but the sourness that runs through her, that she applies to her present worldview, and the activator of her overactive, prejudicing, gag reflex, is the tenderness of her insides and all of the walls she's built to protect them. The toughest skin protects the sweetest fruit. Toni is hard and guarded in this way, but her look keeps suitors bouncing against her shell like anxious sperm cells, with few, very few, with the acceptable makeup for entry.

Being pretty is supposed to ensure that love is found. Physical attractiveness is, without a doubt, the strongest filter concerning pairing, and with all other attributes people are willing to make concessions. Beauty will keep interested parties coming. They will line up for a chance and the length of the line, the consistency, and dependability of it, is the trouble with beauty. Beauty discourages work, self-work mostly. There is nothing so abundant as physically beautiful people with underdeveloped buds of personality that have never been encouraged to blossom. It takes work to bloom, to break through that petal crushing, personality coddling, thick skin that they hide within. They stay within it so long that the skin becomes thick and stubborn. They refuse to break out of it to unfold into who they truly are, and be judged by the blossoming of their maturity because it's easier to just dismiss another in the line who does not appreciate their immaturity. This is the immature game that beautiful people play with one another and with those who are not as aesthetically engaging, until they are forced to face themselves. Some people spend a lifetime without being forced to face themselves and develop into their potential. Beauty is often the cause, being Black doesn't help, and being Black, poor, and a woman definitely doesn't help. Gay doesn't help either. Toni is all of these things along with being sensitive and desirous of love, feeling deeply. She's cognizant of it, at least. This is why she is not beautiful, regardless of what others may think.

The first thing Will thought when LaTonia Adams stepped off of the prison bus was, *Fuck you, America,* because there was no way that she deserved to be in prison. That thought was wrought with sexism, beauty discrimination, and size discrimination, and Will initially wrote off this looker of a little lady, having no clue as to what she was capable of. He was right though, she shouldn't have been in prison, along with thousands of others who'd done nothing but commit victimless crimes, but not because of her shape, size, and look. Toni had accomplished a lot of negative, as in anti-society things, with her small, cute, unassuming package, and to this day she adds to the list. No one ever sees her coming, so their defenses are down, and if it's a man, he's usually busy thinking with the little head, and thinking there was no way she could be any harm, just like Will, once she hopped off of the bus. She raised his brow a bit, but those were the days Will wouldn't dare risk his job by giving residents he found attractive much more assistance than they requested. It would only take a year or so to mature into that version of himself. Will's inability to actually do his job, bumping his head with the higher ups, reduced his ability to care about performing the job professionally. Fortunately, Toni missed it. Their relationship would be entirely different and presently nonexistent, possibly, if Will had found his way into her most intimate spaces, because Toni can't help but to hate those who do as soon as the infatuation fades. She feels not as if they'd shared something, but as though something had been stolen from her. If she'd discovered this disgust in Will, and symbolically bitten his head off like a widow when the music ended and their dancing was done, there would be no Legion, so something good did come from him keeping it in his pants.

Toni met the old Will, awkwardly social because of his long military service, doing his best to relate to people who lacked the structure he was accustomed to. He wasn't an organizer; he was just highly organized. He was also a highly stressed house manager of Harmony, a money making venture disguised as a halfway house. Toni had a year to do at Harmony. Will missed a good eight months of it and would have never noticed her even then if it weren't for Janice's insistence that he notice her. Toni really impressed Janice in their sessions with her openness and ability to relate to others. Relatability is both a gift and a curse. Those who relate best do so as a result of being challenged with the same struggles of those they relate to. As a Black woman with an alternative lifestyle, attractive, intelligent, poor, and a felon, there is nothing anyone can throw at her of an oppressive nature that she cannot relate to. She's the zenith of oppression, and has been high ranking in the category ever since she slid out of her mother's birth canal. Arguably, her ability to communicate so well was honed through the difficulty she's had her entire life with making others see her, not as Black, not as attractive, not as a woman, not as poor, but simply as a human and as an equal. Toni never blocked, even in the initial sessions and she had a way about her that helped the other residents open up. It is the same character she brings between the Will and Tuck dynamic, removing the dangerous edges of them both making compromise possible. They are not nearly as proficient without her, neither were Janice's sessions,

301

and that is how she caught Janice's eye. Along with relating, her ability to create a compromise in others, and her inability to compromise herself, Toni having a constitution and sticking to it, also impressed Janice. Will didn't care to be impressed. Harmony was a job, one he wasn't good at, and one he didn't particularly like, but one that paid well enough to keep him, so he was there but he wasn't, just like he has been recently.

Will didn't notice Toni, but she noticed him. She mostly noticed that he didn't notice her. Attractive people are hyper sensitive to not being noticed, even those who choose not to be noticed, and who have determined that they are not attractive. What's up is down and what's down is up. Will was gay, Toni was convinced. There was something a little too conservative about him, too neat about him, and too nasal about his voice, along with him not sending her any rhythm. It wasn't a problem if he was, as she'd dabbled herself in an alternative lifestyle, but he struck her curiosity, like all powerful men, powerful people, do. Attraction to men, physically, was never the problem as much as having to adhere to western roles and submit, take on the subservient role to make them comfortable when she was often smarter, more disciplined, and more dedicated than they were with things they claimed mattered to them.

Men, on one hand, men in the culture, artists, and self proclaimed teachers and revolutionaries, were quick to call her goddess, queen, empress, the mother of civilization, and say things like, *the Black woman is God*, all while treating her like a servant. When the ego is being stroked liberally enough, it is difficult for one to notice his or her servant status, and Toni was fooled again and again. Men, many raised by their mothers, knew how to reach her, and she was afflicted with falling quickly and deeply, so she decided it best to just stay away from them. She didn't respect them enough anyway. Many had the nerve to blame Black women for the cultural problems, and she found it cowardly. She blamed the softness of Black men. The same men who would say the Black woman is God cannot be satisfied with just one. How weak of a God is that? Toni is still attracted to men though, but she retained more control in relationships with women, and that makes the sacrifice worthwhile. Often though, she's reminded of her attraction to men. She was reminded by Gray's presence at the Temple of Morality, upset by the reminder, and forced uncomfortable in his and Will's presence.

She wasn't initially noticed, but Toni made her presence known. She fights like, thinks like, acts like, and she even rebels like a girl, and with all of those supposed disadvantages, she is the least expendable part of the Legion local chapter, with the exception of Will, like queen and king in chess. Once she was noticed, she made sure she kept his attention, learning him, and assisting him, and this is why she's being checked on without her knowledge. She's Will's right hand man, and although he isn't worried, it is worth confirming. Toni helps Will relate, and she also, by example, made him appreciate the strength of a strong-willed woman, which helped him throw all standard out of the design, his militaristic chauvinism, and his bias for those who think like he does, since he wanted to represent everyone in his antiestablishment collective. Toni helped him to see what his privilege disallowed. She was a couple of decisions away from being a drug addict, a single mother, a prostitute, a low wage worker, or even a college graduate, but her choices landed her in prison. It really wasn't a question of intelligence. She hadn't spent a day in higher education and she easily challenged the argument that where she was from doomed her to being ignorant and undisciplined, and she was the example making the argument to Will. Tax fraud was the official charge, but she really went to prison for getting caught trying to leave her cell. Those born in the ghetto are supposed to stay there, and only a tiny percentage are allowed out, usually by escort, and Toni wasn't part of that number. Years later, she still hasn't officially left, but she's party to an organization that seeks to one day break all of her people out of their cells, and Toni is the liberator her oppression created her to be, should she still be of sound body and mind.

"Toni!!" Tuck calls out to her as soon as he enters The Fifth. Will sighs and shakes his head. The light from the open door cuts into the haze, that and the heavily filtered light from the stained glass. Nothing appears out of place or different than normal. Will looks back at Gray to see if there is anything he notices. Gray shrugs to signal that there is nothing special. He's in a new place, which makes it difficult for him to look for anything out of place because he doesn't know what *in place* even looks like. All three men hover around the doorway, already further in the building than they'd been invited, so no one was comfortable in trying to make themselves comfortable.

Toni appears, she walks from the back scratching behind her right ear with a frown, and brow wrinkles so deep she can hide anything in them but her concern. "Fuck is going on here? What... What are y'all doing here?"

"Talk to your man, here." Tuck immediately places the pressure on Will, and walks over to the nearest table, slides a chair out from under it and takes a seat, throwing one leg atop the other like a defiant laborer striking. Tuck's work was done, and he was removing his involvement as far as he possibly could from the mess that they'd pilled high, the most terrible of walls, unpleasant and imposing.

Toni takes Tuck's advice, "Will, what is this? What makes you barge into my home like this? This is my home."

"Well..." Will is hit by a rush of embarrassment. He didn't visualize this confrontation beforehand. "I heard something, so I wanted to check on you. Make sure everything's ok. The nature of it stopped me from calling first..."

"Heard what? Who's lying now? You men are like babies, I swear! And I don't know how my name keeps coming up in your power struggles." Toni is very short. She shakes her head trying to digest the apparent betrayal that has literally invited itself into her place of residence. "What Will?"

"Well..." Will scratches his forehead. "Since all of the niceties are out the way, and I take full credit for that and how we arrived. Moving right along..." Will paces deeper into the darkening haze, away from the doorway, towards Toni smoothing his thighs and hips with his hands. "I got reason to believe you're smoking dope."

What?!" Toni responds piercingly.

"You know I know the people at the carwash, right?" Will presses, also placing all of the responsibility on himself instead of including Gray in his story. He had no reason to believe Gray over Toni's word and she could exploit that, but if she thinks his knowledge is first hand, it's her word versus his. This is a completely differ-ent strategy than Tuck's, *Talk to your man here,* upon entry, and surely Gray can see the difference between the two leadership styles. Will is as in pocket and neat as the fit of his clothing this hour, placing everyone in difficult spaces with little to no harm to himself.

"Who? What people?" The outsides of Toni's eyes become claws as she searches to understand, but a subtlety beneath her tone is a pleading to be understood. Her edge softens, and it is telling.

"So, is it a lie? ... If it's a lie we drop it, and we don't have to worry who or what people? But if it is, you shouldn't mind us having a look around, right? I mean, it's up to you." Will waits. He crosses his arms across his torso, gripping his upper triceps with his top arm.

Toni freezes. She looks down and around herself, then at the men scattered around her bar, and stopping back at Will. "Well..." Her palms become earmuffs, and she makes a fist of surrounding hair, shutting her eyes, and pressing her lips tight. See no evil, hear no evil, and speak no evil become one. Placed in check, Toni turns and calmly retreats to her living quarters as if nothing at all had just transpired.

3:3 *Some people are killers, some are not. The ones that are not are natural, right in the head. No one should be born lacking the empathy that makes pointing a gun at another human and pulling the trigger effortless. It should be painful. It should release toxins that inflame the flesh and poison the host when they fire and connect successfully, like their finger is the stinger of the honeybee, ripping away their own insides as a consequence of sorts for the preservation of the species. Maybe it happens in a way. Anyway... I'm of the natural stock. I'm no killer. I've tried it. I hate it, and even if, by some cursed necessary purging, it happens to be the only path to liberation, I'd still pray for another way. I've even attempted hiding behind altered states to decrease my sensitivity. Doesn't work. I'm no killer, it's just not for me, and I'm fine with that.*

Toni excused herself from their disrespectful, uninvited presence, and locked the door to her chambers. Will attempted to follow, only to discover that he'd been locked out of that chamber and possibly others belonging to her. Tuck sat in a raised brow smirk, disappointed not humored, but he could be save for the connection with those involved. Gray scanned the bar, mostly ignoring the dramatic scene and confirming that it was, in fact, a church at some time with the weathered cross resting upon its head in the back corner. It should've been trashed. It's trash to any that have no belief in its power. This told him more about Toni, but its orientation created a conflicting narrative. Will knocked and knocked and called to her, but received no answer. He received no response from Toni rather, because he'd received an answer with her decision to become hidden while he yelled through the door like he was giving orders to a subordinate. The men, placed in an awkward space, each took their turn in moving to the front door, with Will being last. They returned to the blinding afternoon light, the glow behind Gray's porch dove threshold, which they crossed in silence, in a trail to Will's car.

With the Toni development, Tuck walks with a new resolve. Legion is a sinking ship, and the Temple of Morality is his lifeboat.

The signature on his resignation was in telling Will, "The heavens wait, and another angel loses its wings. Good luck to you, Will." Will mostly gets the gist of his riddle at the end of yet another quiet ride, only confused by who the angel is, who's lost divinity and become mortal, the whole of Legion, Toni, or himself? Tuck is gone, possibly Toni as well, and the gamble of Gray, who now knows too much is the hand Will is left with. A bird in the hand is worth two in the bush, instead of holding on to the problem he has somewhat learned to manage, Will released Tuck to the skies, thinking the bush would provide something more tangible than the two question marks he's captured instead. Tuck will test his wings by flying to the sun. He'll prove to Will his wings are not made of wax, and should they be, Will has no interest in catching him, not anymore. Will has more pressing things to think about. This Toni thing is really important, and he is immediately engaged with how to solve it as soon as they make it back to Harmony to go their separate ways, with Tuck heading to his post, and Gray in the backseat dialing his phone and upon it summoning his ride as they exit the vehicle.

"Don't forget to sign out, Gray." Will reminds him. "And I want to talk to you some time this week. I'll catch you in the morning before your job... hunt." Will shakes his head at the idea. Gray nods.

Predictably, Toni refuses answering Will's phone calls. He gave it a couple of days to confirm, but he expected as much. There was no way to avoid returning to The Fifth, at one time his refuge, but now the place where all of his conflicts occur. He finds more peace at Harmony. The Fifth is conflict and turmoil, a spirit that has been consistent since they spoke in confidence about the death of that boy. Irony speaks to Will in his knowing he must face her to save her, and that he doesn't want to do it too soon for being unprepared, or too late when she can no longer be reached. He could wait forever and never know the best time, and there is a lesson in it for him. She is a metaphor for the present struggle, their revolution. Will decides he'll check in with Janice first, and see Toni before the day's end, prepared or not, driven by both his love and his discomfort.

"Just the woman I've been looking for." Will peeks his head

in Janice's office.

Janice looks up from her paperwork and flashes Will a disappointed mug. "Well, used to, you had no trouble finding me at one o'clock in the conference room. Used to."

"Yeah, I've been kind of busy as of late."

"Come in Mr. Bunting. What do you need?"

"Mad at me? ...You look nice today. I like your blouse." Will is lying, she is fully circus-ready this morning, but his charm needs to be thick like cream gravy, and poured on liberally. He's been a missing part of their team, so he has to suck up a little to ask her questions that only someone of her experience can answer. He could use the Internet instead and end up with the opinion of anyone interested in the subject, maybe an expert, maybe not, but he has an expert in-house. It only takes him swallowing a tiny bit of his pride, and he has plenty, a surplus even, so he will not miss that bit. He walks into her small office and sits on the edge of her desk.

Janice smiles like she knows she's being played. "What is it, I'm listening? And I'm glad you finally started shaving again, by the way. I had you on suicide watch. You know we have counselors for that, right? ...We haven't talked in a month, easy. So what brings you by to break the spell, Mr. Bunting?"

After a sigh, he responds, "It's Wilbert, my first name... never been fond of it because I think it sounds a little country, but yeah..." He smiles softly. Janice stretches her face in surprise and closes it with a sharp smirk. Will continues, "I need help, Janice. It's about addiction. I think... I really don't even know how to tell if someone's addicted. Honestly."

"Ok. There are a number of factors, but they require an intimate relationship to observe. Everyone doesn't get addicted and completely lose their mind, so drug use, by itself, is difficult to measure it with, without knowledge of the frequency and, the crazy behaviors that come along with addiction. We get most of out data from those who sincerely desire to stop using and the difficulty they have doing so. May I ask which drug?"

"Heroin."

Janice's eyes widen and she nods slowly. "That's highly addictive. Depending on how long they've been using, I'd put money on addiction setting in. How do they use it? Shoot it up, smoke it, snort it?"

Will shrugs. "I've been told it's smoking. I didn't even know it could be snorted. There are no visible tracks."

"So, if it's addiction, you want to know the best way to break it?" Will nods. "More drugs. Weaker drugs that replace the craving. I prefer cold turkey myself, and it's much cheaper. If you can control their environment, it's the best approach. Well…" Janice digresses. "Some say it's not the best approach with heroin because of how detox attacks the nervous system. It just really depends, Bunting. It's difficult to assess without knowing the patient and working with them in a clinical setting."

Will sighs and stands. "Alright. I really don't know enough to even question how to help. I'll find out more… maybe it's nothing. Thanks, Janice." Will rises from her desk and begins to walk out. Janice stops him by calling to him. He turns.

"Mr. Bunting! Now, I know you've been going through whatever you've been going through lately, just doing your day to day, unable to get any better acquainted with new residents, but you might want to pay some attention to Gary Dixon. I think he has a lot of potential, and we'll lose him if we're not careful."

Will smiles. "I'm like three steps ahead of you on that. Told you I got eyes behind my head, but you never believe me. It's why I don't wear hats Janice, or hoodies." Will winks at her. "Definitely a revolutionary spirit in him, and he wasn't doped out of his mind in the pen. Not sure how they missed him, but I'm not gonna… Oh, and I ran into LaTonya. Saw her at Robert's church, or whatever it is. She's doing alright. Told her she should stop by and she said she'd consider it. Not sure if it's a yes or a no, but she looked well." Will lies.

"Would be nice, if she does. I kind of miss her."

"Me too…" Will reveals with an empathizing nod. Ok, Janice, thanks again."

There is a new case of police misconduct happening weekly.

Cellphone cameras and the Internet are keeping the events in the public eye, one event after another, with many being lost in the shuffle when too many occur in too short of a time interval. The cops are averaging two murders per week, and on a pace to beat their astounding murder numbers from the previous year. Every murder is not a case of poor police work, nor is every treated as such, but many cases, most of which reached the viewfinders of cellphone cameras, were clearly abuses of power, and those obvious cases, tried by the court of public opinion, served in making the public question all of the police accounts that they did not have the liberty of viewing. Police getting murdered is at an all time low but the media plays up each occurrence like the sky is falling while downplaying the number of citizens they murder. The battle is decidedly one sided, and the citizens are the victim. It isn't a good time for police morale, their integrity questioned with each new incident, yet they are still killing citizens at the rate of two a week, collectively saying, *So what,* to the public disgust of their actions.

Not only is America taunting the Blacks, but there is a swell developing showing poor nonBlacks how powerless they are as well. The bulk of the deaths are Black males, percentage wise, but a few events against the pattern, including other races and genders challenge the potential safety of them all, disturbing the secure space their minds hold for them concerning how the cops will treat them. The police are playing their hand rather recklessly. Legion's local chapter is working through its issues, and the affiliate chapters are either doing under-the-radar work, doing nothing, or waiting for a signal from the local chapter. If they are waiting, it is Will hurting them all, because those locally are waiting for him as well, whether he's the leader or not. The police have done a wonderful job of making distrust the general sentiment. They are making the job of those organized to create a systematic loss of faith easier, if they would get out there and assume their position. Tuck has a valid argument, but its validity made it no less a death wish.

Throughout the country, in the north and the south, the pattern is incident, public outcry, mostly online, and protest, and one story fades seamlessly into the next, wash, and repeat. There is very little follow up and by the time prosecution comes around, which happens rarely, the public has completely forgotten about the incident connected because they've been acquainted with many more. If the energy doesn't see it through to the end, it is rendered ineffective. Also, with the frequency of the events, two deaths a week, the people suffer from overstimulation and desensitization is the only logical result. Eventually, it will only be easier for police to kill with impunity, and it is already easy at present. The nation is on a fast track to a police state, and the few revolutionaries on hand are sitting upon them, arguing both philosophy and strategy. Neither philosophy nor strategy will matter when the window of opportunity closes and people no longer care that they are being murdered in the streets like animals, left to bleed out for hours, and they accept it as just another part of their horrible reality. Humans have proven to be able to adapt and accept even the most debasing and life-threatening conditions as normal, look at prison, look at slavery, they only need to develop within the culture long enough, as if in a Petri dish.

The people are losing patience and losing power, and they haven't the organization to do anything about it or even diagnose what is happening. Their anger rises and falls like a diaphragm; it is the respiration of daily living for the poor and no other options are being offered to them. They either breathe or decide not to. The choice seems simple enough, obvious indeed, but there are definite advantages to not breathing. How many heroes have chosen death instead of submitting to an oppressive reality? Part of Will's freedom or death demand was unplugging. The more the negative events began to happen, or as their public exposure increased, the less Will began logging onto the Internet and watching the news. His *see no evil* mode was only disturbed by the streets, while keeping up with Gray, and the streets don't care nearly as much about events that do not directly affect its blocks. When being bombarded with emotionally stirring events, Will finds it difficult to be objective. He has to guard himself against becoming emotional, because under the grip of emotion people tend to act irrationally. An irrational Will enjoys his guns and planning ways to hurt people, although sometimes that can also happen with rational thought.

With each new event, the conversation is diverted. People would rather discuss Black on Black crime, which actually isn't higher than White on White crime, and the same with any race because most petty criminals target who they know and have access to and they live around those like themselves. If Black on Black crime is really dear to their hearts, how exactly is the mention of it in any way related to the number of Blacks being murdered by police? It is completely unrelated beyond the police directly being responsible for the reduction or eradication of Black on Black crime, or crime in general. Will encounters that argument and finds the humor in seeing more than one way the police are unnecessary and doing a horrible job. People would also rather victim blame, stating that if the victim would have complied, they would not have been murdered, as if murder is the proper response to noncompliance. If the police officers weren't cowards, always in *fearing for their lives*, there would have also been no murder, and many times the victim has been in compliance and still met his or her end to the murderous hands of a trained coward.

From all of the examples and the classical conditioning of constant media exposure, the time should be approaching where Black males themselves will be able to use the, *I feared for my life*, defense when encountering police, should fight or flight be the resulting action, and the law should make accommodations for them as much as it does for cops. It is just the slave breaking of old, with special emphasis on the lowest and the weakest. The cops subconsciously flex, not their power, because they haven't any and they are only the extension of, but the power lent to them by the elites to make examples that will keep the entire herd at bay. Will knows exactly what is happening and why, so the constant exposure to it does nothing for him, and he opts to holding his breath instead of inhaling and exhaling with the massive lung of the destitute. Harmony has placed him center stage, and he sees the effects of the breaking regardless, and feels them.

Man choked to death for selling cigarettes illegally. Child shot to death for playing with toy gun in a park. Man shot to death for holding toy gun in a retail store. Man shot to death holding toy sword. Couple shot to death because their car backfired. Man shot to death for allegedly trying to take an officer's taser. Man shot for allegedly trying to take a cop's gun. Man shot for allegedly trying to take a cop's gun. Man shot for allegedly trying to take a cop's gun. Man shot for reaching for his waistband though unarmed. Man shot for reaching for his waistband though unarmed. Man shot for reaching for his waistband though unarmed. Man shot for reaching for his waistband though unarmed. Man shot for reaching for his waistband though unarmed. Man killed in the back of a police van. Man pulled off of his horse and strangled to death. Teen murdered for not listening to cop's orders while wearing headphones. Teenage girl shot to death for allegedly trying to run a cop over with her car. Woman shot to death for allegedly trying to run cop a over with her car. Man shot to death for allegedly trying to run a cop over with his car. Man shot to death for allegedly trying to run a cop over with his car. Man shot to death for allegedly trying to run a cop over with his truck. Man shot for reaching into his truck to grab his license as he'd been instructed. Man shot to death for reaching for his seatbelt. Man shot to death because prescription pills were mistaken for a gun handle. Man shot to death when ordered not to exit car and he decided to anyway. Child shot to death while she slept in her grandmother's arms. Man shot to death. Woman shot to death. Child shot to death. Wash and repeat.

What will another unarmed, innocent, Black, Native American, Hispanic, poor White, woman, or child, wiped off of the planet by the hands of a cop mean to him when he hasn't built the power base to properly stop it from happening? This is Will's logic. It is healthier for him to work his plan than to allow the sky falling around him, as people pretend that what's happening has not been happening for over a century, to interrupt it. The results are disastrous when one tries to fly before one's wings have fully developed, and unified thought must precede unified action and some of his most active and dedicated membership have allowed the looks of the world around them to rattle them and force them to make poor decisions. Toni is on drugs... Will has to acknowledge his alcoholism in the same light, the occasional joint, and the manner in which he uses sex, but his level of functionality is nothing short of impressive while juggling his addictions. The reality is that without his escapes, while being subject to constant stimulation reminding him of his worthlessness, he'd go crazy. Rational people in irrational conditions cannot help but to find escapes while trying to reconcile the two extremes. He's watched enough of the craziness his people have exhibited, metaphorically poking the bear, pretending that an attitude, sharp words, or a good hand game are ways to challenge extensions of actual, definition controlling, resource hoarding, power. It just isn't worth breathing for Will, and his heart has yet to stop beating for his refusal to participate, so he is fine. He only logs into the network to send important messages, and he hasn't even done that in a while.

Gray is just as ignorant to the depressing national respiration because he doesn't give a damn, and he represents the honest sentiment of the street. There is only one person's death, and a couple of possibles, he's concerned about, no matter how many of the others dying match his description. It's a tough world, and the best way to fall victim to it is occupying one's mind with those things that have no direct effect. Gray has too many personal worries to adopt the worries of others not in his immediate circle. He's returned to, *if I can't eat it or beat it, I don't need it… unless it's money*, mode. He actually never left it, but it was a difficult mantra to stay true to while in prison. Sanity is even difficult to stay true to while in prison. Many inmates would go crazy, and many others would play crazy, pretend to be, to keep people afraid of them, and end up doped up and made crazy as a result. There is a way to get legally high in prison, state sponsored, and inmates were becoming the walking dead riding the crazy train, but many never return from the trip. It's already a psychological gauntlet and although facing it with an altered state appears and even feels easier, the proper orientation of things can be lost forever. Gray could stand the challenge of prisons reversal of truth, up being down and down being up, but he never wanted to be stuck asking which way is up. He's seen it too many times in the addicted, and he saw it mostly outside of prison because prison itself is just a smaller, stricter version of the ghetto.

Gray, fortunately, never got heavy into drugs, even the legal ones. If his mind his cloudy, it increases his chance of becoming a victim, even with alcohol. Lena thought it square of him that he never wanted to smoke or drink with her. His excuse was easy with smoking since Harmony did frequent urinary analysis, and he even got her to stop smoking around him because of that. He isn't sure whether secondhand inhaled smoke in close quarters shows up in tests, but he convinced her not to smoke anywhere near him. She likes him enough to comply. She doesn't even function well without being high. She's built a dependency. It allows her to do things that her sober mind would question and regret. In the moments they shared together while she was sober, she seemed not to know what to say, struggling to express herself. While high or drunk that was never a problem. Gray isn't one to carry a conversation, so the sober Lena created some awkward moments, but him being nice to look at and adept in body language helps in those times. She could then hide behind their sexual attraction to one another. She is fine as long as she is hiding. Gray is too, but Gray is compelled to, not for embarrassment, but for the safety of being an unknown. People have trouble hurting what they do not know, not knowing where or how to attack, so Gray stays guarded should someone desire to harm him, because some have desired to and some have been successful.

"I wonder sometimes if this is all there is with life, you know?" Lena is speaking from Gray's chest. She gets introspective and vulnerable after sex, like she's reverted to who she would be if life had dealt her a better hand. Before sex, she's cocky, tense, and aggressive, and Gray enjoys removing her tension, pulling her, taking her, shaping her, making her elastic, or the sweet and sour ecstasy of folding taffy rolling across his tongue, but afterwards, she's soft and demure, wanting to explore her emotions and the dreams she'll never return to. Gray is no fan of this pillow talk, but he understands her vulnerability in these times. She's just shared half of herself with him, with no financial transaction, and the least he can do is allow her to share the other half of herself with him, the person she misses and would rather be. Gray doesn't like that kind of thinking, the could haves, should haves, and would haves, because his focus is always the present and not the potential. He has no interest in alternate realities where Lena grew up in a great neighborhood with two loving parents, was a good student in good schools with teachers from the community who had a vested interest and cared, where she was surrounded by people with similar upbringings and value for life. There is no use for it and all she does is makes him think, not of her fantasy, but of his own and who and where he could be if things were different, and it's even worse for him because he has two children that he tries desperately to forget that always reappear in his should be, could be, and would be life.

"No. I don't wonder stuff like that."

"Never?" Gray shakes his head *no* and Lena can feel the vibrations through his chest while listening to his heart as if she could tell if he were lying or not. He doesn't want to open that door with her. The less he shares, the easier it is to deal with people, and the easier it is to deal with himself. "Well, I know there's more to life than this. To think we just born to do this for some years and die, makes it a waste of time… I went to the liquor store over off Moreland to pick up a couple of things. Walking out I recognized a lady at the bus stop. She used to babysit me when I was a girl, 'cause Mama worked so much. Good lady. Church-going. Kind. I don't have no bad memories of her… Well, she's old now, and one of her feet been cut off. Diabetes, or *the sugar*, like they call it, I bet. Sitting at the bus stop, so she probably alone. Good people, bad people, all end up the same. Gotta be more to this, Gray. It just makes me think."

"You speak to her?"

"Hell no. I don't want her to see me like this… Funny, as bad as she looked, I think I look even worse. Nothing like the little girl she used to read nursery rhymes to and put together puzzles with. Not sure who would be more embarrassed if she saw me. I don't even talk to my Mama, so I don't see no reason in talking to someone who might still. I'm glad she didn't see me. Not my life anymore." Lena's words get increasingly softer, and she digs her cheek deeper into Grays chest. He feels a drop of wetness fall upon his body, probably after rolling across the bridge of her nose and squeezed out of her tightly pressed eyes. He acts like he doesn't feel it.

People looking for some deeper meaning in life always end up disappointed. The meaning of life is to live it as long and as easily as possible for Gray, and he plans to live in the moment until he's out of moments to live, the moment he dies. There is no need to plan ahead when nothing's promised, and the disappointments are less disappointing with no expectation. Gray reduced his scope of who he worries about, nearly no one but himself, and when he worries about, nearly no time but the present. The simpler he keeps life, the better. If he gets into talking about dreams with her, it won't be long before she questions why she isn't a part of his. Every woman wants to be a part of a man's dreams and feel like a part of his life that isn't replaceable or expendable, and Gray has always found it easier not to enter the arena where those discussions will come up. If the woman introduces the subject they look desperate and Gray's silence is often enough to show that it isn't a subject he is interested in discussing. He doesn't have that out if he walks the path into the world of intimate wants that dreams provide.

"Life is just about living, Lena. Don't put so much thought into it, baby." Adding *baby* was his way of comforting her. Gray doesn't talk like that, and every time he does, it's a treat. "Find a way to appreciate and be appreciated for who you are, what you do, and when you do it and you have the secret to happiness. If you feel good right now, where you are and who you with, then life is good. Don't complicate it."

"You think I'm your baby, Gray?" Lena questions.

"I gotta get out of here soon. You know I gotta curfew," Gray answers.

"I know." Lena sits up as if rejected. Gray recognizes it through her body language. She clears her face of the wetness it accumulated, and begins the process of hardening again. Her softness is just a grace period immediately after orgasm, and her suede is turning back into leather right before his eyes. Many times Gray has experienced the transformation, but this evening he decides to slow it.

"Of course you're my baby. Why else would I say it?"

Lena smiles. "Are you leaving, going back home when your time up? I don't have nothing holding me here. Just putting it out there since I'm your baby and all." She pinches his chest and laughs to make what wasn't a joke seem like one, and Gray laughs to play along.

"Not sure I have a home anymore. There's no one back in that city I'm interested in seeing again. Here might be just as good a place as any, depending what kind of deals I can get my hands on. My life there is the old me just like who you were with your babysitter is the old you." Gray recognizes the direction of the conversation. It's not where he wants it to be. He changes the subject. "I'm not going to do this weak shit for long. I gotta get on some real money and make some moves. This ain't me. This is me under wraps, but soon as I get clear of that house, and the regulations, I'm pushing the gas."

Lena nods her head. "I got shotgun. In case you need someone to hold the map or hold the gun." Lena shrugs her shoulders and smiles again. She slaps Gray on the chest. "Come on. Get up before I end up getting you in trouble."

There were two conversations occurring at once. One where they shared small pieces of their present reality and one where Gray was telling Lena the sacrifice she'd have to make be with him. They both knew which conversation was the real one. It wasn't one Gray was interested in having and the direction was switched to affirm to her that he wasn't a square no matter how square his present situation was. They weren't about to talk about a three-bedroom house, a white picket fence, and girl for her and a boy for him. Lena was still showing her hand for Gray to play his as he wished with full knowledge. She knew he was in the process of getting his life back together, and she was willing to act as glue, placing more parts of him back in functioning order and connecting him with the right people than the government sponsored program whose curfew he must respect.

"We can make it each moment mean more. You and me. I believe in you, baby." It was Lena's way of signing the contract.

*   *   *

Will first needed to see where he was with Toni before addressing Gray. She's probably blamed him for everything. The most consistent character trait Will has found in others is their ability to deflect and place the blame away from themselves. It is Will's fault that they entered her home unannounced, but it isn't his fault that he cared enough about her to do so. That is her fault. Sometimes friendship requires behavior unbefitting of a friend, and although they did not catch her in the act, they found out more in the manner that they approached it than Will could have with a phone call. Toni knew the seriousness of the charge and the quality of the intelligence - which was really only Gray's word because the entire trip was about Tuck and not Toni, but she didn't know that - so she could only have properly challenged if it were, in fact, false. Will really killed two birds with one stone, except he had no interest in killing one of them. There is no one he wants to protect more than Toni, but the collective is more important than the individual and he had to make that point to her and to the others.

The conversation would've have had an entirely different tone if he didn't have an audience. It will have an entirely different tone shortly. She doesn't answer, he left no messages, and it's a better conversation to have in person. Will has had enough of these high stress conversations to last the entire year. The thought of this talk plays with his stomach, and he wishes he could turn to drugs himself, or even prayer. The ice between them has been thinning and he can imagine it breaking with him falling through into a coldness he can't return from. That side of Will is no help to anyone, and he is so proficient in manning it. It's the side that found it easy to be a soldier. It's the side that only went home after leaving the army just to check in and never return. It's a comfortable side, but Will recognizes it as unhealthy, and he needs as many people as possible in his circle that he does not have to be that side with. That side is death, individualistic, dark, and disfigured, and people like Toni, when they are on proper terms, pull him away from it and back to life. He needs Toni's compassion as much as she needs his, escaping and chasing a fantasy. How could chasing the dragon mean anything but?

Losing touch or being forced to lose touch with his people, however far that banner stretches, is his terror. He's been effectively trained as the enemy of people, and he traveled the world planning the demise and the destruction of communities, making them as dysfunctional and dependent as the ghettos and trailer parks in the states. It was a crime against humanity, and he'd participated in it for twenty years, losing his humanity shard by shard to fit the posture his controllers needed him to be. The drugs and the women made it easy. It's amazing what a bump, a toque, or a pill can do for those reticent of taking a human life. Some couldn't get through combat without being in an altered state, the most human of them. Will didn't need assistance in that manner. He wasn't the best soldier but he'd been gifted with a natural numbness that kept his mind in tact. Pulling away from humanity is easy, too easy, and his self diagnoses, as a man in his mid forties, is he'll probably shrivel and dry up in his coldness, disconnected and alone without intervention. He'll become something like his favorite uncle, his father's youngest sibling, born into an environment he didn't quite fit into and forced to live life in the margins because of it. The brother that didn't like women among a group of brothers who loved them too much, or were loved by them too much, in a time and place where his sexual orientation wasn't socially acceptable. The circumstances doomed him to a life of loneliness, and Will's social orientation is dooming him the same. Keeping those he can be close with, close, is important, and he's down to very few, the most important of which is Toni.

Toni needs him too. No one respects her like she deserved because of her lifestyle choices, and how she looks, but Will. Just like Will, she decorates herself with numerous relationships, shiny, entertaining things, that hang upon her like Christmas ornaments until she tires of them or they tire of her because she feels too deeply too quickly. It's the same thing but the opposite for Will, as he never feels deeply enough. For people so dedicated to the collective, they surely struggle with satisfying the individual. Will is a successful experiment in rugged individualism, or he was, or he possibly is still depending upon how he's able to handle the present conflict. Muscles get stronger through resistance, so should he be able to salvage the health of these relationships and the health of the individuals, the local chapter will be stronger.

Will left Harmony after a normal day of almost working, thinking about how he'd approach Toni the entire time. He relaxes at home thinking the same thing, deciding not to head to The Fifth until after the sun sets. Will sits in his living room, drinking wine and waiting for the day to die. He looks at the television remote but he chooses instead the stereo remote. A music recording is much better background to his thinking than a disturbing screen. At the very moment something is probably happening that will piss him off and the news will only alert him to it. Music works. Sundown isn't until half past eight. It is six. He has time to eat, drink, and mellow out. He's tired. He's always tired. He's never allowed to rest his mind, and thinking can be as fatiguing as physical activity. He lets the women sing to him through the speakers. They teach him about love, loss, and heartbreak, all things he knows little about. Just having that range of emotion available is attractive, even while knowing the possibility of it in him doesn't exist. Will's left wondering if heartbreak is better than not knowing love at all. One is at least life changing and worth talking about. On the other hand, one is so flat it will hold no one's attention.

His phone rattles upon his coffee table, and Will just stares at it a moment before deciding to reach over to see who it is. He looks at the screen with little excitement, but he decides to answer. "Dee. What's up, lady?" He turns the stereo down a little while listening. "What do you mean, do I have any work? You used to call me to talk to me, see how I was doing, and now this is how you treat me?" Will laughs. "Oh yeah, I get it. You don't love me anymore." Will is extremely relaxed and the tone of the conversation is playful. "Ok. I'll see what I can do… Well, let me ask you something. Your last job, what did you think? … I never ask because I never care. I mean, I really just avoid the thought of it because you've been with me before." Will grabs his drink and sips it as if padding for her response. "No. Insecure about what? It's not like you're my woman or anything. I was just curious. Forget I asked. Didn't know you had a client confidentiality agreement with your service." Will laughs again. "But I'm the client though, right? I paid you, not him." A soft smile crawls across Will's face while listening to her response. "So modest of you not to kiss and tell, Dee… Did he ask about you? Ha! You do like him! You've never asked me that before." Will is speaking through a huge grin. "If he has, it hasn't gotten back to me. He's kind of quiet. I like him though… I've been out of it for weeks now. That's why you haven't heard from me, but I'm getting better. Have you heard anything on the streets?"

It is time to face her. Will grabs his phone and his pistol, slides it into the small of his back, cuts the lights off, and leaves his house a quarter after eight with a nice buzz and his mind made up about how he will approach this issue with Toni. He didn't grab his gun because he needed it for Toni. Never. He grabbed it because he doesn't leave in the evening without it. He's licensed to carry, and it's better to have it and not need it than to need it and not have it. It's the closest thing he has to a dedicated woman, and she has his back again. Dee's phone call helped loosen him up more than the music and wine. She's an acquaintance he's known for years. He started off as one of her customers until it got old to him, but they stayed in contact. She's a native, so she's one of the people he can count on for information. She's an Ear, unofficially, because she's not a member of Legion or aware of its existence, but she is acquainted with Will's revolutionary side and knows that he has his hands into something other than Harmony. Will has a number of people just like her that keep him informed at a small cost, but the transaction is worth it to keep eyes behind his head, and as in the case of Dee, some can be paid to do more. Between the carwash, the barbershop, bars, other than The Fifth, his favorite women of leisure, and Legion, Will stays plugged into the hood's happenings.

Traffic is light and the heavens are pink like red dye has been dropped into a bowl of liquid sky, growing deeper and darker by the minute. His windows are rolled up. It's still over ninety degrees out even though the sun is falling. At midnight it won't be any cooler than eighty. There is never any cool in the Texas summer unless one has an air conditioner or a cold front comes in. All of the windows on the road are rolled up, except the ones with defective air conditioning systems and the state of their windows are the signal. The hot summer has arrived in all of its glory, and temperatures are high as well as tempers, for they are combustible gasses and the heat is a spark. There are many more fights and murders in the summer in the hood. Will never leaves home without his gun in the summer, mainly because few others are leaving home without theirs. Never does he want to be faced again with having to take a human life, especially not with those through which he identifies his struggle, but if it's his life or theirs, he won't hesitate. His trigger never shakes, never hesitates. He's well trained; he doesn't even emotionally react to using lethal force until long afterwards. He's just as dangerous to the people as the police are, possibly worse, should he be placed in a high stress situation where self-preservation is his only flashing thought. Startled by the sight in his rearview mirror, self-preservation is his only flashing thought.

"Shit!" Will immediately glances at his speedometer to see if he'd zoned out and began traveling too quickly. No. His speed is fine. He's also legal so nothing on their computer is an excuse to pull him over, and he figures it's just a harassment stop. He leans forward so he can remove his gun from behind him. He places the gun between the console and his seat instead, just in case he needs to reach it, while pulling over to the side of the road. The sky is now a deep magenta and soon to be black. It's dark enough to impede vision. Will can't make out the cop in his vehicle any more than the cop can make him out, especially with the darkness of his tint. Should one, or a community declare war upon the police like they have appeared to do so on the poor, with particular interest in murdering Black males, the police would be easy targets by their very job descriptions. For example, a police officer walking up to a car with tinted windows at night is at an extreme tactical disadvantage, and a stop such as this does not have to be by chance. Some slow down by known speed traps, but others can speed up should they have a plan to get stopped, prepared to be, in a car the police can't see into. They'd be staring at their own reflection, waiting for the window to roll down, with a barrel behind it pointed at their heart or face. Simple. Car windows are easily replaced, and can be done in-house. The same can be done with 911 calls that only have the purpose of leading police to locations already prepared for their removal. It wouldn't take too many such events before they changed how they work, refusing to pull people over in certain communities and refusing to respond to calls there. They are humans, and the instinct to self-preserve is as strong with them as it is with everyone else.

They are lucky Will is not as emotional and quickly angered as Tuck. Very lucky. With his experience as a retired first sergeant, over a company of two hundred, he could cripple the police impact in any community, having them too terrified to fulfill their job description, with a tenth of the men in a company the size of his. He has more than a tenth of that number at his disposal in the local chapter alone, but it isn't time, and they are not the targets unless they decide to press the issue. The officer exits his vehicle. Will rolls down his window and he has his driver's license in hand to make sure this harassment is as seamless as possible. The cop is approaching with his hand on his sidearm, which Will views as threatening, especially concerning the nature of the offense, if there has even been one. It's just a traffic stop.

"Good evening, sir. License and registration, please?"

"I have them right here, but may I ask why I was stopped? Was there a moving violation?" Will likes to engage them just to see what lies they will tell. He's been pulled over for not wearing his seatbelt, in a car with electric seatbelts, pulled over for not using his turn signal when turning into a parking lot, and even pulled over, if it can be called that, while not driving. Parked on the side of the street, legally, he's been asked for his license and registration, because the climate is such, and has been such in the ghetto where they really don't need a reason any longer to harass the inhabitants.

"Sure thing. You didn't make a complete stop at the red light on Allen before making your right turn." The officer smiles. He's skinny, young, blue eyed and blond with a military crew cut. His tone is polite, so he is politely being an asshole. *Complete stops* are always bullshit excuses to pull someone over, and one Will has heard many times. They never give tickets to people for not making complete stops, because that is never the reason they pull them over. It's an excuse to harass and to make sure the driver is sober, legal, or paranoid, at times they get lucky finding drivers that have committed a recent crime and they expose themselves in the nervousness or aggression expressed in minor traffic stops.

For the untrained, average citizen, the police have the power and the advantage at a traffic stop, so no matter how much of an asshole the cop is, in recognition of power dynamics, the citizen should be worried about de-escalation, not escalation, if he or she is interested in making it home. Will hands him what he's asked for, and the officer takes it to run it. Will is playing the role of the average citizen. He reminds himself often that police are not power, but extensions of power and wastes of ammo. Although they target the poor and the powerless, it is a failure in their class consciousness, they belong to the group they target, and the poor and powerless targeting them in return will do nothing in acquiring power, but only in keeping the extensions of power at bay. Police are pawns for the elites, protecting property not people, unless they are people who own property. With few exceptions, the same landowners recognized in the Constitution are the same class of people ruling the country, not police. The poor need bigger targets to get the power they want, and this is what Will struggled to get Tuck to realize, as he continued to plan to target a symptom and not the problem. A revolutionary is planning and patient, much more than emotion, and a reactionary is the opposite. Every revolutionary is a potential reactionary, but every reactionary is not a potential revolutionary.

According to all his hood sources, since the cop got shot, the police are making a lot more stops, but it has not resulted in any extra violence. They have possibly understood that everyone is not scared of them. The officer returns and hands Will his information. "Okay Mr. Bunting. I'm going to let you off with a warning. Just make sure you make complete stops. It's easier to slow down and coast on through, we all do it, but it is against the law. Have a nice night." He smiles and nods, Will smiles in return, and waits for him to start walking off before raising his window. The inconvenience caused all his cool air to escape, but he kept his personal cool to the benefit of the peace officer. Will pulls off and continues his travels to The Fifth, only minutes away.

There is no more red left in the sky, and it's a lighter shade of black with tiny white holes poked into it so the planet can breathe beneath its cloak. They'd all suffocate without the stars and the moon.

The Fifth has patrons. There are four cars in the parking lot besides Toni's. It's not an ideal situation for an intimate discussion, but Will parks anyway. He misses Toni, he worries and cares for her, and just talking will be satisfying, just showing he cares. He hasn't even done that in the past weeks as he's felt burned by those he trusted, including her, not recognizing the difficult place she was in concerning her disposition in trying to please everyone. He salutes the Archangel Michael, illuminated by the lights inside the pub, while passing on his way in.

Toni's behind the bar. She looks up and meets his eyes immediately and greets them with an embarrassed smile. The patrons are at the tables, talking and laughing. The bar area is empty. Will takes a seat at the bar.

"Scotch, please. Dry."

"Like I don't know what your conservative ass drinks." Toni opens the floor with a welcoming tease. It's almost an apology in itself. Will grows a smile across his face, and his heart is released to beat normally.

"Right. But if I would have just sat down and waited, or flashed some cash you would've thought I was an asshole."

"Too late." Toni jabs. "I know that about you, too, but I love you still… Will." She starts making his drink. "Been keeping up with the news?"

"Nah. Not really. Been going through some personal stuff. Worried I'd lost someone important. She wouldn't answer my calls or anything. Tore me up something serious."

"Sorry to hear that… Wouldn't worry if I were you though. She's fine. She really is. But seriously, the news might interest you." Toni slides Will his drink and freezes upon him with a look of concern.

"What happened?"

"Tuck…"

Will interrupts, "I don't even fuck with Tuck anymore, Toni. Whatever he's doing, doesn't matter to me."

"Ok." Toni shrugs.

Will carries his drink up to his lips and frowns in a quick recap. "Wait. He made the news?"

"We made it. Well, you weren't there yet, but I was..." Toni grabs her cellphone from under the bar. This happened at the Temple the day we saw each other. Toni pulls up an article from the city paper titled: Local Hate Group Targets Police. Will's heart drops. He shakes his head and begins reading. Toni removes it from his line of sight, and he looks up at her puzzled. She sweeps down the touch screen with her index finger, and puts the phone back in his face. "And there's video." She pushes play, and Tuck's, *fuck the police,* rant is on display for the world to see. The officer sat in the middle of the street recording him, gaining for himself, or rather his team, the public support they need to target the Temple of Morality. Will can't believe what he's seeing and hearing, he fits the heels of his palms into the pockets of his eyes. It's evil; he refuses to see it. Toni adds, unenthusiastically, "Picked the perfect time to cut ties, I guess."

3:4 *The Lord works in mysterious ways. The pain of change appears as failure, and will be if it is not pushed through. Muscles do not get stronger without first ripping, and the gained strength is in the repair. People do not get stronger without first nearing their breaking point. They break down then break through, those that continue to push. The same works for collectives. At least in theory it does. I've broken down many times, and transformed into a stronger me as a result without fail. I'm so used to it, I almost welcome the dark times, the small muscle tears, foreseeing the strength that will result from the repetition.*

Will is out in the hallways early speaking to the residents. He hasn't done this in weeks. There are a few new residents that do not even know him outside of the initial tour. His hard bottoms click around the facility, popping his head in and out of offices and dorm rooms smiling. It looks fake, but it might be genuine, because Will's way often looks fake, but it can easily be argued that beyond his reconciliation with Toni, he hasn't anything to smile about. When he reaches the front lobby, he flashes his smile at Ann. "Ms. Ann!... Now I'm only asking because you're usually in the know, and it's a subject of interest for you as well. Have you seen Robert?" Will smiles like he's part of a mint chewing gum advertisement, and Ann immediately blushes and waves him off. "I'm sorry. Seriously though, has he been through here?"

Ann nods in affirmation. "He's outside."

"See! I knew you'd know. Thank you, dear. I'll tell him you said Hi, as usual." Will winks and walks out of the door. Ann shakes her head. She enjoys Will's social side, although it only makes appearances occasionally. Will can hide a lot behind a smile.

"Well, look who's famous now." Tuck is working up a sweat with the hedge clippers, shaping the bushes on the side of the facility. He doesn't hear or notice Will's approach or words. Will stops and stands about four feet away from him on the side he's facing so he'll easily notice him when he looks up. The tiny leaves flip, float, and flow between the branches that are still in tact, some make it all the way to the ground, and some get hung up and do not. Tuck creates the illusion of conformity; he creates lines and corners where there are none. The closer the viewer gets, the less sense a straight line composed of hundreds of tiny twigs and leaves makes, but this is what he's paid to do. From far away it looks straight. Those viewing the campus from the street will be impressed by the neatness of its shrubbery, and might even imagine the same kind of discipline in its residents. Tuck shakes an annoying sweat buildup off of his brow with a quick head jostle and notices Will in mid swing. He looks up, releases the trigger, tightens his jaws and presses it again as if it would not engage alternating blades and instead drive a bullet through a chamber and ring out loudly. Tuck releases the trigger again.

"To what do I owe the pleasure?" Tuck lets the hedge clippers fall to his side as he addresses Will with an emotionless expression.

"Well… I was hoping I could come out here and get your autograph before, you know, all the fame consumes you. You got fans now, Tuck. Some crazy fans."

"I ain't break no laws. Them motherfuckers can't do shit do me, or they already would have. And what it got to do with you, anyway?"

Will shrugs off Tuck's defensiveness. "I'm your employer, Robert. I'm surprised no one has contacted me yet. I mean, I got your back when they do, if they do. I'll make up something, because… it was clearly you on the video."

"You ain't got to make up shit. Fuck 'em. I meant what I said. They think somebody scared of 'em. Hell, I'm glad it's on tape. My recruiting's up. And we gonna…" Tuck stops himself. "Yeah. I wasn't trying to hide anyway. That's where we differ, Will."

Will nods. "Ok. I just wanted to get an autograph before the fame got to your head, and one of those crazy fans made you lose your mind… I truly hope you're not missing the metaphor here. Cop recorded that video for a reason. And it was released to the press for a reason. That was the beginning of the operation, gaining public support. Your piece has officially been placed on the board, and for what? What you think the next move is?"

"Maybe I'm not waiting for their next move. It's my move now, and if the people on my side, I got the advantage. Told you it's gonna be a hot summer." Tuck pumps the trigger a couple of times to alert Will he has work to do.

"Remove you from the board of play. You were placed upon the board to be made an example of, just so they can remove you... in front of all of your fans, Tuck. All of them." Will illustrates with his hands. He pivots his torso and head and opens his arms with, *in front of all of your fans,* as if gathering them around.

"So! What I'm supposed to be scared now? That's what they want. What they need! I've had a target on me my entire fucking life. I'm Black, I'm poor, I don't talk... like you. Like them. They been looking for an excuse to put a bullet in my head since I dropped out my momma. Nothing's changed. Fuck they move. It's my move now, and this is my hood, these are my people, on my streets, and they the fucking invaders. As long as I got the people, I'm good."

"Let's hope you got them, then. I don't think you would've had a shootout with a drug dealer if the people were with you like that. Just my observation, though. If I get contacted, I'm not throwing you under the bus. We have our differences, but I just see us as comrades on different fronts. I'll feign ignorance. You have my word that I won't sell you out or sabotage whatever it is you're trying to do, but I need the same concerning your affiliation with Legion, past affiliation, in case you get caught up."

Tuck shakes his head and smiles. "Oh, that's what this is about. It's always something with you, Will... I have a code. I ain't no snitch. Nobody getting nothing out of me but some more *fuck yous,* because fuck them, and fuck you too, Will. Respectfully." Will nods. Tuck sounds more distant than convincing. Will is unsure as to who of the two Tuck is even trying to convince. Regardless, Will's satisfied. He's given the information he wanted to deliver, and he's been given the information he wanted to receive.

"Alright. I'll let you get back to it. You're right. It's your hood, and they have to come to you, and should they, it gives you the advantage. We've trained on this. They're too many vacant buildings and too many people that look like you for you to be predictable, if the people are with you. But the moment you become predictable, you're dead or back in jail, but most likely dead ... Bushes look good." Will grabs a couple of loose branches that had fallen atop the bush when cut and tosses them to the ground. He tilts his head to Tuck and walks off.

So, Tuck has plans. Will walks away with this thought that is not at all surprising, but confirming it was worth their talk. When anyone is content in making themselves a target, Will is content in getting away from them. Tuck makes good points, but Will thinks the foundation of his awkward confidence is his belief in a higher power. Imaginary friends are beautiful confidence builders, whispering affirming thoughts into the imaginer's ears in the best way the imaginer can imagine. If the collective God, the people, do not agree, he's in trouble, and there is no telling with them as they move on emotion not logic. Logic would have had them at odds with the police and the elites long ago, but one thousand police shootings will only be seen as one thousand isolated incidents to the emotional, jumping from victim to victim, zoomed in so tightly they do not recognize the resulting pattern. Tuck won't even make a hashtag, as his innocence, which was long removed by his criminal record, completely disintegrated, never to return, with his recorded behavior. He can start feeding the homeless, saving endangered species, and reversing the affects of global warming, and he'll still be seen as nothing but a angry nigger, or violent thug, deserving of death, to the establishment. His being a good father, teacher, and caretaker won't even be mentioned. Moving away from the target is intelligent for anyone not willing to also become a target. Will's timing was divine. He felt as if things were falling together.

Toni told him more than he thought she would. They spoke as if nothing was wrong, hiding the issues at hand, while Will consumed a healthy amount of liquor. He was content just talking to her and watching her smile. It was a good moment for them. The stress of social pressures and ideally trying to do something to remedy them can be hell on any relationship, even platonic ones. Everyone in their circle watches one another, as to not move too soon, say the wrong thing, do the wrong thing, endanger the collective, an apprehension that keeps them all still, but, conversely, this makes them all blame each other for their lack of motion as a collective. It is not that they do not want liberation, and it isn't just fear, it is not truly knowing how to achieve it and the risk of losing the few comforts they have in such a gamble.

Comfort is the enemy of revolution. As long as Will can sit back, cut on his stereo and sink away from the collective struggle with a stiff drink, or dial up a woman and sink into her and away the same, he's not prepared. If he's not willing to lose that, he's not willing to fight for better, because better is the destination at the end of the road of much worse. They have all been pacified by the comfort of just enough, and the fear of not having it keeps their feet still. At The Fifth there were three tables filled with laughing friends, of mixed ages, sexes, and races, enjoying the company of one another and ignoring the problems of the world. They are of the sleeping class, the sleeping giant as it is often referred as, and over ninety percent of the planet are members, with few recognizing it. Their lack of class-consciousness is to the advantage of their oppressors and no accident. Instead, compulsory schooling teaches them to divide along lines like race and sex, mentioning those often in the social sciences but never class. Many don't even know the distinction of class exists, although it is arguably the oldest of them all.

Social animals even separate themselves into classes. It is indeed natural at that level of engagement, but mankind and the point of technology and the massive means of organizing resources and manpower through government is to break the necessity of class stratification, not reinforce it. At least that is what they are taxed to do, or why else would the poor place their money into them to be just as powerless as they would be to the rich without them? Governments, instead, tell them that they matter as much as the wealthy and their collective wants will outweigh the wants of a powerful few. It looks great on paper documents, but the expression of the supposed design falls short as the middle class continues to shrink and the popularity of legal and illegal drugs rises with the depression of all those that find themselves outside of the American dream.

The bar business is a good one to be in. Good call on Toni's part, even with a poor location. The drug business is also good to be in. Good call for all of the inner city merchants and soon to be prisoners and possibly residents of Harmony. The prison business is a great business to be in, as the jobs continue to get worse and wages continue to fall in comparison to inflation while companies are more profitable than they have ever been; people are going to have to makeup the difference somehow and crime is often the how. The halfway house business is a good one to be in. It's government sponsored, and it looks like admirable work geared to make better people of those who were caught into the system, but as it turns out it is just a great way to make money because they are not preparing felons to be successful in a system that many nonfelons cannot navigate through. The healthcare and funeral parlor businesses are the best ones to be in. Sick and dead is exactly where these struggling, stressed, drugged, angry, and aggressive people who cannot find work and satisfaction in life eventually end up. Will listened to those people laughing, drinking, and being merry, knowing that soon they all would die.

One of the White guys who charged the bar to order another round of drinks called Will *pops*, and told him he looked like a military man. Will smiled it off and refused to engage because there is nothing more depressing than military talk, especially between those that have seen action. The conversations turns into death, as there is only really death to talk about, deaths in the field and deaths back at home. The excitement degenerates quickly when the reality sets in of what they've taken part in, and the inhumanity of it that sets in is easily measured by the number of soldier suicides while at home, safe and away from conflict. More die from self inflicted measures than do in combat. Will didn't want to have that discussion. He was enjoying his talk with Toni, so he played dumb and took looking like he was military as a simple compliment on his sharpness. He saw in the man's eyes that he was laughing to keep from crying and opening up that door was a negative. He had enough soul-draining residue to concern himself with, like the lack of class consciousness and class identification of his type, his comfort in his position, and how it made what Will was trying to do so difficult. *Just eat, drink, and be merry, young lad, for tomorrow we shall die.*

There are those that are uncomfortable without enough, many, and with nothing more to lose except their lives, that are more dedicated and ready to move, but often they are the dimmest of the lot. Only the dimmest have nothing, whether it is a lack of education, opportunity, or drive, therefore a willingness to fight would be useless in the hands of those who'd not know what they were fighting for. Preparing a suitable collective is a struggle with comforts and entertainment, no matter how many times the hands of the powers that be, the gods, reach down from on high and strikes another meaningless life from the record of the living. In the first world, with its comforts, this hand is seen as isolated incident after isolated incident, but in the third world, it is more deliberate, striking people by the thousands to maintain profits. Those starving and sick from unclean water are in no shape to fight and haven't the education to, and Will sees that same future in the first world United States with the quickly eroding middle class and supremely aggressive elite class – the same class responsible for most of the world's poverty through multinational corporate decisions. There is a buffer of comfort in the states because the poor are so near to these rich. Keep them entertained, they must, at least until they are too weak to do anything but complain, and never have the time to make the connection with things like the how poor the people on the continent of Africa are while its land is he richest on the planet by measure of acreage and natural resources. They don't see themselves in those people, and others of the world's poor, by design, while they're dumbed down and weakened. So, fighting before they reach that weakness, was always Will's plan while watching the degeneration, but, admittedly, he was so damned comfortable.

So, as Will sat in one of his many comforts, he reached his limit before his limit, the point where he knew he could still drive, rose to exit, and he was stopped by Toni.

"No Liam, stay. I want to talk more. Really talk. I just don't want to while I got customers."

Will obliged, reseated himself, but he stopped drinking anything but water while awaiting the exit of the other patrons. Toni and he continued to shoot the breeze, and he went into specifics about what happened with Tuck. His retelling of Tuck's refusal to fight amused her. She showed her teeth often, and probably aged years in the growth of crows feet with just the wrinkles the night's laughter caused along with the reassuring hand squeezes she gave Will, proof of her warmth and softness. They dropped the politics and fell into the comforts of ignoring it to pay attention to feeling good, instead. It lasted until the last of her patrons was left, Will. When everyone else left, she locked the doors, and she began.

"Ok... about the drugs... Let me start at the beginning... Whoo." She exhaled nervously. "Can't believe I'm about to talk about this. I'm thinking talking about it is what I need to do though, and you're the only one I've been wanting to talk to. Wow. I'm so nervous." Toni poured herself a drink. Will didn't notice what exactly, but it was something straight, and nothing fancy with fruit flavors added. She downed the shot in one swallow, like the kind of drink that puts hair on a man's chest. Not what she was going for. She followed gulping the drink with a raspy gasp. "Now, I'm trusting you more than I trust my own mother..." Without any recognizable question words, the statement was posed as a question, and Will nodded in understanding. Toni continued. "Well, yes, you were right about the... the heroin, which I'm sure you know by now, and I'm sorry, and it was stupid, but it's not as simple as that. It wasn't even based on desire. Really, Tuck is only guilty of verbalizing what I've felt for years now. I see your side, too. Of course I do. I always see your side. I think you're brilliant... I do, but at the same time, I look at myself in the mirror daily, watching new wrinkles form. I read constantly, make plans in my mind, posture myself for this battle that I'm terrified of but that I've also placed my entire life on hold because of. This here, this is not for me, and if it has to be that's more of a reason to fight than anything. I'm not as comfortable as I appear to be. My body's going crazy, hormones... Ha. Can you see me with a baby? Obviously my insides can, no matter what my conscious-self has to say about it." Toni shakes her head in disappointment. "So yeah, everything has been crazy with me, and I got you on one shoulder saying one thing, and Tuck on the other saying another, both well-meaning and both just as anxious as I am. This is where the heroin comes in, and my point… I know it wasn't right, and I know it didn't fit into any big strategy, but…" her lower eyelids filled immediately, and the water vibrated with her nervousness, "I shot the cop, Liam."

Tears eclipsed her stronghold with a blink. Will frowned up with the revelation. "I knew where he was going to be. Where he is always. I got high. I waited, and I shot him." Toni blossomed into a full cry, still talking. "It was the worst feeling in the world… He moved. Split second before I pulled the trigger or he'd be dead, and I'd feel even worse. That's why I went out of town. Flight… There, I said it… and no, that wasn't my last time smoking that junk, I'm ashamed to admit, but I think holding on to this story has something to do with it… I hope."

Will stood and reached across the bar to pull Toni in. She needed him. "I'm so sorry, Toni. Forgive me, please. He pulled upon her like it was possible to remove her pain through diffusion. He hurt as well, and released some stubborn tears of his own. They stayed statuesque in that embrace while they calmed. Once Will returned to his seat, face damp with a case of the sniffles, he tried to regain his composure with a question. "So… why didn't anyone know? You set that up, too?"

Toni shook her head, *no*, regaining her composure as well. "I don't think it was so much a lapse on our part as it was the police keeping it under wraps for several hours. It was early. No one heard the shot, and even emergency vehicles arriving don't tell the story unless they want it told. That's my guess. Wasn't anyone involved but me, and here I was thinking it would be the spark to ignite the collective locally, and it appears the opposite happened. We fell apart 'cause of it…" Toni batted her eyes like one beating down their tears, and chewed upon her lower lip in search for words. "That's why I wanted you to stay. I know how much this all means to you, and I care for it just the same. I'm sorry. I'm so sorry, Will." More tears flowed.

Will was stuck in a brow-raised state like the wind escaped him and refused to return. The longer the space he left, the more insecure the space would become, so he said the first thing that came to his mind that could change the mood. "Look at you, all secret agent and shit. I would've never guessed it..." Again, his bias exposes itself. "So, with the out of town?"

Toni quickly began shaking her head at the mention of *Out of Town,* and it cut her tears. "No. That was just my excuse to get out of town." She shrugged her shoulders and smiled as if self-collected, with a face still soaked from the baptism of her tears. "So, that's it. It was my confidence builder, to help me become who I was not. Worked well too... I haven't touched the stuff in a week and I flushed all I had left when you confronted me. No real withdrawals, so I guess I wasn't hooked yet. I didn't get sick. I've thought about it, but I think of you in concert. I've honestly just been drinking more... I think I'm good, so how about you?"

"Honestly, I can use another drink. Let's just start with that, Ok?"

"Sure thing. Whatever you need, but I'm not letting you drive home fucked up no more. The last time was the last time. So, you sure?" Toni remained in the raised-brow honesty of her revelation. She was being herself, unapologetically.

"Oh, I can't hold my liquor now? You know how much I used to drink in the service?" Misdirection began sliding the tone of their meeting, to keep it comfortable because they were both exhausted from stressful interactions.

"No. You can't." Both Will and Toni laughed.

"Yes. I'm not through drinking. I got that last hour of water taking up useful space. Let me go and get rid of it. Pour me another, and let's see where this goes... I don't feel upset, just sad, if that's saying anything."

The reason Will was smiling going from resident to resident and door to door at Harmony may have been caused by how he awakened. He woke up on the right side of the bed beside a woman he'd not planned to lay with, a woman he didn't pay, a woman he respected, a woman he loved and honestly loved him in return even if it's questionable as to if it's in that way. The life of the revolutionary is lonely, making it rather unpredictable and highly reactive like valence electrons. Will has made love for the first time in years, but he didn't intend to make anything of it. It was just the highest degree of camaraderie expressing itself and dispelling the loneliness in them both, successfully, with alcohol as the accomplice, the wing man, and who to blame just in case.

Toni also told Will what Tuck had been planning with her help, and that it would be in his best interest to assist, even if from afar. She knew enough that should Will decide to assist, he would be able to without direct interference. Will, with both his community and Legion influence, could be the unseen God that Tuck and his team called upon. Their work was hasty, but their work was positive, needed, and visible, and it served a needed purpose for the spirit of the people. Will could not deny that, and the least he could do was support the TOM Center for the liberation it represents, even if it's not practical by the numbers. If Tuck had the support of all of the Blacks or even all of the people of Cottonwood, he could be quite successful in creating a self-sustaining philosophy and reducing the often negative outside influences. He'd still have no control of the means of production, but one step at a time.

A pronounced and aggressive separation from society would only gain him the negative attention that would cut the utilities, water, electricity, and gas, the food, and the fuel shipments to the community, and then a very short waiting game would begin. Will's *cowardice* is extremely practical. His time in battle showed him how easy it is to cripple a community. People have needs, and if they cannot get those needs within their community, fight over. Separatists in the inner city operate by the generosity of the hand that feeds them. Dare they bite that hand, as Tuck so clearly has, and he doesn't even control a city block, much less a community, and that hand becomes a fist.

Toni is right; Will needs to help. He's a strategic necessity with a network sparsely reaching throughout the country yet laced across the city quite intricately. This web of his might be better considered a cobweb for the dust it's gathered from lack of use, but he stays on good terms with people, and the softest spaces in his network are from his refusal to work closely with criminals. It isn't so much a personal choice, all capitalists are criminals in his eyes and the wealthiest are the biggest and often legal, but the illegal associations he just cannot justifiably have with the industry he works in.

Toni wasn't going to allow him to get away without committing to help. She doesn't have the ego that Tuck has, that Will has either, so she had no trouble in asking one for the other. Will can lead where he's not wanted yet needed, and be a presence without recognition, as if answering prayers. Besides, what was he doing with his life anyway? He is not the Robin Hood he imagines himself to be, nor is he leading a merry band of thieves. It is going to take decades to raise class-consciousness and do what truly needed to be done. Will wants to awaken the poor and alert them to the class war they've been losing for centuries. It is no easy task, and it will take thousands of dedicated class-conscious artists, especially writers, to give the skilled class an understanding and class context to counteract the thousands of presently active artists doing the opposite. Toni understands this, everyone does, Will made sure they did, but what she finally got Will to understand is the emptiness of the present, asking, "But what in the meantime?" How many scotches could he drink? How many women could he lay? How many thousands could he save? How many felons could he recruit to rest in this same limbo that Toni had been in with him for years, while their kind were steadily dying in the streets? It's what Tuck had been trying to say, and what Toni understood, but without the ego it made a much better impression. Toni has a smile that can stop time, a mind that arrests thought, a body that can command attention, and she can be very convincing.

She said a lot, probably too much. She lured him with her rhythms and forced him to notice her like he'd always refused to. She openly invited fear into their discussion, and how with a disposition like they both shared, it was fear robbing them of life. The Fifth provided mood lighting, musky and woody were the smells. Toni's hormones were relentless, beating her and giving her little mercy is what she confessed. No matter how baggy her clothes, or how much she dressed to hide her shape, she was one hundred percents woman underneath and the corresponding urges came along with her plumbing. What would she do with a baby? She posed the question to Will, too intoxicated to even consider answering. He was smiling at everything at that point. She'd melt and be driven to tears when near a baby or seeing one on television. The urge for self-preservation is strong, and Toni admitted to Will her struggle and that she deep down desired to succumb to the drive. What else was she doing? What in the meantime? If they were not going to fight, and they were just preparing for a battle that was easily generations away, what exactly were they keeping their lives on hold for? This was Toni's argument to get Will to move physically for the struggle at hand, but it moved him in more ways than one, and not only was she fine with that, she, passionately, welcomed it. It wasn't like he was allowed to leave anyway; his alcohol content was too high. He needed to sleep it off. The floor was no place for a friend, and there was only one bed.

*   *   *

Gray stands at the juice bar filling his decorated paper cup to the brim with apple juice to complement the breakfast he has on the tray beside him, rubbery eggs, watery grits, along with a meatlike substance that's supposed to be sausage, but Gray knows better. Harmony's food isn't good, but neither was prison's so there was no adjustment phase necessary. The trick to it is to eat it quickly while it is hot and having a cold beverage, flavored works best, to wash it down with. Gray makes short work of his meals because he's never wasting his time conversing with other residents. He even times his arrival to eat in the last minutes of mealtime so he can find a space to eat alone. He's been at Harmony well over a month, and he's made zero friends. Randy gave up trying to interact with him, which was perfect for Gray. More friends meant more baggage, and more people in the exact same sinking boat that he was in who were not equipped to assist his condition. He needed to be pulled up by those not drowning, either those in better boats, or pulled out of trouble entirely by someone on land. Birds of a feather flock together, and without the visible bars, Gray had nothing to make him identify with a group he wants no part of. Flying away has been his goal since the day he was first released from his cage.

Will returns from his short meeting with Tuck. "There you go." He peers into the dining area and locks eyes on Gray. Gray looks back puzzled. "Dixon! Hurry up and eat. We need to go."

"We?!... Go where?!... Fuck!" Gray slams his hand on the table and some of his apple juice rims out of the cup. Will is his Jody, as every time he sees him it's a *Fuckin' Jody* moment.

Will smiles at the display like he's holding down a belly laugh. "Oh, I'm sorry if I'm disturbing any plans you had, but I did tell you that I'd catch you in the morning this week. Right? Unless you've picked up a job, got an interview or something?" Will waits for Gray to respond in the positive. Gray doesn't. "Well alright then. You work for me today. I'll be back through here in a couple of minutes. Don't worry about signing out." Will disappears down the hallway making a sound reminiscent of a shackled inmate with his keys clipped to his small-pocketed khakis. Gray begins enjoying his food even less than he had already, chewing through a newly formed scowl. He likes the hands-off Will much more. Gray wonders *where to* and *what now* while smacking through his breakfast. The last outing was entertaining enough, and the thought of Tuck coming along again humors him.

Will returns, keys unclipped and jingling in his hand, as if he'd freed himself while down the hall. The keys make an entirely different sound unclipped. The unchained sound is a better match to his energy level. Will has been chipper all morning, both walking and talking at a faster clip than normal. It's a marked improvement to the undead version of himself that dragged itself down the halls periodically; he's been given life like he'd snorted a bump of cocaine. Tuck is out, but one monkey doesn't stop the show, and Will appears to be feeling better with the monkey off his back.

Gray is dumping his trash and adjusting the toothpick in his mouth with his lips. He uses it to work the meatlike substance out of the spaces it wasn't meant to be in. Maybe five minutes had passed between Will's departure and his return. Will stands at the entrance to the dining area with his hands on his hips, keys in one hand, smiling. "You ready?" Gray nods slowly, repelling any transference of the positive energy Will is sending in all directions. Gray doesn't know what he's so happy about, but he's sure it's not any business that affects him, personally. Will's jubilance didn't make his breakfast taste any better, and Will drafting him to come along on another fantastic voyage didn't make his morning start any better. In fact, Will made both worse. Gray has spent over six years of enduring what he didn't enjoy, so there was no way Will was going to be able to break him in these last four or so months of doing similar, if that is even his goal. Gray has just been trying to stay out of his way because he works best with authority by avoiding it, but that is a difficult task when authority wants to develop a relationship. Gray can ignore nearly everyone in Harmony, except those with the power to refuse to be ignored, and Will is the only one enforcing it.

"Where to, boss?" Gray makes his best slave impression, even wrinkling his forehead and allowing his bottom lip to hang.

Will is amused. "Boss huh? Boss because you ain't got a job yet and I say you're working for me? Or boss like I'm the overseer? Definitely sounds like the second. You got the posture and everything." They walk towards the door, and in front of Ann, Will speaks, loudly enough for her to hear him. "Shhhh. They's gonna be an insurrection. Ain't that right, Ms. Ann?" Ann is puzzled and in mid shoulder shrug when she meets the confidence of recalling her joke about Kenny from weeks back. She nods energetically. Gray is lost, but he's fine with being lost. It's familiar when he's with Will, and he's decidedly unmoved by the show. Will quiets Ann in dramatic fashion, with both arms spread and his palms patting the air beneath them down delicately, "Shhhhhhhh." Will pinches his eyes and leans in towards Ann and places in index finger in front of his lips. She's tickled immensely and turning red, happy to be allowed a role in his little game, where she's obviously no longer a White woman, possibly what she enjoys most about the charade. Ann received momentary Negro status for the part she was playing, because no fool of a slave would be dumb enough to tell a White woman about a planned insurrection or dumb enough to shush one. Ann was Black for the moment and she beamed with enjoyment, just to be able to identify and be accepted on the victim side of the battle and not as the aggressor. Will is full of fun and gifts this morning, and he's also well versed in class struggle so Ann's inclusion is no accident. He pauses, staring at Ann, where usually his wink is placed, and he turns and walks out of the front door with an indifferent Gray trailing. As soon as they cross the threshold of Harmony, Will repeats himself in his standard voice, nasal and stiff, "There is going to be an insurrection... and there is no better way to hide it than to talk about in jest, and I want you to be part of it."

Gray looks at Will like he is crazy, but he stays in character, silent, while walking across the path to Will's parking space. The electric hedge clippers can be heard growling at the side of the building, and Gray is sure Tuck will not be joining them this time. There is nothing as uncomfortable as one on one time with a man he has to respect yet isn't sure he even likes, a man that wants something from him. Gray doesn't know what Will is talking about, but he hopes he will find out shortly, unlike with the last outing, which still confuses him. Gray finds that the only blessing in learning about things he has no interest in knowing about, is in the angle of how he can capitalize. It initially places him in a defensive position and forces him to crunch numbers quickly to see if it's worth his time, but he has no doubt that Will is willing to use his authority to make him an offer he can't refuse. This won't be an honest negotiation, and Gray braces himself for it. He hasn't any idea what Will could need his assistance doing. Gray failed his last task, getting intimate enough with Randy to find something to hold over his head, miserably, by not even attempting it. Gray doesn't even like Randy, just another punk White boy in his eyes, but he dislikes authority and systems of control even more, so although he considered being of assistance, he saw his participation as a level of selling out he couldn't succumb to without considerable financial compensation. He'd rather just take his infraction, and that's exactly what he was prepared to tell Will should he have brought it up again.

Will needs Gray's fear to control him, yet he's never secured it. His world falling apart around him had lots to do with it. Gray's arrival was horribly timed with horrendously significant life events, but what is meant to be will be. His will be done. Gray's rebellious-ness and refusal to obey Will or even pretend to fear him is exactly why he's highly favored for Will's blessing. That spirit is exactly what Will has been searching for, without knowing he was searching for it.

It was a crazy suggestion, made to himself, but maybe the amount of respect and control he had, hands free, was a portion of the problem. Maybe someone willing to ignore him, yet intelligent and self-sufficient, is the energy he needs. Will doesn't have the time to train Gray, nor does he want to, not in the way he's trained the oth-ers. His plan is to set him free, with conditions, of course, but this is as close to *No gods, No masters* as Will may ever get, working from a faith all his own because time is not on his side. This is his way to let go and trust the competence in others, even those he deems incom-petent. Tuck was freed, Toni was as well, and he has planned to do the same with Gray, who was never firmly in the clutches of his phil-osophical leadership, and curtailing his disappointment, hopefully, to the benefit of them all. In his disciplinary meeting, Gray's request to be released so Will could lighten up his job and watch one less person has materialized into a great idea. Will credits himself with the idea, for how it figured into a broader picture, but it is Gray who initially placed the idea. Will's struggle is to get Gray to buy the idea, whether it was initially his or not. Rebels lose their essence when they follow the rules, even those rules that are in their best interest.

Will and Gray enter the car, and as they buckle in Will ad-dresses Gray without looking over at him. "I'm serious, you know? Something big is about to happen in this little city, and we're already a part of it."

"We're?" Gray questions.

Will nods in affirmation. "Yup. Can't help but to be. You can try to ignore it if you want, but it's not going to ignore you. Not as long as you're poor. Not as long as you're Black. Damn sure not as long as you're a felon. Really, it's nothing new from the side of the oppressor..." Will starts his car. "Picture the boot stomping on the human face, and they're the ones wearing the boots. Add a little pres-sure here and there, let up a little every once in a while. Nothing new on that side of it, but on our side... Yes, us, you included, we're doing something a little different than just wincing this time."

Gray responds while shaking his head. "I'm just trying to do my time, Mr. Bunting. Don't know nothing about your *uss* or *wes*. I just know about *Is* and *mes*. Tell you like I told Robert, I'm not into all that Black stuff, power and love and all that. I'm into money. I'm into women. And y'all don't even like my type, last I checked."

"True." Will is listening, nodding, and pulling out of the parking lot into the street.

"I mean all this shit can burn for all I care. Black people too."

"Really?... Interesting." Will isn't startled by any of Gray's spiel.

"For real. Can't save this shit, and these people..." Gray shakes his head in disappointment. "Just let me do my time."

"I'm trying to help you to... But I do hear you, though. Basically, you don't give a damn about anybody but yourself. And... as I process that, number one, I don't think it's completely true, but that doesn't matter because of number two..." Will looks over at Gray. "Conveniently, that happens to be exactly what I'm looking for right now."

Gray coughs out a laugh. "This is game. I know what game sounds like."

"Nope. It's not. I'm serious."

"Serious about what? Need me for what? A better question, what do I get out of it? I'm not doing no Black power shit. I'm telling you. You know how much reading I did in prison? Nothing else to do... I'm up on more than you think I'm up on. I read that Black shit, too, and I built with cats that knew it like the back of their hand." Gray cuts his eyes with a shallow smirk. "Don't mean shit without money."

"Understood. About what, to answer your question... about what's about to go down in this city. For what? I need you to do the things you are already proficient at, and presently doing from what I hear. What will you get out of it? Whatever you want out of it. Depends upon what you put into it. I'm not telling you what to do. I'm just trying to free you to do what you do, in the interest of getting information from you."

"An informant? A fucking snitch?"

Will snaps. "Do I look like a damn cop to you?"

"Is that a trick question?" Gray snaps back and chuckles. "For what, then?"

"Look. I'm about to relax your curfew. Let you get out into the streets and do whatever it is that you do to make your connections, make your money, and whatever you need to get a foothold in this community, in this city. If you can pull some stops on the west side that'd be nice too, so I can know what you know, and, no, it has nothing to do with cops. Best way I can explain it is when hunters capture a wild animal, a lion or something, and they put a chip on him and send him back into the wild to gather data. I need you to be that, because you can see what I can't, hear what I can't, say what I can't, and do what I can't. I got people in the streets, so I already see and hear things, but no one as prepared as you to do things. No one as skilled. No one as selfish. And I bet the way the ladies look at you doesn't hurt."

Gray stares at Will with questions in his expression. "A'ight. I still don't really get it but uhh, fuck that curfew. We can start tonight."

Will had to make it as unrestrictive as possible to lure Gray. There was more to it than he led him to believe but that more will not be important until or unless bullets start flying. Gray has to develop a network of respect at the lowest level in the city, where the criminals, too, will avert their eyes when needed or assist if needed. The city, especially the east side, is going to respond in unison, like an organ, should any threat approach. Will nodded with Gray's last statement while tossing around how he could actually make this all work, and, most importantly, stay safe.

They both process the verbal agreement they've made, who's the winner and who's the loser, for the duration of the trip. Gray recognizes the street they turn on. "Headed back to that bar?" Will nods. "Whatever happened with that?"

Will shrugs. "Only time will tell. She's on my team though regardless what time has to say about it. This we're doing now ain't about that, and I'd appreciate it if you didn't mention it."

They reach The Fifth. It's still in the a.m. and many hours before it opens, but Toni is expecting them. She is outside cleaning the windows with a rag and a spray bottle with music playing as they pull in. A speaker is sitting in front of the doors with a wire trailing, and Toni appears to dance as she meets the rhythm as she reaches as high as her little arms can, with her arms circular motion carrying throughout her body, especially in her hips. Toni's clothes aren't baggy, for a change. She wears terrycloth sweatshorts that sticks to her hips, only giving an inch of slack a couple of inches above her knee where they stop, and a frame fitting T-shirt. They are both workout clothes and work in clothes, but Gray takes in the sight as quite a reveal. He didn't know she was built like that, he imagined her built like a teenage boy under those clothes. The revelation is slightly embarrassing and too, disappointing. He's usually up on the physical attributes of women, within seconds of meeting them, but her black baggy clothing and her tattoos distracted him, which suits her purpose in dressing like she does. He likes what he sees. Nothing is prettier to him than a woman that is trying not to be, and he has no idea how hard Toni tries not to be.

Toni walks out to the car as Will parks. She has a darling smile across her face, and again Gray is embarrassed and disappointed in himself. Toni walks straight to Will's side. He rolls down the window and cuts the car off. Toni leans against the car with her forearm and speaks. "Perfect timing, gentlemen. We'll have plenty of time to talk, strategize, or whatever, but right now I'm putting you two to work… Starting with you, pretty eyes." She points at Gray. "All that height you got is perfect for window duty, and Will I want you to sweep for now. And yes, it's hot out here, and it's only going to get hotter. This is Texas. Ok?" Toni raises her brows.

Will turns to look at Gray, who of course wasn't expecting any of this and says, "She's the boss, not me."

They are three, sitting beneath the same table with the cone shaped lamp hanging above it as two of them did months earlier as they released anger and discussed their next move. No one is smoking this time, and there is light, and all faces are an easy make and there is no reliance on sound. All are as sweaty as the glasses of ice water that accompany them.

Toni starts. "Well, so you know, I've never been the type of woman that says she doesn't need a man. I think men can be extremely useful..." She bites her lip and squints her eyes. She's pulling out everything cute and torturing Gray with it. At least in his mind she is. She follows the squint with, "Thank you guys. I really appreciate it. Ok... Ready when you are, Will."

Will nods, clears his throat and takes a sip of his water. "Well... I'm ready when you are, Toni."

Toni protests. "I just said I'm ready."

"I know."

"Ok?" Toni shrugs, spreads her arms, palms up, and curls her forehead.

"You're ready. You've been ready. Right? You've been playing behind me for years now, and dare I say, *waiting* for me. I trust you. And you basically know what I know, and as far as this, your passion is in a better place than mine, and you know what Tuck got planned. I should be listening to you right now." The unexpected rush of responsibility robbed Toni of some of her color, and her expression of surprise melts into deep thought. Gray is sure that there is something weird about everyone that Will brings him around. He's not sure what, but something is off with them, including Will. He also wonders why Robert is often called Tuck. He wonders as well why he is there, but he's losing hope on ever getting a sufficient answer to that question from such peculiar, passionate, people.

"So... The police aren't our targets. We know that, and if we don't, we do." She looks over at Gray to bring him up to speed in a manner. "But we also must understand, we are targets to the police, and we can't get to our targets without going through the police. To me this means, we're going to have to deal with them sooner or later and there is really no getting around it. I want to raise class-consciousness just like you, Will, and hope they eventually understand which side they belong to, but until then they must be treated as the threat they are, and we must protect ourselves against them, teach others to protect themselves against them, and stand in solidarity against them. Not even calling them to come into our community, meaning we need to set up a way to police ourselves, and making them fear entering our communities without invitation."

"We've talked about how to do this Will, and pretty eyes I'm sure we can catch you up." Will is not at all fond of Gray's nickname, but he says nothing. "But right now the issue at hand is creating a collective consciousness, right there on the east side in Cottonwood, getting all hands on deck, knowing the play is zero tolerance for police and police participation, and should they bring aggression to us, which we are expecting as they beat the bushes to find our comrade Tuck, we need to match that aggression. If we match that aggression, collectively, that aggression will stop. They want to go home to their families just as much as we do, goddammit, and they have to know that that's the chance they are taking when coming into our community sideways... If they do, they not gonna park in our community or ride down our block, 'cause we won't allow it. Have 'em running scared. I hate to say it, but they might not respect us until a few fall, and... that's a sacrifice we have to be willing to make, with those most prepared to execute, but that has to be the last resort. Hostile environment is what we are going for, in hopes to wake them form their sleep."

"This is the thought I can't get out of my head for any that think I'm heartless or irrational for my present stance on police, and the class issue developing because of them. From their entitlement and from who they protect, look at it this way... If that baby, that dear sweet twelve year old, playing in the park with the toy gun who was murdered, who was innocent and died and it was still his fault. Picture for a second if his gun *had* been real, and he was approached the same way with no verbal warnings and shot at by the cops, and say the cop missed and the youngin' shot back, connected, and bagged him a cop... He'd still not be innocent of a crime, and it'd still be his fault! Does that make sense? In self-defense even." She claps three beats with *self*, *defense*, and *even*, "...because there is no balance when one life has a value and another does not. Is that not the problem we face with class already?" Toni looks at Will. "This is definitely our fight."

3:5 *It is a natural mystery how a group so predictable, and so controllable, can be feared. Fear is product to threats to health, life, or comfort. One that cannot impact these things is not feared. The danger is not in how deadly a threat is, for example, but how unpredictable the threat is or the amount of difficulty in learning its ways. Cars are extremely dangerous, yet rarely feared. Driving drunk is extremely dangerous, but Will doesn't fear it. There are many life-threatening and dangerous undertakings people do not fear. Death is feared because of the difficulty in predicting it, and for the mystery of what lies beyond it, not for the many things that can produce it. The most efficient killing machine is fear; it's killed billions without them even knowing it, walking around, dead.*

The lightning strobes and captures the insides of his room like a camera flash. It paints Will, again he's white, like in the lather before a shave, and it sticks a hard etched silhouette of his shape against the barren bedroom wall like his blackness is being blown out the back of him, staining it like ink. Will couldn't find but two hours of sleep. His insomnia is getting worse. Ideas hold him hostage, forcing him to work though impossible age-old conundrums without the use of magic, and it doesn't help that he's in an unfamiliar bed. His company troubles finding sleep as well, all of them; the lightning finds their curves. Being able to predict tomorrow would be Will's super power, if he had one, and he'd use it to wage war on the system and the millions of reactionary minions that defend it. He's calculating, and he pays attention to details, but at present he hasn't even a moderate grasp on what is in store a couple of hours ahead, much less several of them.

Every new development seems to confuse him like someone counting aloud while he tries to do the same in his head. His reality has slipped into another gear. It's found an alternate method of propelling itself, and it is disconcerting for one so conservative and disciplined. He never asked to be exposed to the gamble of a life of insecurity, but his immediate environment and people who decided against such security by making highly questionable decisions make his life volatile. Will's uncomfortable when he cannot predict. His power is prediction, and randoms, as far as he defines them, make him apprehensive.

He's in no emotional position to lead anyone, so it's good that he's not a leader, at least not a static one like in the traditional, western, and classic sense. Toni leads now. Tuck leads now. Hell, even Gray has been given autonomy should he choose to use it. Everyone leads now. It's awkward and not exactly what Will had planned many years ago, but what did he really know about creating a culture of rebellion back then? His only example was the little he'd done to rebel within the military system and the grand ideas that formed in his mind while doing so. Just like agri*culture*, creating any culture is trial and error. Planting ideas is the easy part. Everyone has the ability to plant an idea, but few can develop the environment best for its growth. Some crops produce, reaching maturity, and some are ruined by weeds, eaten too soon, or destroyed as seeds. This is not what Will planned for his paltry plot, but the results fall in line with his philosophy stating that competent individuals with similar goals need no leaders. The next life change, his or the entire community's, could come as quickly, as damaging, and as random as the next lightning strike. Individuals who move like liquid, finding their way to the collective destination, around, above, or through the barriers that have been placed in their path, without waiting for orders, is the goal. This is the complex seed that Will carefully buried years ago and nurtured to mature to the present result. Beautiful, it is not, but it is what he planted, and the starving will be fed by it.

The same that has upset him, is evidence of his success. Some of his closest operatives are doing just that, moving without need of leadership. It is as if they entered the process of becoming the leader they wished Will would be. Will's failure, in this sense, could not have been outdone by his success. The outcome was meant to be, and he can even concede in calling it divine. The collective God has spoken and delivered. It appears that way in his limited foresight, stymied by his lacking ability to predict what's ahead, but how can anyone predict what they cannot control? If they are in control, are those they control their equal, and are they liberated themselves while seeking the ultimate goal of liberation? There is no static leadership without oppression. This thing he's been building appears to have come together, and he is so secure that it has, he cannot sleep. Secure, he is not. There are others in other cities, and others in this city who move like liquid towards a collective destination, in calming rhythmic footfalls until they join as a lightning strike. Lightning is not completely random. Where it strikes can at least be confined to the space beneath rain clouds, and these social rain clouds have been gathering and rumbling for all the while and they've spread far. A small portion of his discomfort is welcomed; it feels like living, and to plunge himself into it fully, blindly, is a satisfaction akin to ridding the fear of death by welcoming it and looking it in its cold eyes, smiling, while falling to it.

It's not even the bad stuff, not the bad that's usually considered bad by most. Sure, all of the events have affected his comfort, but his anxiety has a bias. Their attempts to pry his hands away from the only thing he's created on this planet worth loving, was bad. Tuck's shootout with Chase in the abandoned apartments, was bad. The revelation of Toni's drug use was a definite blow, it was crushing bad news, but, again, it's not the traditional bad that has his insides stressed and hooked together in a thousand tiny knots of unpredictability. Will sat and listened to Toni's familiar brilliance as she took his suggested lead, but he might as well have not heard a word. Will was engaged in another conversation, quite irresponsibly considering the weight of what was being discussed. He couldn't help it.

Will has no clue where to file what happened between them two, what they shared. Was it substantial? Did it matter? Does it matter still? Was it an accident? Was it a result of the alcohol? What did Toni think it was? Was it, even through the haze of intoxication, possibly the best night of his life? Was he making more of it than what it was? While she spoke, he wondered if she was just so focused on the task at hand, or if what happened had not impacted her as much as it had him. What were Toni's thoughts? Will hoped she was just as conflicted, just as curious, and just as afraid to mention it. Was this his first hit, Toni his drug of choice, Will the emerging addict, and the entire engagement poetic justice? Was he being foolish entertaining that they could be anything more than what they are, and in the midst of a war possibly brewing that can strike as unpredictably as lightning? He now wanted to protect her even more, if such a degree is even possible. He wanted to know her even more, but he also didn't want to risk losing her trying to. Meaningless sex is easier, even for one who compels his partner to pretend it has meaning, than the meaningful, at least potentially. Toni didn't even need his coaching.

It's the first rain of summer, and possibly the last in a season that never promises much rain. It promises the opposite of rain, pulling whatever moisture inside and upon the ground away from it and not returning it until autumn. Precipitation occurred one other time after the year's summer solstice, summer's official start, but it was during the heat of the day. The droplets were turning into mist before reaching the ground, so instead of rain, the sky became a miniature display of the water cycle with the drops being juggled amongst themselves in suspended animation above the Texas desert. If it weren't for the water delivered by pipe and pump, the summers here would be nothing but sand and longhorn skulls. The initial almost-rain smelled like rain, but it didn't feel like it. The water just danced in the sky, refusing to let the ground cut in. This time, the rain chose a better time. Few things can compete with the Texas sun, and moving in the late night or early morning darkness increases the chances of success. Will packed some guns and ammo in a duffle bag, called Dee, and also dialed up some Legion transportation, The Feet, for his departure beneath the cloak of darkness and rain.

Will called Dee because he was feeling nostalgic. They'd known each other for years and she was one of the few people who knew about his double life. She didn't know everything about Legion, not even what to call it, but she knew Will had men that he worked with in secret that he wouldn't tell her much about, for her own safety. If he'd called his young one, Erica, she would have just asked a lot of questions. He didn't want to call either, not for an intimate touch, another woman now invades his thoughts about that, and that isn't the reason he'd made the call. Will needed someone to check into the motel room that he would not be in, officially, the one he is in presently. Will also left his phone at home to complete the alibi, carrying a burner instead – a prepaid cellphone with no ties to him, nearly impossible to track. He purchased Toni one as well. They will be home, if their phones have anything to say about it.

Dee had called him recently giving him the, *Why you don't call me, what you don't love me anymore,* speech, made in jest but not, so she was perfect. She wouldn't even question the invitation concerning the circumstance, and the fewer the questions the better. All he had to do is make her think it had something to do with her, and pay her for her services, which unfortunately weren't much. Will could not get into the mood with her, making her do most of the work in just keeping him *ready*. Deloris knows what he likes, and has passed as a costar many times. Will blamed it on the rain, uninspired to give a better excuse, and Dee responded with the standard, "It's okay, baby," that millions of women have quoted word for word. Any man who cannot get it up or keep it up for a sexual performance knows that how understanding she is, only makes it worse. Will had had other things on his mind, three better excuses, one about the anxiety from the coming day's events, another about her excitement when she inquired about Gray, and the third was about Toni, all of which were better responses that would have only complicated things. It was easier to just take the hit on his pride, pay her, and send her on her way. None of it was really about her anyway.

In the blackness of early morning, often mistaken as night, the rain falls heavily. It's dark. The stars, whose luminance usually offer a tiny assistance, are blocked out by the wet rolling smoke of the clouds of the storm, the moon as well. The lightning is the light and the only light for some. Storms routinely knock out the electricity in the poor areas with their aging infrastructure. Will is wide-awake, and his state has nothing to do with the crack from the lightning strikes or the rattle of his windows from the thunder. He hasn't been sleeping much at all. He's been an early riser since his military days, but stress makes it difficult for him fall asleep. Regardless of how long it takes to fall under, he still rises early. He sleeps short, awakens, and awaits the inevitable that lies outside of his vision. He's been purchasing ammunition, he's cleaned his big guns, and now his usual bed partner, black and cool, has company. Some are in his duffle bag, suffocating, a couple are not. After he sent Dee on her way, he unpacked and played with his toys, while drinking, until he tired. The drinking is what gets him to sleep but its effect only lasts a couple of hours. He's up sitting in the dark in the early morning, listening to the rain and suppressing thoughts of Toni. His timing couldn't be worse.

Thinking about living has no place in a time of dying. The decay he encouraged within himself with years of alcoholism, fighting, and meaningless women were supposed to rot his insides and keep him selfish enough, sharp enough, to take lives with no regrets. To love and nurture himself, seeking genuine love creates a fertile space for empathy, and empathy does not belong in war. No soldier has time to think about what others think about, which in itself is the essence of love. It's an arresting undertaking. To the contrary, some say a soldier not deeply loving another as he loves himself, or she herself, is not convicted enough to fight with life-preserving passion. Love songs are some of the most revolutionary, as they craft that that is worth sacrificing for into the minds of the would be warriors. Are national anthems not love songs? None are willing to die for what they do not love, including ideas. Will prefers the dead inside philosophy, knowing he can love strongly as well. Ideas don't hurt and disappoint, so he prefers to love them more than individuals. Legion itself is a labor of love, and he loves his people and his class, and he's willing to make the ultimate sacrifice for either or both if the collective can benefit from it. He's dead inside and he knows love, in the collective respect. It's the individual respect that's rotted out, but decay can create a fertile space for new life if it is allowed to grow.

Will knows strategy like Gray knows hustling. With a dedicated team, he's confident he can push out any oppressive force. Cottonwood is a microcosm of what can be done nationally. Will drew it up on black boards long ago. He learned it by watching native populations do it to his soldiers, and there would be major advantages to urban combat on US soil for the indigenous populations compared to a foreign campaign. It's not like the powers can just pick a neighborhood and start carpet bombing it, not without lots of justification and priming the American public of the danger the target caused. Without a homogenous community, that argument would be impossible to sell, no matter how many enemies of the state resided there. They would have to put boots on the ground, giving the natives an immediate strategic advantage because it is their home. Creating a dangerous habitat and a culture of secrecy is all that's needed, not superior weaponry. Superior weaponry is not going to happen, neither will better training, because poor people, by definition, just don't have the resources. Training as if a face-to-face fight can be won is a failure in strategy. Legion trained to learn how to use weapons because weapons are necessary in defense, but they haven't yet the power to use them offensively in gaining ground. It doesn't take a supreme strategist to understand why, so Will gave it to the Legion membership in a language they could understand. He repeated the same to Gray while assisting Toni in their abbreviated meeting and training with why his assistance was needed.

"Territory, what you sports nuts call *home field advantage,* can mean the difference between wining and losing, living and dying. It's more than a psychology that makes it difficult for you to take a loss on your own turf. In my home, I know where everything is, should I have to use some territorial advantages like where I keep my knives, the iron, guns, which doors lock, whatever. I can only do that at home, and once I leave home, I leave that security. The same can be done in a community by those that know it. You have to be extremely strong to take the fight away from home. The further out you go, the weaker you'll get. You follow?"

Gray frowned up with the question to let Will know that he wasn't an idiot. "Yeah man. I get it."

"Good," Toni took the conversation back over. "That's what we're doing as soon as they make their move. If they make a move."

"They been moving the whole time!" Gray laughed. "I'll leave the revolution up to y'all, but this make a move shit y'all talking… They steady making moves. You play chess?" Gray looks at Will, dismissing Toni as a woman and as one who probably doesn't, guided by his experience. Will nodded affirmatively with the lazy smirk that usually precedes a batch of peanut butter cookies. Will has never been much for ideas contrary to his own. He's tolerant of them, but his facial expressions tell more than his voice ever will. The shape of things, organizationally, were created, by him, in the interest of checking his own ego. Will will check himself, but his face has no discipline. Gray continued, "Keep letting your pawns die, and it won't matter how many major pieces you got left. Cats in prison talked this same shit. War was *coming* and they were always preparing for it. They in prison, talking about the White man this and the White man that, even locked up behind the White man, but talking about the war *about* to come. About to? I couldn't take them seriously. Y'all neither, if this not war already, and they not prisoners of war, and these ghettos ain't battlefields, because we ain't looking at the same game of chess. Y'all gonna keep losing pieces waiting for a game to start that started forever ago. Fuck that. But that's your business. I'm not invested like that."

Toni looked over at Will like, *I told you so*, and closed the topic. "Well, we're about to stop them from moving here, well Cottonwood, or make them lose pieces as a consequence. And we're going to need a lot of people to…" She uses her fingers as counting props, "not see shit, not hear shit, and to not say shit as far as authority is concerned. If we get that, we all won't be dead or arrested in a week. So, little old ladies, the squares, and yes, even White people, anyone with eyes to see, ears to hear, and lips to speak with access to a phone is a potential threat if they do not indentify with us and what we're doing… The common enemy is the gods, the wealthy, and the police are directed by their fingertips and pulled back by their leash." Her hands gestured as if she were a puppeteer. "Not truly the enemy because they're poor they damn selves, but they're the enemy's mindless puppets. Let's see if we can't break the spell and wake a couple of them up. Even the most obedient dog will refuse to walk off of a cliff no matter how much his owner demands it."

"And…" Will cut in, still watching Toni for any signs of anything other than official business. "Understand why we need the cooperation of so many, even those who are not really involved. Besides them being able to expose us directly, they can also indirectly, if they do not appear to be a part, just through their behavior. It has to be one nebulous mass. A community, all kinds of people concealed by our ability to not be identified one from the next. That has always been the goal, and it creates a terrifying effect once achieved. The Mau Mau did it Kenya. They achieved being hidden in plain sight because they had the support of the community. As far as the community was concerned, they didn't exist, and no amount of interrogation could change their minds. They were like ghosts. That's true power. Being unseen, rather than a walking target, like an officer... military officer, out on the battlefield, waiting to get clipped. So, no, no uniforms, tattoos, and identifying slogans, because that kind of identifying would assist the enemy as much as it would us, if not more. This is the essence of guerilla strategy, not being seen."

Toni cut back in, snatching her ball back. "I was going to get to that. Thank you." She gave Will a look to remind him that he'd given her the lead. They were giving Gray a crash course in their organizing style, detailing things that both were well versed in. Still, they conversed as if they were enlightening one another, as well, as not to alienate him. "And, look at it this way, if we are concentrated, and not spread throughout the community, among the seemingly innocent, we are just a utility off switch away from being waited out. If we could be pinpointed on one city block, utilities would be cut immediately. No fighter can survive without water, and there are no natural sources around. And nights without electricity are an easy way to get slaughtered when others have low light and no light equipment at their disposal. We can't make it that easy for them. We have to be indistinguishable from the residents. This is a failure of the some of the Black Nationalists, in my opinion. The beauty of identifying and joining amongst the wave of unity is undeniable. I've been there, but it beacons to the enemy. Black Panthers were easily identified, Philly's MOVE were easily identified, and they infiltrated, burned, murdered, and bombed them into extinction."

Gray nodded while listening, appearing halfway into it, into it at least enough to decide to speak once more. "Yeah, I get that. That's still not what I'm getting at, exactly. Say all that works. Then what? For how long? There has to be more. Just like the prisoners I mentioned, they'll still be stuck in their cells, their world, whatever."

Gray appeared to both want to and not want to offer an argument. His eyes searched, and the others waited. "This is why I'm like fuck it, I think..." Gray shrugged. "As long as there are puppet strings, they don't have to touch us to control us."

Will, familiar, pounced upon Gray's apathy with a syllable that he had to catch in the roof of his mouth as the balls of his eyes panned over to Toni for clearance. Amused, Toni smiled and granted him access with a side head nod. Will continued, "Correct! They don't have to touch us, and even when they have to, they won't be able once we discover that..." Will began tapping his index finger against his temple, "all of the strings are in our mind." Gray's brow raised like an antique cash register's flag indicating a sale has been made. Will continued, "It's not about winning. It's about destabilizing, and while they scramble to adjust, taking back some power in exchange for their respect and fear. We win by carving out a comfortable enough space to make winning possible for those who can, our children, or our children's children. Consciousness is a product of our desire to live, fully, completely, nothing more... the dead and the unconscious have no spirit." Toni smiled even stronger, enjoying Will's words and the feel of the weight of her presence, her opinion being valued, and Will gifting her the leadership role. Will had done well, because she swelled in happiness and glowed on the inside, and on the outside it showed.

The spirit was positive. Toni knew her stuff, and she grew quickly in her comfort. Her posture shifted from timid to regal in less than thirty minutes, and her body language shrank Will with each subsequent interjection. Will acquiesced fully, relaxing his shoulders, his forehead, and his jaws, closing the bakery. Toni could do a better job of making a convincing argument than he ever could. It's what artists do, spend their days finding, logically, the best ways to get others to emotionally submit, and Toni effortlessly made art of his science. He looked at her thinking, *just look at her*. He couldn't stop looking at her. If she hadn't changed herself, she'd changed Will, as she artfully spoke his words better than he could with her velvet voice and seductive gestures. Will is nasal, with an awkward squareness that switches between his hood upbringing to his military years.

He'd made an excellent decision in her leadership, and probably should have years earlier. "That's not going to happen to Legion. Because you cannot hunt what you cannot see. You cannot prepare for what you can't locate and can't count. We are many, even when we are not, and we can turn Cottonwood upside-down with the snap of a finger should anyone be bold enough to test us, especially the police."

If the people are willing to see no evil, hear no evil, and speak no evil, they won't have to raise a finger in an effort to increase their freedom, because the work has already been done. The foundation has been laid and the infrastructure developed for years with nearly no one's notice. If it is Will's fear that caused him to shape it this way or his genius, Legion's placement is ten times stronger than that of the TOMs, and Will has the opportunity to prove it by protecting them as well. If the community stays oblivious, Legion will have no trouble holding a commanding position and winning the respect of the people. Or better, the people will win the respect of themselves, because they're not aware Legion exists, but that works even better. Give the credit to the community and their ability to trust and depend upon themselves while Legion operatives intermingle invisibly amongst them. They've been doing that for years, waiting, like sleeper cells. Everything is in place locally and possibly nationally. Several pockets across the country are prepared to erupt just like they have in protests but not just like the protests, and not asking this time around. No one heard them asking, the police ignored it, their handlers ignored it, so the intensity has to be turned up to get their attention. Asking works better once one gains the subject's attention, and threats are taken seriously once asking is revealed as not the only option, but the least damaging option out of several, and Legion can project that circumstance.

The Black Panther Party won respect by fighting back against the police who had been terrorizing the Black communities in Oakland. Adversity develops its own adversary. Had the police not created that climate, the people would have never desired to be a part of an organization to liberate them from it. The lack of job availability, rising prices without pay, terrible road conditions, community facilities, services, and education, are a taxation without representation, and constant oppression, but subtle. People find that brand of oppression negligible, but when police are in and out the community like terrorists, cracking heads, and murdering its residents and hauling them off to prison, while never solving the crimes asked to by residents, the oppression becomes painfully apparent. The citizens of Cottonwood and every other ghetto should feel the same as they did in Oakland. Overt oppression is a consciousness-raising, congealing force for the oppressed, and Will hopes there has been enough time for the people to trust each other instead of the media and the police. It is one of the things he has trouble predicting. Being calculating demands a certain amount of cooperation, and the community has failed him in that regard. He never knows what they desire. They are under so much heavy manipulation and experimentation by those in control, it's a miracle they're able to collectively identify with anything. The many protest eruptions prove that a collective pulse still exists; they are still alive. After centuries of abuse the poor still have a pulse, and the Blacks do as well.

Tuck wants to take the lead, and he has Will's support, anonymously. As luck has it, Tuck has been waiting for this support for the longest, and he will now get it without even knowing it. He should thank Toni for this. All Will wanted to offer him was a, *Good luck, and make sure you keep Legion's name out of your mouth should they try taking you alive.* The no snitch code of the streets should keep Legion protected, but Will needed to be sure. Toni's influence made him desire to do more. She can be very convincing. His ego was the only thing standing between him seeing it was the right thing to do anyway. Toni never fully understood their inability to get along. It was more than differences in philosophy and method. They were both alpha males refusing to become beta for the convenience of progression. Tuck played beta long while learning, but at a certain age the lion cubs must either leave the pride or risk death. Pride is a perfect name for the collective. The Legion needs to assist because the people need to see a win, and Tuck taking a public loss will affect much more than the Temple of Morality. Tuck stands as an example of people tired and ready to fight back. The better he does, the more he will inspire others. Where Will's ability to make predictions and plan for the future falls short, Toni's stands tall. She knew how to play chess as well, even without Gray looking her way to acknowledge it.

Will recapped everything about the meeting in The Fifth and everything about Toni, down to the rustic smells of the wood furniture and the sweat of their bodies, they'd just cleaned the bar, while he watched the lightning strike in the darkness in his small motel room. He struggles to recall how Gray received Toni's message. Will was too caught up into watching Toni talk about what he already knew well, so it wasn't because of the information. More than anything he was stuck wondering if she thought of him any differently. How unprofessional and undisciplined of him, but he couldn't help himself. If there is any consolation, Gray didn't have much else to say. That could mean he was in agreement, or it could also mean he was just being Gray. Will admired the rebelliousness in Gray's eyes as soon as they'd met, and he's yet to disappoint. That spirit cannot be created or controlled. Will doesn't desire to control it. The rawness of his life experience has its own legitimacy and can find its own way. Too much is based on control. Less control is probably what is needed. It's worth a shot. Whether Gray agrees, philosophically, or not, his participation is insured by the extra freedom away from Harmony Will offered him, so actually Will gave up control of him just to gain control, albeit loose, of him. It was such a smooth move that Will himself didn't notice its strength until later, so of course Gray didn't recognize it. The square seems to know a little about hustling himself.

*   *   *

The air is sticky and hot like Cottonwood is beneath the skin of a blister. Humidity abound. The sun pulls the early morning rain back up into the sky. It is hot enough to keep people inside, but the poor are still out. Some travel to church. Some take refuge under the shade from trees, drinking beers, and having their own church. No one wants to waste their weekend staying inside no matter how hot it gets, so even triple digit temperatures are met with an audience. Once the work week starts again they all lose their voice. At home they have a voice, and they are able to stand instead of kneel. It may appear that they are wasting their time and not talking about much, but their conversations are therapy reassuring one another that they matter no matter how poor they are or how Black they are. Men are men in the streets, and some overcompensate because of all the man they can't be while away from them. Most are uncomfortable in the hood. It is the general sentiment, but it is the only place the hood natives find comfort. It has the inverse relationship with up and down that prison has, and it is more than a coincidence. In the only place they have to call their own, where they have been designated to stay, where the quality of life has been purposely made worse, where they are questioned and treated differently once they leave, they are also questioned and treated differently when they stay. Still, it's better to stay and just deal with the disturbers of the peace, the police, but all of the negatives the residents are subject to, create quite an unhealthy regard for outsiders, especially for cops.

There is violence in the ghetto because it was designed to be violent. Anytime there are more people than there are resources, there is a high propensity for violence. The entire nation is violent in the same regard, particularly when compared to other nations. The citizens are fluent in the language of violence, and where the resources are the scarcest, they are the most violent. Society labels the people while ignoring the conditions, making no point about classical conditioning and what people become, any person, when denied the basic necessities for a comfortable life and forced to fight for them. The true nature of a crab cannot be measured when they are grouped together in a barrel, because barrels are not their habitat, but the Black man in the barrel of a ghetto he's been forced into, is judged indiscriminately, building a social case for his extermination, and allowing the police to execute, literally. The days of little Black boys and girls wanting to be police officers when they grow up are long gone. Police are no longer the good guys and even the children are aware. They see the way their parents react when the police drive behind them, when the police ride down their street, and when the police kill yet another citizen and the news informs them of it. The police are violence, yet somehow they are given the power to come into the community and stop others from being violent. They cannot out-violence the people of the ghetto; they have just long been allowed to believe they can. Those of the ghetto are born of it, born to do it, and they have nothing to lose in the behavior; they are already in prison.

Inhumanity is what the general public screams when those rarely treated as human consider returning the same savage treatment toward the cops. Places like Cottonwood are quickly nearing indifference concerning what those who never respect them think of them. The same society that barely shudders when yet another unarmed Black male gets murdered by a police officer, loses all rationality when a cop is murdered instead. The greater society are truly the mystic apes, with all senses cut off, refusing to see the pain of the victims of capitalism. The higher up one climbs, the more remiss they become to the suffering of those at the bottom. The Internet fills with posts about how niggers are animals and should be hanged and shot. Should *niggers* suggest the same of the police that terrorize and murder them, they are less than human. It's a longstanding truth that's regularly forced to the surface of the American disposition, *niggers are less than human*. It's what the Constitution supports, and amendments are just Band-Aids, unable to heal wounds, just used to reduce the flow of blood and reduce the chance of infection. Only a healthy immune system can heal, an immune system without the proper nutrition is not healthy, and all of the Band-Aids in the world will do nothing but cover up the ugliness beneath them.

A couple of cops died in the line of duty and the country mourned. Cops continued killing unarmed citizens, especially Black citizens, and the country sympathized with the police and inquired about the criminal history of the deceased and argued that if they had followed the cop's orders, they would not have died. It's revolting, and it's a wonder Blacks aren't revolting. The double standard is apparent, and so is the disrespect, and it has done nothing but amplify everyone's anger. Blacks get mad and people get mad because the Blacks get mad. Citizens were already dying as a result of the climate, and cops dying would only be the result of scales finding balance, irrespective of what the public, those with a voice, thinks about it. The overwhelming number of people ineffectively agreeing and promoting that Black lives matter, provided a wonderful cloak for the rising surge of those planning to prove that they matter through creating consequences for those who believe otherwise.

The physical temperature isn't the only thing that has been increasing all year. The heat isn't easy to beat. Less clothes, colder drinks, and shade are remedies for reducing one type of heat, but those things are powerless when the block is hot, meaning the police are out in force. They ride up and down the streets doing to the residents what suppressive fire does to the enemy. It's for their own good. They're savages and the police are protecting them from themselves, even killing them to stop them from killing each other. Nothing came of the many protests. Nothing. As it turns out the police are not worried about picket signs, hashtags, and people shooting off their mouths. It may have seemed as though the police killing an unarmed man or woman was a problem, but it wasn't really, or at least it was not a problem as grand as disrespecting or threatening a cop. Cops kill an unarmed citizen and the people say, "Well, it's a difficult job," but if an armed citizen kills a cop the people call him an animal undeserving of life. One doesn't even have to go as far as killing a cop, a simple threat will do and the cavalry pours out of the woodwork. Cop lives matter. They can almost do no wrong and a citizen, especially a poor Black one, isn't even allowed to say, *Fuck them*, not in a public space. It is not even received by the general public as a threat to cops, but a threat to all things good in the world like liberty, spring rains, butterflies, and sweet baby Jesus.

Tuck's tirade hit the media, and in a little under a week, it was the biggest news moving from the city on the Internet. Tuck was trending. He became a local celebrity, an antihero of sorts. He was revered by some but hated by more, and the video of his rant became a polarizing instillation, or evidence rather of how polarized the city is. He received a number of threats and he fired back the best he could, anchoring his behavior with the rising death toll of citizens being murdered by the police. The same that argued against him cared not for his reasoning. They cared not for him or the group he was representing. It was really a waste of an argument, but still he tried, while enjoying the swell it brought to his image. The negative energy he received created better examples for him. Tuck would point out the obvious racism, classism, and bigotry of those who came for him. If they were looking for an apology, they left looking for more apologies than they had been searching for initially. They turned the spotlight upon him to make an example of him, and he recognized the light, flexed his stage presence, and made a bigger example of himself and how to be a man in the face of *the man*. He refused to back down. His pride wouldn't allow it. His audience deserved more than that as well as his children.

Will recognized his activity online, his escalation of an already dangerous situation, his becoming the enemy they needed him to be to murder him without excuse or recoil, but could do nothing but respect it and distance himself. His plan, before Toni persuaded his editing of it, was to simply stay away. Tuck was growing faster than the foundation he'd built could handle, but there was no anchor to his ego. He used the energy as a means to recruit for the Temple of Morality. Tuck promised his followers and soon to be membership a breathtaking show, and Will couldn't miss it.

Tuck kept his normal routine. Gray saw him Sunday morning at Harmony gathering the chairs he needed for his service. Tuck spoke to Gray but didn't bother inviting him out to the Temple, to Gray's delight. Gray made it clear the last time he asked that just them looking similar had nothing to do with their goals. Rather than save the world, some would watch it burn because it isn't worth saving. It can't be saved, so Gray's plan is just to grab all he can before the fire consumes them all, watching the thrashing flames as they crawl towards him. He had to give up on the idea that anything outside of himself was worth the effort the day he lost his life.

All players get played, is more than a saying, it's a realization. It is never spoken or believed until it happens, because the victim is always blind to the possibility. Gray's eyes might as well have been matte gray like that of the blind, because he never saw it coming. It was a plot twist with no foreshadowing, poorly written, and debilitating. It killed him. She killed him, his blood ran blue from that day forward, possessing only enough oxygen to sustain his vital functions and nothing more. Hearts were only for pumping blood, and she forced him to realize it while crying herself in immediate regret for what she'd done and who she'd killed. His life left his eyes right before her eyes, killing her as well, so he would not have to physically because his children deserved to have a mother since she'd taken it upon herself to replace their father. As much as Gray was in the streets, he never neglected a moment of taking care of his children. He was to be a better father than his father, and there for them when his own father was not. He was good there, but not as good as a mate as far as the media told what the ideal mate should be, as if she was by that same standard.

So while he hustled up on a way to remove his family from their condition, his other half, concurrently, was hustling up on an escape from his plans and taking the children with her, because she could not control him like she wanted to. All the while she told him about how much she loved him to bide her time in planning her escape, or either in planning an event big enough to grab his attention for him to notice how special she was and go and retrieve her. It's amazing how long people can live together and still not know one another, because not only did Gray not know she was capable of such, but she surely didn't know Gray in expecting something positive from him is his response. She got off easy. She made sure of it. She was the hustler, learning from the best, thinking she'd beat him to the punch, though leaving her was never in his plans. His family was his world, no matter how far she and he had drifted apart.

She worked her plan. She left him, and before leaving she'd already prepped his children by introducing them to another man without his knowing, and laid with another man while in their presence without his knowing, a hoe as far as he knew to define it, mostly because the involvement of his children. Gray had been with too many hoes to accept that he'd settled down and began raising children with one, so he dismissed it all, the entire engagement, as she called herself trying to explain it once he'd found out. He'd disgraced his children by choosing such a mother. One who forced them to keep her secrets, and showed them how easily replaced a father, a good one, who never failed in providing for his family, could be. His children would never be the same. She contaminated them with another man's scent. Killed him to them, killed Gray, killed herself, killed it all, because Gray was not who she wanted him to be. A good father he was, but she desired a good man, who'd do the things she defined good to be, basically someone who'd kiss her ass. Gray refused to fall into her definition as well as anyone else's, he didn't play well with authority, no matter what form it came in. She realized this after years of attempts, so she needed someone who would, and damn the children.

While he was out working hard, hustling to make sure his family ate, she had a hustle of her own: Operation erase daddy from their lives. She'd show him, and that she did, and she'll never know how close she came to a death that was not metaphoric. He's not even sure how close himself, he'd drowned himself in an intoxicating haze to deaden the pain, that only seemed to fuel his rage, from being placed on public display like she'd done. He won't even call her by name. She's dead. The dead can't answer. She's just the woman that murdered him and murdered his children before killing herself. They all must be dead, or Gray has to make it so, so this psychology of his works best for all parties involved. Gray's initiation to the *all players get played* club landed him in prison. He received considerably less time than what he should've gone to prison for. Murder should've been the charge, not possession with intent to distribute. The possession charge intervened between Gray and any plans for possible revenge, and that was her official parting gift. She knew what no other could have about his business, worried about his instability, he was going to kill somebody, possibly even himself, so she protected herself, her new man, and her children by giving the police all of the information they needed to put him away with. While the story was unfolding, Gray only found out a little at a time, she kept him at bay with lies about her love for him and wanting to work on herself so they could reunite the family and make it work, while designing the final blow.

He was played, completely, from start to finish, with his

guard down, because he'd been taking care of her and his children. How dumb of him. Gray didn't put it all together until the prosecution made his airtight case, and until an extremely important piece of his life did not show up for his trial. His children never again saw their uncle, their dying grandmother, or their father. Gray's brother kept him abreast in his letters. Gray's side of his son and daughter's family became a figment of their imaginations, and they were young enough to eventually believe it. He was being replaced completely because love and hate are siblings, one creates the naiveté necessary to unlock the heart for the other. Gray knows this first hand. If he returns home, it will ruin the effect, and he might relapse and show her how closely related love and hate are as well. He died for the safety of it. He had to. It makes it easy for him to sit back and watch the world burn, letting his children go means he can release anything, because dead men don't feel pain. They have the privilege of stepping out of the world and watching it spin. It is how his respect for his mother and trying to treat Black women better, especially the mother of his children, came back to haunt him; it came back to kill him.

Tuck was a dead man as well. He just didn't know it. Gray knew, thought it was just a matter of time, and a waste of time trying to protect someone with an ego the size of his with a mouth to match. He didn't mention this to Will or Toni because he didn't care to, and he got the feeling they didn't mind wasting their time just with the amount they'd dedicated to their liberation efforts to awaken a giant that rather enjoys his sleep. Besides, Gray had reached and passed his talking quota, and he would have just moved himself into the discomfort of them learning more about his perspective on things that he doesn't want them to know. The more people know, the more access they have to controlling their subject. The dead woman he had dead children with showed him this. Gray wanted to wrap up the meeting and take his newly earned freedom back to the streets with him. Every new objection he offered was only going to give them more opportunities in correction and convincing him otherwise, lengthening his stay. Gray was going to cooperate because he is a man of his word, he'll do what he can, but he refuses to take on the stress of saving anyone. He couldn't even save himself from his present condition, so it would take a lot of nerve to extend his hand to assist another; he'd be pulling them down, not raising them up. He'd already established the connections they needed access to, and running down to them that something big was about to happen and that they needed to be cool about it was an easy task. Hustlers don't call the cops anyway.

Gray was now in the know, knowing much more about Tuck and his plans than Tuck was aware of, and fitted with the task of doing what he could with the influence he'd gained with the underworld to keep Tuck safe. He talked too much to be kept safe, but Gray would do what he could. He'd already campaigned on Tuck's behalf in the streets the night before in telling the young dealers to keep an eye out in the coming days because something big was going down. Gray wasn't specific enough. They wanted to know who, what, and why, and how did he know as fresh as he was. He hadn't been around long enough to be privy to information that they weren't privy to, so he had to give up some kind of connection to not appear a lie, or put up to this by someone. The street merchants aren't dumb, no hustler is dumb. Their lives are full of constant value-based decision-making, because their next move, if a poor one, can have them removed from the board of play. Gray had to play along. He had to preserve what respect he'd already built amongst this particular group. He had to give them something more, a name or an association that had footing in the community worth listening to that could back Gray's prediction. Gray couldn't mention Will. How could that help, if they even knew him? He couldn't mention The Legion. They didn't know anything about The Legion, neither did Gray, not by name at least. His only option in drawing from what he knew and what they would too, was to mention the Temple of Morality.

The corner erupted in laughter. One choked mid drag upon a blunt and coughed and laughed until he started projecting mucus, and another lost his balance and fell off of his stoop. "Them niggas? Them combat boot, bead wearing, smoking up all the good weed, back to Africa ass niggas?" The eruption sustained and it was a perfect indictment to what some pockets of the community felt about Tuck and his movement. Gray was uncomfortable, but he laughed along with them. It wasn't like he disagreed. His discomfort was in wondering if he had compromised the mission. In an attempt to add some legitimacy, as he'd taken some away, Gray let the laughter die a bit, and then he tried to fix what Tuck's poor reputation had broken.

"The cops are probably about to hit. Hard. That's what I'm talking about, not them. I mean I heard it through them, but it's probably accurate because they the ones that caused it."

"Well what that got to do with us?" One inquires, sincerely.

"Shit. We all look alike. If they come, they coming to harass us all, like they always do. They may have triggered it, but it's going to affect everybody. And that ain't nothing to laugh about. You ain't got to believe what they believe to protect your hood." Gray offers a strong attempt at a save.

"Man them dudes ain't shit. One of them motherfuckers tried to get me off the block talking that Black shit, and I bet that's the same motherfucker who tried to take me out. So, fuck them." Chad was convicted, dismissing Gray's attempt.

"I'm saying, it ain't about them though, Chase. If something goes down, and the sirens come full steam up and down these blocks, they won't be looking for you, for a change, but you *can* be looking for them. This is a heads up for you to be ready, because we all got the same enemy right now, and we get a head start if it happens like I imagine. I'm with you. Fuck that Black shit too, but this ain't about that. It's about showing them evil ass cops who own these streets." Gray made a solid argument and the guys agreed, each with a different intensity, included Chase, who nodded in agreement through a questioning face. Gray sold them on helping, knowing they were not a threat in snitching, and told them to inform others the best they could. He made good of Will's gamble, doing exactly what was needed of him.

Gray watched Tuck as he tried carrying too many chairs at once, and he decides to go and assist without being asked, floating over to him like a guardian angel, and Gray had already used his sword for him. Will was going over the many possibilities of what could happen in his head while sitting in the motel room with the best exposure to his, respectfully named, TOM center, an angel with his swords fully loaded. Toni was making phone calls all morning with her replacement phone, she locks the doors of The Fifth, and angelically walks past the traditional angel imagery with a couple of swords of her own en route to her car, soon to be en route to Harmony to pick up Gray. Assuredly, Tuck had also summoned winged guardians himself. None could deny the local or the national climate and they were just waiting for an excuse. There were troops of angels spread throughout the city in the name of Legion, in the name of the streets themselves, and in the name of God, prepared to protect the idea that those blocks, that small slice of heaven to the right type, belonged to them and no one was going to threaten their ownership on this day of their Lord. The giant is slowly awakening.

3:6 *We need those who lead by example, not leaders. Just point me in the right direction. Show me my potential and show me the problem, and I'll show you my answer… The enemy is nowhere near as large as it appears. It just casts a large shadow, and the darkness it covers us with makes it difficult to organize beyond it or even imagine existence without being beneath its cloak. Examples are like strong light sources pointed in a manner that makes the shadow disappear, showing the enemy and its power as merely a figment of our imagination. The enemy within us, estimating the enemy, is actually much bigger than the enemy itself. It only takes a good example to expose it. One event can return God, in calling all the dead… where all is heard, and saw, and said… the floor awakens the sleeping giant once he's fallen off his bed.*

Without an agitator, a washing machine is just a box of water. As easy as it is to find someone to disagree with Tuck's tactics, there is no denying his ability to agitate and grab people's attention. He has a fire inside of him. It is impossible to tame. It's like those ancestors he speaks of, speak through him, with the rage of a thousand lynchings. He acknowledges more than their names. He acknowledges their pain, along with his own. Tuck is angry, and his anger is justified. When the world was unfolded before him, decoded, and it was explained to him that his condition and the condition of his people wasn't at all his fault, anger was the result. He knew the world hated him without picking up a single book, but to learn the of level of dedicated planning invested into that hate, and into keeping him powerless and ignorant is rage inducing. Rage boils within those that do not understand the whys as well as with those that do; those that do just control it better. Tuck controls it better than the kids upon the block releasing it upon each other, but he doesn't control it as well as Will, the person responsible unfolding the world and decoding it for him.

Discipline has always been Will's strength. If he allowed his rage to drive him, he wouldn't have made it out of boot camp. Being cool headed has allowed him to survive as long as he has, while being hot headed has done the same for Tuck. There is a time to debate and philosophize, and there is also a time to fight. As a product of nothing but fighting, Tuck hasn't an issue with continuing to do so. Those who would inflict and ignore his pain would only understand better when in pain themselves. The way he saw it, the Creator was not going to assist the people in their efforts unless they gave all of their effort, so an honest emotional response to aggression is divine.

It is the language of the warrior class, *liberation* their rallying cry every time they are revealed to still exist after so many attempted exterminations. Many warriors in Africa were never captured, preferring death. Of those, many warriors never made it out of the dungeons, preferring death. Of those, many warriors never survived the slave ships, preferring death. The sharks that follow the paths where the slave ships traveled until this day, had their bellies filled with the blood of the strong, not just the weak. Of those, many warriors never made it past the torture of humiliation, rape and mutilation, of the breaker islands, created specifically to weed out and reduce the warrior spirit, preferring death. Of those, of that small number that remained, many warriors never made it past life on the plantations, preferring death; their lives squeezed from them by the rope, or released by the blade or the bullet and placed on display for all to see because the master, at all stages of the journey, preferred their deaths as well.

The loudest, the toughest, and the most rebellious made the best examples. The slave master even sometimes allowed them to grandstand, gather an audience and gain respect, building a false sense of hope amongst their people, allowing them to become giants, because when giants fall they level spirits exponentially. Their deaths made the jobs of the slavers easier. No amount of individual whippings, maimings, bludgeonings, rapes, or murders, could compete with the collective discipline gained from publicly felling a giant, so they almost encouraged their development, or at the least, the intelligent master didn't discourage it by trying to dispel the energy, he observed it instead, because allowing it to blossom before chopping it down created a better harvest.

Will recognized it as identical to killing a military officer in combat. No matter how religious they are, people actively worship other people, not spirit beings. They make heroes of one another, and place their faith in the ability of others they deem more worthy to lead them than they are to lead themselves. It's part of the issue Will has with leadership, the natural reduction it causes to those being led and the increased relevance and danger of the leader who quite often is no more equipped to protect anyone than any other, just sounding better about the attempt. Charisma is a major leadership quality, but sounding good has nothing at all to do with creating sound strategy. Powers have been waiting, creating these leaders for centuries, and chopping them down one by one. It's a dangerous strategy for power, but as yet, effective. If they let them get too big before murdering them, they'll inspire many more than they'll reduce. Because of the numbers they inspired, their timing with both Marcus Garvey and Malcolm X has to be among their worst.

Proverbs 16:18, *Pride goes before the destruction, a haughty spirit before the fall,* comes to Will's mind concerning the building and destruction of idols. He finds value in the bible, even though he isn't a believer in it beyond its ability to give accounts of human nature like any well-written story, and there are better written fictions than it as soon as the *Word of God* stigma is dropped. That scripture has a stronger social meaning than individual. Everything is collective for Will. The sacrifice is always collective for anyone investing their time into something bigger than themselves. Tuck and Will are both sacrificial, one just as genuine as the other, but should either serve their purpose of dying for the greater good of their people, the fallout with Tuck will be much worse. Tuck's example falling will be much worse, because no one knows Will, and giants amongst men, Gods, fall harder than men.

The often untold side of Nat Turner's rebellion is the estimated around one thousand or so Blacks who died as a result, when Turner and his clan only killed fifty-five Whites. Even after his eventual capture and crucifixion, where he was flayed, beheaded, quartered, and refused a proper burial, eerily in a town called Jerusalem, the damage had already been done. The slave owners had graduated to a new level of suspicion of their property, and they had to increase their level of aggression to preemptively deter future rebellions. More adversity creates stronger adversaries, and the same dance has been happening for centuries, and here Tuck is now taking the stage to rebel against the master's henchmen in blue, no different than the lynchmen once knew.

Toni was correct; much more was riding on Tuck's success than Tuck's success. He has the charisma to attract the necessary attention that can bring the community together. Even with his missteps, he can do what Will can never, and also what Toni can never. Tuck is Toni's polar opposite. Toni is about synergy, taking opposing views and finding the similarities within each, while Tuck amplifies differences. Enough energy has been expended with ignoring the negatives and highlighting the positives, with no honest advancement. The whites and the colors were just sitting in a box of water, stewing with the hate the unsatisfied life produces, desiring an agitator to assist their cleansing. Will's disappointment in Tuck is his inability to see the big picture, not understanding the roles the poor Whites and the cops played, and often adding to the confusion making them, in their powerlessness, a target.

No matter how much he hates Blacks, if he in fact does, Randy poses no threat. His kind is the biggest fool of all, feeling as if they share in power by proxy, acting as a buffer between the poor and the true power as the only ones facing the threat of death in the name of White supremacy. With their numbers, poor Whites, in the US, they are undoubtedly the segment of the population, defined by both race and class, that could turn this country upside down without becoming the target any of the racial minorities would become. They are too busy celebrating their Whiteness to concern themselves with real power though, and looking at the Will's of the world who have something to offer in the direction of freedom with their noses turned up because he's Black. Their energies have yet to be redirected toward the forces that oppress them. The stress of the poor and the lack of access to resources is caused by the rich, and not the other poor, regardless of race, but Will couldn't reach them with this message, or the natural progression of it which details the advantage of abolishing private property altogether in exchange for use, instead. Will has many shortcomings, but he has successes as well, and they are materializing before him, if he can protect them long enough for them to be considered as such.

The majority has been working harder and longer to achieve less, all while tolerating an existence many honestly hate, mostly because they believe God has more promised for them, if they're patient. It's a recipe for violence, and if the victims are ignorant, misdirected violence. Hurt people hurt people, even those that have not hurt them. It is no mystery why those high up on the hill are not offended by Tuck's hate speech, what many have begun to call it. The rich are too satisfied to care one way or another what the poor bicker about, as long as they stay properly programmed to bicker amongst each other. They are completely oblivious. It is beneath them. They didn't have to bother with it, see it, hear it, mention it, or touch it at all, ignoring the reality that the decisions they've collectively made are the reason so many are so unsatisfied. It is rare that anyone points up to them upon the hill, though. Their hands only point down to direct, never touching the pieces. They matured beyond direct involvement in the affairs of the mere men. They invested in industries and politicians that do the touching in their name, without saying their name. They are gods, touch has become a luxury, and similarly, people fight each other in their name, never giving them the blame. The poor aren't even allowed to riot near them, contained in their cells when they've had too much, terrorizing one another.

The pieces are still coming together. Will is secure and prepared in his motel room, and matching the label, *disciplined*, he was first to show, arriving the night before. Toni pulls into Harmony not long after Tuck leaves with his borrowed chairs. Gray sent him on his way, reading his demeanor. Tuck was nervous, which can be a bad or a great thing. He's aware that this wasn't going to be his typical Sunday sermon in front of his typical audience. He also didn't sell it to be. He is no longer bound by Will and what he'll think. A declaration has to be made in his symbolic move from beneath Will's shadow. It's Tuck's coming out party, and Toni is at Harmony picking up Gray to attend the show from afar. No one knew exactly what to expect, so the plan is to be close to the event, but not in it. This is why Gray couldn't go with Tuck even if he'd asked. It is good that he didn't.

Toni arrives and she's buzzed into the front lobby.

"Hey, LaTonya. Long time, no see." Ms. Ann greets her.

Toni smiles, leans against the counter, and speaks slyly. "Hey. Yeah, haven't had the time to check in like I used to." She's wearing dark lipstick and eyeliner, an athletic jumpsuit, and running shoes, all black. Today she's a ninja, instead of a genie. Gray watched as she walked in from the lounge area.

"I'm sorry, Will's not here. He almost never comes in on the weekend." Ann's energy drops a level as if sharing in the disappointment of the disclosure.

"That's okay, Ann. I'm not here to see Will. Picking up a resident."

"Oh. Ok. Do I need to contact them?"

"No. Here he is right here." Gray walks up. "Hey pretty eyes, you ready?"

Ann is puzzled, curious about the connection. Gray nods, and addresses Ann. "I didn't sign out, but I figure riding with LaTonya is something like riding with Will." Gray smiles and winks at Ann. "Let me make it this time, Ms. Ann. If anyone asks, I'm with Mr. Bunting, and if he asks, tell him I walked out upset, cursing his name, and looking for him."

Toni laughs, and Ann flashes a worried smile. "No you don't Ann, but don't you worry, darling. It's gonna be cool. You'll see." Channeling her inner heroine, Blacksploitation era, Toni calms a worrying Ann with a coolness that should have closed with *Annie baby*. Ann nods. She's powerless to do anything but. She can make a phone call, but she can't stop him from leaving. The idea that she has some control over his actions is only illusion. She only has control whether or not to tell someone who has some control, which would be Will. Will doesn't actually have anymore control over him than Ann, but he has the authority to enlist those who can control Gray, physically, legally, against his will, because power exists not in the metaphysical and the idea realm, but in the physical. Power is the ability to place one in shackles. Power is the ability to deprive another of food and other life sustaining resources. Power is the ability to make one believe a truth that is not their own, such as those truths that support immaterial ideas such as power itself to the benefit of those who made themselves the embodiment of its definition. It is a power that is projected heavily, creating imaginary barriers that appear solid, but are as material as state and national borders.

Toni takes the lead, heading to the parking lot. Everything is green and moist. The air is full of steam. They quickly leave the sidewalk in making the shortest trip, and the ground gives like human flesh as they walk upon it, and blood rises through its pores with each step. Walking behind her, Gray speaks, actually uncomfortable with silence for a change. He needs reassurance. "So, Ms. Toni, how you feeling?"

"Alive!" She says it with conviction.

It's the worst possible answer for Gray. He's always had trouble conversing with artist types with all of their riddles and taking the long way around to get to a point. Gray has no time to take the scenic route when making a point or awaiting one from another. What he needs is a read on if Toni is scared, should something actually happen, and here she is being eccentric and poetic. "Unless you been feeling dead, I don't understand what you mean," Gray responds in a near mumble.

"I feel like I had a new sense of importance when I woke up. Like a surge of energy in me, like walking into the unknown and away from the monotonous day to day. I feel good, Gray... How about you?" Toni twists to watch Gray's response, and his reply is simply a shrug. More than anything, he's curious as to how he's gotten himself caught up into whatever this is that's about to happen. Trying to stay out of trouble, kind of, big trouble at least, he's potentially walking into more than he's been in in a long time, and not sure he cares enough to be involved. He can't go back to prison, not when he's so close to the threat of return being removed from above his head. He's left feeling like he's placing more faith into a small group of strangers, who themselves don't appear to have it all together, than he's comfortable with. While Toni is feeling alive, Gray's stomach is in knots. He's only an extra set of eyes, but is it even something he wants to see? He's less numb than usual, or less dead, while Toni feels alive.

"I spoke to Will right when I was pulling up. People are already gathered. He saw picket signs and more White people than there ever are in Cottonwood. You can bet there are some second amendment rights in the mix... I'm not sure what to expect, but don't be too nonchalant. Too much has been building for something not to happen, and if I know Tuck... Well, let's just say we're going for a reason, and it's better to be over prepared than unprepared... Were you able to talk to anybody about it?"

"We're good on my end. They listened. The streets are watching."

Tuck pulls into the vacant lot where the Temple of Morality services are held. Over forty people have already gathered, mostly faces he hasn't seen before, both friend and foe, easily discernable from their visages. Voices strain to grab his attention as soon as he exits his truck. There was, *go back to Africa*, which matched one of the signs waving. A portly Black man in a tight fitting button down and jeans brashly yells, "The police are fine, but fuck you!" Tuck ignores direct engagement. He only addresses his members, helping to set up with his instructions. They remove the chairs from the bed of the truck. No membership engages, per Tuck's orders. He ignores all of the negative energy as well, holding his face tight while setting up, surely curious as to how he'd manage to have a productive service. The tent had already been erected when he pulled up; there were just no chairs. The chairs were being lined up beneath the tent in rows while Tuck set up his speaker system. He would need the volume at its max this Sunday morning. His audience appears hard of hearing and lacking the discipline to respect a person who has the floor. Tuck expected as much, though.

Will has been looking out of his motel window for the past thirty minutes in hopes of discovering suspicious activity so he can give Toni the heads up. Everything looks suspicious. He's counted at least six possible plain clothes officers, and he has the feeling that the entire arrangement is arranged, and not just a group of angry residents that gathered as a result of Tuck's inability to keep his mouth closed. What other reason would there be so many cops, if they are cops dedicated to watching a Sunday sermon? Angry residents are in attendance as well, but there appears to be a level of organization at work by Will's judgment. He's amused by the thought that those who have organized for that side of the board, who can easily be called the white pieces since they moved first, haven't a clue as to how organized black is this time. No black pieces were about to be captured this day, if only this day, without a fight, and white losing a piece or two was not beyond the realm of possibility. Will had a perfect exposure, weapons that know how to whisper, and an easy escape route. He'd been thinking of it all night. Should it come to that, and he has to show off his military training, and the room should be investigated, it's a cheap motel room registered to a known prostitute, an alibi in itself.

Toni and Gray pull down the street slowly enough to make the view panoramic. The parking lot looks like the cheap carnival with the bodies gathered, and the sun presses down upon them all. Will's motel is at is to the east of the TOM Center, and Toni pulls into the carwash next door to the gas station across the street directly to its north. Gray watched Toni the entire trip out of the side of his eye to see if any action of hers matched what he was feeling inside. She stayed in character. It was a quiet ride besides the music she played. Gray imagined being alone with Toni playing differently, something more magnetic, but she kept her eyes on the road and her mind on the task at hand, leaving him with no choice but to do the same while measuring her sincerity. Calling him, *Pretty Eyes*, is as far as her interest in him has been revealed, if that is even a result of interest. Naturally, Gray saw the entire occasion as a product of overconfidence and underestimation. He's been under the wicked thumb of the system for over six years and he has no illusion about the extent of its wickedness. Going back beneath it is far from his plans. Fighting the power is shortsighted. He'd rather hide from it. His perspective of what they are doing is limited by the length of time and level of intimacy he's had with Legion, because fight the power they will, and hide from it, both. Will is hiding at present, as are many comrades throughout Cottonwood, some with no knowledge that they've been deputized and enlisted into the present struggle.

Toni pulls around and into a parking stall where the service can be viewed through the windshield like a drive-in movie. She kills the engine and looks over at Gray for the first time of the short trip. She smiles.

"Can you open that glove box for me?"

Gray complies. There are two handguns. He isn't sure about the kind or caliber. Guns were never his interest to the point of study. He only needed to know if they worked and if they were hot or had a body on them back when he would carry before his conviction. Fortunately, he didn't have a gun on him when the cops ambushed him, or he'd still be in prison, or dead. A gun charge is always good for some years. He's reminded of that fact while peering into the glove box he's just opened. He looks back at Toni.

"Help yourself."

Gray turns up the corner of one side of his mouth, shakes his head in negation, and leans back in his seat.

Toni shrugs. "Suit yourself, then. You know where they are in case you need them. They're loaded. They work. I even got gloves back there. It is a glove box and all." Toni sucks her teeth with the joke. She's uncomfortably comfortable to Gray, and he considers the possibility that she'd gotten high before picking him up. He didn't see it on her. There were no signs, but he needed a justification for why her stomach wasn't in knots like his own. Toni had rid herself of her jitters upon a rooftop one early morning several weeks back. This is nothing in comparison. This has an audience, and nothing is more scrutinizing than self-talk, or more convincing that the wrong decision is being made. With an audience, there are images to uphold and impressions to make. Even in making him uncomfortable, Toni's confidence and calm is a show for Gray.

Gray nods. "Cool… So what now?"

"We wait on the word." Her brow rises. She is all kinds of clever right now, even having space for producing double entendres in the midst of the building tension. The word can be Tuck and his sermon or Will and some sort of signal. Gray knows not which, but again, he's not in the mood to play along with the artist and her *take the long way around* games. He nods. Toni opens the center console, exposing her gun, and Gray watches. She pushes the gun aside and grabs a bag of sunflower seeds. "These things are like drugs." Toni laughs at the irony. Gray cuts his eye with a grin showing he follows. His comfort increases a tick as a result. "Probably not the best metaphor... Want some?" Gray shrugs and nods simultaneously. He likes sunflower seeds as well. Toni tips the bag and fills his cupped hands about halfway. The salt from the first seeds upon his tongue calm him more, like the drugs Toni compared them to. They both dig their backs into their seats, chewing and spitting out sunflower seed shells while looking through the front window awaiting the main feature to begin. Across the opposite street, Will is looking out of his cracked window, enough space for a riffle silencer, waiting on the same.

*   *   *

"So y'all gonna let me talk?!" Tuck is on crowd control and battling hecklers. He couldn't get into the first minute of his welcome without being interrupted several times by protesters. The volume of his sounds system helped, but there was too much noise for those sitting in the audience, who'd come to support him, to hear his message. The Temple of Morality is in a vacant parking lot, and not a building owned or leased where he could better control who attends. Besides not having the money, Tuck aspired to be a street preacher and among the people. His traffic includes the entire spectrum of the impoverished. The location is prime, it is downtown Cottonwood, and where his intended audience gathers at the carwash, the gas station, the barber shop, the beauty shop, the bus stop, and the cheap motels, all within an earshot from his Sunday sermons, but the openness is now a gift and a curse.

"Ok. I'm done asking. People came out to learn, fellowship, and I gotta make sure they able to do what they came to do." Tuck snaps his fingers on his right hand, raises his fist about the height of his shoulder, and all the men of his membership rise out of their chairs. "If they won't shut up, shut them up! Walk the perimeter brothers. Pace around, and if someone next to you wants to test you and yell out, let 'em know how serious we are about our liberation." Immediately, the yelling shrank down to mumbles and surprised expressions. The picket signs, no more than eight, with basic statements in support of law enforcement, stopped bobbing as energetically. Toni sat up attentively with a mouth full of seed splinters waiting to be spat, and Gray stayed relaxed while sucking a batch. "Thank you." Tuck can be heard much more easily at both the carwash and the motel. "Visitors! We have more seats available now, and welcome to The Temple of Morality. Come on and have a seat. Don't be shy." Tuck waves people in, without prejudice. Some comply. Others stand and stare at the men that he's sent around.

"I hope the ancestors forgive me for rushing them and abbreviating libations, I imagine their presence will still watch over us. It is surely needed. We won't call them by name individually but as a collective. I'll call them, and you give me an ashé. Ancestors!" The membership responds with Ashé, while the nonmembership looks on. Tuck continues. His men are still pacing the perimeter. "Let's get to it then... I expected you. Now everybody talking about ol' Robert like I'm the problem. Like I'm out here killing folks because I said fuck the police. I done ruined your city now, huh? Obviously, some of you don't understand, so let me explain." Tuck pauses and takes a sip of his water. The audience is still at a mumble, abated but as though they awaited the perfect time to erupt, those that had not come to listen. They are listening and still not listening, just waiting for the best time to respond like poor conversationalists. Of the men instructed to pace, some stopped and stood beside audience members with the most active potential energy, judged by how active they were before the level of intimidation increased.

"We talked about this, if he's about to go where I'm hoping he will go with this. I did a lot of the research, actually." Toni takes the short break in the action to narrate, giving herself due credit and piquing Gray's interest. Gray listens, nods, and spits a couple of seeds into the brick wall of the wash stall.

"I'm from the ghetto. This is the ghetto right here... Welcome to the ghetto, those of you who traveled from other parts of town. You who I'm talking to, and anybody from the ghetto, this'll just be a refresher. The ghetto has a unique relationship with the police. Oh they might solve crimes on the west side and come when called. That ain't how it works here. Hell naw." Tuck laughs, and some of the audience joins him. "That's really the problem. You think the cops you get are the same respectful members of the community that you know on a first name basis when they here. Nah… they wreck shop over here. They don't like us. They tell us they don't like us. They beat us up. Harass us for no damn reason. Intimidate us. Incriminate us. Hate us… Oh, I got personal stories. I bet everybody from the hood do, but I got a better one to tell you. Although I know you hate to talk about it, let's go back to slavery…"

Toni nods her head and blushes. Gray sees it as a signal that her input follows.

"Paddyrollers is what they were called or slave patrols. Groups of White men would go around at night, making sure slaves wasn't trying to escape. They put in work whether they caught an escaped slave or not. It gets boring at night, walking around, drunk, so often they had to rough up good slaves too, and use the excuse that they were killing the fighting spirit before it really developed. Like, catching a group of maybe three or more slaves was a problem. Sound familiar? Black folk can't gather in public to this day without arousing suspicion unless we dancing and singing in certain areas. And slaves did get together at night and plan insurrections. Them White folks knew. Nat Turner and his people met in secret, and he stayed in secret for weeks until they finally captured him. They had to make sure we didn't get no ideas about storming the big house, and they used more than their fists and sticks. They used their dicks, too. Oh, rape was community business. Poor slave girls wasn't just master's unless he kept them in the house. These disgusting, immoral, vile, drunks, patrolled nightly, and were active nightmares, like demons in the slave quarters. These are the first police! This is how our relationship started, and you want me to love them? Three hundred years later, they still coming here to the slave quarters starting shit. Killing and arresting innocent people to kill our spirits and quell rebellion. They don't do this on y'all side of town! And until they do, you can't tell me who to love. Can't tell me anything. We still getting lynched, and they still trying to keep us quiet, scared, docile, happy, singing and dancing, so we won't be perceived as a threat, so they can fear for their lives and kill us, and still keep us from storming the big house, but like I said, fuck them."

"No fuck you!" There is a rustle of commotion from the outburst. Will leans heavy upon the window ledge as if bout to dive through. The fat Negro reengages, but the comrade a couple of paces away quickly subdues him. He is grabbed not struck. His anger fell from his face in the surprise in how efficiently he was manhandled and taken to the ground. People just watched. It didn't start a wave of resistance. Most must have been interested in Tuck's continued speech. The heckler is escorted to his vehicle by two members.

"Sorry about that. Like I was saying, and why I'm glad you're here, those not from here. My guests… They stopping you from getting to the big house, too. You too busy worrying about skin though, and maybe I might be too, but at least I have hundreds of years of oppression by people who look like you to blame… You need cops to protect you from me. I'm angry, Black, dangerous, savage. Right? I know. But up on the hill, people with real money say the same about you, and need cops to keep you away from them. The same kind of thing went on between the house and the field slave, when both were slaves. If you can convince the lowest White man he's better than the best colored man, he won't notice you're picking his pockets. Johnson, one of your presidents said that. Hell, we ain't got to be friends, but y'all slaves too. So what you in the house? That house is falling one of these days. I promise. Field slaves been talking about it, and that's why cops are so amped up trying to rid us of our revolutionary spirit. You might want to make a deal, 'cause we storming the house."

Will is both surprised and impressed at the direction Tuck has taken his message. Maybe Tuck had listened to him about power and the importance of only expending energy to get more of it. It is turning into a discussion about class, a concept Will thought he'd failed in delivering to Tuck. He'd made an amazing transformation in the months Will chose to ignore and dismiss him as emotionally driven and incompetent. Tuck is doing a fantastic job in Will's eyes, or whoever speaks through him. Toni is beaming. Gray is entertained. The audience, even in its awkward mix, seems to be as well.

"Centuries of pain ain't done nothing but bred warriors. Sure some spirits were killed along the way, but those of us who made it are tougher than anything those in the big house can throw at us. They weak! And they got all the bread and we fighting each other over crumbs. The rich…"

Three squad cars, sirens blaring, speed down the street directly towards the service. The cavalry has arrived. Will suspected as much. They were speeding to increase the intimidation factor, and it worked. The Whites and nonmembership stay put, but the membership begins to shuffle as soon as they hear the sirens and see the flashing lights. They know it's a shakedown and the cops do it just because they can. Tuck was probably dumb enough to allow them to or encourage them to carry, knowing few of them can do so legally, because most are felons. The audience starts to move and Tuck tries to settle them. "Wait a minute. Wait a minute. We ain't broke no laws! They just trying to scare you." Tuck is wasting his time. A lifetime of programming made their response involuntary, and anything illegal found can make everything illegal with police who have a chip upon their shoulders. The city cops are probably no fans of Tuck and his organization, and it's in the heart of the side of town where they can most closely channel their drunken, paddyroller, forefathers. They're already speeding through an area with a high consistency of pedestrian traffic. No respect.

"It's go time. I knew they wouldn't let us have all of this fun without them." Toni wipes the salt powder from her hands by sliding her palms back and forth against each other. She starts the car. She looks at Gray. "Don't worry. I won't pull out until they all park, or chase whoever. They sent multiple cars to make sure they don't leave out empty handed. Calling being on that parking lot trespassing isn't even beyond them." The first car parks, and Tuck's audience continues to disappear like sand from an hourglass. Some people dart across the street, others to their cars, and others still, those from the other side of town, wait patiently. They can be assured no harassment. The second police cruiser pulls up to block the parking lot exit.

A small SUV, heading toward the exit, turns to jump the curb instead and the third police car pursues. Seemingly defeated, Tuck stands watching, shoulders low, as his team of soldiers, over twenty strong, scattered from three police cars, which meant six police tops. It was a fear many generations deep, not to be broken in one moment. The police were already returning his, *Fuck You*, in a grander fashion.

"Robert Anderson." The first car addresses Tuck through the intercom. "This is private property, and unless you have a permit to..." While the driver speaks the officer on the passenger side steps out of the vehicle, scanning his surroundings carefully before walking away from the safety of his vehicle and towards Tuck. After the cop on the intercom finished stating his *why*, he continued with orders. "Show me your hands. We don't want any trouble now." With no backing, Tuck deflates, drops the microphone, and puts his hands up, palms forward.

Toni dials Will, and he answers. She asks, "What now?"

"I was about to ask you the same. Who knew the TOMs were such cowards? We had numbers. I didn't expect him to be alone at this point. Just hold tight. We really can't do anything but watch... No. You leave. They're parked and occupied. Fall back a couple of blocks. Maybe over by the apartments." Will is forced to strategize in real time. Toni responds immediately, pulling out of the carwash. Two cops exit the second vehicle, and they begin moving towards the blocked in parked cars. "I'll keep an eye on this, call and rendezvous with you in a little bit. Cool?"

"Yeah. Now if there's a problem, call."

"Shit, there's already a problem. I'll call if it escalates. You alright?"

"Uh huh. A little nervous, but a good nervous. Don't you do nothing stupid without me is what I'm saying. We're a team, Will." Gray hears a deeper sincerity than that of a simple friendship in Toni's voice.

Will does as well, and it abates his insecurity concerning what they'd shared. It helps him focus. "Yes, ma'am. I won't. Tuck is known for doing the stupid stuff, case in point, not me. See you in a little bit."

"Put your hands behind your head and lock your fingers." The officer is still speaking from the intercom while his partner cautiously approaches Tuck. Tuck complies, even dropping down to his knees, knowing what the next instruction will be. He's been in similar situations enough times and the more obedient he is, reduces the chance of him getting beat up along with arrested. They had nothing to hold him on if they arrested him. He is out powered. He'd only make a target of himself resisting. Of the people left standing, some smile and talk with each other as if justice is being served. One walks up to the car using the intercom and leans upon it. He's a plainclothes officer. There are at least three, all too comfortable to be civilians, all too satisfied by the unfolding event.

"Yes, you know the drill…" The intercom acknowledges Tuck's move to his knees. "No stranger to this, I see… Oh shit!!" The driver is dashed with a rush of glass from the passenger window. "We got a shooter! We got a shooter!! Back to your vehicles!" All three officers begin to duck, scan, and run back to their respective vehicles. Those left to watch retreat to their cars as well. The back window is shot out of the second police vehicle, and the cops running toward it stop in their tracks. After recognizing that an open lot offers no safety, they are compelled to continue to the car. Tuck is dumbfounded, eyes peeled, looking around himself trying to find where the shots are coming from. The initial shot startled Will just as much as it surprised everyone else. He reasoned that some of those who retreated, did so just to put room between themselves and their newly formed targets. If this was the plan, it is much better than he'd originally thought.

The police are caught completely off guard. As soon as the police begin their retreat, the parking lot empties with the rest of the vehicles jumping different curbs. As soon as the second car is reached a bullet makes a spider web of the windshield. The cops duck beside the vehicle. The third officer enters the first car safely, forced to sit in the broken glass. The officer driving the first vehicle pulls forward and signals for the other two hop in the back. They comply. They speed off. The car they abandoned is used for plinking. It is filled with bullets from several directions and rendered undrivable.

There is no better exposure than downtown Cottonwood. It's a sniper's paradise. Four or five strategically placed shooters would never be found without helicopter assistance, which is probably soon to come. Too late. Tuck stands and wipes his knees off in the vacant lot. He's arrested with curiosity, and his expression makes it plain. Like a soldier in shock, he begins to fold and gather the chairs. He'd no reason to make an escape. They know who he is, and he's going to be blamed for what has transpired, without a doubt. He is safer in this parking lot than anywhere else at the moment, so he uses the cushion to retrieve Harmony's property.

Will dials Toni. She doesn't answer. He occupies himself instead of worrying. Worrying would have him thinking the worst. He begins packing up the stuff he's yet to, thinking about the next move. His impulse is to leave. He wants to be swept away to a safer place where his return to the comforts of his life won't be challenged. He wants to bring Toni along, have her pick him up even, so she'll be safe as well as the east side of the city transforms into hell and becomes a Sunday to remember where the spirit grows within the hood in the form of wind ripping projectiles with the power of possession, demon casting, soul saving, and damnation. He didn't want to become what he'd have to become, individually, with the numbness that will surely expand, and socially, he'd be forced to take command. Will is no leader, not in the traditional sense of pointing, instructing, and standing firm and fearless with his chest out with all of the answers those beneath him desire, a God. He doesn't even believe in God, besides the expression of the collective will, so why should he feel comfort in assuming such a position, knowing his insecurity better than any?

Toni heard the phone ring, but her calm escape turned intense when she started hearing gunshots. She had no way of knowing who was shooting or where. She just heard shots from multiple directions. Her driving became jerky and her phone slid off of her center console to either beneath or behind her seat, from the sound of the ring alerting her to it. When she was parked safely, safely away from traffic, so she bent back to dig for it while the sky slowly began falling as Gray watched in awe. Gray is extremely uncomfortable. He feels like one set of flashing lights away from a trip back to the penitentiary, seeing young Ervin and Ol' John again, or people like them, or one gun flash away from death. He preferred his wars confined to the chessboard, because the real life equivalents of capture were much worse. He'd lost so much of his life already that he'd determined that he no longer had one, but the fear of death is the best reminder. When death's cold hand taps one upon the shoulder, reality sets in, and Gray had become so cold that Death's prickly fingertips felt warm. He sits beside a woman who's scared to be a woman, scared to be scared, when they can die at any moment.

Gray had become scared to care about anything outside of himself, with everyone he's given his all to betraying him and making his investment pointless. Almost everyone. He'd turned away from a world that had turned away from him. His mother never turned away, he did the turning, and his children weren't even given the proper chance to reject him, and he likely has a son, skin berry black as his own, and a daughter, almost as intense in tone who shares his eyes, who miss him like he misses his own father. Death reminds him of life and that he's living. He recognizes the speed of his heart, the rapid rise and fall of his chest, and his eyes water. He rubs the heel of his palm through both eye sockets like a squeegee. Toni looks up from searching beneath her seat to see Gray with wet eyes, streaked cheeks, and hanging mouth looking up through windshield at the light of the day like he was having a religious experience, in jaw dropped awe.

"You alright?" Toni's concern was understandable. High stress situations leave little room for flipping out, yet many create the space themselves with their craziness. Toni didn't know Gray well enough to share a small crazy space with him. She doesn't know him at all besides his skin and eyes both being time-stoppingly gorgeous, but that's not nearly enough to make a woman feel safe. His esthetic appeal actually does the opposite, pretty people make others uncomfortable, and rather unsafe, unsure of how their own impulses will react in the presence of someone equipped to flip all the correct switches. So no, she doesn't feel safe in the presence of a handsome man of few words having some kind of experience, when cops are streaking down streets, streets that fire live rounds at the cops, so she asked. She'd found her phone and found Gray slightly unresponsive, as she rose with it in hand.

"No." He spoke softly and shook his head slightly. "I'm scared as shit. I ain't ever been this scared in my life." Gray gazes at Toni, cheeks like glazed chocolate, face dimpled in embarrassment. She joins him in uncomfortable laughter. "I got kids. I gotta to see my kids again … What's our next move?"

"About to find out now." She shakes her phone like a rattle. "Hopefully, we leave. I'm scared too, but ain't no use in showing it. Fear ain't ever stopped a bullet." Toni shrugs her shoulders and returns Will's call. They are parked in front of the vacant Verandahs, and every time a police cruiser turns upon the street, shots ring out, without fail. Shooters are in the apartments, within the same protective gauntlet the drug addicts share. A few cruisers have turned the corner, and gunshots force them to speed away. Unless their lines of communication are compromised, no more will arrive without a helicopter, but air assistance will be of little assistance. Cottonwood has become hostile, and no one is in charge because everyone is.

Will answers, "Well, all hell broke loose over here. Only a few egos were hurt though. How are you two?"

"Hell is still breaking loose here. Whenever a cop shows, people start shooting. Answers your question about how the people would respond. It breathes, Will. Your monster lives, but can you control it?"

"You and your beautiful way with words… Great metaphor, but it isn't a monster, it isn't mine, and I don't want to control it. It can control itself; it needs no master, no God either." Will plugged a popular anarchist mantra to remind Toni of the creature he'd built and she breathed life into. "Same thing happened here as soon as you pulled off. We got to move Tuck, or he's going to take the heat. They can't put it on anybody else. He's out there loading his truck like he's shell shocked or something. You got to come get him, Toni. He can leave that truck and them chairs there." Tuck is as hopeless in the same parking lot as Will was over a month prior. Overwhelmed just as Will was, and Will could empathize with Tuck for a change. He needed rescue from himself before he required physical rescue with restraints not as strong as the mind's, but a lot less malleable.

"Ok. And you?" Toni inquires.

"I'm going to stay… I want you to come get my guns though. I'll call transport, someone from The Feet to get me out of here later. The cops are going to come back and hit hard, and I want to be here. I have to read their strategy, and I won't be able to do that anywhere else."

"I don't like that idea," Toni grumbles. "They're not retreating, just regrouping."

"Right. We can run for the hills now and this will look like some freak accident, or we can sustain this pressure… I don't know if we can, but look, it's our best shot, and if we can, what kind of message will that send to both the local police force, and the nation when these motherfuckers can't even come into our hood? What a signal it will be for our comrades when this goes viral… It needs to last long enough to appear deliberate, and they're going to need me to ensure that while doing my best to keep them safe."

"Yeah. No. But see you shortly." Toni hangs up and speaks under her breath, "I'm not trying to hear this hero shit." She raises her volume to speaking tone to address Gray. "Leaving it is. Going to get them now."

Toni pulls up to the Temple of Morality blowing the horn. Tuck looks up as if the car horn had broken his spell. "Toni! What the fuck is going on?"

"The revolution Tuck, at least a part of it. Get in and let's go. Will is across the street. Getting him, too." Tuck drops the chair he's holding and get's into the back seat. Will has his bags prepared, standing in front of his room. He's calling Dee to come back to check out, once he's gone. Toni parks with the car idling, and Will begins sliding his bags into the back seat.

"No! In the trunk! That's your seat right there!"

"What? I'm not leaving. Told you that." Will demands, "The people need me."

"Well, they need me too, in that case."

"I don't want you here! Call me chauvinist. Whatever the

fuck you want. Fact remains, I want you back at the bar, and take them with you!"

Toni raises her brow and tilts her head in a, *who do you think you're yelling at?*, manner, and responds, "Well, we've come full circle. It's a good thing you trained me not to depend on your leadership, but I love you too… This car ain't moving without you in it. Looks like you're gonna have to make an adult to decision. The three of us have been to prison before. Want to call my bluff, chance going your first time, sitting here with a group of felons with all these illegal guns when cops are getting shot at?"

"Fuck! Pop the damn trunk!" Will yanks the bag he'd slid into the backseat, back out of it aggressively.

Toni affirms, "Thought so."

"What y'all think about this?" Will addresses Tuck and Gray, more so Gray.

"I'm all in, literally… Legion up? Yeah!" Tuck reanimates himself midsentence. Will looks to Gray while still standing beside the car with the back door open, hoping for some assistance with his argument.

"I was gonna get out the car and roll with you. I know them youngsters in the apartments making noise and in three or four other spots. You don't. Might not even listen to you. I don't really want to, but since I did some convincing, might be good to show my face, if I ever want to around here again."

"Toni?" Will pleads. "Should anything happen to me, I need you to replace me." Toni was better equipped to do so than she was even conscious of, already in the process of, and Will was willing to protect her with his very last breath like his blood ran within her. She turns up her lip, faces forward, and bumps her fist against the horn.

"Don't you dare put that energy into the universe. Let's go."

Will concedes, and he slides into the backseat shouting directions. "Well the apartments are the stronghold right now. We need to first get them to stop shooting, activate some misdirection on other blocks away from there, and even get some people to dial 911 to pull them back. That'll give us some time to come up with something." Toni pulls off. "They're already terrified. This is more organization than they'd ever suspect from the ghetto, and they haven't a clue where to even start to stop this. They should've started years ago in not shooting us dead for no goddamn reason! Too late now. We're after power."

The quartet enters into the Verandahs through the split in the fence. Tuck directed them to it, and Toni conveniently parked in the alley near it. The apartments are quiet. People are around but they are quiet. It would be a nightmare to be marked while entering. If the young hoods have enough ammunition to hold it, the police could never take it short of burning them down. The team saw no one, but they didn't move as quietly as those who were already there. They were spotted, tracked even, not recognized, and not trusted.

"Let's break into one upstairs. They are tactically safer as long as we aren't dealing with bombs and fire. And we won't be. Cops won't ever get that kind of clearance." Will suggests and they begin clicking up the metal steps. "We need an eastern exposure, so a lot of sun will pour in while we plan. A southern too. The sun travels around the south of the sky, so we'll have light all day… Gray, you want to walk around to see if you can find any of your people? At least to let them know we're cool."

"I can try." Gray complies.

Tuck gets his fingers beneath the lip of a loose piece of plywood and cracks it away from the frame. They push the window in. The wood is so old, it doesn't need to be broken, and they climb in one by one through it. Tuck and Will remove other pieces of wood that block the light while Toni makes phone calls, planning diversions. Gray returned in around fifteen minutes after making no contacts. Either no one was around or they didn't want to be found. The advantage of the size of the complex is one not being found if they don't desire to be.

Hours later, Tuck roars with, "Hell yeah!!" Loud enough to be heard. Loud enough to be recognized by suspicious ears that have heard his yelling voice before, in this exact location. It is amazing what trauma does to a person's ability to recall, while at the same time arresting all rationale. "That's perfect, Liam. It's fucking perfect. We good."

"We should be. Not sure what's taking so long, but they'll be back, maybe in the evening. But when they are concentrated here, when they send all they've got, we disappear into the shadows, in the trees, and the vacant houses. No firefight. A gunshot here, a gun shot there to keep them disoriented. We can play this game forever and become the nightmare we've allowed them to become in our minds. When they're all here, we'll send a team to hit the west side to really fuck with them. Have them think the entire city's unstable, and even middle class White people are a part of it, as they should be, and will be if we do this right. I just wrote down our targets. We won't be expected. It will disturb everyone's orientation and make our work easier. Unorganized, anger-driven, savages, don't move like this, and they damn sure don't attack the big house. It's almost an alibi. We'll look five times as large, and under the safety of good ol' White leadership. That's good insulation." Will stands and claps his hands together. "Ok? You all got it?"

"And you, Tuck…" In a long overdue swallow of pride, Will addresses Tuck. "I'm sorry, man… I was wrong." Will walks over to Tuck to give him a one-arm clutch hug to add with his apology. Will was wrong about him on multiple fronts, appreciating his passion even through all of their difficulty, and Tuck received the embrace like a blessing from above. It's a good moment. Toni smiles. She'd done more to make it happen, to make it all happen, this final display, than both of them put together, and it pleases her to watch them working in concert. They are a picture. The frame of the window creates the perfect picture frame of two stubborn men in a half embrace, sharing mutual love and respect as comrades in the same struggle. The picture frame shatters. Glass flies. Toni screams. Gray ducks into another room. Tuck clutches at his shirt. Will falls. Young gangsters are never good shots. Chase tried to offer Tuck an answer to his self-righteousness and struck Will's self-righteousness instead. Chad disappears and no one gave chase.

Toni seals her eyes and wails. Tuck covers his ears in disorienting frustration. Gray tightens his jaws and curls his brow just like Will likes to do. Should his be called cookies, they'd have been cooked much longer. Gray is the tone Will imagines himself to be in his most rebellious mind state. As the popular idiom goes, *One monkey don't stop the show.* The copies are not exact, but they are competent and conscious enough to move without him should they have to.

The wise monkeys panic. Wilbert Bunting has been struck. His torso opens and his heart leaks out. It's a small wound, but from the feel of it, a great shot for it to have completely missed its target. Maybe Will's original plan was best. Tuck would be at The Fifth right now and not being shot at, making Will not being shot in his place, and metaphorically saving him and dying for his sins. Will bleeds, struggles to breathe, and it appears to be time for the watchmaker to leave. He cannot tend to his wounds out in the field. His comrades scramble around him, and they move like interpretive dancers. They slide Will away from the window, their perfect picture frame shattered in effort to destroy such a precious memory, so they can stand above him in safety. Toni pulls him against her, she smothers him, hugging him, loving him. Her tears liberally cover him as if he could actually die, but of course he cannot. Great leaders create leaders and Gods create Gods. Liam is a God, and Gods don't die.

Also from Evolutionary Books and author Devin Wright:

In The Background: (Novel) $16.99
The torture of knowing more than one should to exist or to coexist comfortably, pushes a young artist to the limits of sanity.

From The Background: (Collection) $9.99
A collage spanning a decade of Devin Wright's writing career, mostly his work in verse, compiled to show his development as a writer, his transition from verse to prose, and to provide an emotional background to the protagonist in *In The Background*.

Secondhands: (Stage Play) $12.99
In a bar where every patron is searching for something, they all blindly lead each other to their respective destinations.

If Pawns Could Speak: (Stage Play) $12.99
Four different scenarios, characters explore conflicts that all have a collective relevance as far as class is concerned.

For more information go to:
www.EvolutionaryBooks.com

Let no one determine your value, nor what you should value. You are valuable. No one is more valuable than you. You are the most important person in the world, not because God says so or anyone else, but because YOU believe so. And because YOU believe so, demand more from your reality, your world, even if that means changing it.

The world WILL be a better place.

THANK YOU

Made in the USA
Charleston, SC
22 March 2016